Artful Young Rogues

Liam Porter

For my girls – Isla, Eden and Halle.
May this tale inspire you to persist, no matter the odds.

PROLOGUE

The fishing vessel putted through the protected bay, its engines puffing softly through the evening mist. Inside, by the dull light of cabin lanterns, Carter Cunningham carefully flicked a switch, just feet from his sleeping son. There was a quiet winding of gears as a mouldy timber wall panel lifted, revealing a metal clad radio. Carter's hands removed a series of maps and laid them upon the table before him, red scribbles and flags pock marking various points along the coastlines. With them, he placed a small wooden box, delicately upon the centre. Resting a headset over his ears, he flicked a switch – static replied.

'Crucible one, this is Harvest Actual. Do you copy? Over.'

His eyes perused the markings on the map as he waited for a response.

'Crucible One, this is Harvest Actual. Do you copy? Over.'

A crackle responded.

'Code verification: Weathered. Over.'

His brain knew the answer before he could utter a response.

'Code response: Tempest. Over.'

'It's good to hear from you, Harvest. How are you holding up?' It seemed radio formality was being dropped for the time being.

'Likewise. Situation report?'

'As always, straight to business. Still worried someone may be listening in?'

Carter's eyes flicked over the maps before him. Fresh red lines had been added along the inland routes of landforms. His calloused fingers dragged over a series of coastal towns, their red still showing despite attempts to erase it.

'Alright, the Regime have managed to manoeuvre south via the Contari Ranges. They flanked Frusselle from the west. We lost two Battalions. The night before the assault, a small enemy ground team took out key defences... along with the Commander of the 15th Allied Brigade.'

'From the west? But those ranges were almost impassable.'

'Well, it looks like they have some new tech you weren't able to sabotage for once. Intelligence reports say the assault came by air – with the earlier ground attack being inserted nearby and infiltrating past Allied fortifications.'

'Any idea who was leading the ground force?'

'Reports differ when people are scared witless or dead. It was surgical yet indiscriminate - soldiers, civilians, all gone. All we know is that it was quick. Abnormally so.'

Carter's brow furrowed. His fist tightened, knuckles white. Civilians again, he thought to himself, fighting back images that haunted him.

'Harvest? You there?'

'Air you said?' he asked.

'Yes. The city was decimated. Hells of a lot of firepower.'

'Another one. Any guess the next target?'

'They seem to be holding the ground for now. Possibly planning their next move now that their surprise technology is no longer a surprise.'

Carter felt the cabin rock as the currents shifted beneath the vessel. Flicking the latch to the wooden box, he opened it – glancing over at the young boy nearby, snoozing heavily in a hammock beside the still warm steam engine to defeat the evening chill. Satisfied he was certainly asleep and not pretending, Carter continued to listen.

'The report came in from your last sabotage mission. We intercepted radio communications that claimed those Regime ships went down quickly. They never had a chance to ambush our naval forces. You and those magnetic mines you created saved thousands. Well done.'

'Is it? It seems the Governor is still trying to spread the wealth and prosperity of his nation to the world. Just ask the people from Frusselle,' he couldn't shake the disappointment from his voice.

'Harvest, there's more. The *Left Hand* has acted. They have *The Thorn*.'

His hand slipped, the lid of the box almost snapping shut. His head dipped backward and rested against the panel. He sighed.

'*The Thorn*? What happened?'

'A few weeks ago. Mid mission. His team are MIA too. We think it either wiped them out, or they have split and gone into hiding.'

That changes things, he thought to himself. Another friend gone. One he had trained personally.

Carter shifted aside some schematics and reached into the box. Sifting through the straw lining, he removed a small mechanical contraption, no bigger than a cup. Brass cogs and wheels, machined and interlocking with precision rested in their fixtures, as their creator scrutinised his handiwork before placing it back in its resting place.

Carter turned his attention back to the maps.

'Any reports on the *Sunset Water?*' His fingers measuring out distances upon the map to a significant sizeable port. As usual, he tracked across the large papers the position of the Regime's Western Naval fleet – *Sunset Water* simply being a code name in case their communications were intercepted by Regime Intelligence, therefore not giving away the mission.

'Sitting pretty as predicted. But Harvest, reports suggest that the *Left Hand* is travelling with them.'

Carter's teeth clenched.

'Harvest, things are getting desperate. Without the Thorn and his team, you'll be working alone. Are you sure you want to go ahead with this? Think about what you have to lose. What you have lost already. No one would blame you if you just slipped off into the ether. Think of your future. The Governor's reach is catching up with all of us.'

Carter's eyes removed their gaze from the maps and focused upon the sleeping boy. He watched the gentle rise and fall of the coat upon his chest. A peaceful expression upon his face.

He pondered.

What future do we have? he thought. *This is our last chance to stop the Regime's grasp in the region. How can we live free from their zealotry and control? They don't ask, they simply take. I cannot let that happen. Not again. No matter the cost.*

Carter's hand plucked a small silver locket from the depths of his jacket. Turning it over, he flicked a latch – a sepia photograph of a family filled the frame. A man, his arm around his wife, their two children a boy and a young girl smiling cheekily at the artist.

He grimaced. Carter kissed the image, and returned the locket back inside his jacket.

'Crucible, I have a favour to ask. I need to rendezvous at Cache Point Bravo in two days' time. I have some – 'his eyes lay upon his son, 'some important cargo that I need looking after.'

'Roger that. Rendezvous, Cache Point Bravo.'

'Harvest Actual, over and out.'

Carter breathed outward, rubbing his hand through his hair as though trying to shake a terrible headache.

The sound of metal hooks clunking hard upon the outside deck and scratching for a hold snapped him from his reflections. Many hooks.

Acting quickly, Carter slapped the switch – the false panel once again hiding the radio from prying eyes. He bundled the maps and dove past his still sleeping son, launching the sensitive papers inside the furnace. The dying embers reinvigorating with fresh fuel - illuminating the room. He shut the iron door and turned. With one last look at his hard work, he tossed the mechanical device through the porthole into the deep waters outside.

A commanding voice rang out through the humble fishing vessel, just beyond the cabin door.

'By order of the Regime, give yourself up, Harvest!'

Chapter One

'A fair fight,' scoffed one of the crew.

'Only way to settle differences between sailors the Captain says,' added another.

My ears strained to hear their discussion through the floorboards. I knew the drill. It had happened weekly on the ship for as long as I could remember. Two men entered a makeshift ring under the deck. One left victorious. The other usually picked themselves up, or their own recently relocated teeth. What I wanted to know was, who were the two sailors about to be 'duking' it out and more importantly, what were the odds the bookkeeper was giving?

My mind ran through the possible match ups of those who would be involved, when a sound broke my concentration. Two sets of footsteps echoed down the stairs to my solitary cell in the dark underbelly of the ship.

Hanging from the top of my cage, with my ear pressed to the planks above, I released the iron bars that crisscrossed my ceiling and dropped softly to the floor, dove for the corner and did my best to curl up and appear asleep amongst the rat droppings. I lay in almost complete darkness, save for the brief cracks of lantern light bleeding through the gaps in rotting floorboards above.

The lock to my cage *clanged* as the sailor fumbled with the keys. I lifted my face and looked toward the door. I added in a forced 'yawn' to help sell the image that I had been asleep. The pair ignored me and opened the cell door with a final 'bang'. It was the usual duo of gaolers tasked with minding me. Prebold, an older brute of a sailor with a long sandy beard full of food scraps, and his weedy mate Crispin. It was 'The Weed' who stopped abruptly under the cracks of light. He inspected the cage door with curiosity as it swung open and shut, smooth and silent. No squeak. Not after all these years at sea. That was suspicious, especially aboard The Kraken Krusher.

'Ere, it's still in perfect working order this one,' stated the sailor proudly through his weathered toothy grin. 'Don't think I'll be saying the same for young Flynt ere though after this,' he added slyly. 'The kid'll wish he was back to being bait in the waters with those monsters instead I reckon.'

I groaned at the thought of what he might mean by that, wondering the chores in store for me above deck. What would the Captain have me doing this time? Bird-catching in the topsails for the crew's fresh rations? Shoveling sea monster innards into barrels? Removing kelp from the rudder in shark territory? Whatever it was, it wouldn't be pleasant.

'Stop yer jabberin, and bring im out fer the match,' rasped the husky voice of Prebold, 'An check yer pockets after handlin im. You know what that cur is like.'

He stepped in to grab the keys from Crispin. They struggled and finally Prebold was victorious. Crispin reluctantly entered my cell. I checked the lining of my pants to make sure my locket was still well hidden before he grabbed me by the arm and led me through the dark. We carved a trail through the stale air of the hollow bottom deck of the ship from the hold, to a set of wooden stairs. Crispin's calloused spiderlike fingers gripped my wrist tight. I wasn't sure why this was always necessary. I never had a chance to struggle and there certainly wasn't anywhere to run to. We climbed upward toward the gun deck and moved past rows of new cannons, barrels of black powder and portholes toward the central interior of the ship. It looked as though I was actually going to be allowed to watch this fight after all.

It wasn't unusual. Now and then, they let me watch — just to remind me what'd happen if I stepped out of line. The message was clear: play up, end up in the ring. Not that it bothered me any. Most of the crew on this ship were too dopey to catch me doing anything they deemed worthy of such a punishment. However, they did have their suspicions, and every day I remained on the ship, the dubious rumours grew. All it took was a rumour. A rumour would often end with me strapped to the main mast and having an 'encounter' with a cat-o-nine-tails. Scars were left as strict reminders.

Spectators to the match jostled for positions amongst the shadows. It seemed as though most of the sailors had assembled for the fight, leaving a skeleton crew working the main deck. No one ever wanted to miss a fight. This could explain why I was summoned – to spectate. I sighed in relief at the thought. Perhaps this current outing from my cell wouldn't involve menial chores once again and involve some excitement.

As I approached the masses, the smell struck me. Down here, under the main deck, it was one of salt, fish guts and dried blood. It mixed in a putrid concoction with the bodily odours of men who hadn't bathed in months. Time had made me slightly accustomed to the repugnant stench, but after the odd stint above deck in the fresh ocean breeze, returning to below deck was nauseating.

Crispin pushed me through the sweaty assembly of sailors that had gathered for the weekly entertainment. Usually, I would be 'fanning' them for any valuables, which would be better suited to my pockets than theirs and simply take advantage of the bumping and bustling through the crowd. Not today, however. Today, they eyed me suspiciously as I moved through their ranks. Some chuckled, while others sneered as I looked up at their surly faces. I guess seeing a kid move into a better viewing position wasn't a welcome sight. Especially if that kid was their current 'Prisoner of War'.

A pudgy man, more drenched in sweat than the others, sidled up to me. It was Salvey, the shifty bookkeeper. His hands held the winnings and losses of each gamble the sailors made, which was rather fortunate, as I had some 'acquired' coins I wanted to add to the pot.

'What do ya got fer me today, Flynt?' he muttered not making eye contact with me. 'Pick up anything special on your way here?'

'That depends. Who's fighting?' I asked.

He chuckled at that.

'Well, it appears as though someone has taken a disliking to another person, eh. An that's how it works on this here ship, innit? One sailor dislikes another and they sort it out, don't they?'

'Yeah, so which sailors will it be? Crowley? Butterbean? Two Teeth Joe?'

'Well, to be fair, it's not always sailors, is it?' He danced around the question while managing to scribble wagers on scraps of paper and accept coin like a seasoned croupier on the floating gambling dens in the Southern Isles.

'Tell me kid, do you have any gods you pray to? Any names you whisper as the sea beasts hunt you down?'

The gods hadn't exactly favoured me in my lifetime. Matter of fact, I felt like they were keeping me alive for their own amusement.

I shook my head. 'Stop playing games Salvey. If you won't tell me who's fighting. At least give me the odds.'

'Two hundred to one.'

Those odds made my head swim. My mind began to go over the combinations of fighters. At this rate, it sounded like one of the bigger sailors was up against the ship's cat. Even then, cats have claws.

'You're kidding me. Sounds like some poor sod is going to die.'

Butterbean. I bet it was him. He'd been injured during the last sea monster hunt, and everyone was picking up his slack ever since.

'Tell you what. I'll do a deal with you. If you don't ask who's fighting, I'll double your winnings.'

'Triple. And you hold onto it until I get released.'

'If you get released. Sure. Why not?'

I didn't even need to say who I was backing. Salvey knew I always backed the underdog. Plucking a secreted roll of sovereigns from its hiding spot inside my waistband, I placed them discreetly in his palm. He didn't bat an eyelid. As far as he was concerned, if it made him money, then that's all that mattered. Almost by reflex, my hand felt for my most valuable treasure —my mother's old tarnished locket – to make sure it hadn't slipped out in the hustle and bustle. It was safe, I could still make out the tell-tale shape within my pocket lining. Salvey on the other hand, felt the weight of the roll and could immediately tell its worth. He licked his sun burnt lips as he calculated his cut somewhere in his mind. Salvey was the closest person to a friend I had on this ship. Although, I was aware he only liked me as long as I helped line his pockets. It was a partnership of convenience. I had no misconceptions that he would rat me out to the Captain if it earned him coin. Once satisfied he'd done his math right, he nodded to someone else nearby that I couldn't see through the mass of spectators.

There was a cry from Doleki – the referee for the fight. 'Fighters! Step forward.' I guess I was about to find out.

The noise of the crowd settled immediately to a muffled grumble. Then, slowly, almost in unison, the surly glares of each sailor turned to face me.

They stared. Hungry. Waiting. As though my blood was worth gold.

I gulped.

The fat fingers of Salvey slapped against my back. 'You heard the man, Flynt.'

He leaned in.

Grinned.

'Fighters. Step forward.'

Chapter Two

All the faces glared at me. I could feel my pulse pumping in my ears. Salvey tried to push me forward, but fear rooted me to the spot.

'M-me?' I asked. 'But that's sailors,' I hissed through my teeth. 'I'm a kid. A thirteen-year-old kid. What chance do I have against a sailor?' I felt a lump grow in my throat. 'Isn't there something you can do?' I asked desperately.

'Fraid not, young un,' he replied. 'Me hands is tied.'

Angry protests at my stalling began to spread. The volume and spite began to grow as the crowd bayed for blood.

'Get the Captain. Surely, he would put a stop to this. He needs me. I'm his prized bait for the *Sea Monster Challenge*. He couldn't possibly want me to be pulverized before the final round of hunting.' I was becoming desperate now and grabbed at Salvey's sweaty hand. He swatted me away.

It was true. As far as the *Sea Monster Challenge* was concerned, I was the Captain's best and only remaining bait. He needed me in good working condition, especially if the rumours for his next hunt were true.

'What the Cap'n don't know, won't hurt him. Besides, the crew reckon you're the reason behind all the bad luck we've been havin' of late and they reckon you're a bad omen. Bad

omens need to be dealt with. Now, off with you, and don't
forget to put your guard up.'

With that, Salvey, plucked a matchstick from the folds in
his jacket and placed it between my teeth. I was slightly su-
perstitious, and a matchstick had been my lucky charm for
many years. I relaxed a bit and tried to think more positively
about the situation. If the opponent they chose for me was
one of the scrawnier members of the crew, or perhaps dopey,
maybe, *just maybe*, I was in with a chance. Better than two
hundred to one I thought. That is... unless, I'm fighting *him*.
My mind imagined the particular member of the crew that
made my hair stand on end. The same sailor that was the
reason the Captain almost stopped these fights – because
several members of the crew were used as chum shortly after.

Impatient hands grabbed me, and I was shoved violently
into a makeshift arena amongst barrels of black powder and
cargo netting.

'Time to settle some differences,' rang out the voice of
the selected referee. A stringy looking man with facial hair
similar to a scrubbing brush and a tattered old uniform. It was
Doleki, a disgraced former officer of the 'Regime'. He turned
his attention from the crowd toward my opposite corner.

The noise amongst the crew dulled to hushed whispers as
they waited for my opponent.

A figure emerged from the shadows and through the dusty
beams of light that cut through the above grate. A giant of a
man, who clearly wanted to smooth things over... with his fists.
And my face.

He stopped and stared straight at me.

I held my breath. Anyone but him.

My opponent was Steiger. A towering sailor, covered in as
many scars as he had muscles. His face had the appearance
of a mastiff's chew toy and it twisted in a disgusted scowl as it

looked upon me. He had to slightly duck his shaved head to avoid hitting it on the boards from the upper deck.

'Right now, it is time to pay for your disrespect young one.' His heavily accented voice rolled its 'R's as it rumbled through the cavity. It could've been almost humorous if it weren't for his wild eyes staring at me from under thick bushy eyebrows. The crew erupted in cheers.

My eyes, on the other hand, widened. I felt my heart beat faster. Sweat gathered on my brow and I began to chew nervously on the matchstick that rested between my teeth. Any calm reservations I once had had now well and truly vanished.

Steiger calmly moved his hand in the slightest of 'hushing' gestures. The crowd obeyed.

'Steiger, this is a misunderstanding. What problem could you possibly have with me? I haven't done anything,' I stammered.

Actually, I had.

'I know what you are thinking, you and the others always blame me when things go missing, but it wasn't me. I am always in my holding cell,' I continued.

Truthfully, I wasn't.

'I mean have you looked at it? Cast iron and solid. *Regime quality assured.* How do you think I get out? Do you think I can turn into a rat and squeeze through the bars?' I asked.

To be honest, it wasn't all that hard. The lock to my cell was merely a flick of a pocketed fish bone to exit and enter. The things you find scooping giant fish guts about the upper deck. The sharp serrated edges were perfectly spaced for raking the three tumblers inside to pick the lock. After applying some cooking fat (which I scraped off the 'luke-warm' gruel fed to me daily), to the hinges to stop the door from squeaking, everything else was simply a bit of fun. With Steiger, it was as simple as fishing his months' wages from under his pillow while he lay snoring like a 'bear seal'. His cauliflower ears made him practically deaf during his slumber. Moving through the belly of the ship at night doesn't require much silence though. Through the chorus of snoring sailors and the squeaks and groans of the timber hull, I would sneak out almost nightly. I reckon I could fire off a volley from the cannons and they wouldn't stir from their sleep.

Each evening would hold new adventures and the slight enjoyment of some added freedom. Outings could involve, helping myself to the ship's rations of biscuits and jars of preserved fruit, moving across the open deck to gather some fresh air, passing myself off as part of the night shift in the dull lantern lights or perhaps my favourite; to mess with the sailor's valuables. It was a great way to interfere with the crew's morale and to boost mine from my dreary existence. Quite often, a night of sneaking through the crew ended in the morning with the added entertainment of watching two sailors punch it out. All because one was carelessly found with a prized possession of the other, or a sprinkling of biscuit crumbs across their blanket. The fun a kid could have.

Steiger's eyes narrowed. He didn't buy it. Well, he couldn't — I *had* taken his money.

'Not today, little boy. I have grown tired of your way with words. You are a very tricky one, little man. Very tricky. Ask anyone else here and they will say, "That young Flynt, he is tricky,"' he said with a scowl.

There you have it ladies and gentlemen – Steiger, master of words.

'Alright, I get it. I'm *tricky*. I don't have your money though. You can check me. Heck, check the ship. I'll help,' I insisted, beginning to pull out the innards of my tattered pockets. 'All I have is lint, a fish bone and some biscuit crumbs. It is impressive I know, but it isn't your money Steiger,' I said with feigned sincerity.

At least now I was telling the truth, I didn't have his money. Salvey shifted nervously on the spot gripping his fat sweaty hands tightly, now aware of where my wager had come from.

'I do not need to check the ship, I know it is you who is responsible for all of our misfortune,' he continued slowly in drawl. 'I will take great pleasure in pounding your cheeky, smiling face.'

I believed him. You see, Steiger was the kind of character that would spend what amounts of brain power he could muster on devising a variety of ways to enforce his hatred of me. The looks he kept shooting me through the sheets of smoke were hinting strongly that he must have spent months preparing the upcoming spectacle.

Lucky me.

'The Captain won't—' I began.

'The Captain is not part of this, young one. He cannot help you now,' he cut me off. Steiger shook his finger in my direction like a scolding parent.

The crowd of silhouetted mugs in the darkness surrounding us jeered and laughed.

'Let us get started,' he continued.

Steiger turned his back to me and began wrapping his knuckles in a grubby linen bandage. As he did so, the ship creaked from side to side. The air became even more thick and stale as I began to feel trapped in the shrinking space. The mob of sailors moved away from my corner - as though I suddenly became a target for the wrath of the gods themselves and that any bystander might just happen to meet a similar fate.

With his back turned, the giant sea serpent tattoo that adorned it glared just as menacingly at me as its owner had.

Steiger said something quietly to the other sailors in his corner. They laughed, while looking over at me. I had no doubt that he was going to enjoy this. I had watched him time and again throughout my years on the ship, 'settle' his disagreements with almost every member onboard, save for the Captain. Crispin and his crooked set of wooden teeth were proof of this. Steiger would pound his opponent's heads so hard into the floor, that many slats that created our footing, were exceptionally unsteady. A carpenter's nightmare really.

I cringed at the thought of meeting the same fate.

Two rolls of equally grubby linen wraps were tossed at my feet. I stared down at them laying on the recently scrubbed surface. I pretended to know what I was doing, kneeling down to pick up the cloth. I began a measly attempt to wrap my knuckles.

I nervously looked around. Peering back over my shoulder I saw something that raised my blood pressure even higher. Doleki in a clumsy attempt to be subtle, reached out and placed something in Steiger's palm. Everyone had to have seen it. I shot a glance at Salvey, his eyes looked down. There was an air of guilt about him. In that single moment, I realised Salvey had done what I had always thought he could. *Back-stabber*. You worthless crumb, I thought to myself as Crispin and Prebold joined him in the corner.

Their sly smiles told me everything.

The four of them had been working together all along. Salvey. Prebold. Crispin. Steiger. I had been set up. All this time, Salvey had been feeding them information.

Every coin I lifted. Every pocket I picked.

They must've stacked their bets on me not even making it to the fifteenth *Sea Monster Challenge*. If I dropped dead now, they'd rake in the winnings —every last sovereign the crew had wagered on the fight. And the best part? I'd even added to the pot —with *my own* bloody bet.

So, this was it. The fight was rigged. *I was the payout.*

I knew now what Steiger held as he slipped it into his waistband. My adversary was carrying a knife from the galley.

I looked around me for something of use. As we were on the gun deck, there were cannons, shot, black powder and lots of cargo netting to tie it all down.

Looking back into the crowd, pipe smoke was now so thick, it created a misty veil between us. Steiger began to stretch. An almighty series of pops echoed through the space as he cracked his knuckles and spine in anticipation. I had hoped he would somehow pull a muscle or dislocate a vertebra with his overzealous display of aggression.

I moved away into the darkness.

'Steiger, I understand that you want to include weapons in this little bout?' I said from the shadows.

Steiger laughed, 'What makes you say that, little one? You don't think I'll fight fair?'

'No, I don't. I don't think any of you will. You are all bullies and cowards, the lowest of the low. You think your cause here is noble? You think what you are doing helps the Regime? You're nothing but wannabe sailors wearing old tattered surplus uniforms. A bunch of turn coats and washed-up military rejects. That's why you're stuck hunting monsters for oil. Rear line work for the expendable,' I was trying to sound tough, however the pubescent crackle in my voice defied my best intentions.

'Go on then. If you think I am dishonest, young thief, if we are all cowards, then you may choose your own weapon to fight me with. It should make this... more entertaining.' His accented tongue rolled the syllables of the final word.

Immediately a commotion rippled through the gathering. Hands delved deep into pockets for skerrick of coin and valuables. Salvey licked his equally fat sweaty lips so loud it resonated through the belly of the ship.

I rummaged through the silhouetted objects to my front. My hands frantically felt through the darkness for the object I needed for the moment.

'Hurry up, little one,' he mocked. I felt my temper flare briefly at his irritating remark.

I found it. My hands reached out and I wrapped my fingers around its cold iron. Struggling under the weight, I emerged back into the beams of light hauling it.

The crew erupted into laughter.

I held in my hands a cannon ball. Almost fifty pounds of cast iron, which my young limbs strained under.

Steiger could no longer hold back his laughter. "You are amusing, little one. What do you hope to do with that?" He moved forward. "You need a cannon to fire that, silly." Taunts erupted from the other sailors.

'Look at him! He can barely hold it.'

'Careful Steig,' it might roll over your toe.'

'Want some help with that, little fella?'

'He has bigger balls than you, Steig.'

The ship rolled over a wave. I staggered, then caught myself, trying to regain my composure. This sent the crew into a riot of guffaws and hoots. I ignored them, like I always had. We were now standing no more than two fathoms apart. I stood with a wide stance to help control my balance as the ship moved through more chop. Steiger mirrored me for the same reason.

'What now, little one? You can't be tricky anymore. It is just you and me and— nnnngh!'

I dropped the cannonball onto the loose floorboard. Hitting the tip with the accuracy of a Damarian Archer. The effect on the other end was instant. One side went down, the other went up. *Hard.* Into the poorly protected groin of Steiger. His knees buckled. The crowd reeled in empathetic agony. Steiger's eyes rolled into his head as a pain comparable to the 'fire of a thousand burning suns' pulsated through his veins.

I paused and tried to think of something witty to say.

Nothing.

He curled into the foetal position— probably imagining himself far away from the thought of smashed coconuts or cracked eggs. I stood there, stunned. Impressed by my own accuracy. And realised... I might've actually won. Me — a kid — versus the beast of a man, Steiger. *'Flynt the Giant Krusher'* had a nice ring to it. All he had to do now... was stay down.

Doleki, began a nervous count.

'One.'

I watched as Steiger's veins bulged in his head and neck.

'T-two.'

'Three.'

His eyes crept back into position from within his skull.

'Four.'

By the Gods - could this *eunuch* count any bloody slower?

'Five.'

Steiger shifted. He slowly began to regain his composure and moved onto his hands and knees, head bowed. Even in this position, he was almost taller than I was.

The counting had stopped.

'Oh, C'mon, Doleki!' I protested wildly. 'Your mother teach you to count, did she?'

Steiger shifted. His breathing became faster. I now prayed for the gods to strike the ship with lightning to stop him from getting to his feet.

I realised I needed to make the most of this moment. I moved forward, cutting through the smoke. Steiger witnessed my advance and took a wild swing in my general direction, never quite lifting his head. It swept wide past my shoulder, his weight launching his body forward violently. I saw the knife tucked into the rear of his tassel tied trousers. With a pluck of my hand, the knife became mine. The sailors started to yell and holler at Steiger to stand up and fight.

Steiger responded by shakily lifting to his feet.

His face was cast in shadow. The blow to his nether regions had caused him to sweat and tremble.

He chuckled. Low. Unsteady.

'That... young one. You'll pay for that. Just like your spying father did. The pain that I will make you feel now is nothing compared to what I did to him. The fun I had torturing him,' he spat with as much venom as his body could muster.

Something snapped in my head. He mentioned my father. He, a lowly thug dared to utter a derogatory term about my father? An innocent fisherman. A family man. The one they took from me. A sudden fury developed within my veins. My voice lost its crackle.

'What was that, Steiger? All I'm hearing is something bout losing to a kid.'

He shambled across the decking toward me. A new-found metal pipe had made its way into his possession from a not-so-helpful crew member. I stood my ground and placed my hand into my pocket. I withdrew some more useful contents from my earlier trip to the shadows. It had the appearance of black dirt.

His eyes widened.

With a quick flick of my wrist, I launched a handful of *black powder* into his awaiting corneas. He yelped in pain and frustration. There was a shocked silence from the crowd, but I wasn't done with Steiger or the rest of them.

I turned to the crew.

'By the way, if you lot are looking for your money— check with these four,' I pointed to Salvey and the others. 'They've been getting me to steal it from under your noses the whole time. Just so they could set this fight up and cash in on the Challenge pot.'

A ripple moved through the mob. First shock. Then realisation. Then anger.

Satisfied they would soon be on the receiving end of some jilted form of justice, I turned my attention back to the reeling, blinded brute before me.

'Now... where were we Steig?'

I removed the match from my mouth.

'You've got a little something on your face.'

I struck it on the timber strut to my side. It hissed and crackled between us. 'Let me help you with that,' I said— and flicked it his way.

There was a blinding flash as spark met powder.

POOOMF.

CHAPTER THREE

Black powder smoke still billowed from the grill below. I could've almost smelled it, if it weren't for the muzzle of the Flintlock wedged firmly up my left nostril. The Captain had summoned me via the ship's 'bell' shortly after the 'incident' with Steiger below deck. As usual, Crispin and Prebold were tasked with escorting me, after I had been persuaded to hand over Steiger's knife. A flintlock in your face makes a solid bargaining tool. This time though, they seemed a touch more on edge than usual after my announcement to the rest of the crew. Crispin's finger itched at the trigger. Together, we moved across the deck. Their free hands pinning mine behind my back as they half-dragged me.

'Like a rose between two smelly thorns, eh fellas?' I bantered.

They looked at one another in a way that suggested their revenge on me would have to wait. I wondered briefly if they'd live that long given the comments and threats made by the crew below deck. I'd say there'd be a few more 'fair fights' over the coming days.

I opened my mouth to add to the previous remark, but the hammer 'clicked' back on the Flintlock. I stifled a smile.

Members of the skeleton crew manning the day shift loafed about the rigging and rails. Some turned their attention toward our little group as we shuffled past. Others pretended to focus on their jobs.

Being above deck, the effect on my morale was instant. It soared up with the three tall masts of the ship. A swift salty breeze whistled through my right nostril. The cold sea spray whipped over the edges of the deck onto my face, matting my hair against my forehead while the sails strained in the wind. The sun would soon begin to settle in for the night leaving us with the approaching storm. I looked out at the white-capped swells as they twisted and swirled as far as the horizon.

The view up here always reminded me of the times I had spent with my father. Sailing. Fishing. Trading each catch in different ports throughout the northern seas. I missed those days.

We moved across the 'filleting deck' where sea monsters were drawn aboard and cut into more easily transportable pieces. Red and blue blood had stained the fibres of the timber planks with the help of the sun's baking rays. As if their souls remained long after the beast had been dissected.

It had been weeks since our last hunt and barrels of valuable parts from the creatures lined the decks, tied together in rows. Their fats, oils, bones and scales all fed the war machine of the Regime. One man made sure of that. Not for coin, he wanted his pride back - and a particular monster to bleed for it.

And ahead of us he stood. A lone figure, stoic in his footing behind the helm, while the ship rocked in the rolling surf. He was the reason I was here – 'prisoner of war' the crew called me. More like bait. Collateral. Insurance against a man who made them look stupid. Some might call it bad luck, say we crossed paths by accident. Others, well they'd know better than to think that the Regime doesn't have spies or people willing to sell out anyone for some coin.

The Captain appeared unbothered by the coming storm. He surveyed the horizon, looking for any sign of quarry. Once a member of the Regime's navy, he still wore the uniform. Unlike the crew however, he maintained its dark fabric, red trim and conversation-starting hat in impeccable condition. His mutton chop moustache didn't break trend either, contouring perfectly across his worn features like a well-manicured shrubbery. His main vice, however, was his pipe. Carved from Kraken beak ivory, it was always well packed with the finest of Carvian tobacco. A smell so unique and pungent, you'd recognise it even if you were buried to the neck in mammoth seal dung. Apparently, only the highest officers within the Regime were paid enough to enjoy it.

We closed on his position as Crispin and Prebold forced me up the stairs onto the Quarter deck. The slimy Quartermaster Mordgill noticed our approach and swooped in to relieve the Captain of the wheel. More of an eel with legs than a man, he stooped his head in respect to his master.

Somewhere not too far behind us I heard coughing and spluttering. The distinct boom of Steiger's voice attempted to overpower the sound of the waves. I couldn't quite hear it. What I did make out had something to do with 'making me pay'. His voice drowned in a sea of noise from the angry mob as they sought revenge.

The smirk on my face disappeared as I was launched at the Captain's feet with the combined force of the two escorts. I skidded across the deck in a sprawl of arms and legs, finally stopping on my face in an undignified heap. I made a mental note that my time after this moment would be well spent digging splinters from my chin. My left nostril itched intensely from the pistol muzzle that was previously irritating it. I scratched it in relief.

The unamused expression of the Captain looked back at me, pipe smoke billowing from his mouth. Slowly, he scrutinized me—a seasoned hunter checking his equipment before setting off for the stalk. Mordgill sidled up beside him and leaned in to whisper something. If I were to guess, he was filling him in on what just happened below deck with Steiger. No doubt the eel already knew the score and had held off informing the Captain until now. Hells, he probably had money on me getting skewered too. The Captain nodded and stepped forward, motioning for me to stand. I did so, rubbing the back of my head and cracking my neck. Rough, he grabbed my chin, turned my head side to side and finally, looked me in the face.

'Hello, Bait,' he said.

The title was mine. My heart sank each time I heard it.

I pulled my head away from his grasp.

'Hi.' I said. I peered at his milky left eye.

Mordgill snapped at my lack of formality. 'You will address him as Cap'n sir, Bait.'

'You will address him as Captain-sir-Bait,' I mimicked his nasal voice.

The Captain held back an amused smirk.

It was a good impression, if I say so myself.

Mordgill fired up, 'You'll know fair well what I mean. Would a few extra lashings help remind you? Stan up straight and address the Captain proper like. An quit starin!'

The Captain raised his hand and the Quartermaster immediately fell silent. Like an obedient lap dog, a sneer still lingered on his face.

I can tell when I've stirred the pot enough and this was it... for now. The order to quit staring however, that was always a hard one to follow. I found it difficult to look away from the Captain's scar because it amused me. I remembered the moment he earned it. A fully restrained fisherman—my father—planted a very well-timed head butt in front of the whole crew. A head butt that shattered his beloved pipe into his eye socket.

Over the years though, it was me who had paid the price for that moment. A lackey. A lash-mark. A lure. That's what I was to them.

The aroma of pipe smoke interrupted my thoughts.

'Daydreaming again, are we? Enough of that eh. I need you 'switched on' for your final chance at freedom. The big *fifteen*.'

He turned to the crew that manned the surrounding rigging. Raising his voice and adding in the same theatrical tone he always did when trying to entertain them. 'The big fifteen!' he roared.

They cheered and hollered. Their entertainment was about to begin.

Fifteen.

This was it.

Fifteen times was all I had to survive and the Captain would set me free. Fifteen encounters as live bait to lure the nastiest monsters the seas had to offer. There had been others of course. Other prisoners. None had come close to freedom. The only evidence they had existed were fingernails left embedded amongst the barnacles on the hull of the ship. And now somehow, hope crept into my heart. Maybe the promise of freedom wasn't a ruse. But doubt floated there too, like bear-seal fat on salt water.

'I need you healthy and well for this venture,' he said pacing around me like a shark circling a castaway. 'The recent thefts and allegations seem to have put our young Bait...'

'It's Flynt,' I interrupted.

He paused, letting the correction hang in the air like smoke from his pipe.

'Flynt,' he continued, 'in a spot of bother. How am I supposed to catch monsters if my best bait is killed in a below deck brawl?' The crew laughed again.

I doubt he really cared. A lump of meat would have the same effect on monsters. Live bait just jiggled more.

'I can handle myself,' I replied.

The Captain paused and looked over my shoulder. He considered what he saw behind me for a moment.

'So, it seems. Man and monster alike eh? Let us recount...' his voice projecting to the crew... 'to date, you've faced kraken, serpents, naga, a megalodon. You even escaped a titan-crab. That was a tough one to crack wasn't it lads?' scoffs and laughter surrounded me. 'And now, our very own Steiger. Not that that one counts mind you.'

The laughter swelled into a riot, then died just as quickly when his boots carried him behind me.

'All of it led to this moment. A bid for freedom.' He stopped pacing. 'I bet you've been counting down to this moment, haven't you, boy? Each time the jaws or tentacles of our prey snapped by you, you thought to yourself that you could actually have a chance at freedom, didn't you?' The Captain leaned in so close, I could smell the Carvian smoke on his breath. He peered over my shoulder at the ocean. 'I haven't forgotten about the little incident with your father. An eye for an eye, son of a spy...' the last was purred ever so aggressively.

Anger and frustration welled up inside me. I shouldn't have let the thought slip in – that maybe he was a man of his word. That maybe freedom was real. *Idiot*. I shoved the hope down and tried to find something, anything, to cling to. He stepped back and resumed his stalking circle.

'Son of a *fisherman*.' I managed to croak out.

'Fisherman? Fisherman?!' he scoffed. 'Boy, if only you knew what your father did. The damage he caused. The plans he stalled. The lives he ruined!' But his words weren't for me—they were for the crew, his audience. And he was reveling in it.

I felt threatened. *Pissed off.* It was time someone other than my father humbled this man. And I knew just the secret to do so.

'And what would you know? I raised my voice over his. 'Let me guess, you had intelligence reports. Too bad that intel didn't stop you leading your fleet into a *sea monster mating ground.*'

I felt the collective cringe from our audience.

'Shut your mouth. How do you know about that?' he hissed in desperate disbelief.

'Your crew aren't as loyal as you thought, Cap. 'Specially old eel features there,' I gestured towards Mordgill.

He paled at the Captain's now livid gaze.

'No no Captain. I've never said a word gainst ya in me life. It's Flynt, he's trying to bait you.'

'You sure about that? Come on Cap, they always talk about that day. The day that destroyed your career. How would the rest of the crew know about it if your trusted Quartermaster here hadn't told them? How'd he earn his position beside you anyway? Bet it wasn't through honesty.'

'You shut your mouth, boy,' the Quartermaster ordered from behind the helm.

Boy was I going to cop it after this stint after the amount of people I had angered today, but I could hardly care anymore. If I was going down, then I wanted to cause as much trouble as I could. Even if I didn't get a chance at freedom, at least I'd inspire a possible mutiny amongst the crew.

'What is it that you called it? The biggest blunder in the history of the Regime? And you referred to the Captain here as *'The Laughing Stock of the Northern Seas'.'*

The Quartermaster drew his flintlock pistol and began to aim at me. My eyes widened. Prebold and Crispin grinned at one another. Mordgill stopped suddenly, the Captain's levelled cutlass, was at his throat.

'Let him finish,' growled the Captain.

Everyone on the deck stopped and watched us. Waiting to see what would happen. The eyes of the Quartermaster flitted between the Captain's and mine. A slight smile emerged on my face. I wanted him to lose control. He needed more of a push. The Quartermaster was important to the crew. If the Captain ended him now, he'd find *himself* as the bait for the next hunt.

'Yep, a wealth of knowledge you are, Mordgill. You painted such a detailed picture to the crew on all those occasions. So, what was it like that day, Cap? That alpha male serpent make much work of your boys? I bet that impressed your superiors.'

The Captain paused a moment and turned his cutlass toward me instead. The tip of the blade rested but inches from my mouth.

'Enough! Watch your tongue, child. Or I'll cut it out. You don't need it to be my bait.'

Despite my cockiness, I felt my nerves telling me to shut my mouth.

'Such a waste. All those men becoming monster snacks. How is that hunt going? Still haven't found him yet though, have you?'

His expression of anger suddenly softened and the eyes of the Captain became knowing. He smiled unpleasantly. Lowering his blade, he returned it to its sheath. I felt a disappointed sigh from my gaolers behind me. Mordgill breathed a sigh of relief too. Muttering something about almost 'falling for it' the Captain looked down and began to chuckle to himself and nod his head. The chuckle developed into a laugh that went on far too long to not be forced.

'The answer to that question lies –'

'It was rhetorical.'

'- in these waters. This next prey we hunt is 'Le coup de grâce. The Pièce de Résistance. The *Bloody Big Bastard*. Killing it, ends this chapter of my life. Then Admiralty opens her arms once more. He continued in his delirious ranting. 'It will bring us new wealth, new respect, new status...'

'A new eye. A new boat.' I goaded.

'You dare? This ship is the fastest maiden these seas have ever seen. Weathering the heaviest of storms and capturing monsters–'

'The only reason it stays afloat is because I keep fixing it,' I interrupted. 'Every cannon, every second-hand mechanical addition from your beloved Regime. *None* of it would work if it weren't for me. Your crew are useless.'

There were grumbles and jeers from the crew, but despite my interruption, he hadn't stopped his rant.

'—including enemies of the Regime, such as your father.' He stepped toward me again to drive the word home.

'Congratulations. You and your fast *boat* caught a fisher-man.'

His temples bulged under reddening skin. His eye twitched wildly. That was it, I insulted his pride and joy. I felt Prebold, Crispin and Mordgill cringe simultaneously.

'She's a ship!' he yelled, his pipe struggled to keep its contents from spilling out. 'A master huntress and currently the best monster hunter in these here seas.'

'You think this is a monster hunter?' I shot back. 'Just you wait. One day I'll be my own captain with my own ship. I'll hunt monsters alright. Monsters like you,' I announced turning and addressing the crew myself.

If I'd thought the laughter loud before, it was nothing compared to now. The crew howled, doubled over and pounded the deck—at me. All, except the Captain, who glared at me now like an insulted drunk in a tavern. He seethed.

I didn't stop. 'Besides, it's not too hard to be the best when there's no competition,' I said.

His face purpled, 'There's no competition because of your bloody father!' His voice cracked into a roar, spittle flying, 'But we caught him, that devious bastard!'

'Yeah, that devious bastard,' Mordgill sounded like a parrot.

'He was using that boat of his, to transport reports on our navy. He used it as a *front* for his sabotage operations. What'd he tell you, boy? That he needed to sell fish to all those ports in our waters?'

'Yeah, what'd you think, Bait?' chimed Mordgill.

The Captain continued, 'Every port he visited ended up being attacked sooner or later. Whether from his hand or his spying. He sunk ship after bloody ship. Hundreds of good men lost their lives.'

'Hundreds, eh Cap'n?' The Quartermaster brown nosed some more.

'If not thousands! We caught him because we treated him like a monster, not like prey. We know how monsters think. What, you want evidence? Who do you think messed with my navigation charts and steered me straight into that beast's jaws? Why do you think it was me and the Kraken Krusher's crew who hunted down your old man?'

The crew cheered at the recognition. They yelled expletives and cursed my father's name.

Seriously? That was what this was all about? No one had ever told me *why* my father and I had been captured and imprisoned separately. All this talk of 'spies' and 'sabotage' over the years had me thinking it was just an excuse to capture and torture an innocent man and his son—the Regime and its troops were certainly that cruel. It could've been lies. But some part of me wanted it to be true. Needed it to be true. My father, not just a fisherman, but a weapon. Someone who hurt the Regime. Hurt the Captain in more ways than one. *Good.* They deserved it after everything they'd done. If they had gone to such lengths to break us, then maybe it meant he mattered. Now it made sense. I felt a strange mix of awe and pride welling up inside and it gave me strength. My father, a deadly spy of the resistance. That would explain a whole lot of events over the past few years, especially the columns of smoke on the horizon in the direction of towns and cities we had docked in. The times he had insisted on fishing so close to Regime Navy ships in port. The memories came flooding back. It would also explain why he apologized to me as they carted him from the ship three years ago.

Turning his back to me, the Captain spat on the deck, continuing his rant to the listening crew, 'What did we get as a reward? His bastard child! And that northern sod that took all the credit for his capture, carts off with my prisoner and takes him back to 'The Gulag' for interrogation. You boys could've done a fine job of it here.'

He knew where my father was? Was he dead? Alive? I almost choked up. This was perfect. All I had to do was keep him yapping. So I pinched my nose and drawled in Mordgill's voice: "Where's the Gulag again, Cap'n? He still alive, an' being worked over?"

'Course he's still bloody alive. They have him at the Capital to the nort–' He snapped his lips shut as if trying to suck those last few words back into the vocal vault from which they had escaped.

Gotcha.

My spirits lifted.

They soared.

The Captain, had answered the question I asked myself
every day for the last three years.

My father was *alive*.

— • —

CHAPTER FOUR

No one on the deck spoke. The waves lapped heavy and strong against the ship, breaking the silence. A large smile snaked its way across my face. Cheek, to dirty cheek. I had often laid awake at nights wondering if my father were still alive. If the Regime had realised that he was just a simple fisherman and let him go. Wondering, if any day now, I could be released from this prison of a ship. Optimism had always prevailed. I had tried to never allow the negatives to creep into my mind, despite how persistent they could be.

My father. Alive.

The words kept circling through my mind.

Northen Capital. Captive in a prison. The Gulag.

The Captain noticed me smile. He decided to put an end to my brief stint along the path of hope and happiness.

'Clever child, aren't you? Always trying to gain the last word. Always stirring up the sharks.'

'The only sharks I see are ones smoking Carvian Tobacco,' I said.

'Is that right? Let's give you a better view of them shall we?'

The Captain motioned in the air with his hands. The reaction was instantaneous. The Quartermaster stomped on the deck several times over and a bell sounded from below. The thunderous roar of sailors' boots could be heard 'snapping

35

to' their previously assigned positions. The action was set to begin and I knew the drill well.

Crispin and Prebold appeared and grabbed me violently once more by my arms.

The Captain's boots clunked across the deck slowly as he traced back and forth in front of us.

At that moment, the Quartermaster responded by banging on the bell with a wooden bar. It created a different sound that echoed off after the last strike.

Nothing happened. The waves continued to lap the bow of the ship, the sails flapped in the wind.

There was a pause. I dared to look at the Captain's face. He still appeared confident in the communication of the latest command.

A rumble cut through the ship. The sounds of heavy squeaking wheels reverberated through the bowels of the vessel. The weight of the ship shifted as the bow began to lift slightly from the waters. There was a clanking and creaking of wooden slats and portholes from the stern. Some barrels of black powder were lashed onto the deck for the few cannons that remained at port and starboard.

'The new cannons in position Cap'n!' came a cry from below deck.

The comment was echoed by all crew members to ensure it was heard over the sound of the surf. The Captain appeared satisfied.

This was new to me. All previous attempts at luring sea monsters in the past had involved me being thrown overboard into the chum flavoured water, while the ship remained stationary. All side ballistas would be trained on my position as I had to swim seventy or more fathoms from the ship. At the first sight of a monster, serpent or kraken, the side harpoons would be launched past my head into the limbs of the beast, stopping it from recoiling into the depths. Then, they added cannons to the mix. Their large iron balls travelling faster than the eye could see, proved far more deadly than simply waiting for a creature to bleed out or give up from exhaustion. The cannon fire would erupt past my head as I tried to out swim whatever was chasing me. In the past I had swum under the keel, hidden behind the rudder or climbed the side rigging as fast as I could, just to preserve my skin. It had worked fourteen times for me. All the other prisoners before me had never succeeded past three.

Now things were different. The ship wasn't slowing. In fact, the sails remained fully unfurled catching the wind and propelling us forward. Most of the cannons had been moved to the rear of the craft, according to the sailors.

I dared to sneak a glance out the rear of the ship.

A familiar sickening smell assailed my senses. Chum was being turfed overboard by the bucket load. Mixtures of fish guts, pig blood and chicken entrails polluted the water in a tell-tale trail through the ship's wake.

'New monster, new strategy, Flynt.' The Captain's voice dragged my attention back to the situation.

That was it. The sovereign dropped.

'So, you're going to outrun a sea monster and fire on it as it chases the ship?' I asked.

'As I said, this one is different from the others.'

'Well, I guess you don't need my services then.' I began. 'I can wait for another time?'

'Oh, but I do, my boy. He's a fast one, this beast. The old fella only likes fast moving bait,' he sneered.

Mordgill sidled up beside the Captain. He carried with him a small wooden chest. The Captain turned his attention to the container and fetched a small iron key from inside his lapel.

With a 'clunk' he unlocked the chest and began to withdraw the contents.

'I lost two good men retrieving this from the ocean floor. Your father thought he could hide it from me by throwing it overboard. Nothing a dive bell and some strong swimmers couldn't find I assure you. Ironically, it's the one ingredient that will provide the edge in attracting this beast to the bait and not my ship. You see, he intended to use it against our naval fleets, to attract the largest sea beasts to attack them. But now, with a few additions of my own design, it'll be ever so poetic that it be used on Harvest's own son.'

The Captain pulled a crafted iron and copper bracer from the chest. It was elaborate in design with twists and mechanical additions. It had the appearance of an item of torture, with a clamp and bolts on either side. He nodded to Prebold and Crispin and I felt the pressure of their hold increase. What have they been eating? God juice? Crispin the weed shouldn't be this strong.' I thought to myself. They proceeded to force out my right arm. It was obvious to me what was about to happen. I tried to resist but they easily overpowered me. The Captain grinned and looked at me with his functioning eye, so he could witness my expression of worry as he bound the bracer to my arm.

He sneered. 'The beauty is, I can attach this to your arm now and retrieve it from the belly of the beast later.'

I'm sure he was right. This is something that The Captain – like Steiger -would have put a lot of thought into. But it soon became apparent there was a problem as the Captain struggled attaching the device.

'CLUNK!'

The bracer slipped from my skinny arm onto the deck.

He tried again. This time he appeared slightly concerned.

The solitary sound of waves crashing into the bow of the ship added to the awkwardness of the situation.

The Captain's frustration was evident. He started to mumble various obscenities under his breath. Mordgill, stepped forward with the gesture of providing assistance. The Captain glared at him. The eagerness evaporated and he sank back amongst the other crew with the appearance of a scolded dog.

'Well, this is kind of awkward. No no, don't mind me, I'll just hang out here. I mean, really you've designed it for a...' My comment was cut short by the back of the Captain's open palm across my temple. My ears rang and my vision blurred from the impact. I could no longer focus my thoughts. A second strike made my world go dark.

***

My senses began to return after a while. I peeled my eyes open. My brain throbbed.

I looked around at my surroundings. I was lying upon the deck, my gaolers no longer nearby. I recognised the source of the pain and began to wipe my brow. A new weight on my wrist caused my hand to thud into my face. Blood smeared my hand from a fresh cut on my forehead. My limbs were still wobbly from the earlier strike.

I inspected my latest accessory. The Captain had managed to attach his lure to my limb with the help of wrapped leather to thicken my wrist's girth. A makeshift job that appeared to solve his latest conundrum.

I heard the clunking of his boots once again as he approached.

'Coming to apologise?' I groaned.

Without a word, the Captain crouched beside my splayed figure and tinkered at my wrist. He wanted me to see this. He inserted the key into the bracer, he twisted it several times. It began to make a strange noise.

Tick, tick, tick, tick.

'Stand up Flynt. This is an unbecoming position for a young man.' His voice was eerily calm and almost friendly. 'Maybe we can work something out for you here. Something special for your last moments here on my ship.'

I struggled to my feet, still giddy, like a drunkard trying to face the next day's reality. I looked back and realised I was awfully close to the stern on the quarterdeck. Mere steps from the taffrail. Some of the crew had gathered around us, smiling wickedly at me. Even Steiger, sporting his new look of hairless eyebrows seemed surprised instead of angry. Or maybe he was frowning - I couldn't tell. Meanwhile, the Captain lit a freshly packed pipe, skilfully shielding the matches' contribution from the wind. Satisfied, he flicked the match away.

Tick, tick, tick, tick.

'How about we put all of our problems behind us like two civilised people. Then we can move on with a clean slate and not feel bad. You are not your father, far from it actually. So, you cannot be held accountable for his actions.' His voice was almost sincere.

The Captain extended his hand toward me. I stared warily at it. For a moment, I was disturbed by the sudden change in demeanour, refusing to let my guard down. He kept it there gesturing insistently. I lifted my hand steadily. He lurched forward, clutching and shaking it like a shady merchant closing a business deal.

Tick, tick, tick, tick.

'However, the boys on board have grown tired of your antics and I've got to think about the well-being of my crew.

I am a fair man see. A sporting man. Just to show you an example of how fair I can be, I'll even let you have a choice,' he continued as smoke rolled from his nostrils.

'A choice?' I asked looking into the milky depths of his eye. 'Like, do I get my winnings from the fight with Steiger? Or you're going to set me free?'

'Not quite.' With a sleight of hand, he slipped a noose around my wrist and smiled a large toothy smile. 'More like, Port or Starboard?' he laughed.

'Huh?' I blinked.

And with that, The Captain bid me farewell from his ship, with a boot to my chest.

— • —

CHAPTER FIVE

Hitting the water from such a height in the most ungraceful of 'back flops' isn't the ideal way of entering sea monster territory. In fact, there probably isn't one. In my case however, I didn't have much of a choice. Slapping the water hard, brine punched into my mouth and nose. My lungs spasmed. Convulsing, I tried to regain control of my breathing.

The icy embrace of the waters quickly enveloped me, removing whatever oxygen remained in my lungs. I sank just below the surface in a swirl of bubbles and froth. My body reacted immediately by frogging toward the surface. I gasped, sucking in air between coughs of salty water.

The sounds of laughter interrupted my moment of recovery, bucking around in the turbulent waters. I looked toward the ship as it kept sailing away tacking to its starboard. The crew were lining the rear (now laden with the majority of the ship's cannons), all waving, pointing and providing various other rude gestures well known throughout the nations. I began to think that igniting the black powder stores on the gun deck instead of Steiger's face would have been a better way to say goodbye. Remembering my rough entry into the drink, I felt for the trinket buried within the lining of my pants pocket, only to be reassured by its familiar outline.

42

As I tread water amongst the oily slick surface, the ship moved further from my position, the wind fully fuelling the sails across all three masts. Staying afloat was slightly harder than usual. This bloody device weighed almost enough to drown me by itself. I lifted my right hand out of the water to inspect it, or more importantly, to throw the wretched thing away.

Tick, tick, tick, tick.

Its network of cogs and levers were left unfazed by the addition of salt water. Bloody good engineering that. *'Bugger'* I thought.

Attached to my wrist also, was the noose knot - care of the Captain. I hurriedly tried to remove it, pulling at the scratchy twine of sisal fibres. *Come on,* I thought. *Get off, get off, get off.* Any moment now the rope would pull tight and drag me through the waters. I'd either drown to the amusement of the crew or I'd be the bait for, apparently, the largest, most dangerous sea monster these oceans have had the pleasure of raising.

'TWANG'

It wasn't the noise I wanted to hear. As if in response to my thoughts, the cord pulled upon my wrist, jutting my arm away from my body. I caught a glimpse of the rope rising from the water. It gathered tension quickly toward the pressing ship.

I muttered the only appropriate words for the situation.

'Oh, shi-'

My arm was almost wrenched from its socket. I swore I could feel the ligaments that held the ball and socket joint in place, scream out an expletive under the sudden impact. My body jerked violently toward the origin of the lash and like a piece of meat on a fisherman's long line, I was dragged through the chop and swell.

Taking involuntary turns skimming across the surface and sinking below the wake, I began to feel like a kite on a still day - being dragged by an over-exuberant child with very fast legs. I tried to see if I could angle my feet to create some sort of directional control in the situation – like a rudder. My body went toward the surface. I breathed in some air before being engulfed in the wash once again. This time my body travelled deeper and further at speed. Not the desired bloody outcome. The depths below me revealed nothing but darkness as I torpedoed through the less bubbly turbulence of the swell. The starvation of air began to build more. I almost wished for something to reach from below to put me out of my misery.

Almost.

I breached the surface once again. My body began to bounce across the swells and caps – an expertly skimmed stone. The sensation would almost seem exciting or fun, if not for the fact that I once again struggled to breathe. Glimpses of bubbles followed by cloudy sky began to mix together as my lungs screamed out for a decent amount of air. Salty water douched through my sinuses and eyes. Time and again I tried to reach up and tug at the knot restraining my wrist. Each attempt resulted in failure. I could feel the sting as my flesh began to blister and tear from the cord. I wasn't sure how long I could hold out before no longer being able to fight my way to the surface. And with that realisation, panic began to set in.

Karma is a double-edged sword, I began to realise. If this is how live bait felt of the end of a line, then by the gods, or whatever, I swear I'll never use bait to fish again. Lures on the other hand...

My free hand slapped wildly against my pant leg. A sharp pain snapped into my senses. Instinctively I felt for the barb that had pierced my thigh. Reaching into my pocket was not an easy task as I bucked around. My hand met with the culprit thorn. I recognised the bony texture of my second most prized possession from the ship - my fish bone lock pick. Its thick texture and serrated edges were unmistakeable, even in my current predicament.

I wrapped my free hand around the make-shift handle and stretched my arm forward to grate at the line. My lungs and veins craved air; the glubs and blubs of the water drowning out my thoughts. Not going to make it... *At least I'm not stuck on that stinking cesspool of a ship.*

'TWANG'

The turbulence slowed. My body - weak, drained and tumbling, dragged to an underwater halt. Slowly I began to float toward the surface. Once again, my mouth kissed sweet cool air, after some more necessary coughing and spluttering. My eyes peeled open to view the dark clouds above, the swell kicked and bucked my crucifix form along the surface. I took a moment to compose myself. It still felt as though half of the ocean now resided in my stomach and lungs, along with some rare types of now even rarer tropical fish.

The most impacting realisation after being dragged 'half dead' through the water is the sound. No more bubbles... no more swishing and swirling – just the calm lapping on the currents, the drifting of your hair. A welcome feeling of solitude. My adrenaline subsided and now I could feel the crash in energy as my heart beat returned to normal. I lifted my saviour to my lips and kissed the lock pick with gratitude. Dipping it below the surface, it regained its former position within my pocket. I turned my head to survey my new surroundings.

Looking across the rising and falling swells, I could just make out the expressions of the displeased members of the crew at the rear of the ever-distancing piece of ship. My new-found freedom was not part of the Captain's master plan and he would certainly want back the contraption attached to my wrist. The figures pointed and yelled at me and motioned for the ship to turn back toward my position. Sails dropped and the ship's course began to change. The sailors would know that in the impending darkness, I'd be hard to find and hastened their routine. They had become animated like a bunch of spider gibbons carrying on over the last ripened banana.

I waved with my middle finger. It would take a while for them to return.

The bracer on my wrist clicked. The *'ticking'* had finally stopped. This was perfect for the Captain's plans, not only had his bait slipped from the line, but his mechanical secret lure was absolutely *useless*.

A lever released. Cogs began to turn. My mouth snapped shut from the previously growing smile. The bracer now began to make a deep low humming sound. It was quiet, but quite unmistakeable. The bracer had to be faulty. How could such a pitifully dull sound attract a sea monster? *Dumb bloody Captain*, I thought to myself.

Rain began to strike the surface. Within moments a heavy squall began to pour down. The storms had finally made their way above my position just in case I wasn't wet enough. The last red glow of the day's sunshine illuminated the horizon to the west. So often I had not been allowed out of my confines to appreciate the beauty of a sunset. Instead, I had to admire the pink and orange glows through the cracks in the hatches as the dying light crept its way across my cell. Well, I was going to enjoy this one. Nothing was going to interrupt the peace and quiet of this situation. Not the bloody ship. Not a stinking sea monster and certainly not the bloody annoying noise making contrapti-

'CRAAACK BOOM'

Lightning tore through the sky above. It almost made me jump clean out of the water. I had never really had many positive experiences with it in the past, what with the igniting of sails on the ship, the electrocuting of a few (now) former members of the crew and the fishing town fires I had witnessed it cause in my short time on the planet. My mind knew one thing as certain. Lightning at sea was never a good sign. I felt alone and exposed, and I needed somewhere to go hide till this crappy weather passed by.

'CRACK BOOM!'

Another bolt struck overhead, like the gods were pounding out some sort of bare-knuckle brawl. I needed no more encouragement. Breathing in, I ducked underneath the waves into the darkness below. It would be temporary until more air was required, but temporary was better than permanent death.

Below the surface I often liked to look up and hold my nose to stop the water taking the place of the air within my sinuses. Although blurry, you could make out distorted figures and shapes from the other reality above the surface. This time looking up, light strobed, illuminating the underwater world around me. The sounds of the thunder muffled to a hush. However, the sounds emanating from the bracer had taken on a different tone down here. The resonances were almost... *musical* with lulling deep rolls and high squeals and clicks. The deeper I sank, the louder the noises became.

Another flash.

More thunder.

I turned around and began to swim a bit deeper. The change in the tone from the device became deeper too. Light from above the surface flickered once again, revealing my new underwater haven.

I stopped cold.

Something had moved in the depths below.

Another flicker from above.

I wished I hadn't seen *it*. I wished my eyes were just playing tricks underwater from the salt and bubbles and maybe a rocky shelf below the surface. Surely... I mean... what would *it* eat? Other sea monsters? Low flying Rocs? Naval fleets? No, it was definitely my eyes down here, it's so dark, and how could I possibly have seen -

It lit up once more.

I gulped.

Now there was no doubt in my mind what *it* was, as the gargantuan serpentine figure of the largest sea creature I had ever seen, snaked under my position.

Chapter Six

Oh crap, were the only words in my brain.

On the surface once again, I was now in the middle of the storm. Lightning flashed, thunder cracked and the winds had peaked. Exposed to these elements, a normal person in this situation would fear for their lives, fear they would drown amidst the forces of nature. I did actually feel this fear; however, the particular force of nature causing it, was not *above* the waves.

I froze. My heart had begun a tirade of manic thumps throughout my chest. I foolishly decided to peer below the surface once again, as though actually seeing the beast would stop it from devouring me alive. It was, perhaps, how a fish stranded from its school must feel looking into the eyes of a tiger tuna.

Below me was simply darkness. A deep void of the open ocean. Still, I peered on. Perhaps it had left to go eat something else?

A familiar sound of an approaching bell behind me managed the impossible. It drew my attention from my predicament. I turned my thoughts from the water to witness the most unlikely welcoming sight I had seen. Oh, what a glorious vision it was too. The ship that was once my prison, had returned. With the winds once again fuelling the sails, its beauty was one to behold. The same however, could not be said for the queues of surly outcasts and thugs that would be lining its rails. A motley crew at best, I even felt relief to have them in my presence once again. The ship bucked through the ever increasing swell as it powered toward me.

Now I knew I was a strong swimmer. Heck, that's the reason I had managed to stay alive for all of the previous challenges. It's one of the only reasons the Captain had kept me around and not traded me in as a slave. No one else could dislodge weed from the rudder 'quite like young Flynt', or retrieve other sailors when they fell overboard beyond the reach of a rope 'quite like young Flynt'. I knew it and I made sure I was good at it. My time spent inside my cell was never as mundane as many would assume. Planning your nightly sneak out needed to be thoroughly thought out to make the most efficient use of time. Other times I would practice holding my breath, simply to get better at it. Hiding under the keel from prying Kraken tentacles was a challenge that required minutes below the waterline and speed. I wasn't going to be its cookie at the bottom of a jar. However, right now, I felt as though I couldn't swim fast enough. Even if I could stand on the surface and run across the waves, it wouldn't feel adequate in distancing me from the horror below.

Like two estranged lovers running through a field to embrace after time abroad, the ship stormed toward me and I stroked toward it. The fathoms between us began to dwindle. I could almost feel the sweet splinter filled timber decking I used for a bed.

The ship's bell sounded as the vessel grew closer. I stopped swimming. By now I could just make out the faces of the sailors at the bow. They began yelling and pointing. Not in a 'Welcome back and come aboard, we'll make you some tea and fetch your slippers' - kind of way. It was more of a scared witless, 'we are all going to die' - kind of way, instead.

I turned my head towards my rear. My whole body became gripped in fear.

Cutting through the swell higher than a ship's mast, were the enormous fins of the behemoth. Spines of gnarled bone slid through the waves. The webbing of its hide linked each one, giving the impact of severely sinister sails connected to its twisting and rolling serpentine body. A body so incredibly large, it dwarfed all other sea monsters as a Rottweiler would standing in a pen of Pomeranians. Driven mad and wild, it was surging forward in the seas.

At *me*.

Swimming was now useless, speed was no longer a factor. Closing my eyes, I accepted my fate — drifting below the surface and into my mind.

I was still reeling from the size of the creature.

Massive.

Giant.

And Hungry.

At that pivotal moment, while I lay just below the waves, I had a moment of clarity.

It occurred to me, that I couldn't possibly be a natural prey for this thing. I would likely get stuck somewhere in its giant rows of serrated teeth, and unless it had opposable thumbs, some rudimentary dexterity and a ship's mast for a tooth pick, I'd be more of an irritation than a nutritious snack, and something that large had to have an appetite. To fuel its giant hunger, it had to eat large objects, other sea monsters, ships, heck - no wonder it devoured a whole naval armada. It was probably the appetizer.

Then what was driving it to chase me?

The *bracer*.

I looked at the device in the flashing lights from the sky above. I could see the cogs turning and the gears shifting. The noise under the surface was loud and grinding. It had to be stopped.

I reached into my pocket for my fish bone pick. This time, it was wedged in the fabric folds and unwilling to emerge. The damped report of cannon fire from the ship echoed through the depths. Each blink of flash powder revealed the creature moving closer. It roared in response. The new Regime cannons were definitely far superior to the old Ballistas, but this would certainly be a test of their effectiveness.

I tugged harder at the stubborn pick. Tearing at the fabric. Still, it refused to budge.

More cannon fire. The ship was almost upon me.

The creature too, was now close. Bearing down on me, just eighty fathoms away.

I relaxed. Like a snagged fishing line, I calmly coaxed the bone from my pocket, thrusting it between the moving parts. It wrenched to a halt. The sounds of bone between metal were jarring, however the desired outcome was the same. The musical sounds had stopped.

Without wasting a moment to think, I dove further into the depths. Feet kicking and arms stroking.

There was a show of a lifetime about to erupt on the surface and I had a front row seat.

***

It hadn't been pretty. It certainly wasn't quiet. And from well below the waves, the gruesome encounter between the ship and the creature had been a heavyweight match only the gods could have put wagers upon.

Bodies of unfortunate sailors who had thought drowning would be a better fate than the stomach acids of a giant sea serpent, drifted past me. The terror they had experienced before their demise still lingered in their frozen familiar expressions.

Steiger was among them. The scorch marks across his grim visage didn't seem quite as humorous this time round. Coupled with his lack of both arms, hinted that perhaps the choice of swimming had been made up for him. His corpse mixed with the others as they sunk deep down low.

They were dead snowflakes drifting into the abyss.

I wondered whether or not the Captain had met the same conclusion. I had witnessed glimpses of his temper throughout the years. The deep lash scars across my back were ample proof of his outbursts. Yet I had never seen his focus waver from the retribution he had wanted to instil upon this particular quarry. Losing his beloved ship a second time would almost send a man like him insane.

All of this time below the surface had almost distracted me from the next problem I now faced. Air – I needed it, yet the surface was not a place I wanted to be.

That moment had arrived once again, where air was the only thing the organs in my body wanted. My mind argued back, even my adrenaline had its two copper pieces worth, but the answer was clear. Air. Now. I began to ascend toward the waterline once again. Like a jelly fish pulsing through the currents, I felt lethargic and desperate at the same time. I had to negotiate my way past the planks, trunks and cannon balls that the ship was now spewing from its cavities as the creature tore and ripped away at its new plaything.

I arrived at the surface and once again filled my lungs with air.

Before me was utter devastation. The ship had been crushed to the point of no repair. It had taken on the appearance of a wicker basket whose owner would rather kick it to the marketplace and back rather than carry it. The creature's face was illuminated high above the last remaining upright mast. It was the first time I had seen it above the water.

The elongated snout of the monster was open, revealing rows upon rows of teeth, all angling back toward its throat. The eyes were dark, dead and lifeless as it studied its now helpless prey. It had managed to coil part of its torso around the centre of the ship. Slowly twisting and grinding the last remaining crew through the small openings between splintered wood. The creature began to adjust its jaws. Over the crashing of the waves, I could hear the unhinging of its already massive chops.

A man's yelling cut through the ambient sounds. A figure emerged on the now tilted bow. It was the Captain. True to his creed, he was apparently going down with the ship. Not without a 'fight' as it would seem. I couldn't quite make out what he was yelling, however, it made the monster stop and take notice. It reared back its head to consider this rather annoyed crumb on its plate. Tilting its head side to side, it looked around at the ocean, appearing rather confused and embarrassed by the situation. Still, the Captain kept up his tirade of abuse. In his hand he held a flaming plank of wood, he waved it back and forth with every challenge.

The beast soon appeared tired of the evening's entertainment. It resumed dislocating its large mouth to make it even larger. Slowly it lowered its orifice over the entire bow of the remains of the ship.

This infuriated the Captain even more and he turned his attention to the stores of barrels that remained lashed to the upper deck. Barrels of *black powder*. With one last defiant gesture toward the monster, I watched in awe as the Captain ceremoniously lowered the flaming plank into the stockpile of explosives.

My body reacted before I could think. I was suddenly diving as quickly as I could below the waves.

Within seconds a blinding flash erupted and sent a shockwave hurtling my way. Underwater, it rattled my bones and cleared my sinuses, air ripping forcefully from my lungs. The noise from the creature sounded like a wail of pain and carried through the sea just as loudly as the sound of the explosion.

A ringing sound entered my ears.

I waited a few seconds longer, unsure as to whether my surfacing would encounter an angrier than before monster, or remains of shattered ship. Upon breaching the waterline, I immediately had to cover my head, as chunks began to rain down from the sky. Pitter pattering all around where I floated. The smell of charred fish crept into my nostrils. Flaming debris streaked from overhead and littered the water around me. Equal parts sea monster and wooden plank.

Looking back toward where the ship and monster had been in a not-so-loving embrace was simply a burning trash heap. The fats and oils from previous bounties must have ignited as a flaming slick washed outward from the carnage.

And all at once it occurred to me. As my expression remained lit by the burning embers of my former prison, I realised I was free.

I grabbed onto a nearby floating crate of chickens, which had somehow managed to survive the ordeal.

What happens now? I thought, as the seas continued to rise and fall around me.

CHAPTER SEVEN

Perhaps there are numerous unpleasant ways of being woken from a semi-comatose state. The one I was currently experiencing, was something sharp and pointy, poking tentatively at my aching body.

My eyes peeled themselves open to the blurry surrounds of sand and sea shells. The sun bit hard into my skin. So too did the persistent prods of a stick.

'Hey, dead guy. You dead?' came the voice of a girl – the owner of said stick.

'Unngh,' I managed.

'You look kinda dead,' she said, poking me a few more times for good measure.

My head throbbed and the light glaring off the sand around me was almost blinding. I hadn't had something to drink in a few days (apart from copious amounts of salt water).

'Oi dead guy, I'm talking to you. Where are you from?'

'Sh... Ship.'

'Really? Where? You have a ship? Are you like a sailor or fisherman or something?'

I weakly turned my head from side to side, 'No.'

'Can you take me to it? Are you going north? Don't go north, it's not nice this time of year. Go south, or east, just not north. Do you know how to sail? Of course you do, I mean, you came from a ship, duh. Take me there pleeeeease?!' she spoke fast. It was almost too much to comprehend.

My thoughts began to function properly once again. *Land*. I was sitting on land. I hadn't seen land or felt its touch in years. The Captain had always ensured that I was locked and blindfolded below deck whenever the ship had to dock. I had almost forgotten how it felt. Here I was laying on it. I became as excited as my current weakened state would allow.

'So, are you dead? Or do you need some help or something? Coz I don't have heaps of time to be hanging about all day. I'm looking for something useful in this rubbish. I saw you floating in the water. I was going to leave you, coz you know, zombies are bad juju. But I just had to check you, curiosity, see? Imagine my surprise when you moved. I was like 'PLAGUE ZOMBIE!' Then I thought, of course I would've moved too if I was poked by a stick up the –'

'Shhhhhh, stop talking,' I cut her off. I had no idea who this person was and right now my mind hurt so much I didn't really care, just as long as she stopped the barrage of words. She spoke quite fast and I simply wanted a moment to enjoy the sensation of dry land. It was almost nauseating as my perpetual sea legs tried to transition to steady, stable ground.

I rolled over onto my back and sat up. Blinking, my vision began to sharpen. I was on a white sand beach. The turquoise waters to my front created lines of small crystal-clear waves that lapped against the shore. I could taste the salt on my blistered lips. The storm clouds that had carried me here slunk off into the far horizon. It was a breathtaking sight. Breathtaking and bright.

I held my arm above my head to provide some shade for my eyes. Almost immediately the girl lunged forward grabbing at the mechanical bracer.

'What's this? This is pretty. How does it work? Did you make it? What does it do?'

The bracer. I hadn't even thought of it since the night of the incident with the monster. I had lost track of time clinging to the crate for buoyancy as the ocean spat me about in the last few days.

'It's nothing, it's just an... Arrggh!' I tried to hold back my shock. For the first time I could see the girl's face. At first glance, she appeared almost dead. Her skin was ghostly pale and her hair stark white. Large eyes - so brown and flecked with orange they appeared almost a glowing red, stared widely back into mine. She was roughly the same age as me, perhaps slightly older. What I guessed were once nice clothes of some sort were now tattered rags, frayed and worn. It was almost unclear as to who had been the one clinging to a crate in the ocean for a few days.

'What? You look like you've seen a ghost. Never seen a girl before?'

I wasn't sure whether or not I was witnessing a mix of the two.

'Um, no? I mean... I have... It's just you're... you're...' the mix of dehydration, poor sleep and meeting an unexpected intense character made my head spin and my words falter. I noticed the drag marks from where she had pulled me from the sea. It occurred to me that she quite possibly saved me from drowning in knee deep water.

'A girl?!' she persisted angrily and interrupting my personal space.

I leaned back to a more comfortable distance.

'Obviously. I was just trying to say, that you're very helpful. Thank you.'

An immediate smile peeled from ear to alabaster ear across her face. It was the quickest change of moods I had ever seen.

'Wait!' Her attention changed to the lines of debris spanning the shore. She whisked away and rummaged through a nearby heap of broken barrels and decking. Diving head long through the wreckage until only her long legs waved about above the top of the pile.

'Eureka!' came her cry and within moments she bounded over, landing hard on her knees in the sand beside me. She was hiding something behind her back.

'Close your eyes. No peeking, got it? I'll give you this, but you've got to take me to your ship so I can get outta here, okay?'

I had just met this unhinged character and now she wanted me to close my eyes? All common sense screamed out to resist the request, however, my mind was growing weaker by the minute as fatigue finally doused my initial adrenaline rush from waking up.

I wearily closed my eyes. The girl seemed harmless enough and had given me charity already.

A pop of a cork was quickly followed by the familiar ceramic touch of a jug against my lips. Cool fresh water poured over my face and down my surprised throat. I coughed and spluttered. I had only been on the land for a moment and already I was drowning again.

'Sorry,' she said. 'You look like you need this pretty badly.'

I opened my eyes and grabbed at the vessel. I chugged desperately.

'Slow down. You'll make yourself sick.' She reached out and lowered the jug so the stream became a trickle. 'Just take sips. You'll throw up otherwise.'

'I don't have anything to throw up.' I peeled myself away from the water. 'Again, thanks.'

'You're welcome. So... what brings you here, kid? Apart from the waves and ships n stuff. Speaking of – where is your ship?'

I remembered my mantra from the past few days at sea. My father was alive and being held prisoner at some capital city near here. As I clung to the crate, I clung to the hope of seeing him once again, and somehow, I could break him out. Although, the *how* wasn't quite clear just yet. Well, at all really.

'I need to get to the Capital. Is it near here?'

'Huh? Um yeah, it's four days on foot from here, well, maybe longer for some.' The girl responded. Her voice had a slight concern to it. 'Why would you want to go?'

'You know where it is?' It was my turn to be the excitable one.

'Yeah, I do, but...'

'Can you take me there? I don't have any money, but I will try to...'

Fingers slammed against my lips in a 'hushing' fashion. I stopped speaking. The girl's head was lowered. Her voice took on a more serious tone.

'Look, kid. I don't know why you want to go there. Quite frankly, I don't care. All I know is that I am never going back there... ever. I'm guessing you want to join the Regime. If that's the case, then I should've left you face down in the water. As for now. I've wasted too much time on you. I have to keep moving.'

'I'm not tryi-' her fingers pressed against my lips again. She pointed back up the beach toward a break in the foliage. I could make out a trail of her footprints leading from the bushes. Without lifting her head, the girl turned and stood up.

'Whatever it is you're going there for, you're crazy. Just cut your losses and thank yourself lucky to be alive. Just point me in the direction of your ship and I'll work it out myself.'

'I think this is what is left of it.' I motioned to all the debris along the beach.

She looked up at me astonished. 'You tricked me. You said you'd take me to your ship and help me get out of this place.'

'Actually, I didn't get to say a thing. You did. But, I did stay true to your implied deal though. It's all around you.'

Her eyes flashed with anger. She swung a pointed fist at my face. I braced for the impact too weak still to stop her. The girl's pointed finger stopped just a breath from me. I opened my eyes and looked up at her. The scolding was about to begin, but she stalled. She was still coming to grips with the fact I couldn't help her as she realised I was right. With that, she turned south and began to jog in the opposite direction of where she had come from. I watched as she continued away and around a steep bluff that jutted toward the ocean. Then, as I had been for days — I was alone.

Wind blew through the coastal palms and trees behind me. The waves continued to lap the shore. I sat with my head bowed, taking the odd sip of fresh water. My mind was still fuzzy and coming to grips with the strange girl who had just rescued me and my current location. My stomach rumbled with the unfamiliar addition of actual contents. My father had always said '*When in doubt, follow your gut instincts*' and right now my gut and my instincts both told me I needed food.

The storm had claimed numerous shore birds, reef fish and larger, more decomposed corpses, currently in various states of bloating as the hot sun accelerated the process of rot, allowing a build-up of gases inside the bodies.

After a few wobbly attempts, I managed to stand. Getting my bearings, I instinctively felt the lining of my pants for my family's locket – breathing a sigh of relief at its familiar outline where I had left it. I delicately removed it with trembling hands to see that it had not been damaged in the sea. The seal remained unbroken – and like always I returned it to its resting place without looking inside before indulging my need to eat.

I decided the easiest way to find food in my current state would be to scavenge the animals that looked the freshest. Hunting in the steep cliffs behind me was not an option. If only the crate that had kept me buoyant for the last few days had still been attached to me. The chickens inside - although likely to be dead, would at least be slightly fresh.

I began to stumble down the beach, roughly in the same direction as the girl. Walking was a lot harder than I had expected. Every so often my toes would connect with a sharp stone or piece of coral, which led to my frail body collapsing into the sand. Just ahead on the high tide line, I could see the slightly rotting corpse of a rather large bear seal. Its cause of death was likely the enormous bite from its mid-section, possibly from a large shark. I shuddered at the thought of sizeable sharks patrolling these waters and how long I had been within their domain. Intestines and stomach contents had spilled onto the sand and shore birds were having pride of the pickings.

On hands and knees, I crawled feverishly toward the not-so-gourmet buffet. Decorum would have me at least use my sharpened fish bone pick (still wedged firmly in the bracer) to cut neat slices off and cook them first. However, this was survival and I let my mouth do the work. My teeth bit hard into the blubbery flesh of the beast as the shore birds scattered in protest of my arrival. I gorged on the meat from the rump, and quite soon my stomach felt full. The metallic taste of coagulated blood wedged firmly between my teeth. I felt like retching, but I had to keep the nutrients down.

A noise beyond my meal interrupted my chewing. Angry yelling and the sounds of metal on metal grabbed my attention. I lifted my head to spy on the source. A fight by the sound of it. I rolled over my meal and crawled up to some boulders ahead. I peered over the top to see what the commotion was.

The scene before me made me forget to chew. I choked on a piece of lodged seal fat.

Just a stone's throw away, a group of soldiers were attempting to capture my saviour.

She was tied up in a spot of trouble.

CHAPTER EIGHT

How many soldiers does it take to capture a person? More importantly, how many Regime soldiers does it take to capture a girl? Apparently, their answer to this particular question was quite a few. Still though, it seemed that they didn't have enough.

Just ahead beyond the rocks, it was the girl. Four Regime soldiers were attempting to restrain her with ropes, each keeping their distance, almost as if they were afraid of her, their feet slid through the sand. More stood on standby to add to the entanglement. Others pointed spears in her general direction, shifting back and forth from her attempted lashes. The girl's struggling made them slip and stumble over each other. It almost appeared comical, but I found myself concerned. I realised maybe it was misplaced as my attention shifted to two of her would-be captors lying motionless on the beach.

Dead motionless.

I hadn't seen Regime soldiers in years, just the crew of the ship and their poor attempts to mimic the naval uniform with tattered surplus garbs. Still, I could recognise their colours — the distinct Regime red and black armour and helms. They had all the calling cards of infantry, with their disciplined formation (although that was failing) their weapons and their physiques tipping that they were likely to be elite. Elite soldiers, still struggling to restrain this girl. What had she done? More importantly, what exercise program does she follow?

I made a quick study of the surrounds. It must have been an ambush. The cliffs above and around this small beach inlet provided excellent cover and concealment from an elevated position. With game tracks up high providing access to a multitude of positions and small windblown coastal bushes and shrubs providing observation points. The beach itself had absolutely nowhere to run, no cover to seek. I had often eaves dropped on members of the crew back on the ship. Some were disgraced veterans (officers of failed missions or not-so-tactical retreats) who loved nothing more than telling all the others of the strategic geniuses they once were and palming the blame of their losses to those underneath them. The embellished details were all too obvious with the stories growing more and more stupendous each time they were told. Sitting there, night after night, I inadvertently received lessons on Regime doctrine. I learnt from their mistakes.

Watching the spectacle in front, it occurred to me that they were doing their best to not harm her, just capture her. Perhaps they were waiting for her to tire, but she was showing no signs of fatigue. Instead, the girl found her grip on one of the ropes and launched the soldier on the other end in her direction. With the slack on the rope she wrapped it around the soldier's neck swiftly and manoeuvred him into a human shield.

Stalemate.

'Enough!' roared a metallic voice.

The men braced in position. The girl stopped struggling and firmly held her hostage - peering just over his shoulder to survey her opponents. Although her face still showed her frustration, my frustration stemmed from the fact I couldn't see the whole story. I moved my head around another part of my rocky cover that had been concealing the owner of the commanding voice.

Standing just to the rear of the group was the tall, broad figure. How long had he been there, letting the men struggle with the girl? He stood almost statuesque in the sand. His muscled arms remained folded as though he was admiring a sunset rather than an apparent military ambush. His face was shrouded by a solid red mask that hugged his entire head. Slits concealed his eyes, creating soulless cavities. Horns protruded out and upward from the helm giving the appearance of a devil. Two sheathed swords extended from behind his back. The rest of his attire was a mixture of a type of fitted darkened armour, red trim and various pouches. No fancy flowing garbs, no embellishments – it looked intimidating and spelt business. At his feet lay two, very large, tracking war hounds. They panted in excitement waiting for their opportunity to be set upon the girl.

'Take a look around you,' his voice boomed. 'I have orders to return you unharmed to the Governor. After what you inflicted upon him, I believe he has taken a *soft* approach in your return. However, accidents do happen. We can either do this the easy way or – my way.'

The leader motioned toward the cliffs surrounding the tiny beach. Men armed with crossbows emerged from behind various points of cover. The entire escarpment was peppered with them. Each having an elevated and almost unobstructed view of their target. Unobstructed, save for one of their own – a look of terror swept across his face as he too, realised he was the one factor now standing between the platoon and their quarry.

'Let me make my intentions clear.' The leader of the group pointed his finger at the girl. Almost immediately, it was followed by a chorus of muffled twangs as several bolts punctured the human shield she held in front of her. It was a ruthless approach. Sacrificing one of their own to capture the girl. Her situation was growing ever grim, yet she continued to hold the now limp prickled body in front of her as the only source of cover.

I had to do something. This girl had taken the time to save me – a complete stranger, from drowning. She knew where the Capital was and she was *clearly* an enemy of the Regime. The enemy of my enemy is my friend, and she was the one chance I could have of finding my father. I would need all the help I could get. However, what could I do against a heavily armed platoon (minus three) of soldiers from the Regime? I was just a kid.

The smell from the bear seal corpse to my rear, gave me a sign. Adrenaline began to surge into my body giving me a burst of strength. I moved quickly back to the mass of blood, innards and flesh and held my nose. If this was going to work, I had to sell it and sell it well. With a sharp inward take of breath, I plunged my head and shoulders into the mass of guts and rolled in it like a dog writhing in a strange new stench. The effect was – well – effective. From head to toe I was now covered in dripping coagulated bodily fluids and I'm sure my smell would carry beyond the horizon.

I scrambled forward over the rocks with as much speed as my tired body could muster. This had to be fast to be effective, and it was *show time*.

Like a curtain raising for a performance, I rounded the corner of the headland into the view of my collective audience. I thrashed about with gurgles and snarls. The attention of the girl turned towards me as she looked in my direction. Her large reddish-brown eyes revealed a severe case of confusion as I shambled hard and rapidly in her direction. I tried to wink at her through the strands of flesh dangling from my brow. Whether or not she had seen my message I couldn't be certain.

'A plague zombie!' yelled some of the soldiers as they released their holds on the ropes. They reeled backward. Some holding their noses. Others covering their mouths. A few ran for the safety of the headland. To be perfectly honest, I had actually never seen a zombie before – plague or otherwise, but once again, the stories of sailors painted a vivid picture that I tried so hard to copy.

I lunged forward at the girl and tackled her to the ground. I scrambled on top of her.

'Go with it.' I hissed, winking again.

Her blank look turned to one of realisation. I then proceeded with my best imitation of a zombie sinking its teeth into the neck of a victim. I growled and carried on like my life depended on a top review from a watching critic. Essentially, it did.

The girl screamed out in pain as I 'gummed' her neck harder. The noise she released was blood curdling.

'Throw me off,' I continued between 'bites'.

'Okay,' she responded through gritted teeth.

I wasn't expecting the *inhuman* strength that followed. With a swift motion, she catapulted me through the air. Upside down, I managed to catch a glimpse of the soldiers moving back off the beach. Then – I landed on something. Hard.

The air was forced from my lungs. A pair of collective 'yelps' rang out as I realised I had landed on top of the two war hounds. Although undoubtedly well trained – they obviously were not prepared for a blood and guts covered zombie look-alike to fall from the sky on top of them. With fear taking over, I could hear their cries as they joined the soldiers retreating from the beach.

Trying to stay 'in-character' is especially hard when the wind has been temporarily knocked out of one's lungs. I feebly tried to attempt this by snapping my eyes open and pushing the 'zombie- esque' noises. Sand had managed to mix with the sticky bear-seal remnants all over me. Now, not only was I already a muck covered mess, I could add grating grains of sand to the list of things making this experience unpleasant.

I looked up from my prone position to gain my bearings once more. Standing directly over me, was the intimidating, cold, hollow stare of the leader. He appeared a lot more imposing close up. The empty dark slits he peered through gave away no hint of emotion, fear or otherwise. I felt as though he could see straight through my ruse. His stare lingered. Studied. Scrutinized.

A 'gulp' formed in my throat.

The mask remained emotionless as his hand reached backward over his shoulder.

It returned.

This time it had a rather sharp looking sword in it and he aligned it with my neck.

'Disgusting abomination,' he growled, drawing the sword's equally sharp looking companion from its sheath.

I felt quite helpless. I was just as frozen in fear as the night of the sea monster incident. What had I done in a previous life to deserve this? My mind, usually resourceful - was blank. The figure smoothly drew both arms back as though he were about to scissor my head from my body.

'Reaper Sir! The girl!' A soldier from the cliffs above yelled.

His focus switched to behind me. I knew an opportunity when I saw one. Trying to make the most of the situation, I attempted to scramble away during whatever distraction was behind me. His leg swiftly moved above me and tomahawked down upon the base of my skull. I was pinned by my neck in the sand. It was fast, eloquent and painful all at once. Through my discomfort and my new facing (back toward the sea) I could make out the scene unfolding.

The girl was acting strangely. Contorting about in a sort of dance, her hair was now covering most of her face, save for her mouth. She had already looked ghoulish in a 'pretty' way earlier. Now her appearance had taken on a more sinister approach. It made even *me* shiver and I knew it was a bluff. She was hunched over and staring in our direction. Her pale skin and white hair were stark against the ocean storm clouds still out at sea. Arms dangled to her sides as she stopped and stared through the veil of hair toward the Reaper. I noticed in her hand, she was firmly holding the leg (still attached thankfully) of the pin cushioned soldier's corpse. The panic grew in the soldier's voices.

'Sir, one is bad enough. Now the girl is infected. She'll be almost un-stoppable.'

'Get out of there, boss!' cried another.

His voice trailed off as the Reaper drowned them out with new orders.

'Five bolts rapid,' his iron voice was still absent of any trace of panic.

With that order, the girl snapped into a sprint still dragging the corpse with her. Bolts began raining down in her direc-tion, yet none were finding their mark as she moved swiftly across the open ground. She closed on our position and began to spin. The body of the soldier lifted off the ground, swung horizontal from the force, and circled her. In one powerful movement, she launched the corpse at the Reaper.

With his boot firmly on the back of my neck, he didn't have any space to evade the hurtling dead ballistic missile.

'OOMPF,' the mixed sounds of breaking bones and wind bursting from lungs filled the air. The pressure from my

neck was instantaneously gone. The Reaper had undoubtedly
reaped a dash of Karma. The airborne figure of the girl leapt
toward me. A starving dire wolf protecting its fresh kill —she
positioned herself between me and the remaining soldiers. A
teeth bearing growl emanated from her.

'*THUMP! THUMP! THUMP! THUMP!*' Another round of
bolts embedded themselves throughout the sand surrounding me. It was rather unnerving. One stray bolt, or one false
movement to show I was still mobile and I would meet the
same fate as the soldier's comrade only moments earlier.

Despite the risk of impending piercing demise, I was like a
curious child that had been told 'no' by their mother. I just
had to see what was happening. I hoped the watchful eyes of
the elevated marksmen above would be glued to the girl and
not me. I slowly rotated my face through the grains of sand.
Holding my breath and contorting myself with painful control,
I eventually managed to split my lids enough to see the scene
unfold.

The girl remained standing over me. Her fortitude was
fierce and unwavering. The soldiers were quite the opposite.
Fleeing in the direction of the hills, I wondered if this would
later be referred to as a 'tactical retreat'. Three had returned,
albeit seemingly reluctantly, to gather up the limp figure of the
Reaper some eight fathoms away. He seemed to recover quite
quickly after the crushing sound of the impact. He gradually
gained control of his legs and brushed the minions off. The
Reaper's decision to stay and fight had somewhat changed
however and he joined the other soldiers in removing themselves from the area up over the dunes to the rear.

Then the scene was empty. No characters, save for the girl
and myself.

Turning my head some more, I could see no more marksmen in the cliffs. Instead, the sea breeze aggressively rustled

the spinifex grasses and wind carved brushes along the sides of the re-entrant.

The area that had been alive with tension, now appeared picturesque – if it weren't for the three scattered bodies that littered the shore.

And at that calm moment, as the adrenaline subsided and my less vital senses returned (smell for one), I realised the icky and grotesque contents that lathered me. Bile, stomach acids, chunks of tripe and the odd smear of internally stored excrement all mashed with vigour through my hair and across my skin. Some of the more sinister of which had worked their way into my tastebuds, nostrils and eyes.

I retched.

All of the valuable nutrients that had filled my stomach earlier, now painted an abstract puddle in the sand before me.

I scrambled toward the ocean and leapt over the small waves to get into knee deep water. Desperately I plunged my face under the surface and swished it about in an attempt to remove the muck. I rubbed furiously at my skin and scratched at my hair, only to return to the surface to breathe. I contin-ued to spit out sticky strands of mucus from my mouth. The flavours were terrible, and I scratched at my tongue.

A bodily weight slammed into me from behind. Not a vio-lent and hurting tackle. This was more of an over vigorous hug - slightly endearing even.

'Thankyouthankyouthankyouthankyouthankyou,' the voice of the girl cried out enthusiastically.

I choked on some more sea water.

'You don't know how much that meant to me! I owe you. I owe you. You're not a wannabe Regime soldier. You're a hero,' she was stoked.

A hero? This girl had just managed to keep my head con-nected firmly to my neck. She just dragged me half dead from the ocean and gave me fresh water. She owes me? Oh well, *I can work with this* I thought.

Carrion birds and gulls swooped down at the red cloudy mess I had created in the water. Another fleck of flesh plopped into the currents. My stomach had decided to settle enough for me to speak.

'You... owe me?' I asked curiously, trying to regain my composure.

'Yes, I owe you. You don't understand what you just did. What would've happened to me if you hadn't stepped in? I had almost run out of options,' she said slipping off my back into the water.

Almost run out? That was an interesting choice of words. Perhaps she didn't need my help. I knew that I certainly needed hers. It was at this moment that I decided to seize an opportunity. With the most innocent and endearing expression that I could muster, I turned to face her.

Her face was brimming with a smile from ear to ear. Her bright red... I mean brown eyes, excitedly darted between both of mine.

'What's your name?' she beat me to the punch.

'Flynt.' I replied.

'Mine is Xanthe. Xanthe Bones. Nice to meet you,' she said extending a long thin arm with much enthusiasm. I drew mine up to meet hers. Xanthe slapped her hand into mine and proceeded to give a hand shake that would make most sailors – with their well-worn rigging hands – buckle under the strain.

X Bones. *By name and by nature* I thought.

'So, you mentioned that you owe me?' I queried.

'Sure did.'

'Well, in that case,' I said wishfully, 'will you help me get into the Capital?'

Chapter Nine

My eyes snapped open and I sat bolt upright in a cold sweat. My heart thumped away in my chest, belying the fact I had just been asleep. I felt extremely confused and unaware of where I was. I could feel wooden walls all around me and a sensation of claustrophobia that comes with the feeling of having tasted freedom from incarceration only to be back in a cell so quickly.

A girl's voice brought me to my senses.

'Wow kid, you sure sleep weird,' she said. 'You had another one of your nightmares. You were all like *mrr grr mrrrr*. Plague Zombie noises all over again.'

She was exceptionally close and appeared to be looking intently at my bracer. How long had she been there watching me sleep? - was a thought that still slightly creeped me out.

I pulled my arm away from her and blinked hard trying to see my surroundings.

I could see the silhouette of her face as the last golden rays of the sun beamed through the large fallen hollow we were hiding in. It was perched overlooking a valley of forests and after yet another cold day of rain, the light managed to peak through the cloud cover to put on a spectacular show of colour as it slid behind distant mountain ranges. After several days on the run, we had only stopped periodically to allow me to rest, due to the likelihood of our pursuers being not too far behind despite our doubling back parallel to Xanthe's original escape route. The brief nap I just had had felt luxurious regardless that it was only for possibly a few hours, or maybe just minutes. Yet sleep had its own problems. I often had nightmares that left me shaken.

'How long have you been watching me sleep?' I responded as I tried to regather my composure. I picked yet another persistent chunk of bear seal innards from my matted hair. I flicked it away into the depths of the hollow. There were faint sounds of scurrying as some unidentified critters fought over the morsel.

'Here and there,' she smiled. 'So, what's the jewellery for? What's it do? Can I try it on? I've been looking at it and it doesn't wanna budge much.' Once again, her questions bombarded me as I struggled to fully wake up. And once again it was a little hard to get used to.

'I told you before, it's not jewellery. The Captain of the ship locked it onto my wrist and I can't get it off.'

'Well, if you were trying to use this to get it off, you probably should use it on the lock and not the gears,' Xanthe held my fishbone pick that had been wedged in the bracer to stop it moving. My lucky fishbone pick!

'How'd you get that out?' I demanded. 'It was wedged in there tight.' It was a dumb question. I had seen brief examples of her strength before. Enough to hold several elite soldiers at bay. What did surprise me was that she had managed to pilfer it as I slept.

'You want it? Here you go,' she tossed it into my lap. 'I just thought it looked like it was getting in the way, so I removed it. The bits all started moving and stuff, but I found a switch and it stopped,' she stated curiously moving back to study it. 'Now that you're awake, give it here and I can get it off for you.'

'No. Don't,' I said snatching my arm away again. 'I kind of like having it.'

I rubbed at the bracer on my wrist. Feeling its cogs and gears. It had previously been annoying, but now it reminded me of my father and I felt a somewhat strange attachment to it.

Now, the bracer was certainly less cumbersome. Like a child receiving their favourite toy that had long needed to be thrown out due to its decrepit state, I had wanted the pick back for a number of reasons lately — but first things first. I let out a satisfying sigh as I wedged it between the bracer and my arm for a long-awaited scratch. The relief was amazing.

'Kid, you're weird. Funny, but weird,' she stated slightly disgusted.

I ignored her distaste at my ceremonious picking and savoured the moment some more.

'What is it you dream about?' she asked now sitting closer to the entry of our hide.

'Monsters. *Sea* monsters,' I replied solemnly. They never seemed to bother me when I was awake, however, time and again beasts still hunted me in my dreams.

'I understand. I think of monsters too. Cept mine are probably different from yours,' she stated and turned herself back toward the sunset. I moved to sit across from her and joined in looking out over the valley. We both sat quietly, enjoying a sight that I had missed many times in my years as a prisoner.

The smell of wet vegetation and fresh air gave a slight chill through my newly acquired yet sodden uniform. I pulled the cloak further around my shoulders for warmth. In the moments after the incident back at the beach, we had pilfered the downed soldiers that were left behind. Between us, we had managed to scavenge some coils of thin but very strong rope, a tiny amount of field rations which were far more nutritious than the raw seal meat and more importantly, their uniforms which both of us had badly needed. There was also a map of the surrounding lands which Xanthe insisted on keeping. Not only did the garbs provide us with much needed warmth and clothing, they also helped us to move through some territories without so much as a second glance from the odd farmer or civilian. The masked helmets hid our tell-tale features – my age and Xanthe's unusual appearance.

Xanthe and I were also sporting Regime spears, more for the reason that a pair of soldiers would look out of place without weapons. I actually had very little experience in its use, save as a walking stick through hard terrain. The odd slap across the back of my head from my *guide* aimed to remind me that leaving tracks would make it easier for anyone following us – and according to her, the Regime's elite hunting squad were certainly doing so. Guided by their leader – one of the most feared agents of the Regime that I had managed to meet in the flesh - 'The Reaper'. According to Xanthe, the sheer fact that I had managed to dupe him into withdrawing had saved her from a fate she described as worse than death. Now though, I could expect retribution. Quite simply, after my escape from the ship, it was a case of 'out of the frying pan and into the fire'. *Fantastic*. Still, I had a lot of questions I would like to ask about him – it isn't every day you come across such a fearsome character.

Things weren't all that grim though. The silver lining I did have in all this was Xanthe. Doing this alone would have been significantly harder to say the least. Despite her slightly unhinged personality, I was learning a lot from her actions and guidance. Ever since the beach incident she had led me at a cracking pace.

The pair of soldiers (save for the punctured one) had amaz-ingly remained alive and were simply knocked out by Xanthe.

In an attempt to buy us some time, we buried them up to their necks in the sand. Xanthe had insisted that we should 'finish' the job, however I had protested firmly against it. Thus, wearing only their regime issued under garments they were planted like wildflowers near the dunes. Speaking of — Xanthe had insisted on decorating their hair with a few wildflowers from the surrounds and had placed sticks in each of their mouths, claiming that once they regained consciousness, they would be able to 'dig' their way out if they *really wanted to*.

Right now though, as the sun said its last goodbyes, I wondered about the pair.

'Xanthe?'

'Yeah, kid?'

'You reckon those two soldiers we left buried to their necks managed to dig their way out?'

'Hmmm.' She placed a finger across her lips as she pondered the situation. 'Yeah, I reckon they would've. A high tide approaching your face while you're buried up to your neck would be a strong motivator I would imagine.'

I shook the image of two soldiers panicking as a king tide lurched toward their exposed faces and pulled some field jerky from my pocket. I began to chew away contentedly.

The sounds of bird calls echoed through the valley. In the distance I could see at least three hawks circling various areas of the forest. Xanthe seemed to have noticed them too.

'Drone Hawks,' she said finally. 'They're looking for us.'

'What do you mean? Aren't they just birds?' I asked.

'No. The Regime captures them and puts clockwork implants in them. It forces them to be controlled.'

'That's brilliant and twisted,' I said astonished. 'How much control?'

'They're all kind of like *duuuurrrrr*,' she went cross eyed and let a small amount of dribble pool in the corner of her mouth. We both chuckled quietly in the hollow.

She continued, 'Right now they are no longer birds, kinda just empty shells running on autopilot. They are relaying images of the forest back to the soldiers that are hunting us, looking for any sign of where we have been,' she informed me as she casually flicked a rather large venomous centipede from her shoulder.

'What does 'otto pile-ot' mean?' I asked, feeling somewhat dumb for not understanding.

'Auto – pilot. It means you're moving and doing things, but you aren't in control.'

'Oh,' I uttered, feeling a slight sense of empathy with the birds after my experiences aboard the 'Kraken Krusher'. Most days for the first year at least, felt like I was simply trying to survive, until I made the decision that I was only a prisoner if I believed it.

'Yeah, the Regime have a knack for stealing innocent creatures and bending them to their will,' she trailed off.

There was an uncomfortable silence between us. Until now we had kind of avoided getting to know one another too well. I was accustomed to looking after myself and considering how Xanthe seemed to operate, so was she. I decided to address my curiosities.

'Is that what they did to you?' I asked as nonchalantly as I could.

'Jeez Kid, you sure ask a lot of questions, don'tcha?'

'That was my only one.'

'*Saaay.* You aren't perchance a sleeper agent sent to help capture me, are you?' Her voice now sounded quite stern and menacing.

'What's a sleeper agent? Is that what that 'Reaper' guy is?' I responded, genuinely puzzled. It sounded quite strange that she would be worried about a spy who obviously had trouble staying awake on the job.

'Huh? Oh no, kid. The Reaper, he's bad news,' Xanthe seemed to shiver at the mention of his name.

'Who is he?' I prompted.

Xanthe stopped for a moment and looked at me. Then turned her head back to the view outside.

'He is the right hand of the Governor himself. They say he is *death* incarnate.'

'Who say that? Who are *they*?' I asked. 'The survivors?'

'No no no kid. Just those that serve under his command. There are never any witnesses or survivors after he has *visited* a land save for a handful of his own soldiers. Sometimes there aren't even bodies. Just burning wrecks and ashes. Even members of his elite death squads fear him.'

'How did he become the Reaper?' I queried some more, feeling somewhat engrossed.

'Rumours differ. Some say he was a man who gained the attention of the Governor's agents as he worked his way through the underground pit fighting rings of the Capital. Every opponent, no matter how big or tough succumbed to his tactics and cunning. Then *the man* simply disappeared. Others say that he was selected from a group of handpicked convicts, thieves and soldiers and underwent a series of experiments that changed his body and sharpened and twisted his mind. And then there's the one that says he was an assassin sent to eliminate the Governor. That he almost succeeded in his task, only to be captured and manipulated to the Governor's wishes and altered. Either way, not long after, there were reports throughout the Regime, that high ranking enemies — officers, saboteurs, scientists — began to disappear and that the Governor now had the means to exact his will upon anyone, anywhere, no matter how well hidden or guarded or powerful. Within months, the Regime had spread its borders through several enemy regions that were previously besieged for years. Their armies fell into disarray without the correct leadership.

'And no one has ever stopped him?'

'Many have tried. Some even claim to have bettered or destroyed the Reaper in battle, but he always seems to return. It is almost as though he cannot die. And just like death itself, once you are in his sights, he will find you.'

I gave an involuntary gulp as I stared wide eyed at Xanthe.

'*BANG!*' echoed through the hollow.

I leapt so high from the floor that I struck my head on the roof of the log. I held my head in pain and grabbed at my spear on the floor. Xanthe covered her mouth trying to muffle a burst of laughter. I then realised the origin of the noise was made by her and at my expense.

'I'm just toying with you, kid,' she giggled. 'At least you had the right mind to grab your weapon though. I'd be impressed if I couldn't swear I heard a girly squeal amongst all that.'

I narrowed my eyes at her, unamused at having been the butt of her jokes once again.

'So, you made it all up?'

'Oh no, most of it is true, or just rumours. I'll let you figure out which,' she smiled.

'Why can't you tell me now?' I insisted.

'Mystery and intrigue are so much more interesting. Once you know everything about someone, they lose part of their allure, ya know?'

I sat back, slightly miffed as my heart rate slowly returned to normal and placed the spear back down, although it was a tad bit closer this time. I returned to chewing away at my jerky and offered Xanthe some. Once more she declined with a slight shake of her head.

'What bout you, kid?' She continued. 'In a small matter of time, you manage to escape your floating prison, meet me and then get yourself onto the hit list of some of the most dangerous men in the Regime, including the 'Reaper' himself. Yet spite all that, you keep wanting to head to the Capital. The same place they'd take you if they caught you alive. So tell me, *what* or *who* is it that you're after? You planning on toppling the Gov-nah himself?'

'If I told you, then wouldn't I lose a lure?'

'Your allure,' she corrected.

'Yeah, that.'

'Kid, you already keep things interesting and there are a bunch of questions I have for you. But right now, I kind of want to know the whole reasoning behind me risking my neck to get you to the Capital. Gimme that at least. I can try to guess the rest.'

Her reasoning was hard to argue against. After the last few days it didn't feel as though a change of subject or attempt at humour would satisfy her. I glanced a look at Xanthe. Once again, she had moved into my personal space and was eyeing me intently. This was becoming an interrogation of its own.

'Well?' she insisted.

Xanthe grabbed a metal broach from the soldier's cloak she was wearing and reflected the rays of the sun into my face. It was blinding and irritating at the same time. I used my hand to shield my eyes.

'Someone there needs my help,' I answered solemnly. 'My father.'

She paused and looked at me in astonishment. Xanthe returned the broach to her cloak and slunk back. My eyes slowly began to shake the effects of the bright light and I could see properly once again.

'Your father? Why's he there? Is he part of the Regime?' her tone was once again stern.

I shook my head. 'No, he's in a bit of trouble and needs my help.'

Xanthe spat out of the hollow. 'Kid, you mean to tell me you're going to all this trouble just to help your dad? Boring! Excite me. Like how much trouble are we talking here?'

'Big trouble,' I admitted.

I was still holding a few of my proverbial cards close to my chest. Knowing that my father was at the Capital was one thing, however, knowing that he was locked up and accused of being a spy against the Regime was another situation all together. Somehow Xanthe seemed quite amused with my answer.

'Tell you what. I might be a bit slow on the uptake at times kid, but I'm no mug. He's in more than a spot of bother, isn't he? Like, even the word 'big' doesn't quite cover it. Over the past few days you've been breaking your back to keep up with me and I set a cracking pace. Not once have you complained or moaned through all the rain, cold, mud and mountains. Look at you. You look like a pile of rhino-bear dung, but you keep moving. That tells me you've got gumption son,' she said in a mockingly masculine tone.

'You don't complain either,' I pointed out feeling embarrassed at the compliment.

'Yeah, but if you haven't figured it out kid, I'm a bit different from you,' She admitted finally. 'I can tell this father of yours is someone you care about just from how you've pushed yourself. I mean, you washed up half dead just to get here. You strike me as the kind of person that is driven, but you need some help in more ways than one.' She stated bluntly. 'Especially if you're intending on sneaking into the Capital.'

She raised her eyebrow.

I wasn't sure if it was a statement or a question, however, she seemed to be waiting for a response.

'Were you just gonna wait till we got there before you asked me to help some more? Or did you think you could do it alone?' she pressed.

I felt on the spot being called out like that. Had I been so easy to read over just a small amount of time? Guilt began to hit me hard. It didn't feel fair to be leading this girl back toward somewhere she seemed to be trying so hard to escape. I'd been used to looking after myself for such a long time, I had almost forgotten to have empathy toward others.

'Something on your mind, kid? You've gone all quiet and mopey,' Xanthe observed. She kept on harping on, but my attention wandered.

Just say it Flynt, I thought. *No matter how much you need this other person to lead you there and how much you hate to admit it, just say it.*

I blurted over her ramblings. 'Look, it's wrong of me to expect you to take me all the way to the Capital. Especially since you are being hunted. I'm thinking we are both even on the 'owing each other' front. Why risk helping me out? Why not just point me in the direction of the Capital and let me get on with it?'

Xanthe stopped her talking and studied me for a moment.

'Relax kid, let me finish, alright? As I figure, I owe you and I gave you my word, see? You got me out of a tight spot and for that I will help you get there – preferably alive and in one piece. If I can at least push you in the right direction to sneak in once we arrive, then I will too. Heck I might even come along for the ride. The last place they'd think to look for someone who is supposed to be running away would be in their very own streets, right? They'll think I've gone as far away as I could get. Brilliant. Plus, no one has ever cared enough for me like you do for your father, and a person like you is the kind of person I wanna be a friend of in me new life, ya see? You keep things interesting most of the time. Even when you sleep it can be amusing,' she jibed.

I wasn't sure how I felt about Xanthe watching me while I slept, let alone being amused by it. I guess though, most of the time I was too tired to care and when I needed to rest, she always insisted on maintaining look out. That was another strange thing about Xanthe; she never seemed to tire. It was almost as though she didn't need sleep at all.

'But don't spoil the situation for me, eh?' she continued. 'Keep me guessing. I like guessing. I'll try to work it out by the time we get there. Also, if on the off chance I do get captured alive, which I won't, the less information I know about you, the less I can tell them if they torture me.' She said cheerfully.

'Torture?' I asked concerned.

'The Regime are good at a lot of things, kid. That's why they control so much of the lands. But what they excel in the most is *torture*. They have turned it into an art form. They take you into a chamber in the 'Gulag' – That's their name for their maximum-security prison if you were wondering - and strip you down and have all these shiny, sharp pointy things, and things to keep you awake and that's just for the ones they don't like, it gets worse ... say kid you aren't looking so good.'

In my mind I began picturing what my father was most likely subjected to over the past three years. Perhaps death would've been an easier option.

'Do they treat everyone that way?' I asked.

'Oh no, not always. They save the worst for traitors, enemy officers, soldiers, sympathizers and especially spies.'

'Spies?' I gulped.

'Oh, spies, they get the worst of the – ' Xanthe stopped and looked outside with a sense of concern.

'Can you smell that?' she asked seemingly rhetorically.

I couldn't smell anything except the fresh air.

'Kid, we gotta move. Fast,' Xanthe said as she grabbed her spear and helmet.

I stayed fixated on her expression as my hands gathered up my belongings. Her eyes scanned the forests below. I looked out but couldn't quite make out anything apart from the silhouette of the distant tree tops. Then it occurred to me. There was no noise. All the buzzing and croaks and cooing of the creatures on the mountainside had faded. The silence became unnerving.

'Sooooo should we move?' I asked after waiting what seemed like too long for Xanthe's signal.

She raised a hand in a hushing fashion that told me to wait.

'Move. Now,' she ordered.

Before I could take a step toward the opening of the hollow, she was gone. I exited the hollow, exposing myself to the cool night air. I looked around for Xanthe. Still nothing. The bluish light from the two moons illuminated the precariously steep hillside that our 'hide' had managed to embed itself upon and the long grasses that blanketed it. They swayed and *whooshed* in the calm breeze. I stopped. I didn't know where Xanthe had vanished to, nor did I know what had spooked her from our resting spot.

'Xanthe,' I hissed the whisper. 'Where you at?'

Beginning to feel alone and exposed I crouched down in the long grass and waited for a response. There wasn't one from her or anything for that matter. Even the bugs had stopped their usual chirps and whirrs and the night birds were silent. It was eerily calm. Something had disturbed both the fauna and Xanthe.

It was only now I realised I was in trouble.

CHAPTER TEN

I peered down the hillside. No more than fifty fathoms away, a line of bright orange light twisted from left to right. At first it gave the appearance of a strangely luminescent serpent, as it flickered and grew. Then in complete unison, many small lights split from the line and began to glow and dance. I watched on almost hypnotised by the spectacle as the lights slowly raised together. Then more lights sprouted in a line behind the first. Dazed, I stared more. It was then that a familiar, yet haunting metallic voice boomed something from the tree line below.

The lights immediately took to the air and arced high above. Like shooting stars, they grew larger and larger as they streaked overhead.

A cold hand grabbed me by the scruff of the neck and ripped me with a jolt behind the hollow. As I landed, there was a series of whistles and thumps all around me. I looked up into the panicked eyes of Xanthe. Her face once again lit up almost like the sunset from earlier. Only this time, as I swivelled my head about, I realised we were surrounded by flames.

There were more whistles and thumps as another volley of flaming quarrels peppered around our position with marked precision. The damp vegetation seemed to do nothing to dull the flames as the oils fuelling them burned hard and bright.

With each passing second, they grew until we were completely cut off. There was no retreat uphill, nor to the side. The only
cover we now had was that of the hollow fallen tree in which
we had just left.

THUMP! THUMP! THUMP! THUMP!

Again more rounds of lit bolts fell. Only this time they
struck the timber of our cover.

I turned and looked desperately toward Xanthe to see what
we should do. Behind me, huddled with her head buried
between her knees and hugging her legs in a ball was Xanthe.
She rocked back and forth shaking her head, sobbing.

'Xanthe?' I asked. 'Xanthe, snap out of it,' I said and shook
at her shoulders.

She didn't respond. At least not to me. With despair in her
voice, she kept repeating, 'No, no, no, no.' There it was again,
I began to feel another lump of guilt welling inside of me. This
situation, right now, was because of me. I was responsible for
this. I had to make it right. I had to snap Xanthe out of her
meltdown and get us out of here. But how?

The crackling of the shoulder high flames grew closer. I
could feel the heat from them growing and the fumes entering
my lungs.

It was then, that metallic voice boomed over the sounds of
the fire.

'Young one, it is time for you to come with us. There is
nowhere to run and this game has worn thin.' It was the
Reaper. He had found us somehow.

I climbed the side of the hollow and peered over the top.
I gulped at the sight. Flames had created a runway down the
entire length of the slope to the tree line. The regime troops
that had been at the beach were now standing in formation at
the bottom of the hill and at their forefront there he was; the
Reaper. His arms folded, he stood much taller than his fellow

men. As the fire illuminated his features, it cast a sinister shadow against the tree line behind them.

Trapped like crabs in a boiling pot was a term that came to mind.

I began to scramble back down the fallen tree toward Xanthe, who hadn't moved. The large log bucked and rocked slightly under my weight.

'Hurry now, child. My patience is fleeting. Or do you need some more incentive?' his voice boomed once more.

Again, there was a series of muffled twangs, followed by yet another barrage of flaming quills peppering the log. I thought of my father and what torture he must be enduring. I thought of how far I had come - only to be cooked alive in an attempt to spring him from his prison. He would not have wanted me to be angry or upset, especially in my final moments. In fact, he had always taught me to make light of a dark situation by trying to find a funny side to it. Really? Was there a funny side to this steaming dung heap of a dilemma?

Maybe there was.

'You do know that there are two of us up here, right?' I yelled back down the hill.

'But only one of you matter to me. Give yourself up willingly child and we may let your companion live,' came the booming response.

I was slightly offended. Either at the term *'may let your companion live'* or the fact that he couldn't tell our voices apart I wasn't sure.

'Is that so? Then why don't you come up here and we'll see about that?' I mocked. It was all bluff. With Xanthe out of the equation and no tricks up my sleeve, I was just full of hot air.

The log we were using for cover was now beginning to burn intensely on one side. Time was running out. I tried one more time to climb over to see if the troops were moving up hill.

The higher up the decaying structure I climbed, the more it teetered back and forth. I balanced at the top and peered down the hill. The troops were still lined up and waiting for our surrender. Game over.

I climbed down once more to Xanthe, only to almost lose control of our only cover. The giant heavy log almost rolled away from me before I could get to the ground. If it did that, then we'd be completely exposed and it would...

I had an idea.

Using all the strength I could muster, I dug my heels into the sodden ground and pushed my wiry arms against the side of the lumber. This time, I couldn't get so much as a budge. Again, I tried and only succeeded in digging my boots further into the dirt. It seemed only adding weight to the top of the frame would make it rock. That is unless I wanted to sacrifice myself and become a smear on the hillside.

'Just to add some incentive to your surrender, young ones. In a minute, I'll send up my hounds to assist the speed of your decision. Oh, and did I forget to mention that they haven't eaten in days?'

Great. Now those ferocious war hounds I had seen at the beach would be chewing on my bones in a few moments.

I needed help. I couldn't do this alone.

I turned back to Xanthe in her crumpled form. She continued shaking in fear. 'Xanthe, I know I have gotten you into this. I know this is all because of me, but you have to pull it together. You have to trust me on this. I think I have an idea, but I can't do it alone,' I pleaded.

Her eyes darted back and forth. She needed something to snap her out of this. Something that would break the tension. Something that would be completely ridiculous and make her laugh.

I knelt down and whispered into her ear. 'Hey, you need to check this out. Remember the two soldiers we buried up to their necks at the beach? Well, they're back with the hunting group, and only wearing their under garments.'

Her eyes turned and met mine. I could see her pupils slowly dilate and adjust. It was a registered response, but she needed more to break out of her funk. I decided to push harder, so I started laughing – hard. I laughed and laughed and laughed as loud and as hard as I could. Xanthe's mouth started to twitch. A smile, I was starting to get a smile. I needed to turn it up some more.

I decided to start some loud banter.

'Oi Reaps. You there? Tell me, how does it feel to be hunting us down with two of your blokes in their jocks? It doesn't seem so *elite* now, does it? Having no pants brings a new meaning to the tip of the spear, doesn't it? Hahahaha.'

It almost felt as though the flames intensified from the anger of the Reaper at my jesting.

I looked at Xanthe amongst my forced laughter. Her smile had grown some more. She was on the brink of coming back to me.

I reached down and picked up the cumbersome spear I had come to fondly know as 'my walking stick' by one end. In an undignified attempt, I spun around twice and launched it through the air. Not in the manner spears usually fly, it spun tip over tail out over the top of the now heavily engulfed log toward the ranks below. To top it off, my balance gave way in the effort. I tasted grass - falling headlong into the turf in a mess of arms and legs.

Somewhere over the other side of the log I could hear the faintest cry of startled pain. A soldier stated loudly, something along the lines of 'Well, least you have your spear back.' followed by a few chuckles.

A burst of maniacal laughter came from Xanthe's mouth. Hysterical, she stood up and pointed at my fallen form. I raised my head and spat out a mouthful of dirt and grass and started to laugh with her. Soon the whole valley was echoing with our snorts and guffaws.

'Enough of this. Release the hounds!' The voice of the Reaper cut through the humour. The order was repeated loudly by the men. We could hear the sounds of chains releasing and chinking and the large beasts drove hard up the hill.

'Xanthe! Push on the log. We need to get it rolling!' I ordered.

Without hesitation, she turned and pushed hard on the side of the large structure. It creaked and rocked violently. Xanthe gritted her teeth and her skinny arms flexed and strained. I ran at the log and jumped, using both feet to connect with the side as high up as I could reach. As I leapt at it, the log disappeared down the hill and I was left to fall flat on my back. The second time in a matter of seconds, I had a face full of dirt and grass.

The ground shook and rumbled as the giant flaming tree trunk hurtled down the steep hillside. There was a moment of shock realisation from the enemy soldiers and a muffled order to get to cover, but it was too late. Trapped between the hill, runway flames and the tree line to their rear, they didn't stand a chance. The shriek of the war hounds, and the cries of the men were deafened by the final explosive crash as the runaway trunk slammed into their position and erupted into a spray of glowing embers and burning splinters.

It was beautiful and terrifying all at once. I stared at the carnage as the tree line quickly began to catch fire too. The crumpled silhouettes of soldiers lay strewn across the ground below, and in the centre, pinned to a large tree, was the limp outline of the Reaper himself, head bowed and unmoving.

'Elite hunting force, eh? I guess you just can't get good help anymore these days,' I stated quite proud of myself.

Xanthe cleared her throat.

'Oh, I don't mean you,' I corrected myself hurriedly.

'Kid, you're on fire.'

'I have my moments.'

'No, kid. Like your uniform is on fire,' she giggled again.

I could feel an intense heat building in the seat of my pants and as the sovereign dropped, so did I. I began to manically roll back and forth across the grass with Xanthe once again bursting into laughter.

Once the flames were snuffed on my backside, she helped me from the ground.

'Alright hot shot.' She gave me a devilish grin. 'Now what say we skedaddle and get you to the Capital quick smart?'

CHAPTER ELEVEN

I edged closer along the branch toward the unsuspecting lizard bird. My legs straddled the timber limb with expert care. A slight drizzle of icy rain masked my approach with their noise amongst the branches – at the same time making my position in the tree ever more precarious. A slip now would mean at least one of two things. One, I would fall a considerable distance to a sharp, sudden and likely lethal stop at the ground level. Two, if I did survive, I would go hungry once again - something which my body could not afford to go through anymore. I tried to not let the pangs of hunger and desperation creep into my concentration. Nothing else mattered. It was just me and my prey. The hunter and the hunted.

Now, straddling a canopy branch, I waited patiently for the lizard bird to turn its back to me.

I guess I was fortunate that Xanthe was allowing me some time to hunt an opportune meal after our last run in with the enemy, she said we could afford a little time now we were so close to the Capital. I hadn't tasted lizard bird in years. It wasn't the most pleasant meat to eat, and they were certainly harder to catch than sea birds, but if there was a chance I would be captured or killed on my way to the Capital, then

I sure as anything wanted to at least have had one creature comfort since my time of incarceration.

Finally, it was distracted.

The lizard bird rustled its sparse feathers and began grooming each wing with its nub of a beak. I stopped along the branch of the red pine, just obscured from view by a thick clump of scarlet pine needles. Slowly reaching over my shoulder I drew out the '*bola*' I had made from the pilfered rope and some fist sized stones. I slipped the bowline knot over my wrist, it was attached to the bola, so I could reel in my catch. With the years of careful practice atop the ship's masts, I lifted one hand above my head and with the other, held the stones. Taking aim, I swung the rope around and targeted for the direction where I predicted the bird would attempt to escape. In one swift motio-

'Have you got it yet?' came a loud attempt at whispering from Xanthe below. The interruption startled me.

The lizard bird turned its attention in my direction and ruffled its feathers with a hiss. As with most animals, its primal instinct of fight or flight had been triggered. Unfortunately for me, at that particular moment, it chose the former.

Seconds later I was falling through the branches of the large pine, with a rather pissed-off lizard bird firmly attached to the end of my nose.

A sturdy branch broke my fall, and possibly a few ribs. The lizard bird detached itself, quite proud of its apparent victory and strutted off along the timber limb. I felt warm drops of blood trickle out of the needle teeth marks lining my nostrils. Xanthe's smiling face poked into my view of the cloudy sky above.

'That was spectacular. Did you mean to do that? Do it again. Do it again,' she demanded with childlike enthusiasm.

'Ungh,' I responded slowly. 'Xanthe.'

'Yes?'

'Remember how you keep telling me to be quiet and be patient if you're doing something important? Like checking ahead or finding a spot to lay up for daylight?' I inquired with a grimace.

'Yup.'

'Well, that was a moment where I needed you to do the same,' I said with as much patience as I could gather.

Xanthe was a very erratic character to be around. Often, she would have moments of candid happiness and innocence. However, in a moment she would snap into a serious, calculating creature with stern orders or demands. One minute she would be chasing a brightly coloured butterfly. The next, she would be planning our route through enemy territory without being seen.

She was a wealth of valuable information when she assumed the latter personality. Teaching me how to cover my tracks. How to stalk silently and deliberately through the forest by using the outside of my foot and gradually shifting my weight onto it completely before taking the next painstaking step. The reasons things are seen; silhouette, shine, shape, shadow, spacing and movement.

During daylight we would find a concealed place for me to rest and eat. Although for some reason, Xanthe never seemed to need either of those two things — instead, she always insisted on keeping watch over me. The rations we scavenged from the soldiers were finished by me within a few days. Anything I caught or stole from farmlands afterward would need to be eaten fresh and uncooked, as fire would give our position away. That even meant fresh lizard bird. Any scraps or leftovers were taken with us, or placed high up in the branches so hounds or soldiers wouldn't easily see signs of where we had been.

During the evenings, we moved. It was my turn to use my skills, as years of time at sea had taught me to navigate via the stars. The slightest constellation that peaked through the dense cloud cover would be enough to assure me that we were still moving North West. Xanthe told me that we were only a day or so out from the Capital. I had yet to see a glimpse of a city, despite my best efforts to sneak a look, each time I was allowed to climb a tree to hunt.

That had worked well so far...

Now I lay strewn across a branch, with a rather sore nose and some badly bruised internals, looking up toward the overcast sky.

The sounds of creaking timber and animal hooves snapped me from my painful pondering. As I realised someone was approaching, the cold and firm hand of Xanthe muzzled me. Creating a perfect seal across my mouth and nostrils, I couldn't breathe. Trying to peel her hand off proved unsuccessful – even with her attention elsewhere, she was far too strong for me to even pry away her fingers. So, I did the only thing I could. I licked her hand. Almost immediately, the seal was broken as she giggled. She looked back at me in mock disgust and I replied with the faintest of expressions to let her know that I needed to breathe.

Xanthe motioned for me to wait and not to move. However, before I could let her see how uncomfortable my current position was, she was gone. I was still astonished how well she could silently and swiftly disappear from sight. I returned to my thoughts as the pain from the branch crept back into my mind. Red needle-like leaves slowly sprinkled down from the branches I had crashed into from my fall. Beautiful in appearance, each new crimson snowflake began to itch and irritate my skin as they settled in my hair, eyes and nose.

Possibly the most 'unstealthy' thing one could do when trying to remain quiet, was about to occur. As each needle crept onto me, my eyes began to water, my nose began to twitch and the unmistakable sensation of a sneezing fit swept over me. I tried and tried to snuffle out the feeling, but the more effort I put in, the harder it became.

The creaking of the wooden wheels grew louder. I could hear the snorts and grunts of the animals with it.

The itching grew stronger.

I could hear voices of humans.

More itching.

I placed my hands over my nose and mouth just in time to snuffle an explosive sneeze. My whole body shuddered. A wave of relief swept over me as I brushed the remaining needles away.

'CREEEEAK' sounded the branch I was on.

With an almighty *snap*, the final branch that had saved me from the ground gave into gravity. I fell to the ground with a loud 'thud!'

Once again, air left my lungs for a brief moment. I winced, squeezing my eyes shut in pain.

Xanthe appeared over my prone body once again. A look of concern and disgust were upon her alabaster features.

'We have to stop meeting like this,' I half whispered, half groaned, rolling and rubbing the base of my spine.

'Shhh. We are in a spot of luck.'

I sat up to listen more closely. Some storm clouds rumbled overhead as the cold drizzle began to become heavier. The Regime sure seemed to have a knack for controlling lands that don't like sunshine.

'There is a wagon approaching up ahead. Even better, on the wagon is a man and woman and I'm betting they have some things that could help us out,' she stated eagerly.

'Things like what?' I asked.

'Things like Regime identification papers. Kid, if you even make it into the Capital, you'll need some papers to say you belong there. Otherwise, they'll lock you up without a second thought.'

I thought for a second.

'And how do you plan on getting their papers, Xanthe? Something that valuable wouldn't exactly be easily parted with,' I pointed out helpfully.

'You know, you're right, kid. No Regime citizen alive would pass up their papers.'

I felt a slight moment of satisfaction at having been told I was correct. It didn't last long. I noticed Xanthe's expression change. Her eyes were now fixated on the approaching wagon.

'No citizen alive...' she murmured.

Xanthe placed the helmet firmly over her head and grabbed the spear tightly. Before I could let out a desperate hushed protest, she disappeared into the trees once more.

I made a mental note to ask her to teach me that trick sometime and then I looked in the direction of growing noise of animal hooves and creaking wheels. Sure enough, no more than forty fathoms away a wagon was drawing forward through the mud. Red pine needles smothered the wheels and the legs of the two draught horses moving it. Sitting atop the wagon holding the reins, was a man and beside him a woman, perhaps his wife. They both appeared to be in a deeply animated conversation. Despite this, something shiny caught my eye. Behind them hung a rather ornate looking crossbow, loaded with a bolt and underslung with a round cylindrical cartridge. It looked impressive.

As they approached, I could see more details. The man seemed to be copping quite an earful from his significant other as he tried to steer the horses through the reddish leaf litter. He was rather old and short in stature and well dressed in dark trousers and riding boots accompanied by a smart charcoal shirt and tan vest. His open riding cloak revealed a gold fob chain to a pocket watch. However, the most noticeable feature of his was his finely waxed salt and pepper moustache, which appeared to twitch in irritation to the various points his partner was making. The woman was much younger and appeared far too attractive to be his wife. She had long flowing red hair under a dark grey riding hood, with a light covered blouse and riding pants and tan coloured knee length boots which accentuated her long legs. Perhaps they were father and daughter? They didn't seem to be tired or haggard from a long travel like we were, which possibly meant we were very close to the Capital indeed. Although the man would have probably argued that point.

As they moved closer through the trees toward me, I turned to speak to Xanthe... only to remember she wasn't there.

My stomach felt like it had begun to twist. I turned back toward the couple on the wagon.

From a tree branch above, the slender figure of Xanthe landed ever so lightly on the crates stacked in the rear of the moving wagon. Completely unnoticed. She crept closer to the bickering pair like a spider moving towards unsuspecting flies. The childlike persona that she had shown earlier was completely replaced by something more sinister. It was then I saw what Xanthe intended. She began to reach out a slender hand for the crossbow. Her fingers almost between the shoulders of the couple, I could see her slowly gain a grip upon the butt of the weapon.

No.

She deftly plucked it from its resting place and shouldered the stock.

No. Surely she wouldn't. They were just an innocent pair making their way through a forest.

Xanthe raised the crossbow and began to point the bolt at the nape of the gentleman.

Had I misjudged her? Willing to save the life of a stranger on a beach, but just as prepared to take the life of another in cold blood?

I had to do something.

Chapter Twelve

I stumbled forward through the undergrowth and red pine needles. Frantically I felt time was running out for the strange couple. Any moment, Xanthe could pull the trigger and end the life of a man and his partner. I would have to 'wing it' here, like, well, like the life of others depended on it.

I dropped the mask of the helmet down over my face to cover my most obvious 'tell' – my age.

Mustering my most authoritarian voice, I boomed, 'Halt there!' It was so loud within the helm, that it drowned out my usual adolescent crackle.

Even the horses took notice and ground to a sudden stop following my demand. The woman snapped shut her mouth and both looked at me in shock. Great, I had their attention. Even Xanthe paused and broke out of her predatory trance. She swiftly and silently pulled back on a lever and removed the underslung container, placed the crossbow back into its resting place and plucked the bolt from the rest. It was fascinating.

It was then that I noticed a name emblazoned on a brass crest just above where the crossbow had been. It read 'Balgowan'.

I tried to think of a goal to achieve. Firstly, I needed their papers.

'Mr. Balgowan sir. I need to see your papers, stock you are carrying and know the location you intend to travel.' I continued as Xanthe slipped down off the crate-filled wagon unnoticed by the pair.

This spiel was one I had heard many times over the years aboard the 'Kraken Krusher'. The Quartermaster would yell it at the top of his lungs to the ship they intended to board. It had been so often played out on the open seas, that it now felt quite familiar and gave me a direction for this situation. Did I mention that the ship I was on was also quite savvy at removing people from their valued belongings?

Meanwhile, the woman glared at the man.

'This is preposterous. Don't tell me that we need to –'

'He asked for your papers. Do not make him ask again.' This time Xanthe appeared from the other side of the wagon, helmet over her face. She was getting into the act too.

Xanthe paced in front of the horses with the soldier's spear held tightly and pointed in a fashion that meant business. Each step was deliberate and cut off the route of escape for the couple and their cargo. That is, unless they managed to trample Xanthe under the hooves of the horses. Quite a possible option I would say.

The man changed his tone. He was easily flustered. *Good* I thought.

'May I enquire as to why we have been stopped?' He asked searching for his papers inside his vest and trying to appear more cooperative. A forced smile crept through his moustache whiskers. 'Usually I am recognised and simply waved on through.'

'I'll be asking the questions today, sir.' I replied. 'I'll need to see the lady's papers too.'

'We have some crates of the finest Regime quality mead on-board here. Perhaps we could come to some sort of arrangement?' he said nonchalantly.

I paused for a moment and stared at the man through the visor. It appeared as though he was beginning to regret his comment.

'Go on,' I continued.

'Well, if say, a pair of fine soldiers like yourselves didn't worry about the papers, then those soldiers could find themselves with quite a valuable crate in their possession... hmpf, well um, if you know what I mean?'

'Are you trying to pay me off, Mr. Balgowan? Because if you are, I may just have to seize this entire wagon as evidence against you and your partner here. Such actions would certainly be frowned upon and would likely result in you being keel hauled or walking the plank...'

The butt of Xanthe's spear struck my toe. 'I mean, hanged...'I added quickly.

Cocking his head awkwardly he began 'Did you just say, *keel hau-*'

'The lady's papers, Mr. Balgowan. I need to see them.' I demanded.

Their eyes darted to one another. She glared forcefully at him. Balgowan shrugged ever so slightly. Her grip tightened upon the railing to her front. The request seemed to touch a nerve.

'Um, well you see,' he began as she rolled her eyes and reached inside her blouse, turning away in an embarrassed manner. 'We are travelling from the Capital through to a Meadery I own south of here, in Carbrook.'

'Yes, yes 'The Balgowan Meadery' of Carbrook. I am aware of it,' I lied – but the details were so easy to guess.

'Yes, well,' he continued appearing slightly flushed. 'You see, the fine lady here isn't actually my wife. She is an, um ... business acquaintance.'

I looked at the man through my visor so our eyes would meet. I cocked my brow questioningly.

'Well, you see, we intend to do some business and I would prefer my other partners, business partners to perhaps not know of this, er, um...' he twiddled his moustache nervously.

'Indiscretion?' I added.

'Yes yes, indiscretion.'

He had become flushed.

'Well Mr Balgowan, we are simply travelling through formalities here for a particular purpose. You see, there are currently a pair of bandits trying to make their way through this region. They are experts of using disguises. We needed to see you *up close*.'

'I see, but there are always bandits in this area. Hence the reason we travel with old Gertrude here.' He leant back to pat the unloaded crossbow. 'She can pin a heavily armed bandit to a pine tree so quickly that it scares the wits out of any others.'

He was brimming with pride.

'An unloaded crossbow?' I asked.

'Hmpf what? No, no, are you daft? She has the finest silver tipped bolts this side of – ' his hand reached back over the weapon's rest.

He paused.

He wasn't brimming with pride anymore.

His *business partner* looked back to confirm. She began to slap his shoulder.

'You imbecile, Harold!' she hissed. 'You said you would look after me. You said you were prepared, and we had nothing to worry about.'

Desperate to change the subject, he stammered, 'But he doesn't have a weapon either. Do you, sir? I mean where is your spear?'

All eyes turned to me.

'Ahhh... huh?' I responded intelligently.

'Your spear, young soldier. Where is your spear?'

'Sir, I am trained in a deadly unarmed martial art. Having no weapons within view encourages bandits to attack me and that is the last mistake they ever make,' I said reassuringly.

'What's it called?'

'Origami.'

'Never heard of it.'

'It's from the far east. Very deadly. Always makes the enemy fold.'

'Intriguing,' Balgowan exclaimed.

'Indeed.'

I moved right up to the side of the man and lowered my voice. 'Speaking of being prepared,' I said. 'It is known to the Regime that this pair of bandits are quite brutal in their dealings with travellers. They have been stealing the identities of those they encounter, taking their belongings and leaving them stranded with next to nothing in the forests.'

'Hmpf, terrible. That's just terrible, terrible indeed. Isn't that terrible, Yasmine?'

She responded by folding her arms and turning her back to him indignantly.

'The papers, sir,' I moved closer to his side of the wagon.

'Hmpf, oh right.'

Balgowan complied, handing me papers from inside his jacket.

I pretended to read the various papers he provided, Regime Citizenship papers and an invitation – "*You are cordially invited to attend the airship of*... blah, blah, blah...for an evening of...." It was boring stuff, so I continued and created some distance, while slipping the citizenship ones into Xanthe's pocket.

'As I was saying, these bandits. They are a cunning pair. Before you know it, you will be unsuspectingly separated from your items. However, our outlying garrisons have been given direct orders to combat this.'

'I am listening,' said Balgowan appearing thoroughly intrigued and likely more relaxed that the pressure seemed to no longer be upon him.

'As you can see, our attire isn't quite the usual of the Regime. We are from an elite group of trackers, tasked with finding and 'dealing' with these bandits.'

'Jolly good that!' exclaimed Balgowan excitedly.

'However, they have caught onto the fact we are hunting them. They know our uniforms and know to stay clear away, you see. In doing so, they have taken up disguising themselves. Hence the reason we had to check your papers. But in order to catch criminals in disguise, we have to disguise ourselves too. Chances are, they have been following you and waiting for a time to strike. Slowly disarming you and making it easy for themselves. Possibly, that is why the bolt was missing from your crossbow, you see.'

'Oh, I see. Cunning scoundrels then, eh? I knew I had that loaded. They even worked out how to completely unload the magazine with the extra bolts. Just trying to even the odds with me, were they?' Balgowan looked around the forest, as though trying to see if he was being watched.

'In order for us to capture the unconventional crook, we ourselves need to be unconventional. That is why the Regime is asking for your help, Mr. Balgowan sir.'

Balgowan seemed taken aback at the request, then proudly he puffed out his chest. His partner Yasmine changed her grouchy demeanour and seemed outwardly delighted at the comment. She shook his shoulders excitedly and kissed him upon his puffy cheek.

'Certainly. Whatever the Regime asks of me in a time of need, may I be willing to provide to them,' he blurted out with bravado.

'What we need, are your clothes and papers sir, madam.'

'I beg your pardon?!'

'Our uniforms are giving us away and you are currently being hunted by these bandits. If we swap our uniforms with you and Yasmine, was it? Then not only will you not be bothered by them, because they will think you are us, they will come straight to us for your goods. You will be able to make the rest of the way to your Meadery without interruption and almost completely unnoticed. It is a win for you both you see. And it is a win for the Regime.'

'Ho! That is a splendid plan in deed! You pair of cunning sods!' he chortled loudly.

'Shhh sir, if you will.' I said.

Xanthe and I both looked around over our shoulders as if bandits could spring from behind any tree or stump nearby. Xanthe waved the spear around for good measure.

'Oh, sorry... sorry.' He calmed down, as the pair aboard the wagon followed suite and mimicked our actions.

'Now, I will also take your papers and pass them onto the local garrison, for you to retrieve in a few weeks.'

'A few weeks?' Balgowan paled visibly at the thought.

'We will need them in the meantime. Remember – you will be handsomely compensated for your cooperation. *Very* handsomely.'

Balgowan was satisfied and the deal went ahead at my direction.

To avoid giving away our identities, we offered the pair the benefit of undressing on the other side of the wagon, with the premise of protecting the lady's dignity.

'So, you want us to just throw our clothes over the wagon?' asked Balgowan.

'Yes, sir. And would you happen to have any hooded riding cloaks perchance? Simply to hide our appearance from the bandits from afar.' I asked.

'Why yes, young fellow. Actually, you will find them in the crate on the back of the wagon. Help yourself to some mead too while you are at it. Take your time. Always a pleasure to help our brave soldiers. Such a pleasure.' Balgowan offered enthusiastically amongst a bunch of hushed comments of adoration at his lady friend's assets. 'My dear, they broke the mould when they made you I would say... Incredible... just incredible.'

'Oh, Harold!' she giggled coyly.

I felt a sudden need to sneak a peek over the top of the wagon, just to see what the fuss was all about. I began to climb the side of the wagon and was just about to capture a glimpse of Yasmin in all her beauty when a strong hand grabbed me by my shoulders and yanked me back down. Instead of ogling the lady, I was now looking back into the wide eyes of Xanthe. Her expression was a mixture of sternness and amusement. I almost felt a little guilty. She pushed the riding cloak into my chest with enough force to slightly wind me.

Clothes were flung over the top of the wagon and we began to swap our attire. I started to draw up the trousers, which had been tight on Balgowan, yet were now rather comfy on me. They were indeed impeccable in their make. I was admiring the finest clothes I had the chance of wearing in my entire life. The stitching was almost seamless, and the fabric kept out the chill from the forest. It felt like an odd sense of achievement. It was almost intoxicating.

My foot caught in the second leg of the trousers and I stumbled backward. Oompf! I collided with Xanthe.

I turned to apologise for my clumsiness only to be met by a truly fascinating sight. Xanthe Bones had struck me as a strange and endearing character over the last few days, full of surprises and personality. However, right now looking at her from behind stirred new questions in my head. Her back was littered with deep scars and healed wounds. Amongst the pale smooth skin from her shoulders to her posterior, light purple marks dragged across the pale flesh. Some appeared familiar – the tell-tale markings from a cat-o-nine-tails. Others seemed more foreign, like twisted swirling patterns from flames and the deep gouges of animal teeth marks. Large teeth marks. She stopped momentarily. It seemed as though she could feel my stare. Her wounds were covered as she hurriedly became dressed. I turned and continued to do the same, feeling slightly bad for letting my curiosities get the better of me.

The awkward silence that followed between us was far from the laughter and chortles from the opposite side of the wagon. The horses grunted with impatience.

'Flynt?' Xanthe's voice sounded raw and unsure.

'Yes.'

'How did you get *your* scars?' she asked softly.

She had noticed my scars too?

'Um... well, you know that ship I was on?'

'Uh huh.'

'Well, I wasn't exactly a welcome guest, you see. I was more of a-'

'Prisoner?' She asked in a whisper.

'Yup, one of those.' I replied casually.

'Oh.'

There it was again. Another awkward moment of silence. We had never had problems talking before, but now, in the middle of a subtle heist, we found it hard to continue our words. Feelings were now involved and raw memories. It seemed to make us both seize up.

We both put the riding hoods on and drew our collars up around our faces. All in all, the clothes were a rather nice fit on Xanthe and passable on myself. We decided to sneak a peek at Balgowan and his partner on the opposite side of the wagon. The reveal was quite satisfying as the two, with visors drawn down, gave the appearance of the Regime's elite soldiers. That is until they began to move. Balgowan's moustache protruded through the gaps in the visor and his partner's attractive bust gave true meaning to the term 'breastplate'.

Xanthe tapped me on the shoulder to grab my attention.

'So, Mr. Ideas man, what is the next part of this plan of yours?' she queried. 'We have their clothes, but I doubt they'll let us keep the papers.'

I had been feeling quite proud of my ability to con Balgowan and his partner into swapping their fine clothes with us up until now. 'Winging it' was almost my creed. Right now though, staring at the playful expression of Xanthe, I felt as though she expected more – she wanted entertainment.

'Um,' I began to think. 'I'm not too sure. I guess, I was just acting on a whim?'

The playful spark in her eyes dwindled.

'You didn't think this far ahead?'

'Well, no. I guess we could keep walking to the Capital in our new clothes and with the papers. That would work. I'm also bloody hungry, so I could also try to weasel out some food for us and I really like that crossb –'

'BORING! Are you ready for my turn?' She asked with a smile growing across her face.

Before I could respond, Xanthe opened up a compartment on the wagon and removed a handful of bolts for the crossbow. I began vigorously shaking my head and mouthing a loud 'No', but the silent protests were completely ignored.

She wound back her arm, poised and nodded her head enthusiastically.

THUMP! THUMP! THUMP! Xanthe slammed the bolts held in her fists into the side of the wagon.

'Take cover! We're under attack!' She cried out.

Chapter Thirteen

'Take cover! Take cover!' ordered Xanthe. Using just her hands, she launched more crossbow bolts into the surrounding red pines. Who needs a crossbow with a throw like that, I thought. Each '*Thump!*' echoed through the forest and caused more red pine needles to fall to the ground. It created the impression we were being fired at and with Balgowan and Yasmin unable to see us from their side of the wagon it must have been causing panic and confusion.

The horses reared and neighed loudly, kicking red speckled mud high into the air. It did help that Xanthe had slapped them both enthusiastically across the rump to possibly help '*get them into character*'. I took this moment to crouch down and look under the wagon. On the other side I could see our pair of newly recruited Regime soldiers dive to the ground, covering their new uniforms in red tinged sodden soil.

A riding boot belted across my backside, which almost sent me spilling into the dirt like our friends. Rubbing my bruised posterior, I looked up to see an animated Xanthe motioning wildly with pushing movements and lots of finger pointing. Now I will admit, it took a while for me to catch on, more than would have been acceptable if it weren't for the fact the Balgowan and Yasmine weren't really lifting their heads for anything.

'Go with it, kid. Get in on the act,' she growled.

The sovereign dropped. Xanthe now seeming slightly peeved for my slow reaction, was waiting for my assistance in keeping up the ploy. I nodded and scrambled to my feet.

'There they are! Over there!' I pointed at a thicker than usual clump of red pines to the rear. I picked up a handful of fist sized rocks and threw them into the trees in an attempt to create some noise. Each crack and thump of the stones echoed amongst the forest and multiplied the sound effects.

'What are your orders, sir?' Xanthe responded loudly.

'Huh?!'

'What are your orders, sir?' Xanthe repeated glaring hard at me and nodding toward the pair on the other side of the carriage. I was beginning to understand how Balgowan and Yasmine must feel on the other side of the wagon – confused.

Through gritted teeth and bulging eyes Xanthe hissed outside of their earshot, 'You're meant to be the one in charge here remember? The officer in charge. So, sir... what are your bloody orders? And you better hurry, coz I don't reckon they are going to stay down much longer. Get what I'm saying?'

I ducked another look under the wagon. Xanthe was right, Balgowan was starting to lift his head and look about. Like a dazed rabbit, he pawed and wiped at the mud embedded in his visor, then began to release the face protection, so the visor could be lifted. If he realised that there were no bandits or even saw our faces, the jig would be up and I'm guessing Xanthe wouldn't necessarily want any witnesses knowing that we had been this way.

I stood up abruptly and once more tried to muster my manliest of voices.

'You there, get up on that carriage and take the thingys, wotsits, you know the... the.'

'Reins?' she prompted.

'REINS!' I yelled more confidently.

Xanthe was atop the wagon in a bound. Grabbing the reins, she began yelling down at Balgowan and his mistress. 'Keep your heads down! Stay down! Incoming fire, Incoming fire!' More arrows left her hands as she threw them in and around the ground beside the pair, like an alleyway card shark dealing a hand. The pair slapped their faces hard into the mud once more in terror, likely thinking that they could be skewered any moment by a stray bolt.

Xanthe began slapping the stage of the wagon for me to get up. I ran toward it and tried to make a graceful leap into the seat, just as Xanthe had earlier. The horses had different plans however and lurched the wagon forward in the excitement. I struck the wooden side rail hard enough to knock a considerable amount of wind from my lungs, but desperation and wiry fingers were enough to keep me attached.

There was a strange shaking on the wagon as I realised Xanthe was trying terribly hard to hold back her laughter. I wasn't amused.

Still straddling the side of the wagon, I was now face to rail with the ornate crossbow of Balgowan's. It was even more beautiful up this close. Solid polished timber lines were accentuated by cast copper and bronze mouldings and etchings. I won't lie. Since spying it from my hiding spot earlier, I had made a mental promise to myself I would somehow become its new owner, I just needed the right opportunity. Now was as good a time as any I thought. Up close, it cut an imposing display upon its shelving. Now, without any spears and only my bola as a rudimentary weapon, it dawned on me that this piece could come in handy and it only seemed fair, considering Balgowan and Yasmin now carried our last Regime issued spear. It would simply be bad business to walk away with a loss. In an instant, I lifted the crossbow from its resting place on the stage and clambered onto the loaded tray of the wagon.

Xanthe grabbed my shoulder and hushed into my ear, 'We need this wagon. Try to get rid of them, kid.'

'What? Why?'

'Why what?'

'Why do we need the wagon? Aren't the clothes and crossbow enough?' I asked.

'Kid, just trust me, alright? Gots a plan worked out. Kinda. Sort of. Just get rid of them now!'

'But-'

'You want into the Captial or not?!'

I didn't need any more convincing. I turned and yelled with more vigour than before as I pretended to aim at the phantom bandits.

'Sir, get to cover with your lady. We have you covered and will try to lead the bandits away. Get to your meadery and baton down the hatches,' I ordered in my most heroic tone.

'Well hero, if you're going to shoot anything with that, you might want some ammunition,' smirked Xanthe. Her hand appeared in front of my eyes holding a wooden and copper cylinder filled with crossbow bolts.

I sheepishly took the cylinder and fumbled with it, lucky that the pair below were still too frozen in panic to look up at me. Unable to work out the darn contraption, I took to simply holding the casing underneath to give the impression it was attached and loaded. The pair on the ground hadn't even noticed my indiscretion as they hadn't even moved an inch from their position.

'Sir! Get yourselves to your meadery now! We will draw off the bandits!' I ordered again. This time with more authority.

It sufficed. Breaking from the cover, Balgowan and Yasmine lifted their visored faces up and scrambled to their feet.

Balgowan puffed himself up and began an attempt at sounding bold, 'Thank you, young man! We are indebt-'

'He said move tubby!' Xanthe cut in sharply, yelling at the pair in a voice that was more intimidating than expected from such a slight person.

The effect was almost comical. The couple, turning on their toes, scrambled away with enough speed it made the pair of horses almost redundant. At first, they moved in different directions, then found one another as they scrambled into the trees, snapping branches as they went.

Xanthe took this moment to slap the reins down hard and before I could hold on properly the wagon abruptly picked up speed.

'Hold on, kid. Ya snooze ya lose!' She said laughing.

Chapter Fourteen

'Why are we going away from the Capital?' I asked. 'Isn't that just a waste of valuable time?' I placed yet another matchstick in my mouth, from a packet Balgowan had left in the pocket of his jacket.

Xanthe was musing at some wooden signs in the shape of arrows at the crossroad in front of us. A crow atop the sign that read 'Capital' stared thoughtfully back at us. I kind of felt bad for the bird. For the past day, despite travelling a lot more comfortably, the only scenery had been hillsides littered with lines of scarlet pine tree stumps and the sodden earth of the road. This sign was the tallest landmark for miles.

'Kid, I told you before, we need a plan for getting into the city,' she replied guiding our acquired horse drawn cart in the direction of the opposing sign. Its letters long faded beyond recognition.

'Yeah, and? We've got Balgowan's papers and cart full of mead, don't we? Why can't we just show the guards the papers and give them the mead to sweeten the deal? Easy,' I said.

'Easy? Easy? You have a lot to learn about sneaking into places kid. For starters, as Balgowan pointed out, the guards already know who he is. In case you haven't figured it out, you're not him. So, we'd get arrested under suspicion because we have *his* papers, *his* cart and no Balgowan. Secondly, not all guards can be bribed. You've obviously been spending too much time with bent characters that you've forgotten that there are some diligent military folk out there too. Trying to bribe the wrong guard will likely end you up with your head on the chopping block. That, or they'll simply take the stolen goods for themselves and leave you high and dry. Either way, you lose. We lose.'

It was hard to argue with logic like that. I was starting to realise more and more how Xanthe had managed to escape the Regime in the first place. However, I was still at a loss as to why she had and why they wanted her so badly.

'So, what is the plan then?' I said giving into her explanation.

'Glad you asked. Firstly, we need to get ourselves to one of the hamlets outside the Capital. Especially if it is a mining town.'

'Why a mining town?'

'Because they get worked to the bone for next to nothing. The Regime's lands are full of the disadvantaged and disgruntled. Big militaries need lots of resources and money. Need money? Tax the population. Need more money, tax them some more and pay them less. Put some money into the right hands, or wrong hands as we would have it, and you can find out some very valuable or helpful information. Sometimes it is rumours, other times it is facts. Right now, we are looking for information as to which guards on which entrance to the city are likely to help us for the cost of this wagon of mead.'

'How do you know any of the guards will take a bribe?'

'Balgowan told us himself when he offered you a case. That gives us an indication of the value of this wagon. If a case is worth some guards turning a blind eye, then...'

'A whole wagon should be worth a lot more.' I finished.

'Now you're getting it. Cept it'll be short a case or two for the information we need.'

'And who is going to give us the information? Surely we can't just walk into a mine and ask around?'

'No, silly. We want them relaxed and preferably drunk. Alcohol has a way of loosening the tongue and making haggling a lot easier for ourselves. Or in this situation – you.'

That last point made my head snap around.

'Me?'

'Yep. You're the one sneaking into the Capital, so you're the one who is going into a local tavern to ask the right questions of the wrong people. I can imagine you would have a fair bit of experience with drunkards after all those years stuck on a ship. It's only fair and so far, you've had a decent gift of the gab when it comes to obtaining valuables, so why not valuable information?' she grinned as she pat the ornate crossbow resting across her lap.

The crossbow was a bit of a sore point with me. Xanthe maintained that she should be the one who carried it. Despite all of my previous negotiations that it was because of me that we even had the crossbow, she shut me down every time. I didn't even have a chance to get near it as she almost always had it slung by her side or on her lap.

'Maybe I should take Balgowan's crossbow with me just in case. What do you reckon?' I asked hopefully.

'Nup,' came her quick reply.

'Aw come on, Xanthe. Cut me some slack, will ya? So, I buggered up with the ammo barrel back there. It was the first time I had seen something like this. I'm used to Flintlocks and cannons, not crossbows. At least have the decency to show me how to use it.'

Xanthe pulled hard on the reins and the horses drew to a halt. She paused for a moment.

'Alright, I tell you what. I'll set you a challenge. First, I'll show you how to use it, then I'll give you a simple task of hitting something with it. If you pass, you get to use it from now on. If you fail, I hold onto it, no questions asked. What do you say?'

'Sounds fair.'

'Far from it,' she muttered.

Xanthe picked the crossbow up and held it in front of me.

'I take it that you kinda know the parts of a crossbow?'

'Yep.'

'Well, firstly show me how you hold it.'

I eagerly took the crossbow and buried the stock into my shoulder. It was solid and firm in my grasp. I pointed it around eagerly lining up tree stumps. Her hand pushed the front of the weapon down toward the mud.

'Right, settle down a bit, kid. Not too tight, it should point naturally toward the target. You have that part, but wait until I give you a target or your arms will get tired and start to shake. Then who knows what you'll hit. I want you to grab a hold of the cocking lever and pull it back until you hear a click. That means the bolt has loaded.'

I followed her instructions and heard the click.

'Right, before I give you the challenge, let's see if you can actually hit anything with it first. Call your shots.'

Finally, I was about to have a chance at firing this fantastic looking piece. It felt comfortable resting in my shoulder. I scanned to the left of the wagon for a target to hit.

'Alright. The tree stump over there,' I stated.

'Which one, kid? There are a few hundred over your side of the wagon. Be specific. Give me a distance, a description,' she corrected.

'Umm. Thirty fathoms to our front portside.'

'Portside?'

'Sailing term... ah, left.'

'Ten O'clock.'

'Eh?'

'Call it ten O'clock. Think of it as though we are sitting in the middle of a clock or fob watch. Twelve o'clock is to our direct front. Six o'clock is to our rear. You're pointing to our ten o'clock.'

'Right. Gotcha. Ten o'clock. Thirty fathoms. Tree stump that is darker than the others.'

I lined the rear and front sights upon my target and squeezed the trigger. There was a sudden burst of bolts from the front of the crossbow that startled me. The first finding its mark firmly in the stump and the remaining few scattering over the top right of the target.

Xanthe began laughing. 'Bet you didn't expect it to do that now, did you?'

I looked in amazement at the crossbow. This was more than just a detailed piece of art – it was deadly. Anything I had used in the past from muzzle loading rifles to Flintlock pistols was simply one shot and then it would need to be reloaded.

'It's a repeater crossbow, kid. It holds fifty bolts inside the magazine underneath. If you pull back to the first trigger click it'll fire one bolt. If you pull back like you just did, she'll let rip and keep firing,' Xanthe stated proudly.

'Woah,' was the only word that could leave my lips.

'Yup. Only the wealthy own these beauties. Only ones who can afford em. But don't be surprised though if they start becoming standard issue with the Regime soldiers in the coming months.'

'What makes you say that?'

'Well, for starters, all these trees are being chopped down for something, and I don't fancy that the lumber will be used for paper. Secondly, you have to agree, something like that is far more effective than what other countries' soldiers are equipt with.'

I had been pondering for a long time over the past few days as to how Xanthe knew so much about the finer workings of the Regime and their military for that matter. Once again, I had to open my big mouth.

'Xanthe.'

'Yeah, kid.'

'How do you know so much about the Regime?' I asked.

'Kid, I keep telling you, it's better if you don't know.'

'I know, I know.'

'My former job is... hard to explain. But I worked for them.'

'Doing what?'

'Let's just say, I was a soldier.'

'A soldier?'

I guess that kind of made sense. However, she was only a teenage girl at most, surely the Regime weren't that desperate as to conscript kids.

'And a prisoner.'

'And a prisoner?'

'Are you going to repeat everything I say? Yes. I was both a soldier and a prisoner. Like I said the other day, they can make you do things you don't want to do. Mess with your head and all that. The Capital is where their cutting-edge science happens and let's just say, I was one of their Guinea Pigs.'

'What's a guinea pig? Were you like one of the hawks they use?'

'Not quite. Now no more questions. It's time for you to actually hit a proper target. You ready?'

I was still slightly taken aback from her confession, but I hadn't missed her attempt to change the subject so quickly. Before I could squeeze out some more information, Xanthe began reaching into a case behind us and removing a bottle of mead.

'You hit this and you get to carry the crossbow. That and I'll answer any of your questions that you ask. Whadoyasay?' Her eyes looked slyly at me.

'Alright.'

Before I could even prepare myself, Xanthe launched the bottle high into the air behind me. Startled, I turned as sharply as I could and drew a bead on the glass container as it tumbled through the air. I began to squeeze the trigger.

A sharp pain shot through my leg and I fell backwards as Xanthe's foot connected firmly with the back of my knee. She laughed hard and loud as I toppled backward into her lap.

Looking back up at her I felt a tad jilted that I had fallen for her trick.

'Gotcha. You shoulda seen your face. You never had a chance,' she skited.

I straightened myself up and sat back into place.

'Alright. My turn to challenge you,' I declared.

'Eh?' came her response. She stopped laughing. 'Your turn? Kid, you just had a go. Straight up, I am the winner- winner- lizard-bird dinner.'

'True, but you have hardly demonstrated that you're a better shot than me. Out of the two of us, I am the only one who has hit anything with this crossbow. Therefore, I am the better shot,' I said trying to get her to rise to the bait. Over the brief time we had spent together, I now knew that Xanthe was hard pressed to turn down a challenge or dare.

'Are not. Kid, as I said, I was a soldier. I know how to use one of these,' she snapped.

'But you also said that there are soldiers and there are soldiers. Which one were you?'

A small gathering of crows collected on the side of the wagon and nestled together watching us intently. Perhaps they thought we were hunting wild game and they would have something to scavenge upon. Or maybe they just wanted some entertainment.

'Alright, kid. You're on. What is your challenge?'

I pondered for a moment.

'I'm going to give you a target and you're allowed one bolt only.'

'Wait a minute,' she said squinting her eyes. 'I'm onto your little tricks. Firstly, the target has to be in range of the crossbow.'

'Ok, what is that?'

'One hundred and fifty fathoms.'

'Sure. It will be.'

'Okay, so what's the target?'

I leant back into the case behind our seating and fumbled through the straw padding. Removing a bottle, I held it aloft. 'This will be your target, but only when I throw it. The wagon will also be moving. Savy?'

'Um yeah. Pffft easy,' she rolled her eyes and flicked the reins. In response, the horses began to trot again, pulling the wagon.

'Come on. You said you were a good shot. Get this hunk moving faster! I've seen ships move quicker than this without any wind in their sails.' I egged her on.

She slapped the reins down again and gave a 'yah,' call. The horses increased their speed considerably along the road.

With Xanthe distracted, I acted quickly to turn the tables in my favour. I slipped the matchstick from my mouth and wedged it firmly between the cocking lever and its fully closed position.

'Don't forget the crossbow,' I reminded her placing it in her lap.

Xanthe looked completely focused. She waited patiently for me to throw the bottle. And waited. And waited some more.

Fields and hills passed as we kept up the pace. Her irritation was beginning to take its strain. I laid back with my hands behind my head and rested my boots upon the rail in front of me. A new matchstick had replaced the previous one and I rolled it between my teeth contentedly.

Xanthe looked over.

'Kid, this is ridiculous and it isn't proving anything. We've been travelling for ages now and you haven't given me a go. If you think tha-'

Her outburst was exactly what I had been waiting for.

'Reaper!' I yelled out and pointed behind her.

She spun and aimed in the direction I was pointing. I flung the bottle high in the opposite starboard direction. Sensing I must be playing a trick, Xanthe immediately corrected herself and fired the action of the crossbow. Nothing happened. The matchstick had done its job perfectly. I was almost ready to cry out in victory when a bolt launched past my face, flicking my hair. There was the familiar sound of the smashing of glass some distance behind me.

Her smile said it all. I didn't need to look back to know I had lost, but I did out of curiosity. Sure enough, some fifteen fathoms away I could see the remnants of the bottle lying on the ground. I could argue that the bottle simply shattered when it hit the ground, but there was one defining point that would make that argument invalid. Pinned to a stump, lay the crossbow bolt. As a string threads the eye of a needle, the bolt had done to the opening of the neck of the bottle.

My jaw almost hit the ground.

'Lucky shot,' I grumbled.

'Don't beat yourself up, kid. You're dealing with a master here. Nice job with the matchstick though,' she slapped my shoulder hard. 'Sides, if you walked into an inn around here with this beauty, they'd slice you open just so they could sell it for parts. And your parts too I'd imagine.'

With that image now painted in my mind, I slunk back into my seat and looked out over the hills.

CHAPTER FIFTEEN

'It'll be easy. Trust me.'

I had heard those exact phrases before. They didn't exactly instil confidence in me. The Captain of the 'Kraken Krusher' would often say it to new prisoners before they 'volunteered' to be his bait when hunting sea monsters. It was often the last thing they heard, apart from their own terrified screams or the sloshing of monster digestive juices from within.

'You'll forgive me if I am not convinced,' I said.

'Look how well you handled the situation with Balgowan. It paid up big time. Sides, I can't exactly go waltzing into there looking like I do. People have heard of me, they'll tip off Regime soldiers quick smart. Sides, they are looking for two people with a wagon and horses now, ain't they? Well, one person certainly isn't two, is it?'

She had a valid point. 'There' as Xanthe had referred to it, was a backwater tavern, in a backwater town that we were observing from atop a nearby backwater hill. It was miserable weather, with drizzles of rain mixing with a mist that seemed to be just at home in the village as the occupants. None of which we could currently see, although the dim glow from the tavern windows and the faint sounds of music suggested that if people were to be anywhere, it was there.

'So, what will you do if I need you?'

'I'll be out here keeping watch over our stuff, silly. The horses can have a good ol munch on this long grass and I am close enough to keep an eye on the watering hole.'

'Can I at least take the crossbow?'

'Oh yeah, very business-like. Just rock into the tavern carrying a weapon likely worth more than ten years of their wages and try to strike up a conversation. Like I said before, at best you'll leave with most of your body parts still attached. And, wouldn't you feel better with me covering your back from up here? '

I gulped. It was worth a shot.

'Don't worry, kid. Just mosey on down and act like you belong. Remember you are just asking for some information about guards on the various gates to the city in exchange for some quality goods. I don't know a single bartender who wouldn't dive at that opportunity.'

I nodded and mentally prepared myself. I made my way down towards the muddy road leading into the town.

'Mind you, I don't suppose I know any bartenders, come to think of it...' she trailed off talking to herself once again.

Xanthe was right. We needed this. Any information on an *easy* way into the city would make our chances of success better and push me one step closer to finding and jailbreaking my father.

As I neared the tavern, I noticed something I hadn't seen in years. Searching through the mud and puddles was a large but very gaunt looking dog. It was a mixture of shaggy grey fur and bones. I remembered before I was captured, how I used to pat and sometimes feed any dogs that I would stumble upon when walking through villages or visiting new ports.

The poor thing looked starved. I felt about my person and recovered some secreted jerky from my pocket, care of Balgowan's food stuffs from the wagon. I held it out and whistled to it.

It snapped its head up. Slowly it considered me warily. I threw a small piece of jerky toward it and the animal leapt backward a tad. The dog was nervous. It carefully came closer, keeping its eyes on the food, its nose twitching at the scent.

It stopped a few feet away. I could see scars along its face and sides. The animal had had a rough trot in life. Looking into its eyes, I felt almost a connection with it.

It didn't take much longer before my new acquaintance was eating furiously from my hand. A scratch behind his ears and a belly rub later, I stood up feeling happier and more confident.

Deciding it was time to move on with the business side of my actual task I walked onto the veranda of the tavern and pushed through the door.

The gentle rapping of canine feet followed me inside.

Chapter Sixteen

'Information? You want information?! Bahahaha! Even if I had any, what makes you think I'd share it with the likes of you - a townie?'

Well, this certainly wasn't going as well as I had planned. At least it appeared as though the new disguise was convincing. My attempt at scrounging up some information — less so.

I was now standing in front of a very large and burly innkeeper whose forearms were almost as big as my torso and had the same bodily hygiene as the sailors I had spent three years on a ship with. At least they ended up in the drink from time to time for the occasional wash. My entrance into the dingy, poorly lit tavern had created somewhat of a slight stir as many eyes stared at me from tables through coal smudged faces. It appeared that for the first time in my life, I was a *tad* overdressed for the occasion. The music however, remained jovial and I remained constantly aware that my only real exit was the door and windows now some twelve paces behind me.

The innkeeper levelled his unpatched eye at me.

'I asked you a question, boy,' he sneered, still wiping out a tankard with possibly the dirtiest rag I had ever seen.

I gulped at the question. Then I gulped down some of the watered mead I had been served moments earlier. Looking at the rag again, I wondered if it added or took away from the flavour. The overall effect was gods awful.

'Think of this as a business deal. A small venture in your favour,' I began.

'Hmmm. And what makes you think that I'd be willing to do business with someone such as yourself?'

'Well, this tankard of watered-down mead to start with.'

The innkeeper's large hand slammed down on the bar top.

The noise, like many other abrupt ones of late, made me jump. Surprisingly, my hand instinctively reached for my fish-bone lockpick as a makeshift shank. That, and a growl came from my new companion at my feet. This caught the attention of the bar keep and he eyed me suspiciously, a little warier than before. Satisfied at his reaction, I slid the handle back inside the bracer.

'No dogs allowed in here... sir.'

The sudden change of respect instilled a small sense of pride within me. Making friends, animal or otherwise was definitely becoming something I could get used to.

'Oh, he isn't a dog. He's my associate. And I don't control him. He just likes to make sure that my business agreements are fulfilled. Like a minder, if you catch my drift?'

He eyed me suspiciously. I tried to appear nonchalant and convincing. It wasn't as if a stray dog would impact the high hygiene standards the barkeeper kept so carefully hidden of the establishment.

He caved.

'Aye.'

I looked again around the room to see if anyone else had noticed my mistaken prowess or my protective companion. All members seemed to be carrying on about their business. All except a hooded figure in the corner, of whom I could not make out much more than ragged robes and a finely waxed, yet thin, moustache. I could swear the hood was staring at me, but it was hard to tell.

'Ere, what you be sayin bout my mead...' continued the barkeeper.

My attention snapped back from its brief interlude.

'Now now, what I'm trying to say is, that I could make you an offer that will keep you and your fine hard-working patrons here happy. After all, everyone knows that townships such as this are the hardworking backbone of the Regime.'

An argument in the far corner of the bar quickly erupted into fisticuffs. The inn keeper didn't seem to notice.

His eye narrowed. 'Go on.'

'I have a few crates of some of the finest mead in the Regime that I'd be willing to trade for some accurate and helpful information.'

There was the sounds of glasses breaking and a chair smashing. The inn keeper casually leant over to a slate board resting against a lantern and placed two marks beside a name.

'Is that so?' he mused.

'Um... yeah.'

'An what kind of mead are we talking about here?'

'Well, surely there is only the one that is above all the rest?'

'Birningham's Mead?' he lit up.

'Nope.'

A tankard flew past my head almost knocking the match-stick from my mouth. The innkeeper once again put a tally notch on the board. The music played on.

'Fallaway Hill Mead?' he continued.

'Nope.'

'Crescent Moon Mead?'

'Ahhh... warmer? Look sir, I'm not talking about those sub-par copycat labels that aren't worth the honey their sup-posedly made from.'

'They're the labels I stock.'

'And what fine labels they are. I'm saying that I'm willing to part with two cases.'

His eye narrowed some more.

'Three cases.'

He bared some yellow teeth and leant forward.

'Four?'

'Sounds better.'

'Of superb mead from the Regime's finest mead brewer; Balgowan himself.'

Again, the fist met the bar with a forceful thump.

'Balgowan?!' he spat a hocked-up lump of mucus on his own floor. 'That no good lump of Kraken crap? The same Balgowan that stole away my wife?'

'Yasmine was your wife?'

'Is!'

His complexion was beginning to match the colour of his hair and lengthy mutton chops. I decided to change my tact.

'I didn't stutter. I did indeed say I have three cases-'

'Four,' he grimaced.

'Yes, two cases of Balgowan's finest brewed mead. What I didn't say is how I came across the aforementioned product — nor did I mention how, by trading it under the labels of your current stock, you can discredit his merchandise and improve the quality of your own, thus putting a slur against his name and his business.'

The innkeeper appeared slightly confused at the use of big words. I figured those that he could understand he liked the sound of, mostly because he hadn't throttled me across the bar as yet. I kept up the talk.

'What I mean to say is but the truth. I am not a representative of Balgowan's Meadery, nor am I a competitor. What I am, is simply a pilgrim that has stumbled across some valuable wares that would profit someone such as yourself. And seeing as I am a reasonable man-'

'Kid.'

'Whatever. Seeing as I am a reasonable *young* man, I am willing to ensure that your profit is maximised by only trading over valuable information. Take Balgowan's bottles and steam off the labels. Switch them with your *hmpf cough* less than premium standard drinks. Soon enough, customers won't even take a second look at Balgowan mead.'

The innkeeper considered me for a moment as I continued to nonchalantly swig on my current drink. He served a pair of coal smeared customers and returned to his incessant tankard polishing in front of me. Meanwhile, the dog decided to lay down at my feet and scratch a particularly deep itch behind his ears while the innkeeper considered me again.

'So, you mean to say that you aren't working for that scumbag? At all?'

'Not at all.'

'So, you stole the cases,' he declared, a grin growing across his large jawline.

'Well, one might say he gave it up willingly.'

'So where are these four cases?'

'Two.'

'Where are these... two... cases of the so-called finest mead in the Regime?' he asked through a slight growl.

'Not here. I have them stowed away safely. What I do have are some bottles however.'

The innkeeper reached over and plucked one of the bottles I provided on the bar. Popping off the wax sealed cork, he sniffed the opening and then swigged long and hard on the drink. He paused. Next came a weird series of mouth swishing, gargling and finally a large gulp. I was beginning to think that I had actually unknowingly poisoned the poor sod, that is, until he placed the bottle back down on the bar and smiled.

'I'll give him this. It is a fine quality mead this one, and I admit that maybe the quality of my drinks have been less than their usual potency.'

I held back a reflex cough.

'But it appears as though you've overlooked something boy-o,' he sneered leaning across the counter.

'And what's that?' I asked.

'You've come alone and you're carrying ill gained goods. At least four cases if I am correct. Probably more. What is stopping me from simply hurting you enough that you hand over the mead and I get to hold my tongue still?'

His dirty rag hand disappeared behind the bar and reappeared. It was now holding an equally dirty and blunt looking knife. I looked around the tavern nervously. No one seemed to notice at all. Even the hooded man from earlier had disappeared from his seat. This situation was declining rapidly.

—·—

CHAPTER SEVENTEEN

'Might I interject my fine fellow?' came a rather husky voice from close behind me.

Not wanting to take my eyes from the ever-growing aggression of the barkeep or his blunt knife, I managed to turn my head enough to see the hooded figure, now standing beside me. Even this close, through the corner of my eye it was hard to see the man's face. I could only make out an thin twirled moustache and shapely jaw protruding from under the hood.

The barkeep blushed slightly, his eyes looking downward, unable to meet the stranger.

'Oh, I, um, sorry, your holiness. How can I help thee?'

So, he was a holy man? I thought to myself. Now the barkeep, caught off guard reminded me of a young boy who had been discovered up to no good by a village elder.

'I would like to purchase another of your whiskeys, from the top shelf if you don't mind. One from the Islaeden-o-Hal distillery in the Isle of Darkwater, if you may. The peat-y ones make me rather sleepy.'

'Impeccable taste, sir... your holiness,' bowed the barkeep, and he turned on his heel and made his way over toward a small wooden ladder in the corner.

Once the barkeep had left, the hooded figure leant in toward me a little.

'Join me by the hearth fire. We may be able to help one another,' his voice now taking a very different and stronger tone.

'Um, sure.'

This was not part of the plan. Xanthe would not be happy.

The barkeep returned and the hooded figure held out a pouch of coins with both hands peeking just a little from under his robed arms. As they made the exchange of goods, my new friend pulled the barkeep in close and whispered into his large cauliflowered ear. There were a series of nods and a concerned look upon the barkeep's face. Finally, the 'hood' finished what he had to say and turned and left to his corner.

Once again, it was now me and the barkeep. There was an awkward pause.

He spoke first.

'I would like to apologise for my behaviour just now, young sir. It was not like me at all. See, times have been hard of late and deadlines in the mines have become rather hard to meet for most of the folk who used to frequent here. My customers simply don't have the coin to be my customers anymore. If you could see it in your heart to forgive me...'

'Forgiven,' I stated bluntly. This awkwardness and sob story was borderline unbearable and to be perfectly honest, I was keen to distance myself promptly from the man who had until recently considered filleting me for his own brief financial gain. I made my way past the tables and stepped over a patron who was either dead, unconscious or sleeping, with a new curiosity burning in my mind as to my new contact in the corner. The cliché very evident in my mind of meeting a mysterious hooded stranger in a tavern.

I made my way towards the stranger's table and the ruckus in the background died down. The lute and fiddle claimed the establishment once again. The dog followed me through the room like my own shadow. Watching out over the seats in this part of the tavern's hearth was a rather huge and dusty skull of a large horned reptile, possibly a massive serpent with a rather antique looking sword still buried firmly in the centre of its brow.

As I neared the wooden table, I could see my new contact. He had his back to the fireplace, allowing shadows to once again envelope most of his face, his drink remaining untouched in front of him and his hands rested under the table. Hanging nearby were sprigs of rosemary and bulbs of garlic that, now mixed with the smells of alcohol and the absence of the odorous barkeep, provided quite a homely and pleasant feel to this corner of the tavern.

Tentatively, I removed a seat and went to sit down opposite the stranger.

'Closer,' he stated, motioning for me to pull up beside him.

'Um... no, I think I'll be right here, thanks.'

'Suit yourself,' he smiled with his head still lowered, 'but it'll be harder to help me, so I can help you I'd imagine.'

'Say again?' I asked as I sat down.

'Word of advice my friend, if you don't want to get noticed by half the residents of a town, don't dress flashy and certainly don't sit with your face lit up like a bonfire in the light.'

'Oh, sure. Thanks,' I responded, feeling a bit sheepish.

'Don't mention it. Now let's get down to business.'

Feeling rather exposed now, thanks to his comment. I turned my chair just enough to allow shadow to fall over my face. The dog settled under the table at my feet, sniffing my boots and then leaning into my leg in an attempt to score some more pats. He was rewarded with a gentle scratch behind the ears.

'What's your name, kid?'

'Flynt. What's yours?'

'You handy with this lock pick you have here?'

He brushed his robbed hands over the table, leaving my fishbone lock pick sitting idle on the table beside his flagon.

Flabbergasted, I reflexively felt for where I usually kept the lock pick, as if not believing my own eyes. Sure enough, it was gone from the underside of my bracer.

'How did you?'

'My friend, I picked you out when you walked into this place. I thought that kid is certainly no mead salesman. Look at him. He must be a con. And sure enough, what I heard, satisfied my suspicions. So, I moved a little closer and... ah... assessed you, closer up. Turns out you need some information. I need someone who can use that pick there. I believe we could help each other.'

I'll hand it to him. It was slick. I had been so focused on the barkeep and our conversation, that my attention didn't pick up on his 'light' fingers.

I tried to hide my naivety.

'You were right to suspect that, I suppose. I am no more a mead salesman than you are a holy man. So, before I continue to answer your question, you need to answer two of mine. Who are you and what exactly do you think that I am supposed to use this for?' I motioned to the pick on the table.

'Right now, the name isn't important. As for the other answer, discreetly look under the table, if you don't mind.'

This simple task of approaching a member in a tavern had now become a lot messier.

I pretended to wipe some muck from the bottom of my riding boots on the floor. I was met with the affectionate licks of my canine friend, excited to see my face under our table. I gently pushed him aside and glanced up to see the stranger's fingers pointing at his wrists. A rectangular and rather barbaric set of iron manacles were bolted down fast, holding both hands firmly together. So firmly in fact, his fingertips were an ominous blue.

I sat back up. 'Oh.'

'Oh indeed. Let's not play dumb here, my friend. I know you have a conundrum too and I am guessing that we have similar interests. Getting caught with a lock pick is enough to get you into some serious trouble. Someone who carries one in Regime territory must have a sense of *rebel* about them. So, if you would be so kind as to use what I am hoping is a self-made lock pick to help out a fellow... professional, I'll see to it that I return the favour.'

'Who put those on you? And how exactly can you help me?' I said.

'Well, to answer the first one, let's just say that some new guards posed a larger problem for me and my crew than I first thought and we bit off a bit more than we could usually chew. Secondly, my options are running out. Especially if my fingers fall off waiting for your curiosity to be satisfied. However, I could start by finding out what exact information it is that you want?'

I did the math in my head. It was simple. Sitting here in front of me was a fugitive, an enemy of the Regime. Aside from the obvious, he was now more impressive than I had first thought. He had managed to pick my pockets with hands that looked more dead than alive. Before I committed to any sort of agreement, I wanted to know more.

'I'll get to that soon. What did the guards want with you?'

'Soon. Either you can help me or I'm wasting my time. You seem smart, right? You have the upper hand here. But look at it from my point of view. If I tell you who I am, and you don't help me, I am kind of...'

The large wooden doors of the tavern swung open letting in a gust of cold air from the drizzled icy day outside. Four cloaked guards of the Regime entered the tavern. Their uniforms were different from many of the Regime soldiers I had seen in the past, but they were unmistakably military of some sort. One remained at the doorway, her hands folded across the front of her double-breasted coat that was doing not such a good job of concealing a small but rather mean looking crossbow. Her eyes scanned the room from behind her dark complexion. The other three made their way to the barkeep. I lowered my head and did my best to not be noticed. The room began to feel very small and a whole lot less cozy.

'Guards?' asked my company without turning his head toward them.

I nodded slowly.

'My boy. It is now or never. The name is Arnesto Dubois,' he said lifting his head to reveal a warm smile.

I nodded.

'Arnesto Dubois,' he said again, as if waiting for a response.

'Um, alright.'

'Seriously? Nothing? I am *the* Arnesto Dubois. Thorn of the Regime.'

'Uh?'

I could just make out his brown eyes as they stared at mine in disbelief from under the hood.

'Ladies, lock up your daughters and valuables! No lock can hold him... well, that is until, ah, recently I suppose.'

I shrugged my shoulders.

'Wow comrade. Where have you been? Stuck under a rock for the past few years?'

'In a cell in the belly of a ship actually.'

'What?'

'What?'

'Well, I guess it is never too late to make a new friend. Someone you can trust.'

Somehow, it was a name that rang a bell, but I could not place where from. He seemed slightly deflated by my lack of knowledge. It seemed the simple idea of a single solitary person not aware of his reputation was inconceivable to him.

'Oh well, I guess the less you know, the better. Look at it this way, you help me and you can go back and tell all your friends that you helped the infamous Arnesto Dubois. You will never have to buy another drink again. You'll be the toast of…'

'What did you say?' I asked.

'The part about a new friend, or the part about trust?' His head tilted to regard me from under his ragged hood.

Trust was such a funny concept to me. Often had my father said that trust had to be earned through deeds and loyalty. Upon the ship however, too many times had I seen it broken by people on a whim. This was no longer a matter of trust. It was a matter of convenience. I did not want to be the reason another person had to be dragged away in chains by my own enemy. One of the guards began walking around the tables talking to patrons. With so few members, it was only a short matter of time until he would be beside us and asking questions.

'Do you have anyone waiting outside? Someone who may have already been picked up by these guards?' Arnesto queried.

I nodded once more. Followed by a slight shake of my head. I reached out and retrieved my pick. Leaning forward, I felt for Arnesto's restraints under the table.

He grimaced as I found them. I found the keyhole and began to work the pins inside.

One of the guards, a large broad man with a dark bushy moustache and a patch over one eye spoke to the barkeep. Despite the barkeep's size, this guard appeared to loom over him. He held up a parchment with an etching of a man's face.

One that I would not have even taken note of, if I hadn't just met the man it belonged to. The barkeep looked at the picture and shrugged his shoulders.

'Big fellow walk in? Moustache and eye patch?' asked Arnesto.

I nodded. A pin locked into place. The lock was more difficult than it looked.

Arnesto groaned and rolled his eyes. 'Captain Atticus Mortlock. That man just cannot handle a joke, I tell you.'

Another pin clicked into place.

'Are they the guards you had trouble with?' I asked.

'Ha, no. If only. Old Mortlock there is always one step behind me. He can't quite catch a break. Although, he is a tenacious man, I will give him that. Try a different angle there my friend, the third pin is slightly to your upper left.'

I carefully and slowly moved the pick. There was another faint click in response.

'You've picked this before?'

'Well yes and no. I lost the feeling in my fingers shortly after trying. These cuffs tighten the more you fiddle with your hands apparently. A new development, most likely one of the fine Captain's ideas to keep me under wraps I'd wager.'

The Captain that Arnesto was referring to, now turned his attention towards the patrons of the bar and slammed his fist against a timber pillar. It made a surprisingly loud noise. Mortlock's large metal fist, I had failed to notice prior, splintered the timber, and shook the dust out of the rafters above.

The music stopped.

'He has a metal fist,' I exclaimed.

'That? Oh yes. Part of the reason he doesn't like me very much I am afraid.'

'Brilliant.'

'Listen up.' Mortlock's voice was hoarse and menacing and each word seemed a struggle to rouse any volume. Normally it would be nigh impossible to hear it in a normal tavern, however, he had the complete and undivided attention of every member within the walls. 'By order of the Governor himself, we are looking for the one... *pest*... that goes by the name of 'Arnesto Dubois'.

Arnesto was rolling his eyes and mouthing the words exactly to those that were coming out of the Captain's mouth. The other two guards fanned out and made their respective ways toward other groups of patrons.

'As such, you are all required to provide your citizenship papers promptly and without discussion. Harbouring or helping this fugitive will result in swift and reasonable punishment.'

'What does he mean by that?' I asked as another pin clicked into place.

'Most likely a beheading out the front of the tavern, if any of my previous experiences are something to go by.'

I gulped. My luck thus far had been a saving grace, but I had a niggling feeling it would run out eventually, and this time it seems, my punishment would not involve chains after all - for either of us.

'Wow, you didn't care to mention this before I started? I would very much like to keep my head attached to my body.'

'As do I. And I fully intend to see to that aspiration as long as my hands can be freed. Listen, just relax, my friend. It isn't something to lose you head over... well... not quite.'

I glared at him momentarily. His confident smile did little to ease my tensions.

'Ah quick question,' Arnesto asked.

'Yes?'

'Do they per chance have any rather large mechanical look-ing giants?'

'What?!' I asked.

'Don't make me ask again. Did you see any large mechanical looking giants enter the room?'

'They have those?'

'Verily. For a con, you sure are slow on the uptake, aren't you? Yes, they have them. That is part of the reason I am in this mess. From your reaction, I take it the answer is a resounding 'no', in any case our chances are finitely better.'

'Our chances of what?' I asked.

'Escape, of course. What you thought we'd just sit here in a bar and I could give you all the help you need? If I know that man with the grizzled outlook over there, which I certainly do, he will have back up teams of guards stationed at all exits. Which, for your information is the front door, the cellar exit, that window over there and the two windows by the front door. Just a click of his fingers and they will burst in here with their crossbows. And they are a trigger-happy lot.'

My thoughts jumped to Xanthe. I would have felt a lot safer with her beside me at this moment in time. We had agreed though, that it was best for someone to stay with the horse and carriage of cargo and given her unique appearance, she would be more suited to security detail and I to the simple and easy role of trading two cartons of mead for some information.

Stupid simple plans. Which brings me to my next train of thought.

'Do you have a plan?' I asked.

'I am an artist. And an artist usually needs their hands to work their craft. So, if you wouldn't mind.'

'So, you are confident we can escape?

'There is always the element of risk, but, yes. I have escaped them many a time before. That is currently why we are having this conversation, although my hands would seem somewhat still under lock and key. So, I suppose, I am somewhat still a prisoner.'

'You were in a Regime prison?'

'Not just any prison, my friend. I was in 'The Gulag', the Regime's most heavily guarded prison. Only those they deem a threat to their war machine are ever confined in there. My escape was quite the tale actually and I would revel in telling it to you, but ah...' he gestured to the cuffs again.

I couldn't believe the moment. I was sitting with someone who shared a prison - possibly a cell, with my father.

'Did you... Did you know... do you know Carter Cunning-ham? I stammered. I desperately wanted to question Arnesto further, but now was not the time nor place. 'By the gods, how many pins does this lock have?'

'You know Carter?' he considered me more seriously. 'Oh, and the answer I do believe is six pins,' Arnesto replied.

By now, I was raking back and forth as subtly as I could manage under the table.

'He's my father,' I replied.

Arnesto's mouth dropped open slightly. He leant forward and stared at me more closely, as though looking to see if I was lying.

'What?' I asked.

'You're... Flynt?'

Chapter Eighteen

'Yes, you do have his eyes. My, you have grown. You *are* Carter's son. You're Flynt.'

'So you do know my father. Where is he? Is he alright? Is he-'

The burly guard nearest us, turned his attention toward me from only a few tables away. He must have noticed our reluctance to comply with the orders of his Captain. Slowly and deliberately his boots clunked as he moved toward our conversation.

'I do know your father,' he began. 'But the questions you ask are not simple ones I am afraid. I will need some time to explain them to you and it would seem our conversation is drawing to a close,' he looked down toward the floor.

'Click'. The raking was working, albeit slowly.

My eyes met those of the guard and I cursed myself quietly for having looked up. Now looming above us, he stood behind my companion.

'What eez eet we av ere?' he demanded.

I recognised the accent from the islands of the south. Last time I was there, the region was free of the Regime's influence. Now it seemed that those men and women helped fill their ranks.

'Where eez your papers?' he continued. A low but soft growl protested from under the table. The guard ignored it.

I worked the lock more desperately. I had counted five clicks of the pins. Surely, I only had one more to go. Subtlety had now left my movements as I struggled to locate the final pin.

'What ahh ya doin? I said for ya ta show me ya papers!' The guard now reached down toward his weapon. The other guards in the tavern all turned their attention in our direction. Mortlock stared straight at me and began to make his way over.

'I... ah... well you see.' I struggled to get the words out.

There was a faint clicking sound followed suddenly by a very loud 'CLUNK' as the restraints fell onto the floor. I looked down to the horrified sight of Arnesto's cuffs now resting on the toe of the guard's boot. He too stared down in disbelief.

'By the gods, that is a relief. Thank you, Flynt,' Arnesto sighed sitting back in his chair.

'You two, you eez coming weeth me!' demanded the guard, as he placed his large hand upon Arnesto's shoulder.

'And thank you too, my friend,' exclaimed Arnesto.

What happened next, I am sure, was meant to be a lot more spectacular and impacting than reality. In one smooth and quick flourishing movement, Arnesto spun to standing causing the guard to lose control of his grip. He was only as tall as the guard's shoulders. In a split second, Arnesto was on his feet and pivoting, his cloak extended like the wings of a large bird into the air. This however was simply a distraction as his fist, with the full weight of his body, met the jaw of the unsuspecting guard. It was at this moment, I was certain the guard would fall, rocked by the blow. Instead, however,

Arnesto's hand flopped like a dead fish and merely slapped him.'

'Ahhh...ow, ow, ow pins and needles. Pins and needles,' Arnesto cried to nobody in particular.

The slap stunned the guard momentarily with the reflexive movement of holding his hand to his face. Arnesto, now dancing on the spot flapping his limp hand around, looked as though he were trying to rouse an unconscious puppet. The guard regained his thoughts and with eyes narrowing, wound up for a heavy haymaker of a blow at his assailant. His movement stopped short as Arnesto's boot kicked his front leg out from under him. The guard buckled and the punch fell wide. A second blow from Arnesto's elbow met the back of the guard's head. His temple connected with the timber floor. He groaned momentarily and then fell limp.

Now standing there in the light of the fireplace, without the cover of a cloak or hood was Arnesto, in a pose fit for any bard's tale. He wore a uniform of smudged and torn rags, his feet all but bare. His dark hair was slicked back, and his small salt and pepper moustache and goatee were overgrown yet twisted in a mundane effort to appear neat. To top it off, despite the impending danger, there was a large cheeky smile, framed by possibly the strongest looking jaw I had ever seen. Now having regained his composure, he ignored the immediate danger of the other guards and fired a cheesy wink at me. I do believe it was somewhat of a trademark.

The moment of defiance was shortly lived. Mortlock had stopped mid stride on his way to our table and wheezed loudly the order to fire. As if predicting their next movement, Arnesto grabbed his bottle of whiskey and flipped our table over between us and the guards. There was a pair of whistles and 'thunks' as their bodkin tips slammed into our cover. I grabbed the dog and pulled him in behind the cover.

'My friend, how is your aim?' Arnesto asked.

'Eh?'

'Take this,' he handed me the bottle. 'If Mortlock charges us, which I am sure he will, be a good fellow and throw it in the fire when he reaches that third table there.'

I risked a quick glance beyond our cover. Patrons were scrambling toward the doors or flipping tables as we had. The barkeep was yelling at the guards for the disruption, only to have his protests fall short as Mortlock pointed a small crossbow in his direction and loose a bolt at the shelves behind him, shattering glass bottles and plastering their contents across the wall and floor. The other guards were frantically yet methodically reloading their weapons with another round of quarrels.

'Bravo Team move!' came the raspy demand of Mortlock. 'Alpha has them pinned.'

His guards repeated the command loudly down the line.

Arnesto and I looked around us, waiting for some sort of response.

Nothing.

'Bravo Team move now, we have you covered!' Mortlock tried again with as much volume as his voice could muster.

Again, we peered at the windows and rear door.

No shock troops. No crossbow bolts whistling in our direction.

Nothing.

A chuckle from Arnesto grew quickly into a loud and arrogant series of riotous laughter. It was somewhat infectious. I found myself smiling at the situation too. Then, just as any moment when it feels inappropriate to laugh, trying to stifle it made it worse. Now the Captain had the displeasure of witnessing two fugitives laughing at his misfortune from behind the cover of a mere table in a backwater tavern.

'It would appear your 'Bravo Team' as you call them, have turned tail and fled for the hills, my dear Captain,' Arnesto finally managed between laughs.

More bolts whistled through the air. A bolt pierced through a tankard very close to my head. I ducked down further in response, my laughter dying back to a nervous chuckle.

Arnesto was now rubbing his hands frantically, as though trying to revive them. He looked around the tavern and turned to me.

'I need to get to that sword,' he motioned toward the sabre buried into the serpent's skull above the fireplace. But I need a distraction. Do you have any suggestions, Master Cunningham?'

I was surprised at being put on the spot. Why was he showing so much faith in me?

The simplest and stupidest sounding answer escaped my lips before I could rationalise it.

'You could use the Captain for a leg up?'

I immediately realised how idiotic my response had been. Arnesto stared blankly at me now. No smiles. He most likely believed he was now stuck with a head case on the wrong side of the table.

Then his face lit up.

'Hah hah, you're absolutely right, my friend. That is exactly what I will do! Hold off on the whiskey will you and sit back and enjoy an artist at work?'

'No... wait, perhaps,' I began, but my protest fell on deaf ears.

Arnesto grabbed his bunched cloak from the floor and stood up from behind cover. He gestured a challenge toward the Captain.

I peered wide eyed from behind the table. Was this man actually insane? What was it he was trying to prove?

'Come now, my dear Captain. What is wrong? I am unarmed and you still cannot best me or my young friend Flynt here.'

I cringed ever so slightly at my name now being known by all members still present in the tavern. Especially the guards.

'It would seem that if the question was raised as to whether 'Captain Mortlock' is a man or a mouse, the answer would be resounding and unanimous in the favour of the latter.'

I dared another look beyond our cover. Mortlock fell for the goad, his moustache twitching in anger. Puffing his barrel chest, he bared his teeth and charged. His movements across the floor ignored furniture and danger alike as he made head long for our cover.

Arnesto smiled and shifted his feet on the spot.

The Captain raised his metal fist and swung hard towards his target. Arnesto leapt from behind the cover simultaneously and ran to meet to the Captain, unfurling the cloak and holding it before him. Arnesto jumped and dragged the cloak before Mortlock's face. The Captain's blow narrowly missed as Arnesto ducked away. Now swinging wildly, his face smothered, the Captain was destroying his surroundings. Tables splintered, chairs shattered and goblets became almost as dangerous as crossbow bolts as they flew through the air trailing dregs across the floor. Arnesto danced with the blinded, struggling Captain. He chose his moment and ran toward the blinded beast. Arnesto used the Captain as a step ladder, running up his back and leaping from his shoulders over the fireplace. He landed melodramatically, brandishing the sabre freshly plucked from the Dragon Head mantle and pointing it toward the occupied Captain.

The theatrics were short lived. Even without the use of his eyes, the Captain must have heard the landing of his enemy. His powerful metal arm struck with full force against Arnesto and sent him barrelling across the floor into the nearby remains of tables. My friend wheezed in pain as the guards scrambled toward him, crossbows levelled at his prone form. By now the Captain had finally won the struggle with the cloak and was breathing heavily. His eyes were livid and wide. Standing there in front of the fireplace, he watched as his guards restrained the stunned Arnesto. The moment had happened so fast, the scuffle so brief, I had forgotten myself.

It seemed however, that wasn't the case for our Captain. Slowly he turned his attention toward me. He lifted an accusatory finger in my direction.

'You.'

That was all that he needed to say. No longer distracted, I suddenly felt very alone. Fear rumbled in the pit of my stomach. By now, the guard that had been on the floor was starting to come around and was sitting up holding his head. The Captain ignored his condition and hauled him to his feet.

'Grab the boy and bring him outside with Dubois, we can use the same rope, no point in wasting any more bolts.' he ordered.

Rope? So that was it. I was to be unceremoniously hanged simply for helping Arnesto.

I felt briefly about me. I needed something to protect myself with. I felt a sharp prick and instantly looked down to see a wooden table leg, nails protruding from the end that had previously been attached to one of the many obliterated tables littering the premises.

The guard, still groggy, regained his weapon from the floor and moved toward me. His eyes, though unfocused, beaded at me. He stopped and levelled the crossbow.

'You tere. You eard da Captaan. Move it.'

It was at that moment, kindness rewarded me. The dog which Arnesto and I had been patting, the one that had found comfort at our feet, now leapt forward between the guard and I, appearing far bigger and more ferocious than the timid stray from before. Fangs bared, it growled and snapped wildly causing him to reel slightly.

'And someone silence that gods damned mangy cur, will you?' yelled Mortlock.

The guard looked at his Captain and then back to the dog. A slight smile drew across his face as he moved his aim to the animal.

'No!' I blurted out.

The guard's eyes met mine and narrowed. The crossbow 'twanged'. There was a brief whimper, followed by silence.

Content with his actions, he began to reload another bolt.

My fists clenched and my teeth did the same. My eyes welled with tears.

He finished loading a new quarrel onto the stage, but his aim was lowered. I saw my opening. I felt a surge of anger propel me over the table at the guard. He was too slow raising the weapon, but training must have kicked in. I was stopped, as the butt of his crossbow struck my brow. The room seemed to shake momentarily, but my anger helped me to focus on him and his stupid smirk. I felt the hate. I channelled it. I swung with my full force. He leant back slightly, possibly expecting a closed fist by a young teen. Easy to dodge. He learnt of his mistake too late as the table leg gave me extra reach. The twisted nails turning that smirk, that malicious face, into something a little more 'open plan'. The smile was no more —neither was his jaw.

He gurgled something wet and wordless, clutching at the ruins of his face.

'It was just a dog! What kind of human – what sick – Argh!' Anger had my words twisting in my mouth.

I struck again with an upward swing into his groin. The guard's legs buckled and he collapsed. At least he would never sire a spawn as twisted and evil as himself.

I looked up for my next target and tried to remove the embedded table leg. It didn't comply, it had stuck fast and was unwilling to move from its new resting place in his loins.

By now the guards were lifting Arnesto up. His hands once again bound in the cuffs I had only just removed. He still appeared hurt, but more so crestfallen.

The Captain ordered another of his guards, 'Billingham, check on where the bloody hells 'Bravo Team' are and why they didn't enter on my comman-' he stopped as one of his guards motioned toward me.

The Captain, who had been making his way toward the door stopped in his tracks and turned. He surveyed the scene and looked to the heavens with a pleading gesture of frustration.

'Do I have to do everything myself?' he growled to no one in particular.

I knelt down beside the twitching guard and commandeered his crossbow. As the Captain strode toward me, I remembered Xanthe's words, 'I'd rather be killed than ever be captured alive by them.' Her comments floated around, repeating in my head. Xanthe. Where was she? Surely, she had seen the guards enter the tavern. Why hadn't she appeared? Had she been captured? Had they hurt her?

If she was okay, surely, she would have burst through that door and resolved this situation. They *must* have her. The uncertainty made my anger pulse. If they could hurt an innocent animal like that without a second thought, what must they be doing to her?

'Where is she?' I demanded.

The Captain raised a quizzical eyebrow. He kept moving across the tavern, glass and timber crunching under his boots.

'Who?'

'You know who. Tell me where she is and tell your guards to stop where they are. I won't ask again,' I said as I raised the crossbow.

The Captain slowed to a saunter and began to casually pace in front of the fire. With a slight gesture, the guards stopped dragging Arnesto.

'You know you should watch where you point that, young man. You might just take someone's eye out. It would be in your best interest to lower the weapon and hand yourself over.'

'Is that so?'

'Well, yes. Do I look like a liar? Consider your options. You can come along peacefully, do your time in my prison, even enjoy two meals a day and some labour. It will make you strong, I can guarantee it. At least you will be alive. You might even be conscripted into the ranks of the Governor's forces and receive a shortened sentence for your actions against the Regime.'

'You said they were to hang me. I heard you.'

He stopped in front of the flames. Plucking some dried sage leaves hanging above the mantle, he closed his eyes and drew them past his nose, inhaling deeply.

'Perhaps, but I only have to change my mind and say the word. The more I think about the situation, the more I realise I can help you. Why? Because I know this isn't your fault. You see, I know Arnesto there. He doesn't have friends, only people he can manipulate. He takes innocent people like yourself and convinces them he can provide them things they need in order for them to serve some purpose in his plans. He convinced you to help him, didn't he? He tricked you into committing a crime. He' – he gestured toward Arnesto. 'He, cannot be saved. He is but a mere parasite who steals from the Regime. A dog, who tries in vain to stop which cannot be stopped.' He nodded toward the dog now dead beside me. 'He tries when - as you can see - he cannot succeed. So, ask yourself. Do you really want to pull that trigger and start down a futile path after being manipulated by a liar and a thief? Because, you can, if you want. You can pull that trigger, but you better make sure you kill me, and all of my guards, because if you miss, I guarantee that I will pound your corpse into a fine mince beside your canine friend right there.'

The threat was unnerving. I *was* trapped with nowhere to go. I felt weakened, hopeless. If I hadn't patted or fed that dog, it wouldn't be dead. If I hadn't unlocked Arnesto's cuffs, he may have gotten away. If I hadn't forced Xanthe to help me, then she would be safe, or at least I think she would be. If I didn't slow my father down, he would have never been captured. I realised it had always been my fault. I had let everyone down. Maybe Mortlock was right. Maybe giving up was the only way I could stop people from being hurt.

The fire crackled loudly as Mortlock stoked the flames and added another log, using his metal arm to place it further into the coals.

'Made a decision yet, boy? Because we don't have all day.'

Chapter Nineteen

I looked down at the floor. Gazing back at me were the dead eyes of the stray dog. An innocent animal, it was dead because of Regime guards.

My breathing became deeper. My hand twisted around the neck of the Whiskey bottle and the other gripped and fingered the trigger of the crossbow.

'Boy?' queried Mortlock.

Xanthe too, would have been captured or killed if I hadn't tried to save her. And now, Arnesto, would soon be dead because of them too. Beheaded or hanging from a tree outside.

I felt another surge of hate burrowing through my stomach.

At that moment, I realised, *futility* was *inaction*. Doing nothing made others pay the ultimate price.

'You took it all away from me.' I seethed.

'What's that?'

'You took everything I ever had, everything I ever cared about and you destroyed it. My mother and my sister. Dead. My father, a prisoner. You broke me and now you think that you can bargain with me to save my own skin?'

'Have you been listening, boy? Or is the fire snuffed out in your young head? I represent the Governor himself, head of the Regime. I hold his word as decree and I say drop the wea—'

It was the flames that cut him off. Whatever they distilled on the Isle of Darkwater, seemed to be simply explosives labelled as 'Whiskey'. There was a shattering of glass as I launched the bottle into the flames. Followed closely by a bright flash. Then a wave of heat. It reminded me briefly of my incident with Steiger aboard the 'Kraken Krusher' only now, the effects were more severe. Mortlock was now well and truly alight. Flames twisted and twirled up and down his right side as he screamed in pain. It was a horrid sight. His guards dropped Arnesto and lowered their crossbows to help their Captain. One ran toward the bar, possibly in search of a wet rag or water to extinguish the flames, while the innkeeper backed away with hands raised. The others dove at him and tried to help him roll on the ground.

I stepped forward and pointed my weapon at the guards. The odds had tipped in my favour. They had stopped in their tracks as I was now the only armed person in the bar. My sights aimed steadily at the writhing burning figure of the Captain.

'Stop!' I commanded.

They hesitated under my aim, waiting for an order. Something I am sure guards and soldiers are inherently trained to do in times of stress.

'When he stops, tell him I have a message for your beloved Governor. Tell him that I will find him and I will put an end to his Regime.'

They nodded in unison.

'Now, you take yours and I'll take mine,' I said, slowly making my way toward Arnesto.

Wide eyes stared back at me. There were slight nods of acknowledgment as the Captain's cries turned to whimpers. The flames, now all but out, were replaced by smouldering clothes and the smell of seared flesh.

Still pointing the crossbow at the pair of guards kneeling beside the Captain, I crouched down and hoisted Arnesto onto his feet.

'Keys,' I demanded.

One of the guards looked at the other and answered by sliding a set of elaborate looking iron keys across the timber floorboards toward us. I knelt down carefully and maintaining eyes on the guards, unlocked the cuffs for the second time. Still groggy from his run in with a steel fist, Arnesto leant into me wincing as I put his arm over my shoulder. We backed steadily toward the door.

I didn't take my gaze from the guards, even as we left the doorway. It wasn't until my feet struck something 'meaty' that my attention and senses returned to normal.

Looking down I could see what tripped me up.

A body of a guard lay strewn across the veranda.

Followed by another.

And another.

There must have been several guards, scattered in various uncomfortable positions, each one having something in common with the next –

Each guard had a vital piece of anatomy skewered by a solitary crossbow bolt.

'I say, whoever your friends are, they are certainly good friends to have,' commented Arnesto, between breaths.

'Agreed.'

I searched up and down the misty street. The churning of uncertainty in my stomach became worse. There was no sign of Xanthe.

CHAPTER TWENTY

'Xanthe!' I cried out. 'Where are you?'

My voice echoed off of the surrounding buildings.

'Call to someone else,' Arnesto recommended as his eyes scanned the corpses around us.

'There is no one else.'

Arnesto gathered himself and stood up. 'Hold on. Do you mean to tell me that *one* person was capable of this?'

'Yes.' I called out again, 'Xanthe!'

'By the gods, that is splendid,' he exclaimed.

'I get it, you are impressed, now can you at least walk? We need to move out of here.'

In response to my question, Arnesto stooped to commandeer two fallen sabres from guards who clearly no longer would find use for them. He slung one over each of his shoulders and began to hobble quite quickly... in the wrong direction.

'Wrong way, Arnesto.'

'Understood,' he stated and fixed his direction. 'Oh, where are my manners?' He dipped his toe under another abandoned sabre and casually flicked it up into his hand. Spinning it briefly, he turned and offered me the handle.

'If you are Carter's son, I take it you know how to use one?'

I took it without answering his question.

As we moved through the town toward the hill where Xanthe and I had agreed to meet, the rain became much heavier.
The downpour blurred out the details of the buildings, instead
leaving shadows of the old stone and timber constructions
lining the street. I couldn't help but notice the spot where I
had only moments ago met the stray dog which had trusted
in me, only to meet its demise. I quickly pushed the painful
thought to the side. I had always liked animals. They were
innocent.

People, far less so.

The streets were void of life or the sounds one would
usually expect from a town. Even the steady distant sounds of
a blacksmith pounding metal against metal had ceased. Only
the pattering sounds of rain on mud and shingles resonated
around us.

The rain was becoming so heavy that it became hard to see
more than a few fathoms. The mud squelched up my boots
and the cold water matted my hair to my face and eyes.

'Are you sure you know where you are going?' Arnesto
asked.

'Roughly.'

'Beg pardon?'

'Look, it is hard enough to see where we are going without
you questioning me. Last I checked, it was my turn to ask
the questions since I just saved your neck from having a date
between a rope and a sharp fall. Not to mention the cuffs -
twice. So how about a little understanding, or information, or
if you can provide neither, just keep your noisemaker shut.'

Arnesto considered me for a moment.

'Agreed. I do owe you a debt of thanks. And the answer to
your earlier question is 'yes'.'

'Yes what?'

A steady incline indicated we were close to the hill from earlier.

'Yes, I know your father. Old friends in fact.'

I stopped and turned to him.

'He is the reason I have been able to escape the Regime. He started the riot which distracted the guards long enough for me to liberate myself. It would seem I owe him quite a lot actually, or his offspring as it were. He inspired me to be who I am, to aggravate the Regime, to spoil their plans. I knew him well before my capture, he was a – colleague. A comrade in arms.'

I remembered what the Captain said aboard the *Kraken Krusher* —that my father was alive. But this... this made it real. He hadn't just survived. He sparked a riot. He helped free someone. He had been part of something much bigger than I ever knew.

My mind became full with a rush of questions and excitement. *How in the hells could he be a spy without me knowing? How long ago did you escape? Where is the prison and how do I get there? How can I break him out?* I felt so many emotions stir within me at hearing the news.

'He was a fisherman. A trader,' I said as we made our way up the sodden road to the rendezvous with Xanthe.

'Ah, that is what he wanted you to believe. He worked so hard at keeping you, a child, protected. You had already suffered enough. In the end, it was futile it would seem.'

'But he traded fish. We travelled everywhere together. How could he...'

'Willpower. You don't recall any times that you would wake and he wasn't there. Times when a stranger would approach him in the marketplace? Times where he would sail his boat close to Regime ships at anchor? The occasions where he left you with surrogate families for days and nights at a time?'

Arnesto was providing a sound argument. I could remember all of those moments and more. He had left me on numerous occasions because the weather was predicted to be too dangerous on the seas, or his favourite customer would supply him a package instead of payment for a fish. Life had appeared simple, but now it seemed that the lie had been blown wide open.

Arnesto's hand grabbed me by the shoulder reassuringly. 'Fear not, Flynt. I do believe we have company,' he gestured with his chin to our front.

From the muddy hillock overlooking the town, a hooded figure emerged from beside our wagon. It paced deliberately through the heavy downpour toward us.

'Well, my dear. I do believe a thanks is in order. You are an impeccable shot if I do say so myself.' Arnesto began.

I pushed my hand against his mouth to quieten him.

The figure moved forward. It raised its arms and appeared to grow taller, much taller than Xanthe.

'Flynt,' Arnesto whispered.

'Yeah?'

'Please tell me that is your friend.'

There was a slight creaking sound as limbs of a bow were drawn. The timber shaft sliding against the bow as it was pulled rearward.

'I... don't think so.'

The figure moved forward and I could finally start to see some features. Standing not more than ten fathoms away was a tall, broad-shouldered individual. Then a sense of dread fell over me as I saw a familiar red mask emerge through the rain. The dark slits where eyes should have been appeared hollow and soulless under small horns. A large and powerful bow, already back at full draw, was aimed directly at me.

At this range, he couldn't miss.

I hesitated. Arnesto didn't. Seeing the Reaper's intentions, he moved quickly.

There was a whistle and a thump. I felt a sharp sting across my cheek.

Arnesto wheezed briefly, then dropped to a knee in front of me. The arrow had entered his chest and exited halfway through his back. Its arrowhead had sliced a deep cut through my cheek as Arnesto bore the full brunt of the thick shaft at such a short range.

Thick red blotches welled through the rags he wore.

'Fl-Flynt, run.'

I didn't. Whether it was fear or anger I couldn't tell. My father hadn't abandoned Arnesto. If he showed faith in him, then I would too. Dropping the commandeered crossbow, I threw my arms under Arnesto's shoulders and lowered him awkwardly to his side. His attempts at protests were but mere gurgles now.

The faint sound of the bow being drawn once more made me lift my head. The Reaper had knocked another arrow and was once again pausing for the shot.

I stared back at him. I felt numb.

His pause continued. As though he were rooted to the spot. I could see now, his large gloved hand trembling slightly. Still the holes in the mask stared back at me. His head tilted.

'What are you waiting for?! Get it over with!' I yelled.

As if remembering the task that was at hand, The Reaper shook his head and then readjusted his aim.

I wondered if it would hurt. Would my passing be long and painful? From a young age, I had seen both sides of death. Some sea monsters took their time, toyed with their prey, removing limbs until all that was left was a final screaming bobbing morsel. Others simply cut to the chase and made quick work of their prey. Back on the ship, I knew which I had preferred if my time had come.

A figure cut through the rain to The Reaper's starboard side. He was struck hard in the mask by the full weight of the assailant's boot. The arrow released and whistled past my head. The attacker moved behind the Reaper with animal like speed and landed another heavy blow with a thick lump of wood or tree branch. The crack of timber against the metal helm was deafening over the rain. Any normal man would likely be dead from such a blow.

The Reaper remained standing.

The attacker swung a third time, however, the Reaper dipped below the swing and struck out with his bow as a makeshift club. The attacker winced and coughed briefly as the limbs of the bow thrust under their rib cage. I instantly recognised the cough.

It was Xanthe.

Her balance thwarted, she stumbled no more than a step. It was all The Reaper needed. The heel of his boot slammed hard into her jaw and sent her backwards. The force caused Xanthe's crumpled body to slide through the mud. By the time she finished sliding, The Reaper had restrung another arrow and was beginning to draw. His aim fixated solely on Xanthe.

Thunder cracked overhead. Lightning illuminated the sky. My body responded before my mind could catch up. Moving toward The Reaper with my new sabre in hand, I ducked low and scooped a handful of sludge. From the stories Xanthe had told me, locking blades with this man appeared to be suicide. However, I was used to being the weakest. Years of using underhanded techniques had become instinctive. Being constantly underestimated is a wonderful thing.

'Oi tin head!' I yelled.

As the mask turned its attention toward me, it was met with an airborne squelch of slop, like a well-aimed bowel movement from an albatross with a stomach bug. The mud plastered the whole face of the mask, effectively blinding him. Sprinting with the sabre in hand, I dropped to my knees and slid through the muck, intent on ducking his next swing. Instead, I felt the wind painfully driven from my lungs as his boot stomped perfectly into my chest and pinned me flat.

It was impossible. He couldn't see me, yet now I could feel my ribs on the verge of cracking as he pushed me further into the mud. Water and silt began to mix in my mouth and eyes. I choked for air and tasted blood. I swallowed more sludge. I was slowly sinking, drowning in ankle deep slop.

Despite the pain and mud, desperation helped me see. The Reaper calmly wiped the filth from his mask and realigned his bow. He aimed toward where Xanthe lay and drew the arrow to the cheek of his mask.

Reaching around, I could still feel the slippery handle of the sabre from Arnesto. With my vision blurred, I reached up and took a meagre swipe with the blade. It wasn't much. Barely a swing. It wouldn't have even scraped The Reaper's armour had I aimed at it. It was enough however, to slice the bowstring. I couldn't see it of course. Nor could I hear it now my ears were thoroughly filled with fluid, dirt and animal dung. But I did feel it.

I felt the bowstring fail. I felt the arrow fall beside my head. I felt the frustration of my enemy. I felt his boot lift, so he could drive home the fatal blow into my desperate rib cage. I felt his need for retribution, and in response, I could feel the rapture of laughter coming from my mouth between mouthfuls of mud. Full bodied, manic laughter bellowing from my stomach and pissing off my enemy.

Then the weight was lifted. Air painfully sucked back into the areas behind my strained ribs. My head lifted from the mud.

The Reaper staggered. His knees buckled as he looked down toward his stomach. The sharp point of a sabre was emerging gradually through his abdomen, between the hardened plates of armour, like a fast-growing metallic weed forcing its way into the world.

Again, lightning crackled across the sky and thunder boomed.

The blade twisted sharply. The Reaper fell to his knees beside me and slumped face first into the mud. Standing behind him - well, only just - was Arnesto. Pale from blood loss, he wheezed sharp shallow breaths.

'I forgot to introduce myself. Arnesto Dubois at your service,' he managed before his eyes lolled back into his head.

Arms arrived in time to catch Arnesto as he staggered backward. Xanthe, muddied and bloodied, held him in a seated position.

'Flynt?' she asked. 'Flynt, can you hear me?'

I tried to respond with 'Sure, I am fine Xanthe, thanks for asking,' but a gurgled 'yup' and a thumbs up was all I could manage.

'This one is alive. Just barely. I take it he is with us?' she motioned towards Arnesto laying in her arms.

I nodded.

'Definitely. He's basically family.'

—·—

Chapter Twenty-One

'Next time, if there is a next time kid, don't ever approach The Reaper when you think he is dead. Just high tail it outta there quick smart, will ya?'

'But I thought...'

'You thought he was what? Dead? That a simple sword thrust in the guts would stop him? What did I tell ya? It only slows him down.'

'I just wanted to-'

'Yeah yeah. I know what you just wanted to do. Duck!'

I ducked under a low tree branch as the horses and carriage rattled at speed down the muddy road.

'You wanted to see if he was human, what he looks like.'

'Well yeah.'

'Kid, does it matter? If death herself had red lipstick and braided hair would it make a difference? She is still there for one purpose.'

The carriage jolted as the wheel hit a large stone on the road. Arnesto winced loudly and clutched at the arrow shaft buried in his chest.

'Kid, lean him back over toward the side with the arrow sticking out. He is bleeding into his chest cavity. Keep the blood to one side or both of his lungs will fill up.'

'I am. I am. Just watch the road.'

Xanthe was understandably fuming at me. Shortly after the incident with Arnesto using The Reaper's torso as the scabbard for his sabre, I had let curiosity get the better of me. Ignoring Xanthe's orders to hurry up and follow her as she hauled Arnesto like a weightless rag doll, I went back to check over The Reaper.

I was intrigued. Like seeing an ocean monster up close, I was intimidated despite his stillness. I circled him briefly before moving in for a closer examination. The Reaper was littered with items I had never seen before, all with some sort of combative purpose. It was as though the Regime's finest tinkerers', alchemists, generals and even artists, had all gathered in unison, to see what sort of deadly creation they could devise. The result appeared to be someone - no *something*, which would give their enemies sweat-inducing nightmares and the Governor pants-wetting delight.

The dark armour that clad his body was held in place by sturdy flexible fabric. It was unlike anything I had seen before. The design seemed to focus on movement and concealment rather than specific protection. Small pouches lined his hips and chest, each one easily accessible and mostly streamlined. The bow - it wasn't wood or bone or horn. It was metal and stiff. Levers and wheels acted as pullies for the now dangling bowstring. An arrow lying in the mud was thick and heavy with a serrated razor tip at one end and thick dark feathered fletching at the other. It had small raised bumps on the knocking point, possibly to distinguish it from the others still in the quiver. The two swords, which I had previously had the displeasure of seeing this close once before, were now safely tucked away in scabbards that crisscrossed his muscled back. But it was the helmet that I wanted to inspect most of all. I wanted to see that underneath this phantom-like exterior, that he was human after all. Up close, I could see dark mesh in the recesses of the mouth, some of which still had muck caked into them. It was made from incredible craftsmanship. Admiringly, I had reached down to unclip the helmet.

And that is where I made my mistake.

There was a snapping and a whirring of mechanical noises. The hand of the Reaper lashed out and clasped mine with an iron grip. His head snapped sideways and peered back at me.

A small mechanical hatch, opened from his shoulder and with a *'Whoosh'* a bright red light rocketed forth into the sky. There was a loud 'Pop' and suddenly, the immediate area was cast in a luminous red glow.

That was minutes ago. And now, we were on the run.

The carriage wheels lifted briefly as we turned a corner of trees without slowing.

'What was that?'

'That, was his emergency beacon. They call it a 'flare'. You triggered it when you messed with his body.'

'I triggered it?! I barely touched him.'

'Well, what else would you call it?'

'I don't know. What is it supposed to even do?'

'It calls for reinforcements in the area.'

'And that works?'

'Look behind us. You tell me, wise guy.'

She was right, of course. My stupid attempts to pass the blame from the situation were becoming evidently more flawed. Currently not far behind us in pursuit was a large yet unbelievably nimble airship of the Regime. Without the need to navigate the uneven terrain or steer around fallen trees, the airship was currently closing the distance to us - fast. Its large bulbous form swooped in like an overweight dragon.

'How did this one find us so quick?!' I yelled.

'It... is Mortlock's. It's a... prison ship,' Arnesto piped up.

This was both pleasing and disturbing at the same time. Pleasing because I had kind of thought Arnesto had died a little further back down the road.

Disturbing because Mortlock would be just a little upset with me given the ending to our last conversation.

'Kid, tell me now how the simple task of trading some mead for information turned out like this.'

'Urrgh...' moaned Arnesto as the carriage briefly became airborne.

'And who is this stray you picked up?'

'There is a bit of a story to that actually. But the short of it is, he knows my father.'

'What?'

'He helped me out. We chatted. He knows my father and it turns out that he was on the run from the Regime. So, I helped him out of some cuffs.'

'You believed him? Kid, anyone in cuffs will try to sweet talk their way out of a situation. He could be a delirious drunkard for all you know.'

As if in response to her accusation, I heard the top of a mead bottle being cracked. I looked back to see Arnesto, his finger raised to stop my protest. In a moment, the contents had been necked followed by an arrogant belch.

'Let me guess... to stop the pain, right?' I asked with hope.

'Well, that... and if I end up shedding this mortal coil tonight, I'd rather not go without a drink. Savvy?'

'Like I said – drunkard,' Xanthe interrupted.

'No, it isn't like that. He knows him, alright?'

Arnesto wheezed some complaint to himself about preferring rum. I ignored it.

'Okay, let's suppose he isn't a drunkard. You still just helped a fugitive. That's great. Just great.'

'Are you even listening to me? Sides, last time I checked, you were a fugitive too. I helped you, didn't I? Just trust me on this,' I pushed.

She shot a look at me that was full of fire. She knew I was right. I stared back regardless, despite a slight gulp in my throat. I wanted her to see that this was not negotiable.

'Well, if he dies, you're ditching the body. An' if that is something you don't want to do, maybe take the alcohol off of him. It'll thin the blood and increase the chances of him bleeding out before we can get out of this mess.'

I looked back at Arnesto. He cracked another bottle and put it to his lips. Despite his defiance in the face of possible death, he was pale and his eyes were closed. I had managed to prop him upright with some of the cartons of mead as a makeshift armchair. I had torn some strips from my cloak and packed them in tight around the wound creating an airtight seal. This seemed to help his breathing. After finding another cloak in a small storage chest, it was now draped over him in an effort to keep some life-giving warmth. Taking the one last piece of enjoyment away from him seemed cruel. I had seen many sailors in their final throes of life, guzzle rum to ease the suffering. Still though, if I wanted to have a better chance of being reunited with my father, the drinks would have to go.

I reached out to remove the bottle from his hand.

'Maybe we call it quits with that one, eh?'

Arnesto's hand grabbed me by the face and pushed me onto my back. Seems as though he wasn't in as dire a straights as I had thought.

'Fair enough.'

Meanwhile adrenaline had caused me to forget the swatting sting of the rain and cold as we kept up the pace.

'Does the fugitive have a name? Or do I refer to him as 'Escapee Number Three?'

'Yeah. He said his name is Arnesto Dubois.'

Xanthe's head snapped around, her mouth forming a wide 'O'.

'Watch the road, please!'

'Did you say Arnesto Dubois? '*The*' Arnesto Dubois?'

'Yes,' I replied, but Xanthe wasn't listening. She had flicked the reins to one hand and leaning back, was using the other to lift the hood that was obscuring her visual answer.

'Kid, do you know who this is?'

'Uh... Arnesto Dub—'

'Dubois. That's right. Oh ,wow wee, this is a moment to behold,' she was gushing with excitement. Reaching down, she grabbed Arnesto's limp hand and began to shake it. 'Real pleasure finally meeting you, sir. Long-time admirer of your work.'

Arnesto licked his lips and nodded. A slight forced smile gave him a little glow of life.

'Wow wee. Wow o wow. Aw kid, the stories I could tell you. Oh, the stories *he* could tell *us*! You just hang in there, sir. We will have you out of here in a jiffy.'

'Um Xanthe? Remember we are being followed by a Regime airship?'

'Airships,' Arnesto wheezed.

'What?' I looked back.

He held three fingers in the air and then proceeded to point behind as he bucked about the crates.

He was right. A pair of airships had joined the chase as we rounded another thicket of pines on a hill top. The forest parted back into open fields of felled trees. It occurred to me, that unless airships had the visibility of badger-moles, we now had nowhere to hide as mile after mile ahead was nothing but rolling grasslands scatted with stumps.

I looked behind us. The lack of tree canopy meant I could now see our pursuers much clearer. A little too clearly now, they were but ninety fathoms behind us. The bulbous air compartments and side wings gave the impression of a pair of ginormous overfed rhinoceros beetles about to plunge on their next morsel of whatever it is that beetles enjoy eating...

'Kid, switch on and stop gawking. Start ditching that mead. The horses cannot hold this pace much longer with all this extra weight. At this rate, we'll be lucky if they can handle another hill.'

I ducked toward the back of the wagon and opened the rear tray gate. Using my legs, I began pushing rows of cartons over the edge. Timber and glass scattered across the road. As each box rolled off, I couldn't help but make desperate calculations of how much money we were losing.

Some thirty cartons of mead (about six hundred gold sovereigns, plus tax) later, we were in – or out of business.

Annoyed, I scrambled to my original position behind Xanthe.

'Why are we running from these things? They float, what can they actually do that'll harm us?'

'Glad you asked, kid. Each ship has a crack team of hunter killer guards. Or as we used to call them, 'Black jackets'. A bit of a sadistic bunch if you ask me. They really do love it when their targets run. The ships themselves, well they are always being fitted with new surprises too, because we all know how much the governor loves his cutting-edge technology.'

'Here here,' moaned Arnesto raising his hand wearily. 'And stealing it, is what keeps me in business. Kept... Keeps...Couped...'

There was a 'BOOM' to our rear. A loud whistle. The ground a few fathoms away from the carriage erupted in a flash and a spray of mud. The concussion from the blast made my ears feel like they had *bosun* whistles sounding off.

'What in the seven hells?' I think I said. I couldn't hear the words, nor could my fellow passengers.

Xanthe refocused the horses, who had now found new inspiration and speed. The high-pitched chorus hushed.

'Cannons. They have cannons,' I said.

'Yup. Chances are, they are some of the new ones too.'

I thought briefly of the Captain mentioning the new cannons he had been issued back on the Kraken Krusher. The Regime certainly were advancing their technology for warfare at a bloody fast rate. Speaking of weapons...

'Where is the crossbow? Maybe I could...'

Xanthe glared at me.

'Or you know, you could... hold them off. Shoot down the air tank. Hit the spinny thingies?'

'Firstly, the spin-ny thingies you are talking about are turbines. Secondly, the crossbow? It's empty, out, finished. That, and it's completely useless.'

'Is that why you didn't just plug The Reaper full of bolts like you did to those guards?'

'Yup. What? It's not like it has an endless supply of ammunition.'

'Well, why don't we still have it?'

'It broke. There was a 'clunking' noise and a bunch of screws fell out.'

'I could've fixed it.'

'With what? Your big collection of crossbow fixing tools? Last I checked, all you have is a fishy lock pick and that clap trap on your arm.'

'And these,' I smiled, fishing into the coat on Arnesto and holding up a folded metal rod and a heavy belt with organised pouches.

'What? Did you? ...Is that?'

She knew precisely what it was. As if in response to her question, I flicked the rod. With a spring and a snap, I was now holding the mechanical bow of 'The Reaper'.

'I...' she began.

'Yes?' I smiled.

'I'm... impressed. But that bow doesn't have a string.'

'Well, not yet. But I am sure I can fix that.'

'Kid, you have a long list of things you're *gonna* fix. How bout you help me out in trying to fix our current situation. Otherwise, that list of yours will never be addressed because you, me and the thief of all thieves will be dead. Gimme a look at what's in those pouches.'

There was another thunderous sound. The round felt as though it skimmed just over our heads and slammed into the road a considerable distance in front of us. The smell of the gunpowder briefly reminded me of the incident between the sea monster and the 'Kraken Krusher'. That lasting image of the Captain igniting the only supposed stores of gunpowder the Regime held. The same stores that were meant to take the Regime into the next era of battle, in order to sate his revenge against his nemesis. It gave me an idea.

I strapped the belt around my waist. A simple task made all the harder with the erratic bucks of the wagon. I pulled the strap to adjust it to my waist and immediately began pilfering through the pouches. There were numerous metallic capsules of the same size and weight. The only discerning features they possessed were a singular coloured ring around the middle and a marking of bumps and divots along the side.

'Any of these familiar to you, Xanthe? Do you have a clue of what they do?'

She shot a brief glance from her attention on the road.

'Ho boy. Jackpot!' she stated. 'I recognise some. Others I haven't seen before. The red ones. Those are my old favourites. You simply twist the capsule to set the time and throw it. But two or three or fifteen of those can't drop an airship. Those things can take a beating.'

I looked back at the airships. The smaller of the three had now maneuvered to our right and was steadily creeping upon us. Its propellers whirred furiously as it tried to accelerate. It gave me an idea.

'The airships might be able to take a beating, but their *spinney* parts can't.'

'Turbines.'

'Yeah, those... turbines,' I corrected. 'If we can't destroy it, we can at least slow it down if we manage to take out one of the turbines. It'll give us a bit more leeway to lengthen our lead.'

'Alright, throw it.'

'Wait. We need to hit it perfectly. If I miss...'

I looked back again, both airships fired in response. The crews seemed to be new at their jobs with both shots still sailing wide of their marks. I was curious however, that when the cannons fired, it stalled the airship's pursuit briefly. The turbines working extra hard to account for the recoil. Each one was fitted with dual forward-facing cannons. A number I thought to be very few. Now I knew why.

The turbines whirred loudly again and the smaller gunship kicked forward toward us.

The horses had been travelling on level ground as the incline had eased. Now though, as the tree line to our left began to wane, an open landscape spread out before us. The rain had slowed enough to reveal open fields and paddocks for as far as the eye could see. To our starboard, lay a rather steep and precarious drop off into the swelling river below, with its waters surging from the heavy downpour as they steered through the sheer rocky banks. The far bank of the river, was actually sharp steep cliffs rising upward forming part of a humble mountain range that overlooked the same view as us. The road began to angle downward and the horse's strides became longer. Ahead of us, the road travelled into the open land, where we would have no cover from the attacking ships. We would be 'sitting ducks' as they say.

By now, the first airship was so close, I could hear the yells of the crew, echoing the captain's orders. I could even begin to make out some of their faces, as it began to pull alongside us.

I not only recognised the commands, but also their tactics. Just like the crew of the 'Kraken Krusher', they were preparing for a broadside. Up until now, the odd shot had missed. A broadside would leave but a crater of where we had been. The captain at the same time, was attempting to steer us toward the open ground.

The bloodied hand of Arnesto grabbed my cuff and wrenched me downward. He rasped instructions into my ear and leant his heavy head onto my shoulder.

'Xanthe, when I say so, take a hard right!' I yelled.

'What? But the cliffs?!' She responded. 'That is a massive drop!'

'Do you have a better idea?' I asked over the whirring of the closing propellers.

It seemed that the gunship Captain wasn't taking any chances. He either really wanted to hit us, or he wanted to use our explosive demise to bolster his crew's morale. I recognised the intentions through the airship's movements. It reminded me of a statement a member of the crew aboard the 'Kraken Krusher' had made when the Captain allowed a massive yet elusive behemoth to charge the vessel. 'At this range, a child couldn't miss.' It made one hell of a mess, and so would we I thought as the airship was almost at the same distance as then.

Arnesto appeared to be concentrating as best as his constitution would allow. His eyes straining for a marker or something he could recognise through the whipping rain.

Swivelling my head, I looked up to see the barrels of at least a dozen cannons no more than twenty fathoms away. The airship began to steady its course.

I recognised the lull before the final order.

I looked at Arnesto, his eyes closing over, seemingly unaware of how dire the situation was now becoming.

'Arnesto?!'

His eyes rolled back into his head.

'Arnesto?!' I yelled louder.

His eyes snapped open in recognition. His hand slapped my shoulder hard.

'Now!' I yelled. At the same time, the Captain's voice thundered the order to fire.

Xanthe pulled hard enough on the reins that the horses reacted with a sharp change of course. There was a deafening chorus of 'Booms!' to our starboard and we could almost feel the iron balls skim over our heads and decimate the soil on the other side of the wagon. The turn was so sharp that the wagon lifted its portside wheels high into the air. Only Xanthe and my collective leap to the right, corrected the tip and saved us from being spewn hard into the rocky face that now ran beside the portside of the wagon as it barrelled down a new narrow decline beside the river.

Now we found ourselves travelling at speed on a track certainly not designed for this sort of abuse. The hard-wooden wheels of the cart bucked and squealed in protest as they grated periodically against the rocky face to our left. A wrong move would see us fall into the now turbulent water of the river, sixty or so feet below. We were traversing a ravine that angled downward and while it was dangerous for us, it was certainly more so for our pursuers. I stole another look back to spy the airships struggling to dip into the narrow hallway of cliffs. The second of the pair, lifted upward, seemingly unable to give chase or perhaps allowing the smaller, more nimble craft to continue alone. Or maybe, Mortlock had taken a turn for the worse.

Now the humming of the rear propeller droned loudly as it echoed against the stone walls of the natural pass. It reminded me of a fat wasp trying to chase its quarry through a thin drainpipe.

I stole another look at the ship as it edged ever closer to our position. The stabilizing wings tilted and twisted to within forty feet of us. The crew gunners, madly yet methodically loaded the cannons for another blast.

'Flynt, they're close. Give me one of those red explosives from the belt, will ya? I'll see if I can get one into the ship's magazine.'

My mind flicked back to the memory of the Captain igniting the ship's magazine as he was devoured by the biggest sea monster I had ever seen. Coupled with the thought that whatever was keeping the airship afloat was likely to be a flammable gas, an explosion that size in a ravine this tight was NOT a good idea.

'If that magazine blows up, then so do we. It's too close,' I reasoned loudly.

She looked sideways at the ship and grit her teeth.

'Arrrgh, if only I could get on that ship!' Xanthe growled to no one in particular. 'I'd give those buggers something to worry about.'

I'm sure she was right. But the wings of the craft were just beyond our reach and the constant sharp turns made it all but suicide if she tried to leap aboard.

My body was suddenly thrown across the wagon as Xanthe violently negotiated another precarious corner. I turned and slammed hard onto my back across the almost bare floor of the tray, feeling as winded as the day I fell from the scarlet pines while hunting lizardbirds.

The pain sparked an idea.

I wheezed in air with the sudden epiphany. Reaching into my back pocket, I pulled out the makeshift bola and cord I had used to hunt in the forest.

'You want on board that ship?' I yelled over the clacking of the wheels.

Xanthe glanced at me quickly as I began to stand with a very wide, unsteady stance.

'Sit down, kid. You're gonna get splattered!'

I tied one end of the cord in a rudimentary 'bowline' to her wrist.

'Kid, what in the hells?'

'Trust me,' I pleaded, not really caring if she did or not. I then draped the Reaper's belt and its loaded pouches over her narrow shoulders.

I focused on the wings as they flitted in and out of range. The slippery planks bucked and writhed under my feet, but the years spent weathering out the rolling waves of storms at sea allowed me to maintain just enough balance for what I needed to do next... I spun the cord with the stones attached and waited for the opening I needed.

'Kid, I said –' Xanthe began, but it was too late.

The wings edged steadily in our direction, as the Captain levelled for another volley. The effect of such a blast at this range in this location, would likely obliterate us and half the Cliffside around us, I thought. These distracting thoughts were the last thing I needed right now. I shook them from my mind. Instead I replaced them as I imagined another lizardbird perching upon the wing, ready to be caught for a tasty meal.

I exhaled slightly. This was it.

As the stones around on the bola spun with greater speed, I released the cord. Each weighted rock caused the strong twine to splay like the web of a large spider and wrapped around the metal of the wing. I swiftly pulled it tight and the cable bit into itself for a firm anchor.

I grabbed the reins from Xanthe. 'Go for it!' I yelled at her.

Xanthe must have quickly assessed the situation, because she didn't hesitate. Without looking, she leapt out from the cart toward the crashing rapids below. I couldn't help but look to ensure I hadn't just caused the death of my friend.

Xanthe fell further than I had anticipated. But the cord pulled taught, and like a circus performer, she used the momentum to swing underneath and flicked herself upward and onto the deck of the airship.

A bloodied and weak hand of Arnesto squeezed my shoulder.

'My dear friend,' he wheezed 'she is something else.'

I smiled weakly, having to revert my attention back to the now very difficult task of steering the cart. The horses rasped and spluttered in their continued exertion as the trail made another sudden sharp descent alongside the rapids below.

We dipped below the level of the airship, as it maintained its altitude and powered ahead of our position.

There was an eruption of much yelling from within the ship as the crew began leaving their posts of manning the cannons, to deal with the intruder. Concussive blasts rocked the internals, followed by cries of soldiers. Xanthe must have become reacquainted with the goodies in the pouches to help her assault.

The figures of two aircrewmen fell into view and thudded hard into the rocky path to our front. Without the luxury of being able to avoid them, there was a quick and nasty sounding crunch as the horse's hooves and the cart's large wooden wheels barrelled over their bones.

I pulled back on the reins in an attempt to slow our speed, knowing that it'd be almost impossible for the ship to manoeuvre back beside us given the current terrain, and just in case Xanthe didn't quite stop the crew from firing another blast from the Port-side cannons.

'Ouch, here she goes again,' Arnesto half chuckled, half gurgled, as another, rather large member of the crew was launched from the ship and slammed into the Cliffside eight fathoms above the ground ahead of us and fell yet again into the path of our cart. To his credit, he must've been rather tough, as he sat up briefly to gather himself. But the wooden crossbar between the horses T-boned his skull with a sound of a coconut splitting.

There was the sound of a small explosion within and the craft veered to starboard, struggling to maintain a steady course. Some crew had weighed up their options and must have considered the rapids a safer option. A handful of them leapt through various exits including the cannon holes, and plummeted into the rapids below. Maybe it was a safer option, but now they struggled to keep their heads above the water as they were swept along the surging current.

Smoke billowed out from some of the port holes. There was now yelling coming from inside the bridge, followed by the sounds of orders and the unmistakeable clash of steel on steel as swords were swung.

I felt my stomach lurch with concern. There was more yelling, but no sign of Xanthe. I held the reins so tightly in my hands, the sharp tingle of pins and needles dragged my attention back to my role. The horses still galloped along despite my signalling to slow. Whether it was the angle of the descent or the excitement of the cannon fire from earlier, it was hard to tell, but they seemed to almost steer themselves now, without any direction from myself.

There was the sound of glass shattering. I caught a glimpse of the Captain's uniform as he made the lengthy plummet into the rapids below. Except this time, he didn't resurface to bob along in the violent swell. He simply vanished below the white water.

Meanwhile the airship swayed and bobbed with no one manning the wheel. Quickly the vessel dipped lower toward the water, bumping against the rocky edges with its wings sending an echo of scraping metal through the canyon. The smoke had now cleared thanks to the broken glass, and I could make out the familiar figure of Xanthe wrestling with the ship's wheel somewhat unsuccessfully.

There was another loud bang as the airship bounced of the Cliffside ahead, sending rocks and dust plummeting onto the now levelling trail before us.

A wet cough came from behind my shoulder as Arnesto tried to lever himself up to my ear.

'I don't think... she knows how to stop it,' he managed before another buck in the road caused him to flop back down like a rag doll.

He was right, of course.

I urged the horses under control with the manliest 'Yeaargh' I could muster and despite their exhaustion, they responded in kind. Steadily we gained pace till the cart travelled alongside and level with the unsteady craft.

I stole another look sideways to see Xanthe, pulling levers and twisting the wheel back and forth. We were now close enough that I could see that some smoke still crept from areas on the control panel. A handle that must've been the control for speed had a knife wedged into the groove, stopping it from slowing down.

'Xanthe!' I yelled. 'Xanthe!'

Her eyes snapped in my direction. I could see that she had a bloodied lip and her eye was beginning to puff over. The 'Blackjackets' had roughed her up badly, but she was still standing.

'Flynt! How do I steer this thing? It doesn't seem to re-spond!' Xanthe yelled back.

My eyes darted between the road and the ship as I searched for a way to help her.

Another crunch of metal pierced my ears, as a sizeable chunk of wing dropped off the ship, clanged into a winch along the side and into the waters below.

That was it. The winch.

I yelled at Xanthe. 'Is there a control that says 'winch' on it?'

She quickly responded with a shake of the head.

'Well, what do they have?!' I prompted.

A series of high-pitched expletives were slung back at me, with enough information to tell me that there were indeed *buttons* and *switches*. Bloody lots apparently.

'Dammit. What would they have?' I thought back to my time on the ship. Military leaders liked to make things 'sol-dier-proof' – so simple, that even the densest of fighters couldn't stuff up, therefore minimising the damage soldiers could do to themselves or expensive items.

Then it dawned on me. They wouldn't use words, they'd use pictures.

'Is there a picture of a hook?' I pressed.

She looked around again.

'Yes! She squealed. 'It's above a stick!'

Within moments I had directed her to steer the winch and hook toward us, giving me extra cable to work with for the next step. She had also managed to familiarize herself enough with the steering to avoid most of the jutting cliffs. *Most.* Speed was still against us, and without the luxury of slowing down, it made things all the more difficult. The road had somewhat evened out and lazily wined around slight imperfections in the rock face. A waterfall had caused the rapids to fall much further away, providing a wider canyon to work within.

Now all I had to do, was move Arnesto. However, at this current moment in time, he still had half an arrow protruding from his chest with bubbles of blood forming at the wound.

A large metal hook lowered before us, Xanthe having worked out the controls inside. I swiped a few times as the metal object bounced, danced and swayed before me. The cart bounced along the trail, making the process of looping the thick cord around and under Arnesto's shoulders all the more challenging. By now the colour had drained from his face, leaving a pale and sweaty husk behind. His blood had created a red slick across the floor of the wagon. If it weren't for his occasional forced smile, or gurgled comment, one would be forgiven for thinking he had already gone to meet his gods. Yet he clung to life... just barely. As if sensing my fear and confusion, he grabbed my scruff and pulled me close. He rasped in breathy tones, just loud enough for me to hear.

'Coastline... North... Four stacks... Hideout...'

He pulled away my head and slapped me on the shoulder with a nod. I nodded back in understanding. *Vague* understanding. Arnesto then gestured toward the belt in a bid for me to get on with the job.

Looping the thick cord wasn't easy, it kept snagging on the arrow shaft. He smiled at me again and with a trembling hand gripped the protrusion and grimaced. I could see what he was trying to do, and with a quick apology, I helped him snap it in half. He wheezed, bucked violently and went limp.

'Arnesto? Arnesto? Speak to me. Say something,' I cried out.

He didn't respond. Instead the movement of the wagon caused his body to buck about slightly.

What had I done?

'Kid! Hurry up down there... we have...' Xanthe interrupted over the hum of the engines.

'Xanthe! I think I just killed Arnesto!' I yelled back.

'He probably just passed out! People do that when they have lost a lot of blood! Trust me kid, it'd take more than an arrow to stop him. Now get on with it or say goodbye and get up here! We have-'

I blocked her out. I was not going to leave him on a cart to be picked at by birds. Leaning forward over the binds that kept the horses tied to the cart, I sliced the straps with my fish bone pick to release them. Before the wagon became too unsteady to handle I turned, tightened the strap around the two of us and released the reins. Almost impatiently, the hoist pulled us up. I watched as the horses and cart drifted away below us into the drizzling rain. Soon Arnesto and I were bathed in the orange glow of sunset, moving beyond the shadows cast by the cliffs around us. Now without the ravine for cover, a rather strong breeze began to chill our sopping wet clothes. I felt myself shiver rather uncontrollably and wondered what havoc this was playing on Arnesto's chances of survival.

As the airship lifted toward the coastline ahead, I could see the ocean once more. For years it had been my home and my prison. I had longed to escape and touch land once more. Now though, it was a welcome sight as familiar squalls rolled across the horizon. I soaked up the view one last time before Xanthe, hanging upside down on the metal strut supporting the winch, reached out and wrenched us into the confines of the airship.

And with that, we slid like birthed baby seals across its studded metal floor.

Chapter Twenty-Two

Now inside the safety of the craft, my body ached. I still clutched onto Arnesto's limp figure. With some reserves of energy, I unlocked my cramped legs and he flopped backward onto the studded metal floor.

The welcome face of Xanthe appeared in my view - upside down.

'Having fun, kid?'

She smiled widely, but swelling had completely taken over her eye and a dark, almost black blood had congealed on her lip. She must've noticed my gawking, her eyes darted around for a distraction.

'Ah... welcome aboard the Airship Xanthe Bones!' she announced puffing up her chest and gesturing around the cabin. 'Ensure you abide by our safety rules and commands or feel free to step outside for some fresh air. We've already had a few unruly passengers, and as you can see, strict measures have been taken to keep them quiet.'

I looked around the inside of the ship. It was a rather simple looking setup, with one internal deck now littered with several unconscious... possibly dead crew, slumped in various unnatural and painful looking positions.

From the ceiling, there were handrails and grips. Five cannons lay on either side of what was most likely the interior hold and gun deck, however their rigging was unlike any I had seen before. Instead of standing on wheels, they rested on stands and swivels, with mechanical gears on either side.

The front of the craft was walled off. At its entrance the open metal door lay wrenched inward and hanging awkwardly to the side. To our rear lay several cramped looking cells, complete with bars to keep their intended occupants inside. The dulled humming of the propellers outside echoed lightly down the hallway.

As if his body were trying to remind me that he needed help, Arnesto began to convulse.

'Kid, he's going downhill fast,' Xanthe said. 'I can help with an arrow wound, but this is looking grim.'

I recognised the reaction his body was having. I had seen sailors, missing legs or with sections of their body gone, spasm wildly when too much of their blood had left their body. The ship's physician would often try to replenish lost blood with whatever stores they had gathered that morning, but it was never enough.

Xanthe moved beside him and put her ear beside his mouth and her hand on his chest. Her brow furrowed and placing two interlocked hands over his heart, she began to pump up and down on his chest.

'I need to keep his heart pumping, kid. But we are going to need something to plug up his chest and he needs blood, otherwise this is a waste of time.'

I felt immense pressure mounting on me. Arnesto already appeared dead.

I looked around the ship for something to use. My eyes searched over the piles of dead and unconscious crewmen, the exposed panels in the wall and toward the door on the far wall. There, I spotted a box with a white cross marked on it. It was the symbol of the physician. I made my way to the box and grabbed the latch to open it. Gauze, fat syringes and vials with powder lay in neat little rows. I grabbed the case from the wall and ran back to Arnesto. Xanthe still worked away at his chest, pausing momentarily to breathe into his mouth twice before continuing with the pumps.

I slid in beside her and opened the case.

'What do I do?'

Her eyes darted at the case and then back to her task.

'Take one of the sharp objects there...'

'Yeah.'

'Now take off the cap...'

'Yeah.'

'Now slip it between his ribs over here, but not too far. Once you feel it push into an opening, turn that nozzle.'

'What?!'

'Kid!'

'But what if I go too far and kill him?'

'Kid, if you don't do it, he is dead anyway,' she said, pausing to tear open his ragged and soaked shirt.

My hands fumbled with the needle. A mixture of adrenaline, wind chill and sticky blood on my fingers was making the task more than difficult. I pulled out the needle and felt around his clammy white chest.

'Kid, go for the side and work around me.'

'Alright. I got this.'

I found a point between two of his ribs. I readied the needle. Xanthe stopped pumping. I pushed it inward against the flesh.

The blood filled the clear casing and I turned the nozzle as Xanthe had instructed. The vial squirted the blood onto the floor and Arnesto's chest lifted slightly.

'Good work, kid. Now we have to plug him up and get some blood into him.'

'Get blood into him?'

'Yup.'

Xanthe rolled his chest toward her and with a swift yank on the arrow, it slid the rest of the way through his torso. She cast it away casually.

'I'll plug him up. You find a way to get some blood into him.'

She made it sound so simple.

'How?'

'I dunno, kid. You've always found a way to get yourself out of sticky situations before. Use that brain of yours and find a sack of blood somewhere. Although, by the look of him, you're gonna need a few sacks.'

I stood up and looked around the interior deck once again. But try as I might, there was no 'magical' cure hanging against the wall. No sacks of blood... just several unmoving bodies of bruised, bleeding and battered personnel.

Several.

Bleeding.

Sacks of blood.

It wasn't going to be pretty, in fact it was going to look downright gruesome, but it was the best idea I could come up with. I grabbed the lightest looking soldier under the arms and began to drag him clumsily toward Arnesto.

When I finally arrived, Xanthe was pouring the black powder contents onto Arnesto's wound – the point where the arrow had exited his body. She leant over to grab the smouldering stick used to ignite the cannons and applied it to the powder.

There was a flash and whooshing sound, followed by the smell of burnt meat.

Within seconds she had repeated the process on his chest.

'That should do it,' she said to herself proudly before turning to me. 'Whatcha got there, kid?'

'A sack of blood,' I smiled back.

Her furrowed expression turned to a nodding smile.

In a very brief amount of time, we had slung up three unconscious soldiers by their feet. Using the thick tubing and needles from the physician's kit, we fed several lines of blood from each living 'sack' into Arnesto's body. Clear, flexible tubes ran red with blood as they coiled downward feeding into the veins in Arnesto's arms and thigh.

During the process of rigging our little improvised set up, it turned out that one of the crewmen wasn't quite comatose. This was something which Xanthe corrected quickly with an arm squeezing around the neck for a few seconds. We have removed the warm quilted uniforms from various members of the crew and they now lay as makeshift blankets and pillows to keep Arnesto as warm and comfortable as we could make him.

Xanthe held two fingers to Arnesto's neck. A moment later she turned to me.

'His pulse is calming down which is good. You've saved him for now, kid. Time will tell if he continues to stay alive or goes to meet his makers,' she stated satisfied.

'Time will tell? You mean he isn't in the clear yet?'

'Well, a whole buncha stuff can go wrong. Infection for one. Those arrowheads do a nasty job to your insides when they punch through. They cut through all the organs, blood vessels and connective tissues they touch. That's why he bled so much. Well that and the booze. You can smell it in his blood.'

I couldn't, but I took her word for it.

'My guess,' she continued, 'is that it punctured through his lower right lung and nicked the top of his liver. That's why there's that thick dark blood that was on the...'

My mind wandered off from her ramblings as I stared at Arnesto. Colour had begun to return to his face. His lips were no longer blue and he was breathing steadily on his own once more.

'I did my best to cauterize the wound to stop him from bleeding on the outside, and his body was doing a decent job of clotting up on the inside but now it is down to luck and how tough this guy is. But if the stories about him are true, and I *know* they are, he'll pull through this.

'Xanthe, how do you know all this stuff?'

'All this what now?'

'All this stuff. *This.*' I gestured to Arnesto and the tubes. 'How did you know how the body works so well?'

'Well, it's easy. To kill someone, you gotta know what makes them tick, ya see. The Regime pumped that info inta me pretty heavily, morning, noon and night. I figured, to keep someone alive, you just have to reverse it.'

'Did you have to use it to save people in the past?'

A blank look came over her face.

'No. Never to save anybody. Just the opposite.'

'Did you ever use it on yourself?'

'Kid, my body don't work like that.'

'How so?'

'It just don't. Now are we gonna sit here and pow wow, or is one of us gonna take the wheel and actually steer this thing?' she gestured to the whole ship.

She was right. Ever since we had been pulled aboard the ship, it had been cruising along through the sky.

'Who is steering?' I asked moving quickly to the front of the craft.

'I think you'll be impressed with my handiwork. I managed to rig a lil something special up down there,' she called out.

I made my way past a sign that read 'cockpit' and stepped beyond the twisted heap of metal door cast to the floor. Inside the room, cold air swirled about from the broken windows. Despite the breeze, I could still smell the remnants of gunpowder and smoke. Three more bodies littered the corners of the room, however, from the look of the burnt markings on their bodies, they weren't unconscious. Before me lay a large metal box of a table with the inscription 'Main Console'. It was covered with a series of dials, levers and buttons. But the 'special something' Xanthe had referred to was obviously the unconscious crewman lashed to the wheel of the airship. With his head wedged firmly between the handles of the wheel to stop it from moving, the airship maintained a steady course.

'Like it?' she called out.

'Well, it works. Nice job.'

'Yeah, you like it. But it gets better.'

I untied the man and his body slumped backward onto the metal floor with a hard thud.

'What's his name tag say?' she prompted.

Looking down on the inside of his collar, I noticed he had a metal identification tag hanging from his neck.

It read 'Otto'.

I smirked.

'Annnd what is he?'

The pilot.

The ship was on Otto Pilot.

'Get it?' she yelled. 'Ha!'

CHAPTER TWENTY-THREE

'Is that it?' Xanthe asked leaning forward and pointing.

'No.'

'How do you know?'

'Because that is an arch,' I yawned. 'We are looking for four stacks.'

'Well, what do they look like?'

'Kind of like giant rock tree stumps creeping out of the water near coastal cliffs. Look, I doubt Arnesto would send us on a wild goose chase. Just be patient.'

Xanthe groaned and rolled her eyes. Pouting her bottom lip, she went and sat at the open doorway of the cockpit that dropped into the swirling waves along the rocky coastline below.

It had been this way for quite some time. Travelling through the night we had moved north along the coast as Arnesto had vaguely instructed back on the carriage. Xanthe had informed me that we were now well and truly close to the Capital and had turned the cabin lights off. Red lanterns fixed into the ceilings now illuminated our workspace. Apparently, this was okay because red light doesn't give away your position from a distance. We had taken turns in monitoring Arnesto's condition and steering the ship. For years I had wanted to steer a big ocean-going tall ship, even the 'Kraken Krusher' would've sufficed. Now, it seemed strange that the ship I guided was one that flew in the air instead of travelling through swells.

Using the moonlight outside to make out various coastal landmarks was not easy. A few times we had to double back to make sure it wasn't four stacks near an ocean cave. But we were yet to find what we were looking for, and with sunrise looming, we were running out of time. In the daylight, we would easily be spotted from a vast distance. A half wrecked, maroon and black coloured airship tacking along the coast would surely be on the Regime's current 'wanted' list.

'There it is!' she yelled pointing.

'Where?' I leaned forward and squinted through the darkness trying to make out silhouettes against the white wash from the waves ahead.

'... is what I would be saying if there were four stupid rock trees sticking out of the water...'

'Oh...' I mumbled.

'Kid, how do you know he was making sense and not just hallucinating from blood loss? I mean he might've been groaning 'My poor slacks.' Or 'I crapped my dacks.'

'No Xanthe, he made it clear. He said, *'Coastline. North. Four stacks. Hideout'.* I'm sure of it.' I responded by checking a compass. It was attached by a small gold chain to the lapel of an wool lined aircrewman jacket I had acquired and donned shortly after stabilizing Arnesto in a bid to remove the cold wet garments. Travelling up high in the air with open window and doors was chilling to say the least.

'Well, I'm just saying. He could've, you know.'

Her boredom had been peaking for quite some time now. Hours ago, when we had switched between looking after Arnesto and driving, I walked into an almost empty cabin, save for our patient and his blood donors. I caught Xanthe dusting off her hands beside the open tailgate and looking rather proud of herself. When I had asked her where the rest of the crew had gone, she smiled and gestured to the ocean below. She knew I would've been conflicted about such behaviour, so she did it without bothering me. I wasn't sure whether to be angry or thankful, so I opted for neither and returned to occupy my mind with steering the ship and locating our landmarks. It wasn't long before she resumed her position in the open doorway, legs dangling over the distant ocean below.

'Hey, kid.'

'Yes, Xanthe.'

'What was... is your father like?'

'I thought you said you weren't interested in my background? Something about the less we know about each other, the better?'

She went quiet and continued looking at the ocean. She seemed almost hurt at my jibe. I felt a small pang of guilt. I guessed that this was a sign that she wanted to hang around, that she would stay and help me. After seeing what the Regime was like up close, the chances of rescuing my father seemed more and more fleeting. I knew that with Xanthe's help, I at least had some skerrick of a chance.

Xanthe tapped absent mindedly on the metal floor appearing as though lost in her thoughts. It couldn't hurt to talk, I guess.

I cleared my throat. 'Dad, ah... he, he really cared for our family.'

I noticed her head turn toward me.

'We lived in a village called 'Eden' in the Southern Isles. Dad was a keen fisherman when the snapper and perch were biting and he would take us kids hunting when the ocean was sour or the sea monsters were on migration in our waters. He and mum worked really hard, but they always had time for us.'

'Kids?' Xanthe asked.

'Yeah. I had a younger sister. Elaina. She was dad's little shadow. Everywhere he went, she would follow.'

'What happened to her?'

The memory hurt. My throat swelled and the words struggled to come out. It had been a long time since I had let myself think of Elaina and mum.

My locket still sat firmly inside my pockets. I removed it and brushed my fingers on the tarnished oval shape. 'Ah...' I paused briefly to compose myself. 'Regime came when dad and I were out fishing. Elaina had begged to come with us, but dad had insisted she stay behind with mum.'

My mind drifted back to the memory.

'The seas were rough that day and dad wanted to show me how to navigate through heavier swells. He said that when the seas were like that, it was no place for a young girl. The last memory I have of her was her crying into mother as we sailed away from the jetty.'

I could feel Xanthe looking at me, but I couldn't bring myself to look back. I felt tears welling in my eyes. For the first time in years, I flicked open the small latch that had kept its contents hidden. I looked at the image. Its sepia tones faded, I looked into the picture of my family. My mother's long dark hair. My father's charismatic smile. My sister's innocent expression.

Placing the locket on the control panel, I swallowed hard, trying to hold back emotion. I continued.

'When we returned, we could see the smoke climbing into the sky from the Village. The Regime ships were already on the horizon. Dad wouldn't let me get off the boat and made me hide under the jetty. I didn't listen. I followed him to our cabin, but by the time we arrived it was just embers and coals. I saw him cradling my mother and Elaina in his arms. Just rocking back and forth,' I couldn't continue. The images became vivid in my mind and I felt as though I were there again, a young boy, witnessing it once more.

A gentle hand, took mine from the steering wheel. I was shaking. Without a word, Xanthe held me. In my mind, I could still see my father saying good bye to my little sister one last time.

I forced the images from my head.

'I'm okay,' I said.

I felt embarrassed, quickly wiping tears onto my sleeve. Years spent at sea as a slave to an enemy crew, it didn't pay to show weakness of any kind. I had forced myself to put on a brave face day in day out, until I believed I couldn't be hurt emotionally anymore. I had bottled up those memories and buried them deep inside until I almost forgot what my mother and sister looked like. Now it stung me.'

I pushed away from Xanthe and wiped my nose on my sleeve. She held out my locket, a solemn look upon her face. I snapped it shut and hurriedly placed deep within my pocket once more. Trying to maintain some toughness, I cleared my throat and hocked up the snot onto the floor and continued to steer the ship, distracting myself out the window.

'Kid.'

'Yeah?'

'I'm sorry.'

I didn't respond.

'You wanna go get some sleep? I can steer the ship. I know what to look for now.'

In the reflection of the window in front of me I could see Xanthe and shook my head. She slowly headed toward the doorway to the interior deck. She paused momentarily and leant back in.

With a gentle voice she spoke.

'That pain, kid. Use it. You're gonna need it for what comes next.'

CHAPTER TWENTY-FOUR

'Is that it?' Xanthe cried out from her position dangling out of the airship again.

I strained my eyes to look ahead. Although the sun was supposed to be rising, there had been a drop in temperature through the night and now a thick fog hung low over the cliffs. Visibility was so poor, I could only make out thirty or so fathoms ahead. Now we moved very slowly to avoid crashing our transport into the rock walls somewhere nearby.

'Ah, where are you looking?' I asked.

'There. Right there,' she pointed excitedly, seeming somewhat frustrated with my lack of perception.

It had become more apparent of late, that while I considered myself to have decent vision, Xanthe, like in almost everything else she did, was on another level.

We edged closer to where she was pointing into the fog and I slowed the speed of the craft even further. I had dropped our altitude considerably to use the fog as cover but it had its disadvantages. For example, every now and again, I would have to steer hard to starboard to avoid the odd jutting cliff or rogue stack. Now, as the noise of the engines lowered to a hum, I could hear the waves crashing not far below us.

'Careful kid, you're getting real close,' Xanthe directed, leaning right out of the open doorway.

A set of four large rocky pillars emerged from the mist into view. I had to remind myself to pull back on the lever (which I had earlier fixed) to lessen the speed to a crawl, instead of barking at a non-existent crew to hoist the sails.

The airship responded by gently gliding toward the rocks.

'Xanthe, keep a look out for a cave nearby.'

'Yeah, I can hear it over there,' she called back immediately.

'Port or Starboard?'

'What the what now?'

'Port or Starboard?' I insisted hurriedly.

'Left, mate.'

I could just about hear her eyes roll as she said it.

'Rightio, Port it is,' I muttered.

Readjusting our approach, I too began to hear the hollow roar of waves belting into the stone walls of a cave entrance. Steering toward the sound, a large opening in the cliff face appeared. Standing at least one hundred feet high, we were lucky, it was more than large enough for the airship to fit inside the opening at least, thus hiding us from prying eyes on the ocean.

Xanthe left me at the helm to man the anchors. This was something I had found quite intriguing, because I had wondered how a floating craft like this, managed to secure itself without drifting away on the breeze. Xanthe had located the solution in the form of two modified cannons, engineered for firing massive harpoons into the ground or switching out the tips for massive grappling hooks.

I had familiarised myself with the various dials, switches and knobs on the console. Now as we drifted into the darkness of the cave, I flicked the switch I had identified for 'lights' and several wide beams of light spilled into the cavern. Immediately I could see that the ocean had carved out this particular section, with the waves below still swelling and lapping at the rocky edge. Granite lined the walls and ceilings, with large stalactites reaching down from above threatening to deflate our floatation bladder in one big pop. Edging inward, I noticed a defined ledge, wide enough to walk around and running the length of the wall. I made a mental note that that must have been the way Arnesto had entered in and out of the cave.

Xanthe yelled out distances to the walls in a bid to guide me in. The cave was becoming narrower as we rounded a bend in the rock work. Now that we were definitely shielded from the view of the outside world, I located a stalagmite large enough to hold us steady. I turned off the power to the turbines and let the craft drift gently.

Just like when I used to help Dad dock his steamboat to a jetty, I leaned out the side doorway and looped thick anchoring ropes around the sturdy spike of rock. The craft kept moving a few more fathoms, and I lashed another rope near an equally big jutting piece of rock. Xanthe leapt across and slid out a gang plank. It clunked onto the surface with a slight grinding sound. I dimmed the lights of the ship. Looking outside, the vessel was 'docked' perfectly. I felt somewhat chuffed with myself, I was really getting the hang of this airship sailing.

'Kid, stay here. I'm going to go check this out. Knowing the stories I've heard about our friend here, I'd say there would be a few 'surprises' in store for any unwelcome guests.'

Before I could respond, Xanthe had leapt onto the rocky ledge and disappeared from the reach of the lights. That sucked the wind out of my sails a little bit. Surely this hideout would hold a whole range of exciting knick knacks for me to discover. I had imagined rooms full of stolen treasures and artworks in the time we traversed the coastline. Now I was delegated to sitting in the ship.

Hurry up and wait, I thought to myself.

I made my way over to the pile of pilfered aircrew uniforms we had kept and rifled through a few pockets. The stress of the last few days had caused me to forget the little things I had once done to amuse myself. Now, it seemed, I had some time on my hands once more. I reached through several pockets before I found what I had hoped would be there. I felt the familiar flat card sides and pulled out the packet for inspection. There it was in my hands once again, a packet of striking matches. Not just one to last me for weeks, but an entire packet. Quietly pleased with myself, I pulled one from its hold and gave it a new resting home between my teeth.

I checked on Arnesto again. He was breathing steadily by himself and Xanthe had recently relieved the pressure from the drainage syringe still embedded in his lungs. Colour had returned to his lips and cheeks. Xanthe said this was a good sign, as it showed his body was 'topped up' with blood. We had enough dressings in the kit to last two more changes, but I hoped Arnesto had the foresight or sense to stock his lair with extra stores for a day such as this. I would have to ask. Oh boy, I had so much to ask him, but for now he slept and that was a good thing. With wounds like those, he had a long road to recovery and being awake would be a painful experience.

'Okay, kid...' came a voice from right behind me.

'WHAA! JEEZ, you scared the living innards out of me, Xanthe!' I almost bit the matchstick in half from surprise.

I was becoming more and more aware of her ability to creep about undetected. I thought I was good, but she was so quick and silent, it left me for dead... and probably a fair few enemy soldiers in the past, I gathered. I made a mental note that I should definitely persuade her to teach me how to be as good as her.

She laughed. 'Calm down kid, I wasn't even trying to scare you.'

She *was*.

'So, what did you find?' I asked.

'Oh well, you'll be surprised.'

'Were there any traps?'

She nodded and opened her hand. Resting in her palm were a handful of sharp sticks the size of tooth picks. Each one had a fluffy feather tied into its end.'

'What are they?'

'Poisoned darts.'

Poisoned?! How poisoned?' I stammered.

'Oh, I dunno. Pretty bloody poisoned, I reckon. Want me to stick it in your arm and find out?' she smiled.

'I'll pass, thanks. So, did you get all of them? All the traps I mean?'

'Yup. Arnesto is good, but you're dealing with a professional like me, you have to wake up pretty early in the morning to get the better of this girl,' she smirked proudly puffing up her chest. 'So, he's looking better,' She motioned to Arnesto laying on rolled up crew jackets on the floor. 'I say we go check this place out some more, then we come back and get him set up so he can continue sleeping. Whadoyareckon?'

I didn't need any more encouragement. I popped out one of the lanterns and adjusted the dials. The oils inside mixed. Red glow was replaced with a warm white glow and became brighter, stretching my field of view out to fifteen fathoms or so. I held it out to see where I was going.

'Lead the way!'

Xanthe turned around and began to skip out the doorway of the cabin and onto the gang plank.

'Oh boy, this place looks pretty decent, kid. Wait and see.'

As she left the ship, I noticed two darts embedded firmly in her shoulder.

'Xanthe! Your shoulder!'

She stopped and looked back. Like a dog unable to catch its own tail, she began to turn around in circles reaching behind her.

'Stop,' I instructed and plucked the dart out of her flesh. I looked at her with wide eyes.

'Meh, I'll be good.'

'Aren't you worried you're going to drop dead?!'

'Well, you could suck the poison out if you like,' she said grinning. 'But if you have a cut in your mouth, I wouldn't advise it. Poison gets into your bloodstream... Then it's you who's in trouble.'

After the events of late, I had several cuts in my mouth.

She laughed at me. 'Relax kid, I'm not gonna drop dead from this old stuff. You sure have grown uptight over the last few days. We can afford to relax just a little now.'

She was right. I felt bloody stressed. At least aboard the 'Kraken Krusher' I knew the routine and the rules. It had been that way for years. And with knowing the rules comes the ability to exploit them. On land however, it had been a different story. Everything seemed new and nothing was as I expected. Now I had an almost unstoppable assassin chasing me, I'd partnered with some sort of super soldier and half of the Regime were probably out looking for us for a range of reasons, none of which I could've anticipated in a million years had you have asked me a month ago.

'Come on, kid. Quit staring into the other dimension and let's get on with it.'

'What is a diamond-shun?' I asked.

I wasn't sure what was more surprising, the fact that she didn't care or that she didn't pass out or die on the spot. Not wanting to hold onto a potentially lethal and sharp object in my pocket, I threw the darts into the swirling waters below the ledge. I hurried along to keep up with Xanthe as she disappeared around the corner into darkness.

I felt the need to remind Xanthe that I cannot see in the dark - something which I was beginning to think that she could. But as we rounded the corner, there was an iridescent glow illuminating the way. Surprised, I looked closer to see that the walls of the cave were covered in thousands of small glowing worms, giving the impression of a starry night.

'Wow,' the word rolled out of my mouth.

'I know, right? Betcha never seen anything like that before.'

'Nuh huh.'

The glow from the worms was almost enough to illuminate the entire cavern. I could see shapes and textures along the walls and make out the edge of the stone walkway before the drop to the waters below. I studied that surface for a moment. If Xanthe *had* managed to be struck by a few stray darts, then it would seem that I still needed to be extra vigilant. Unlike her I didn't have the ability to shrug off poison.

The wall had become smoother and I could make out an indentation every ten fathoms or so. I moved closer to one of them and used the light from the carrying lantern to inspect it more thoroughly. Just like the lanterns on the ship, here too were oil mixing lanterns embedded into the wall. After close scrutiny, I couldn't see anything which would be considered a lever or trip to a trap. I decided to take my chances, and I tapped the globe gently.

Nothing happened.

I figured it may just be slow to start since being left idle for so long. So, I gave it a firmer tap.

I could see oily substances begin to mix inside and swirl creating a warm glow of light. I had heard of refined Kraken fat, when mixed with that of other sea monsters – created a chemical reaction that gave off light. No open flames. No threat of igniting nearby gas leaks, timber or people. Convenient. That was when I noticed the mixture spread very quickly along the wall through an indentation. The next globe began to illuminate, its light gently filling out its section of the walkway. And the next one. Within a short amount of time, the several sections of the walkway and down below us had lit up.

Now for the first time I could make out my surroundings in greater detail. The walkway led to an iron studded door. Beside it a staircase went down several levels to a small makeshift jetty below. The jetty even had globes on fixed on extended poles, each one providing its own shaft of light onto the timber decking below. At its base, the jetty lay amongst calm waters, protected from the harsher currents around the corner. Lashed to one of the pylons, floated a small wooden row boat.

'Xanthe, this looks like it was designed for smugglers. Look at the stairs carved into the rock. They must've brought goods in from the sea and kept them in the crates over by that door. Oh boy, I hope there is some dried beef or something edible. I'm starving. What do you say?'

There was no response.

'Xanthe,' I said louder this time and waited.

Still nothing.

'Cmon Xanth, quit trying to scare me. I'll bloody choke on this matchstick if you make me jump again. This is getting old.'

Still there was no response. I quickly looked around the cavern for any sign of her. Apart from my footsteps as I paced forward, the only others sounds were those of the waves around the corner and the wind blowing through the open cave entrance echoing against the stone.

Something caught my eye. Up ahead, laying on the floor awkwardly near the iron door was Xanthe.

She wasn't moving.

CHAPTER TWENTY-FIVE

She was snoring. Not the sort of snoring you'd expect from so slight a person. These were deep and rumbling inhalations that rivalled those of any sailor I had ever witnessed. Even ones with broken noses I thought.

As I had run over to her to give aide, the snoring had stopped me in my tracks.

Xanthe had *never* slept. She said that she didn't work that way. Now though, she reminded me of the times my father had picked up my little sister when she had drifted off on his lap of an evening. A peaceful smile and long eyelashes, she would stay awake as long as she could when he returned from a long stint out at sea - as though catching up on the time she had missed out on spending with him.

It appeared the poison on the darts did indeed have an effect on her, although not the one Arnesto had likely intended.

I considered waking her. But if she were right, and this was indeed the first time she had slept in ages, then I felt it best to let her continue. I rolled up my jacket and gently propped up her head on the makeshift pillow.

Once again, I felt a slight chill as I rummaged through the contents of a few barrels stacked outside the doorway. In some of them, the contents had long rotted and opening them was a mistake. But sure enough, amongst them lay rewards in the form of some dried meat and some stale crackers. Indeed, the best find I had was some bottles of mead, fine wine and brandy packed in securely with straw. I mentally 'marked' the barrel before moving to my next task – opening the door.

Making my way to the locked iron door in front of me. I inspected it for any sign of danger. It was set firmly into the rock with its solid iron rivets and metal box lock. From what I had witnessed earlier, Xanthe probably could've kicked this in without so much as a worry. Instead, I reached into my leather bracer and plucked out my trusty fish bone lock pick. Going to work, I felt several pins inside the lock and raked at them in succession. There was a familiar popping sound and the fishbone turned within the cylinder. The iron door creaked outward.

I was in.

CHAPTER TWENTY-SIX

I'm not sure what it was that I expected. Having only just met Arnesto in a little tavern not even one whole day ago, all I cared about was that he knew my father. But when Xanthe had become excited at the mere mention of his full name, I began to think that indeed Arnesto was a man of mark. Someone special.

Beyond the doorway, this was made all the more evident.

It wasn't a mansion of course, how could it be? Buried inside winding coastal caves, it was impressive what Arnesto had done to make it homelier and more sophisticated. Upon immediate entry lay a fully laden wine and whiskey cellar, complete with barrels marked 'Governor's Reserve'. Adjacent the cellar was a room with comfort in mind, with rugs of wonderful and colourful exotic mosaic patterns laying upon the stone floor and a leather-bound armchair nestled in front of a sea serpent oil fire – burning clean and steadily without the by-product of smoke. A dusty crystal tumbler lay resting upon a round wooden table, a nip of whiskey resting inside. The walls were lined with shelves. They were packed full of leather-bound books and a variety of curious mechanical items within display cases.

Chewing on a tough strand of meat jerky, I quickly explored the rest of the hideout, which was a series of chambers of various sizes. A few appeared to be storage for crates of differing shapes and depths with easy access back to the iron door. A singular room with some sleeping pallets provided a resting quarter and another larger space appeared to be an improvised galley with a variety of knives and even serving plates and crockery placed in select positions around a central alchemical cooking hearth. It was simple, but well thought out. The oil mixing lanterns throughout provided a steady and dependable source of light within the cave, while the self-heating cooking hearth, like the fireplace, required no chimney or flume with its lack of smoke, relying on the clean burning refined sea serpent oil. In the corner of the room, a steady fresh water stream made its way from an opening, across the slanted slate floor and disappeared into an adjacent hole.

To the casual observer, this was likely a sparse way to live. To me however, this was luxury.

All my years at sea, I had bars for walls. My floor and bedding had been splintered timber planks. Finally, I had a bucket for my 'waste', which often tipped over in heavy swells. If food had been placed in my cell, it was a fight between myself and the large rats which roamed freely throughout the belly of the ship.

Now though, I was happy enough.

Finishing the last morsel from the strand of dried meat, I left the tunnel to retrieve Xanthe and Arnesto. Now that the evening had subsided and we were somewhere comfortable, my body felt weary. And just like them, I too needed some deep sleep.

Chapter Twenty-Seven

The coughing happened again. For weeks, Arnesto struggled through his recovery. Twice already, Xanthe and I had needed to revive him, through chest compressions and Xanthe's extensive knowledge of both providing death and reversing the technique to give life.

This time, I could tell it was bad. The rasping wet coughs echoed down the carved stone hallways of the hideout.

I rose from my sleeping pallet and hurried toward his. Rounding the corner, for the first time, Arnesto's door was shut. This was never the case, as Xanthe and I had both agreed that keeping the door open was the best option for me to hear his calls for help. Xanthe on the other hand, could hear almost everything.

I went to open the door, but the handle held firm.

It was locked.

Strange.

I slipped my hand into my bracer and retrieved my lock pick. Lately I had busied myself training to become faster and quieter in its use. A skill which I considered would become extremely useful if we managed to find The Gulag within The Capital.

The coughing grew worse.

Within a few seconds, the lock popped in response to my prying and I swung open the door.

Xanthe jumped in surprise, something which I had never managed to do to her. She stood over Arnesto, providing him assistance and wiping his brow of sweat. For a brief moment, she appeared nervous at my entrance.

Arnesto's coughs began to subside.

In the dimly lit room, I noticed something new. Upon the floor lay piles of bloodied gauze and bandages. Very bloody.

'Xanthe, do we need more blood? Why was the door locked?'

Xanthe held her arm sideways out of my view. She was hiding something.

'No, I have it under control, Flynt. I didn't want to bother you. You've given a lot of blood to him already. You need rest yourself.'

'I know, but...' I began to protest.

'I said, I have it under control,' she shut me down.

'Xanthe, what is going on? Be honest with me. What are you hiding?'

She closed her eyes and sighed. Dropping her shoulders, she turned slightly and raised the arm that she had been hiding.

A needle and intravenous tube were embedded into her pale flesh. Dark, almost black blood ran from her arm down into Arnesto's veins. As I watched, Arnesto's cough began to subside.

'You can't afford to give him anymore blood,' she continued. 'Arnesto had another bout of bleeding – too much for you to save him. I could hear his heart beating. We were going to lose him, Flynt. So, I had to do something,' she spoke like a scolded child explaining their actions to a disapproving parent.

'Xanthe, I thought you said your blood wasn't...'

'It's not.'

'But...'

'Look, it's not normal, but it *can* save him. We need him right now. If you only knew what this man has done, you would understand. Just trust me.'

I considered her for a moment. Xanthe had never given me reason to believe that she would harm my chances to find my father. Despite having lived three years aboard a ship where not a soul aboard had a skerrick of honesty, Xanthe was more than deserving of my trust.

'I do. I do trust you,' I said softly.

We stood in silence for a few moments. I watched as Arnesto's complexion went from feverish and red, to a paler colour. His consistent sweating subsided to nothing.

Satisfied it was enough, Xanthe removed the needle.

'I'm going to clean this. Maybe you should stay with him. Call me if he lapses again, will ya?'

I nodded. Xanthe awkwardly side stepped past me.

Now, Arnesto and I were alone.

I waited briefly before I pulled over the wooden stool that I had spent plenty of time on over the last few weeks. Again, I watched his chest struggle to rise and fall as his battle for life continued.

I exhaled long and slow. Something had been bothering me for some time and instead of disturbing Xanthe with my woes, I found it easier to confess to my unconscious comrade. At least I could get a word in without being told to do one hundred push ups to take my mind off of my troubles.

I looked at his arm dangling downward after the transfusion – as Xanthe called it – and lifted it, placing it comfortably on his stomach. For a moment, I could have sworn that the injection point had already healed over, with no sign of puncture whatsoever.

'Arnesto, it's me again. Flynt that is... if you hadn't worked it out. I ah... I'm worried. What in the hells have I gotten you and Xanth into? I mean, look at us. You have died twice already according to Xanthe. That's two times too many. And it's because of me. And Xanth... she doesn't deserve this. From what I gather, she's finally free of the Governor and his control. And what do I do? I convince her to help me. To go back to the very place, she is trying to flee. What kind of person does that make me?'

I lowered my head at the thought of the answer.

'Coz that's all I'm good at, Arn. Words and tricks. Even if we ever did get into the Capital... what then? If what Xanthe says is true... it'll be impossible to break him out. You had so much faith in him. Why? Why is that? I always thought he was a simple fisherman... but a spy? That is something else. How could I ever live up to something like that? I'm just a kid. A kid who has been a prisoner for three years of his measly life.'

I dropped my head further, under the weight of my confession.

'I just... don't know if I can.'

A hand grabbed mine feebly. For the first time since being aboard the cart, Arnesto looked back at me... awake.

'Arnesto! You're awake. You're alive!'

He smiled weakly in response.

'Indeed. Flynt, you will never know unless you try. Fear is crippling, yet confidence is empowering. Find your confidence my friend,' he managed through a croaking voice.

'But I am not confident, Arnesto. I have just 'winged it' to this moment.'

'Then keep 'winging it' as you say. None would be the wiser. You have done a fine job until now. As for Xanthe, I do believe that more than anything she needs a friend. You are not the only one to confess their fears to me during my recovery.'

'But what about you? Look what happened to you.'

'I was a dead man anyway. You stumbling across my path was a blessing by the divines if ever I saw one. Mortlock knew I would be there. It was you who saved me. And the incident with the Reaper? One of my finest achievements to date — to skewer The Governor's newly found weapon on a Regime sabre was worth every moment of pain I have suffered since,' he smiled.

Hearing him speak gave me hope. Hearing his words gave me perspective.

'Flynt, there's something I would like you to do for me.'

'Anything,' I replied.

'Believe in yourself. When I am better, I will have something to show you, something to assist you in your endeavours. Until then however, I would have you attend my bookcase and choose the tome - third row from the top, fifth book from the right. I take it that your father and mother taught you to read and read well. I need some rest, but I will tell you this. I am feeling much stronger now than I have in a long while.'

Slowly Arnesto closed his eyes. Within moments his laboured breathing became rather normal. The slight sound of snoring began to resonate through his quarters.

I waited some time, wondering if he would be okay and wondering if he had been delirious in his instructions. I went to the bookcase in the living room as instructed and located the book he had described.

It was a basic hardcover in appearance. No embellishments, no fancy print. No print at all for that matter. Opening it, I was welcomed with information and tales of Arnesto's exploits against the Regime. A journal. It contained dates trailing back more than a decade, his plans, his executions and his thoughts on his work. It was a detailed account of how he managed tremendous attacks and sabotage against the biggest military super power the world had ever seen.

Feeling a sense of privilege at having this one of a kind set of records, I returned to his bedside and filled my mind.

A common theme I saw in Arnesto's work was self-doubt.

Another was the dependence on allies.

Despite all of this, another interesting thing happened. For the first night since arriving at his hideout, the hallways were no longer filled with the coughing of a man clinging to life.

For the first night since arriving, Arnesto slept soundly.

CHAPTER TWENTY-EIGHT

Hanging upside down, I gripped the silk rope tight. With my feet wrapped up and controlling my speed, I slid downward toward my target, careful to avoid any noise that would give me away. I descended smoothly, uncoiling the rope like a silent reel from my shoulder, a knife held outward in my opposite hand.

Below me, my quarry had stopped briefly to scratch their own backside. Almost within reach now, I could see the fabric fibres in the top of their hat, as they hocked up a rather stubborn sounding lump of phlegm and spat it to the floor beside their boots. Pausing, I waited for the soldier to stand upright again.

Now.

In one swift movement, I released the rope, using my full body weight to drive the blade of the knife into their neck and muffle any cries for help.

...Well, that's how it was supposed to go.

Once again, I was too eager and overshot my mark. I plummeted awkwardly and hard into the stone floor of the cave, just brushing the shoulder of my disgruntled mentor.

Rubbing the now throbbing bump on my head, I looked back up into the unimpressed pout of Xanthe. Her hands were on her slim hips. That wasn't a good sign.

'Seriously, kid? How easy do you want me to make this?'

'I dunno, is there an easier way?'

'No, there's not a bloody easier way.' She gestured toward the gods in frustration.

I sat looking at the ground. Time was ticking and at this rate, I wouldn't have the skills I needed to bust out my father until I was in my late thirties. There had to be another way.

'Can't you show me some of your moves? Like the stuff you did back on the airship. Or how you picked off the soldiers outside the inn?' I asked.

'Kid, time is *not* our friend. What you're asking is almost impossible.'

'Aw c'mon, Xanth. I need something more than just hiding in the shadows. We've been at this for hours and I still can't get it right. I just need to focus on something else for a bit and then I can get my head around this.'

She shook her head. The frustration in her expression was evident.

'Kid, you're crazy, you know that?' she asked.

'Yeah, I guess.'

'Listen, let me explain this to you in a way you'll understand. You're attempting to sneak into the Capital City of this region of the Regime. You will be going up against hardened soldiers that have dedicated the better part of their lives to military drills, hand to hand combat and physical and mental conditioning. Soldiers who are practiced in battle and are wearing armour. Soldiers who revel in the thought of fighting to the death. And you think that a mere couple of weeks of training and a move or two are going to help you defeat an army of these guys? And did I mention they have mechanical golems too? They don't feel pain and they don't sleep. Annnd then there's the Reaper.'

'Well, when you put it like that...' I said, feeling crestfallen.

'Yup, you sir need to keep using your brain, coz it's worked for ya so far and if you don't use it, you'll find it splattered onto the floor beside you... Kinda like that hunk of phlegm I hocked up before... the one you're lying in right now.'

I sighed. I was either too dejected or too concussed to care about the sizeable lump of spit smeared somewhere on my clothing. I fiddled with some pointy pebbles that had helped stop my fall.

She pat me on the shoulder, 'Relax, kid. Like I said before, we'll keep at the basics coz they'll help you. By now, you're getting stronger and fitter and you're doing well with the climbing stuff... not so much the abseiling. You gotta work with your strengths, the things you're already good at, the things you know. Up until today, you haven't been half bad at sneaking around and doing things your way. Don't try to be something you aren't. Be you.'

I looked at her, not really feeling better about the whole situation. She was right. I didn't have time to become something I obviously wasn't. But what was I good at? So far, everything I did had felt like I just made it up as I went. I was literally just a kid who had been stuck aboard a ship for a very sizeable amount of my life.

Noticing my demeanour, Xanthe piped up. 'Don't worry about it too badly. I will show you a thing or two, but remember your best weapon in all of this.'

'What's that?' I asked lifting in spirits. 'Lemme guess – my brain.'

'You got *me*,' she smiled so widely, I thought her cheeks might pop. 'Sides, your next bit of training is going to be far more useful. We're going on a field trip.'

'Wait, seriously?' I asked, picking myself up off the stone floor.

'Yuh huh. I found Arnesto's hidden tunnels. They lead right into the Capital. You and I are gonna go in and gather intel.'

'Intel? How are we going to do that unnoticed?'

She went over to one of the crates near the small jetty. Opening the lid, she retrieved the contents and threw it at my chest. It was the clothes we had stolen from Balgowan and Yasmin, now dirty and slightly on the 'pongy' side. We had since replaced them with items we scrounged up from the various footlockers in the sleeping quarters.

'Well, once you've washed and dried those clothes, we'll have some nice suitable disguises to help us blend in with the common folk.'

I looked back at her. 'Fair point,' I said, feeling slightly less redundant.

'Well, what are you waiting for, servant? Chop to it! Those rags aren't going to clean themselves!'

She promptly spun me around and sent me on my way with a kick up my backside.

'Might I interject?' came the long-not-heard voice of Arnesto.

I looked up in disbelief. Sitting casually at the top of the stone staircase, wearing a regal looking robe and holding a rather fancy glass with what I could only assume was whiskey, Arnesto smiled. He looked almost fresh, despite the matting of hair across his brow and the slight hoarse crackle in his voice. Since the night Xanthe had given him blood, his recovery had been exceptionally fast – though not without limits. He moved like a man on borrowed time. Still, he'd set himself the challenge of moving farther each day ...and apparently that included sneaking in and spying on us unnoticed.

'If you two intend on entering The Capital without being noteworthy, you'll need clothing that is both practical and discreet. I have both, if you'll follow me.'

Without wasting time, Xanthe and I made our way up the stairs and through the winding stone hallways to the room containing the crates.

'It has been a while, but with a bit of luck the rats shan't have made themselves at home in these boxes yet,' he spoke more to himself than anyone.

He made his way to a particularly tall trunk with a lock on the front. At least I believe it was a lock, for there was no hole for a key, simply some dials with numbers. Arnesto fiddled with it, grumbling something about his fading memory and finally the lock popped open.

I wasn't sure what to expect, but in my mind it had been fancier than this.

Hanging inside the trunk were some very ordinary looking clothes. They were the clothes of commoners for sure, complete with dirty marks and even slight tears in places.

'Ah, thanks Arnesto, but I think I like the clothes we already have.'

'Young Flynt, if you don't want people to look at you while you wander their streets, then you need to blend in. Don't let the garbs deceive you as they would a casual observer, for indeed there is more to them than meets the eye.'

As if to demonstrate, Arnesto removed a jacket from its hanging spot and proceeded to put it on.

'What do you see?' he asked raising both hands as if waiting for the answer to come in the form of punches from invisible attackers.

'A crazy old man that shouldn't drink while he recovers,' Xanthe answered dryly.

'A grey jacket...'

'Ah, not just *any* grey jacket. This is the grey jacket of the 'City Watch' – the lawmen of the Capital. Notice the red trim? The rank insignia?' he gestured to each detail.

As I nodded, Arnesto performed a flamboyant twirl, although now he was again wearing the jacket, but this time it was of a different colour and cut.

'Woah...' mused Xanthe with wide eyes. 'Do it again. Do it again.'

'All in good time, my dear. Each one of the clothes in these trunks was designed for infiltrating a district, factory or guardhouse within the Capital. This is now the jacket of a regular dock worker. It even has papers to show your qualifications in the inside pocket.'

Xanthe wasted no time, diving past Arnesto to eagerly pilfer through the trunk.

'There are even costumes in there that will conceal noteworthy appearances such as yours, young lady. But Flynt, there is something I would like you to see first.'

Arnesto turned and walked across the hallway to the 'book room'. I left Xanthe to try on the clothes and pick out what it was that we would be wearing on our so called 'field trip'. I could hear her happy noises and exclamations as we moved on. Ahead of me, Arnesto inspected the spines of some books in his shelf. As he reached to collect his choice from its resting place, he coughed and clutched briefly at his chest. It was a wet gargling cough. He turned briefly to inspect the back of his hand and quickly removed a handkerchief to subtly wipe away what looked to be blood. Seeming slightly embarrassed, he continued his task.

'Arnesto, are you alright? Really, you should go back and get some res-' I began, but he held up a finger and gathered himself.

'I will rest soon, but first I wanted to thank you. You truly are your father's son. If it were not for your help, I would be in one of two places right now, and both of those ended with myself meeting my makers,' He paused, slightly out of breath. 'Young man, I thought about how I could repay you in my current state and it dawned on me. Did you enjoy that journal of mine?'

I nodded. 'I found it very helpful.'

'Good. For I have another, which may either answer more of the questions you have floating in your mind – or add to them,' he said.

Arnesto reached into the shelf and removed a book that had no writing along its spine. Instead it appeared as a basic and well used leather parcel. He placed a hand on top and handed it graciously to me. I recognised the leather immediately. It was bear-seal skin. I had seen sailors wrap their valuables in similar coverings. It was completely waterproof and protected materials that were not-so resistant to moisture, such as photos of loved ones or more likely, exotic women they had paid for the privilege of knowing - briefly.

I looked down and flicked through its pages. In them were hand drawn blueprints of various buildings, schematics of ships and airships, guard signals and drills. It was an absolute treasure trove of information about the Regime and the Capital.

'Arnesto, this is incredible, how did you get this?'

'Check inside the cover,' he said.

I flicked back to the inside of the cover. There was a hand-written message.

'May these records find you well, my friend. They have been gathered from all of our available sources in the hopes of giving you the means to success.'

I stopped. There was something familiar about the handwriting. As if in response to my expression, Arnesto provided the answer.

'Yes, what you are thinking is right. This was given to me by your father. It was to help me and my team in our mission to sabotage and steal from under the very nose of the Governor.

Now, it will help you in your mission to find him. In there, you will find the blueprints for 'The Gulag' along with any other details you may need to assist in planning your break in and escape. I hope you will find it as helpful as I did.'

I didn't know what to say. Arnesto had just put me one step closer to my father.

'Thank you.'

Arnesto smiled briefly, then stopped as though remembering something. 'I heard Xanthe saying that she found my secret caves. Those were decoys I'm afraid. Riddled with traps for would be assassins and a few routes to freedom should we ever be compromised.'

Before I could feel the slight pang of disappointment, he continued. 'However... I believe she may have been looking for this.' Arnesto pulled upon another book. There was a clicking sound and the bookcase swung gently toward me revealing a tunnel with hanging serpent oil lamps lining its edges. They ignited in response.

Arnesto sipped his drink and grinned.

'Now, how about we get you prepared to learn the family trade and send you off for your first lesson in espionage?'

CHAPTER TWENTY-NINE

I wasn't sure what I expected from the Capital. Perhaps a dark metropolis under a never-ending thunder storm, with evil characters on every street corner wanting to cut my throat. However, this was far from it.

The city was built all around the edges of a large protected bay. The paved streets bustled with life. Women worked stalls and shopfronts below multistorey sand-coloured buildings as ivy vines wound past white shutters and cast-iron balcony railings. The buildings had begun to take on an orange shade as the sun began to set beyond the distant haze. Although I hate to admit, it was actually all quite beautiful in its own way. Children played in the alleys, chasing one another or amusing themselves with sidewalk games. Old fishermen laid out their daily pickings for potential customers while gulls cried out and fought over the rejected scraps. Strangely enough, the only military aged males seemed to be those of the City Watch, whose ranks appeared to be made up with a range of nationalities assimilated by the Regime. They patrolled casually up and down the streets, chests puffed, more on the lookout for attractive women they could flirt with than any possible infiltrators. Which made our job, all the more easy.

Arnesto's tunnels had travelled for a considerable distance before joining some underground paved catacombs and rat-ways that, as he informed us, led to most areas and districts. He informed us that the city had once suffered an incredible plague, so the dead were buried in the underground tunnels beneath the city. Superstition and time deterred anyone from ever venturing far down here. Up until this point, Xanthe had appeared sceptical of Arnesto and his wild claims - his drinking dulling her previous impressions of his reputation, but this seemed to completely change her opinion of him altogether. The sheer amount of work that had gone into mapping or memorising these 'rat ways' would have been substantial. Genius even.

Arnesto explained how often the catacombs had helped him and his crew sneak into districts or escape. Something which seemed to peak Xanthe's interest as she listened intently to every word. Before long, we had navigated to a make-shift ladder that led to a loose paving stone in a shaded alleyway. We cached our oil lanterns at the base of the stairs before slipping into the empty lane between buildings. As simple as that, we had infiltrated (as Arnesto kept calling it) into the districts of the Capital.

'Are you ready, my friends?' Arnesto had asked with an air of melodrama. I nodded enthusiastically, while Xanthe rolled her eyes. 'Remember, we belong here, this is the theatre and we are but the actors in the wings,' he smiled before turning toward the street.

Now, to the casual observer, I looked like any other kid in the area, wearing very plain, and even grubby looking clothes. Xanthe had chosen to don a dark coloured wig and make up, to give her a more discreet, albeit exotic appearance. Arnesto led the way, with a much more complex disguise. Barely recognisable, he now sported a very realistic looking salt and pepper beard and the clothing of what looked like a humble fisherman. He walked on the opposite side of the street, saying it would help with not raising any suspicion.

'Xanthe, where are we headed?' I asked as we made our way down a steady slope of a street.

'Relax kid, we are heading to the harbour to get a better view of the Gulag. You know, the prison? Right now, we are in the housing district, where the common folk live.'

'Why is the 'Gulag' near the harbour?'

'It isn't *near* the harbour, kid. It's *in* the harbour. The Gulag is part of an Island in the middle of it.'

'Why?'

'To stop the captives escaping. See the size of the sharks those fishermen are hanging up for gutting? They are from out there,' she pointed to the waters at the end of the road. 'Even if a prisoner does escape, they are more than likely to get eaten once they step foot in the harbour.'

I considered the sharks. Flies buzzed around the barrels of offal the fisherman were filling. After the monsters I had seen out in the big blue ocean, these were nothing but bait-fish.

'Pffft, seen bigger,' I scoffed under my breath.

Xanthe gave me a sharp look as though I were crazy.

'So, what are those large spinning things up ahead then?' I was referring to the tall structures that lined the opposite shoreline. Through the salty haze I could see their large silhouettes, their tops turning steadily.

'Jeez kid, are you gonna keep asking stupid questions or am I gonna have to cross the street and join old mate over there? They have somethin to do with generatin power for the factories and houses or whateva. Now give it a rest, we are almost there.'

Xanthe had become more and more uneasy since we made our way into the Capital. I had grown to know her quite well over the past few weeks, even to the point of knowing when

she was hiding something. Right now, walking the streets, I
could see that she was nervous. Her eyes studied everybody
carefully, as though any moment one would recognise her and
the jig would be up.

'How does my wig look? Is it sitting right? Can you see any
of my hair?'

'It's fine Xanthe, relax, really. You heard Arnesto, we fit in
well. Sides, you yourself said that this is the last place anyone
would look for you.'

'Yeah. Yeah you're right, kid.' She breathed out in an attempt to calm her nerves.

I placed a hand on her shoulder. 'Xanthe, level with me.
What has you so stirred up? Are you worried the Reaper will
pop out from around the corner?'

'Kid, you know how we talked about the Reaper being the
right hand of the Governor himself?'

I nodded.

'Well, he has eyes and ears too -everywhere. I should've
mentioned it before we came into town, but I didn't want to
spook you, because next thing ya know, you're acting weird
and standing out.'

'Who are the eyes and ears?' The thought of a man with
literal eyes and ears all over the lands would've seemed quite
humorous if it wasn't for how unsettled my stoic companion
now seemed.

'His secret intelligence agents. Anyone. Anywhere. Even I
don't know much about them – only that they exist. Especially
in the Capital.'

Now my eyes searched the people in the streets too.

'Gee, thanks for the boost of confidence, Xanth. I kind of
wish I hadn't asked.'

She seemed to ignore my quip and continued with her
silent scrutiny of the street.

I watched as Arnesto turned a corner. Xanthe and I kept walking a little further before crossing the street to join him. We rounded a spiked iron fence and came to a stunning look out over the harbour and the adjacent headland. Before us lay a long, wide, set of stairs leading down to what was clearly a large-scale operation of cut stone docks tiered into two levels. On the lower tier, crowded market stalls lined the waterfront, each tent with its own wares for sale. Many stalls had begun lighting their lamps for the evening, some shop keeps even had tall poles with permanently placed lanterns illuminating their unique merchandise below.

The higher tiered level opposite us appeared to be a mix of towering cliffside and man-made splendour. Higher than almost anything within view, crafted balconies jutted out, pointing in various directions over the bay. Small shapes of people lined the railings that were cut into the cliff and looked out from observation decks over the bay. Their casual strolls and movements were juxtaposed by the orderly and quick movements of the personnel manning the dock that jutted forth from the face creating a large sculpted overhang. I say 'dock' because that is what it appeared to be with its crates and crew, although it remained well above the waterline. It wasn't long before my suspicions were answered however, as a very large and elaborately adorned airship putted around into view from behind the enormous structure. The orange sunset that had painted the markets, all but disappeared as the bulbous hull eclipsed it. The airship manoeuvred into position just above the raised dock, her crew throwing heavy ropes from the edges for the waiting personnel below to grab. It was a well drilled process, within moments, the airship had steadied herself and docked into an elevated platform, side gates opened outward as aircrew and ground crew went about their delegated tasks. The whole process only took a minute or two, but everyone seemed to stop briefly to witness the spectacle. I felt the need for a closer look, but the only way to the raised dock however, appeared to be by crossing through the lower tier, something which the wallahs and sellers on the waterfront seemed to capitalise upon.

We made our way down to the lower waterfront markets and were immediately swept up in the atmosphere. Shop keeps cried out, claiming to have the best deals for their goods, their attention devoted to scoping any whiff of a potential customer. Speaking of smells, many wafted from the various spruikers of foreign cuisine. There were locally caught fish, imported spices and various creatures in cages from the Isles, ready to be butchered and cooked to your liking. Hanging along the walk way were elaborately patterned rugs from the Eastern Regions and rare fabrics from the furthest reaches of the Regime. Xanthe gave a delighted squeal and left me in the blink of an eye, delving into the various lean-tos and tents, trying on items. The scene was almost overwhelming for someone who had spent the better part of the last few years locked in a ship. But the feeling was short lived as a sobering realisation crept into my mind. Among the shops and prospective customers, the dock was riddled with various uniforms. I made out members of the City Watch, Regime Sailors even members of Air crew and Infantry, all scattered amongst a sea of civilians, going about their tasks. A group of uniforms rounded a set of crates before me. Scratching my head to hide my face, I casually turned to face the view of the water.

The harbour itself, was strewn with ships of various kinds. Familiar Tall ships lay at anchor in the deeper waters, their sails furled, while smaller fishing vessels travelled in and out of the massive port via a huge gated wall between the harbour and the open ocean. Then there were the less familiar airships that floated lazily over various distant parts of the city. But the strangest of sea going creations were some downright absurd looking steamboats that were devoid of any sails or timber whatsoever, clad in metal and sporting large wheels on their sides. They reminded me of slightly of my father's old vessel, but were more like windmills welded onto barges. There wasn't any real beauty in their design – just industrial bulk. Beyond these curiosities, the opposite shoreline appeared to have an array of large buildings with tall chimneys that sprouted out plumes of smoke casting a slight haze across the distant reaches of the city.

I sidled up beside Arnesto. He had stopped by some crates on the edge of the jetty and lit up a pipe casually, as though he had just finished a big shift at sea and now required a decent break for his efforts. After Xanthe's admonishing, I decided to try my many questions on him.

'So, what are we doing?' I asked under my breath as the crowds swept by.

'We -' Arnesto gave a long exhale of thick white pipe smoke, '- need a way to move around more freely, young Flynt. There are too many prying eyes here, too many of the Governor's men patrolling the streets. I haven't seen it like this before. It's busier for some reason. Getting closer to the Gulag is going to be more difficult than I thought.'

Arnesto's words trailed off. He continued to puff away at his pipe, his eyes searching the surrounding crowds.

'Well, if we see the uniforms coming, can't we simply avoid them?' I asked.

'Perhaps. Perhaps. It isn't those in uniform that I am worried about though, my young fellow.'

'Wow, first Xanthe and now you? I thought for the slightest moment that she was trying to fool me. This isn't some sick stitch up, is it?'

Arnesto turned toward me but didn't answer. But he did show something in common with Xanthe. A quiet sense of concern.

I watched as he scratched his nose briefly, but I saw it. Arnesto used the gesture to peak through his fingers at the surrounding stalls. His eyes had quickly gauged the various workers and customers before deciding whether it was safe or not. Feeling somewhat redundant in the ways of espionage as he called it, I tried to casually tie my bootlace, while briefly trying to mimic his methods. But to me, customers were customers and sellers were... you guessed it – sellers. Arnesto did have a flair for the dramatic from what I had seen. Perhaps he was simply overreacting.

The main thing that grabbed my attention was floating across from us. I found myself gawking across the bazaar toward the massive airship once more. The look outs from the cliffs seemed to have a brilliant vantage point over the bay.

'What if we were to go up there?' I suggested, motioning toward the towering structure. 'Wouldn't that provide a decent view of the bay, away from prying eyes?'

Arnesto mused for a moment, his eyes scanning the various ledges and the people that lined them.

'Indeed, it would, young Flynt,' he said thoughtfully. 'I tell you what, you head on up there and I will follow shortly behind. Having spent such time as mine in incarceration, there are a few vices I would like to indulge in, if you catch my drift?'

I smiled in feigned understanding. Something was 'off' about his sudden need to disappear, but before I could bring it up, Arnesto had disappeared into the bodies cruising through the bazaar.

Now with no one to talk to and feeling rather alone in a crowd of strangers, I took his advice. I swept through the crowd looking for any sign of Xanthe to let her know our intentions. Stall after stall revealed no results.

A shoulder bumped hard into my back, pushing me slightly off balance. Too hard to be accidental.

'Watch where you're going, *commoner*,' sneered a red-haired boy roughly my age. His messy freckles contrasted his clothing, which appeared to be of a finer cut than my outfit.

An older balding man in a double-breasted waistcoat who I picked as his father, joined him in half perusing nearby stalls of exotic looking artworks. The man considered me briefly over the rim of his gold wired spectacles.

'Don't fraternise with the 'simple people', my boy. You might catch something. Just look at the ghastly company the boy keeps,' he sneered, turning down the corners of his mouth. I realised he was referring to Xanthe as she re-joined me draped in a newly acquired silk scarf. My fists tightened at the comment.

'Flynt, I got you something. Look, there was a stall selling water proof matches. *Water proof.* So, you can chew on them in the rain and they will still light and stuff. And check this out,' she turned this way and that flaunting her new bright red scarf. 'Isn't it beautiful? I've never had something so nice.'

The boy and his parent laughed openly at Xanthe. They made no attempt to be subtle in the nasty comments that followed, regarding Xanthe and their disapproval of her ap-pearance.

Words like 'disgusting' and 'ugly' began to be slung in our direction.

The lively spark that had filled her briefly with happiness was immediately snuffed out. Her shoulders dropped and she quickly removed the scarf, letting it fall listlessly to her side. Xanthe's head drooped slightly and began to turn and walk away. I could've begun throwing hands right then and there, if the threat of being caught by guards didn't loom over me.

Instead, I knelt down and scooped up her scarf, arranging it back around her neck. I smiled at her.

'It looks great, Xanthe. That colour suites you. Where did you get it?'

'Yeah, you think?' the spark ignited again slightly. 'I ah... acquired it from a guy over there with the twirly whirly moustache.'

I dared a look back towards the stalls to see the merchant in question, none the wiser for his missing items. Xanthe giggled and before I could tell her of my plan, she disappeared into the crowd once more.

Regarding the boy and his father, I felt a tingle of hatred begin to fester within. The boy and his freckles scowled at me before scampering off behind his old man.

A hand upon my shoulder gave me a friendly squeeze. I turned to see Arnesto before me.

'That wasn't very sporting of that pair now, was it? Flynt, I know what I said before about splitting up, but I must admit, I am a sucker for an eye for an eye. What's say I give you a lesson here and now, so that we may settle the score with that pair of miscreants?'

'What, here? Now?' I was taken both by Arnesto's sudden appearance and his attention to the incident that had just occurred. He eyed the boy's father like a predator stalking prey.

'You were already planning on marking them, weren't you?' I realised.

I was unsurprised.

'Indeed. People like that were made on the back of industry built by the Regime war machine. The money they have is taken from the countries they invade and the investments they make in profiteering from war. This is my speciality and my pleasure to pay you and your friend back for what you have done for me. Just follow my lead and enjoy the pickings,' he winked at me before starting off in the direction of the duo who had upset Xanthe. I moved off behind him, attempting to keep my distance without losing him in the jostling crowd.

Had I have not been aware of what Arnesto was up to, I don't think I would have seen it. Moving past the stalls, his finger dipped into the bottom of a cage of furry looking possum hawks. A few paces later he passed the pair and moved further a few stalls ahead. It was at this point, Arnesto ducked down and I lost sight of him.

Without meaning to, I almost bumped into the back of the boy's father as I tried to duck around a lady carrying a large basket of fruit.

'Shine your shoes, sir?' came a familiar voice from below. Arnesto had set out a handkerchief before him, his beanie upturned with a scattering of sovereigns inside. He crouched beside it and tugged at the man's trouser leg.

'Hands off pauper, I have important places to be,' the man scowled downward, pulling his leg away from Arnesto.

'Well sir, if they be important places, perhaps you should look the part?' Arnesto gestured towards a smear of what appeared to be animal droppings on the man's boots.

'Ugh!' he stated out loudly, before trying in vain to scrape the brown and white goo onto the ground. 'This is what I get for mixing with the poor. Curse this place.'

'Sir, if you like, I can have them shoes of yours looking rather splendid before your important meeting. And your brass embellishments too,' he motioned toward the man's fine-looking buttons.

The man went to swat away Arnesto's hand once more but turned and looked up toward the airship. Impatiently he fumbled through his pocket and removed a shiny gold watch on a chain, flipped open its lid and then returned it. With a visible grinding of his teeth, he turned impatiently and thrust his foot into Arnesto, almost toppling him backward.

'Get on with it then. And don't expect a tip.'

Arnesto produced a pair of procured stools from a nearby stall without so much as a glance from the owner and wiped them to the man's liking with his handkerchief. The pair sat uncomfortably as the crowds pushed by.

Rolling up the man's trousers, Arnesto went to work with his rag of a handkerchief, whipping it back and forth with an element of showmanship and flair. The man and his son busied themselves in a heated yet hushed discussion ignoring any attempt at small talk from my friend.

As though reading my thoughts, Arnesto looked up briefly at me and with a wry smile, he winked. Though his hands moved quickly over the man's shoes, I watched as they deftly swooped in and around the pockets of the jacket as it drooped nearer the ground. Every flamboyant whip of the rag and items returned – moved into Arnesto's own back pocket.

Things were moving smoothly, that is until the man once again reached into his pocket to check for some unknown contents. His impatient fossick within his coat pocket became more frantic. Arnesto motioned subtly to me with his fingers gesturing toward his own coat. I pushed through the moving crowd and casually picked it up before slipping into a slightly more distant position inside another stall. He watched me as I cached his new belongings. Now, without any evidence on him, my comrade leant toward the man to offer assistance. His polite offer was answered - the man pushing Arnesto aside before diving into his jacket. Desperately he began pulling the insides of every secreted storing place inside out.

'Where is it? No, no, no... I need it!'

'Where is what, sir?' asked Arnesto with the face of a bewildered child.

The man's eyes snapped at Arnesto and began to bulge wildly.

'You! You have something to do with this no doubt! You... you... charlatan!' The man lunged at Arnesto, his arms outstretched for my friend's throat. With a slick movement that belied his current appearance, Arnesto zipped forward and twisted an incoming arm around behind the man's own back. Legs went upward, and in a split second and a sharp painful sounding thud on the stone ground, the man lay face down, Arnesto's knee buried in the nape of his neck.

'Guards! Guards!' the man half squealed, half gurgled. His son too began to shriek for assistance. People from the crowd began to turn toward the violent interruption to their casual perusing. Customers and shop keeps alike reeled away from the scene as the sounds of yelling could be heard making their way closer through the masses.

I looked frantically at Arnesto. Why wasn't he running? Maybe he couldn't with his injuries. He'll be arrested for sure. I searched for any sign of desperation or concern on Arnesto's face, but he simply smiled and remained calm, holding down the man with ease. The man's son, took it at that moment to run away. He barrelled wide eyed through the edge of the crowd in my very direction, leaving his own father at the mercy of my partner. In a moment of disguised vengeance, I waited until I could see the spots on his face, before raising my arm like a tree branch. Well... a young tree branch of sorts. His face stopped on my arm causing his legs to spill upward. His body gave way to gravity with a thud. As his diaphragm spasmed for air, wild eyes of recognition looked up into my grinning mug. Before he could recover, I dragged him in behind some elaborately decorated hanging tapestries and tried out one of the techniques Xanthe had taught me during training. With my arm pressed against his carotid artery, the blood flow to his brain slowed. Within seconds his body went limp – unconscious. I quickly went to work removing anything of value from the now-much-more-compliable boy from before. The only problem was, everything appeared to be of value! His clothes were of even finer quality than those of Balgowan and his mistress. So, I did what any respectable thief would do – I took them. Don't get me wrong, I'm not a savage and even though the boy had upset my friend Xanthe, a crumpled pair of trousers were left beside him.

By now a pair of guards from the City Watch had approached Arnesto and the man and were questioning the pair. Arnesto once again saw me from the corner of his eye and winked subtly toward me before looking upward toward the lookout. I got the picture. He had the situation under control. As I walked past I caught wind of the stern talking to the man was now receiving from the leader of the pair of city watchmen.

'Well Lord Stravovich, as you call yourself, we've checked this gentleman here and he does not have your papers, nor your invitation -so drop the lie or the only important meeting you are about to have is in the forced labour mine for impersonating a noble.'

The comment caused him to pale and temper his anger considerably. Imagine if he would have noticed the boy he had insulted earlier slinking past in his own son's clothes.

Chapter Thirty

I've made a few big mistakes in my short life. There were the little mistakes, like the time I used the wrong bait when fishing with my father and causing sharks to swim in and eat up our potential profits. Then there were bigger ones, like believing the Captain aboard the 'Kraken Krusher' and his empty promises. The particular mistake this very day, however... was a doozy.

But let me explain.

After failing to find Xanthe back in the bazaar, I thought I had noticed something strange. I had caught a woman staring at me. She had a stern appearance, with her dark hair tied back firmly and lips that seemed permanently pressed together – unable to smile. She stared at no one else but me. Not in the he's-a-handsome-lad kind of way, her eyes scrutinised me firmly from behind a stall cooking unusual looking dumplings. But when the cook lifted the lid to his steamer, and a cloud of vapor billowed forth - she disappeared.

Now, usually it wouldn't have bothered me. However, given the circumstances – what with the fact we were in the Capital city of the Enemy Regime and Arnesto had just swindled with some important looking locals, it played on my mind.

I thought I had seen her once more when climbing the stairs to the lookout. But, as the groups of people bustled past me on their way downward, I lost sight of her in the crowd.

When I had arrived upstairs, within the carved hallways and balconies, only people who appeared to have the wealth of a small country gathered, mingled and chatted the way I guess those sorts of people do. Yet despite my not having much money, my new fine cut jacket and shoes where enough to give the appearance of their kind. That fact, paired with my age meant that I didn't so much as earn more than a casual glance from the groups as they schmoozed the afternoon away. It did occur to me that they appeared to be milling around waiting, not enjoying the views of their city skyline or harbour from the lookout platforms. Just beyond the confines of the lookouts, dock workers shifted and moved large crates onto trolleys heading for the tethered airship. Using a series of hydraulic contraptions, they lifted and shifted the stores onto a rear loading point of the enormous docked airship, before crew then moved them within the bowels of the fuselage. Separated from the workers, the nobility appeared to have their own red carpet leading to the airship, from the edge of the stone dock, along an elaborately adorned gangplank to the ship's portside deck. People everywhere were either working or socialising, each with their own job to do. Me? I realised I had to get down to business. I began to search for an ounce of privacy and considered stealing away to a private balcony and do what I came here for – to find the Gulag and try to work out a way in. Moving to an archway before a balcony I chanced a final look up and down the hallway, that's when I spotted her again.

The woman.

This time she had a sizable entourage of guards in tow, and they joined her in scanning the crowd. At least four of them had blocked the top of the stairwell back to the bazaar. The remaining guards were split into groups of three at the command of the woman and began filing towards the various social circles.

Great.

My eyes widened as a group of guards made their way toward my balcony. I turned my back and popped the collar of the boy's jacket to shield my face and quickly took stock of my surroundings. The light-coloured sandstone of the cliff-side had been cut away expertly, with wrought iron fencing providing chest height safety for those wishing to admire the city below. Way below. I considered momentarily the idea of leaping from the balcony into the bay, but at this height, it would likely end poorly for me.

The winds had begun to pick up allowing the coastal birds to ride their currents above the bay in the orange light of the slowly setting sun. From this vantage point, the city was both mesmerizing and distant. As I looked to the Northwest, I could also see the enormous form of the airship, with its wide decks, elaborate designs and red and gold floatation hull. Standing on a private side deck, I could see a man in fine military attire, admiring the same view as I.

I wondered briefly if he was aware of the trouble the boy on the nearby viewing platform was about to face.

Before me, a rectangular brass panel was framed into the railing beside me – an outline of the bay and its buildings etched deftly into the metalwork. It provided a perfect scale view of the buildings lining the water's edge and beyond. Each notable building in the artwork had a switch beside it. Like nothing I had ever seen before I found myself curious as to the purpose of this creation, when simply looking further than the perching posts for the gulls would provide the same – if not better, view. I pressed one of the switches.

The board crackled with noise, causing my hand to reel back as though bitten by something. A metallic sound of a woman's voice came from a tight knit series of holes nearby.

'The 'Stravovich Arms Company' is the factory where all of our latest weapons and armour are produced. Some two hundred units per day, creating the latest and most deadly weapons for our soldiers.'

You're kidding me. Shouldn't this sort of information be secret, not publicly known? I tried another switch for a rather large structure across the bay.

'Standing at well over one hundred and sixty feet tall – one of the tallest buildings in our fair city is the factory for manufacturing our airships. Currently it produces six a month, which with new found resources and man power will eventually produce double that volume, making it the foremost producer of airships in all of the Regime's territories.'

I heard boots just a few fathoms from the entrance to my balcony. The guards were close. I needed to know more. I pressed another switch.

'Our major protector from any threats - the fortifications to the bay, combined with the impassable natural cliffs surrounding the city, provide complete protection – particularly from Allied Navy and the occasional sea behemoth.'

I felt footsteps behind me. Three sets. Now my only safe escape was blocked and an unsafe one lay before me. How could I play this out?

Oh, hey there... just a kid here, checking out your important military installations...

I stole a glance backward. Two male guards stood just past the archway entrance to the balcony, while a third female moved toward me. Her footsteps were deliberate, yet cautious.

'Young man, I would like to see your papers.' Her gruff voice was devoid of any promise of negotiation.

'Um, sorry?'

'Your papers,' she insisted impatiently. Now I understood how Balgowan must have felt the day Xanthe and I fleeced him in the forest.

'Oh, right, I ah –' I reached inside the lapel of my new jacket and began to fish around for anything that might help my situation. My eyes once again considered the distance to the waters below. At least three times the height of the Kraken Krusher's Crow's nest, I reckoned. And even that hurt when I hit the water.

'Young man, hurry up. I don't have all day.'

Despite her words, I could see her reflection in the brass information panel before me. She signalled to the other two guards to approach. My heart thumped, my breathing short-ened. I stepped toward the railing and began to mentally prepare myself for the fall. I felt her move behind me. My foot lifted for the railing.

'Step away from the-'

Her words were cut short by the sound of gurgling. I turned to see an arm wrapped firmly around the guard's throat. Her eyes rolled upwards as she struggled to remember her train-ing, instead pawing desperately for air.

Within moments she went limp, her head lolled forward to reveal one of my colleagues behind her.

'Xanthe!'

She was wearing the same uniform as the guards she had just beaten the snot out of.

'Kid, you were really gonna jump, weren't you?' she smiled.

Behind her, the other two guards remained slumped into uncomfortable positions on the ground.

'I ah... considered it,' I admitted sheepishly.

'Yeah, that wouldn't have worked out so well.'

'It might've,' I protested weakly, but was cut off by Xanthe's finger pressed into my lips.

'Listen kid, we don't have much time. They are onto you and have your scent. The stairs have guards posted top and bottom. If we make a commotion, they'll sound the alarm and every military and law enforcement resource the Regime has will be on us. You've got to find a way out of here.'

'Well, I was working on that. Have you seen Arnesto?'

'I lost sight of him in the Bazaar. He was headed up this way, but I had to get a hold of a uniform.'

'How did you manage that?' already suspecting the answer.

'Well, if old crone features out there actually counted her troops, she would realise that she lost two back by the rug merchant in the marketplace. But that means, I filled the role of one... which means she'd be short by one... but now that's three... no four...'

'Xanthe.'

'Oh yeah, so to getting you outta here before they realise...'

I started to think. Feeling trapped was not unusual to me, what with the times I had to hide behind the ship's rudder or deep in a kelp forest to avoid nasty jaws or searching tentacles. But this was out of my comfort zone, so to speak. I looked around to any vines or places outside that I could climb away to. Meanwhile, Xanthe busied herself with searching the guards and casually disposing of the evidence over the railing – an unconscious form flopping out of sight.

Xanthe mumbled away, half to me and half to herself, 'See, ya wouldn't have made it to the water. Oh man, that's a mess...'

I felt the strong urge of a cringe, but my senses were suddenly charmed.

That's when it hit me.

The most amazing smell that had sucked up my nostrils in years. Food. Not slop, or gruel or sludge. Beautiful, savoury and sweet recipes wafted from the archway, almost mesmerizing me and hijacking my thoughts. I peered toward the source... or sauce... back inside the hallway. Trollies of cloches, serving plates and wines were being wheeled past by smartly dressed wait staff – uniforms uncannily similar to the guardsmen. An almost endless line of fine foods made its way from a distant doorway - previously unnoticed by me, all the way to the wide gangplank of the airship.

My stomach took control of my rational thinking. I would do almost anything to eat whatever was upon those serving dishes. I watched, openly and blatantly from the archway, entranced. Suckling pig on a spit, pastries filled to the brim with evidence of tasty innards, steamed fish coated in spices, and more than my eyes and nose could discern. Each brass trolley was covered in a long flowing white cloth, almost brushing the floor.

It gave me an idea.

Turning back to see Xanthe dusting off her hands after the final guard disappeared beyond view, I asked, 'Xanthe, have they spotted you yet?'

'They have no idea I'm here, kid. You on the other hand – she really is interested in you. Hey, I know that look. You got an idea, dontcha?'

'Yeah, well, not really. Kinda... maybe. Probably I should rethink this one-'

'And you need a distraction, dontcha? Well, that's fine, I got this.'

Xanthe held up a knife in front of her face with childlike enthusiasm.

'What? Wait, no, you don't. How are you going to...?' I began to protest, reconsidering my options briefly, but it was too late. Xanthe threw the knife across the hallway with incredible force. Unfortunately for one guard scoping the eastern balconies, she was aiming at him. Fortunately, though, the knife hit him in the base of the skull - butt first. The sound of the 'crack' echoed briefly through the hall. I watched as all of the guards were alerted as one of their own plummeted to the floor unconscious. Groups up and down the hall abandoned their tasks and bee-lined for their downed partner creating a slight sense of panic. Soon, everyone's attention was drawn to the commotion. Even the orchestrator or my would-be-capturer, the stern-faced agent, had turned her focus to the downed guard from her entourage.

With a slap on my back and an 'Off ya go kid, what are you waiting for?' I made for the nearest trolley. The waiter, thoroughly bemused with the spectacle unravelling to his right, was none the wise as I swiftly ducked under the cloth draping the trolley and delicately sat upon the lower tray.

I waited with gritted teeth for a moment to see if I had alerted the trolley pusher.

Nothing.

I breathed a sigh of relief.

I didn't have time to consider my new predicament. The trolley began to file forward. Its dicky wheels rattled upon the cobblestones, sending short and sharp painful bumps up my spine as I tried to hold steady beneath the glorious smells from above.

Oh gods.

Perhaps this was a bad idea.

A really bad idea.

A terrible idea.

And as the trolley began to make its way across the gangplank, onto the polished timber decking of the massive air-

ship, I realised, I had indeed made one of the biggest mistakes
in my life.
   At least now I might get a better view of the city.

CHAPTER THIRTY-ONE

Wooden decking was replaced with fine maroon carpet as the trolley I hid upon was wheeled into some sort of room. Immediately the temperature became cosy and warm compared to the slight chill that had begun outside. Music played and the sounds of people chatting and chinking glasses filled the air beyond the confines of the cloth I sat beneath.

Like a mouse looking for its chance to steal across the pantry, I lifted the covering slightly and peaked through the gap. To my immediate front, were legs in trousers, long dresses and fine boots. I repeated my actions to the rear and was pleased to see no one nearby.

Breathing in and collecting myself, I tried to remember Arnesto's words upon entering the city.

Something, something, actors... No, what was it? Just pretend like you belong here, Flint.

With a brief muster of courage, I slipped awkwardly from beneath the trolley and stood up. A few strange looks were thrown my way – as a boy in fine clothes had just seemed to appear from nowhere. Slipping my hand across the table, I raised a nearby pastry upward.

'There you are,' I muttered out loud before distancing myself from the group.

Moving to a nearby corner, heart beating wildly, I wondered if I had just given the worst performance of my life. The adults from before had barely registered a response, turning back to their conversations.

Adrenaline subsiding, I realised I now stood inside the finest looking room I had ever laid eyes upon.

Finely dressed people mingled and exchanged pleasantries around tables piled high with some of the nicest smelling food to ever assail my nostrils. My mouth started to water at the display of pastries and meats upon the tiered serving trays. It took most of my self-control to stop from simply launching onto the table and holding it all ransom with a butter knife. Men and women in dark uniforms appeared from a back room and replaced the emptying silver trays with new ones, stacked high with even more delicacies. It was a never-ending supply of food. Piano music filled the mahogany clad cabin, while the dignitary's body guards lined the walls, standing to attention beside the glass doors to the viewing deck outside. With the setting sun, the sight of the Capital was cast in an orange veil as the clouds to the west began to shed their colour to pink. More and more of the city stretched into view as the airship drifted on its course lazily above the bay.

'Hello, son.'

Hello, son?

My eyes bulged wildly. Shaking, I turned.

I looked upon a familiar brass buttoned jacket, immaculately cut. With a crystal tumbler in hand, it raised to the smiling face of Arnesto in gold rimmed spectacles - finishing a final swig before having it immediately refilled by one of the passing men in uniform.

'By the gods, Arnesto. How did you?' I felt like hitting him square in the jaw, if it wasn't for the sudden wave of relief at having a friend with me in this unfamiliar setting.

'Now now, son. You must remember to refer to me by my proper title – Lord Stravovich. I think you'll find my newly acquired title, paperwork and invitation to this fine evening is more than enough to explain my being here,' he smirked.

He was enjoying this.

'And remember, your name is Igor Stravovich. Although I would have thought a name such as that would suit someone with a much spottier complexion.'

'All right, you've had your fun. I swear, between you and Xanthe, I can't keep up with you both. Speaking of – did she make it aboard?'

'With an agent of her skills, I would imagine so, though I am yet to see her. And as for keeping up, don't be too hard on yourself, you are learning. Never mind the situation. We will find your father soon enough. But for now...' he trailed off.

'For now... what?' I asked.

'Now? Now we wait, my boy,' he responded. He stared toward the front of the room where people seemed to be moving about. There was a slight tone of apprehension that had crept into his voice. It made me feel uneasy, but it didn't stop my hunger.

'Well, in that case, can I eat the food?'

He smiled knowingly and nodded in response before turning to a well-to-do looking lady in a slim fitting dress and casually striking up a conversation.

Her laughter became distant as I turned and faced the array of laid out delights. Instead of following through with my earlier desires, I restrained myself. Barely. I pocketed a circle shaped pastry that was dusted in a white powder and indulged in one for myself. A sweet pink goop oozed from inside. Within seconds, I had polished off another, before searching the hall of a room for any sign that Xanthe too had made it aboard. I know that Xanthe claimed she didn't need to eat, but I had a feeling she would actually enjoy this food.

After scanning the crowd, it didn't take long before I noticed her familiar slight form. Xanthe had joined the rest of the wait staff by the open glass doors.

Making my way through the schmoozing members, I closed the distance between us. But as I neared, not more than a few fathoms between us, I noticed her attention was elsewhere. For the first time since the night on the hillside, I saw a different Xanthe. Her eyes darted around the room from face to face.

Who was she looking for?

The music stopped.

A deep and refined voice cut firmly through the festivities, 'Ladies and Gentlemen, might I have your attention?'

On the opposite side of the room, a man wearing a dark red and charcoal officer's uniform with slick black hair addressed the people around me. I recognised him as the same man that had been standing upon the airship's private decking when I was confronted by the guards earlier. Almost immediately, the crowds ceased talking and turned their attention toward him. Whether it was to marvel at the array of medals neatly assembled in ranks along his chest or his immaculately trimmed side burns, was hard to tell. He stood before a large painting with an extravagant golden frame. When I observed the oil painting, I realised I was looking at a double image. The man now addressing us and the man in the painting were one and the same.

The Governor, himself.

I almost dropped the morsel from my hand in surprise - a sense of dread passing through me.

'I'm sure you are wondering why I have invited you all here aboard my personal vessel on the verge of this fine evening. I assure you, that point in particular I will address very shortly. As you all know, you represent the elite members of this fair city, which have benefited the most from the Regime's rise as a superior nation. Our very own lords and ladies, investors and trail blazers of industry. Each and every one of you have lined your pockets with the profits of our expansion and the spreading of our prosperity and technology. An expansion which I have personally driven forward into the heart of the world. An expansion which I will personally see lead us into the future.'

'Recall our nation, but mere decades ago. A crippled and starving society, recovering from the ravages of a plague released upon the world. Thousands of our dead citizens, lay burning in ditches to stop the spread. Men, women and children of our nation suffered from a disease released by our neighbours, our supposed allies. Traitors and conspirators they were. And when we were at our weakest, they attempted to leech from us in return for aid that never came.'

He began to walk through the crowd, moving closely past the nobility as they gave him their undivided attention.

'But you stopped that fine, sir!' one of the men in the audience called out raising his glass. Everyone else replied in kind by toasting theirs.

'Indeed, I did. We did. Through garnering our resources and turning on those that would drain our very lifeblood and wipe us out, we rose from the clutches of annihilation and took back what was rightfully ours. On this very eve, those many years ago, we struck back and squashed the *leeches*. In a matter of months our people had recovered, our resources had multiplied and our borders had expanded.'

'Since then, we have steamrolled forward in a manner that has shaken the world. We have become a respected leader amongst our people and a feared enemy of those who would stand against us. The blood of our nation courses through the world and enriches those who welcome it and drowns those who do not. Resources and brilliant minds have allowed us technological advances that have made our nation stronger than any foreign alliance could hope to stand against. And yet they do stand against us—trembling.'

'As I speak, alliance fleets comb our western waters, in the hope of finding a chink in our armour. A weakness. But they are mistaken, because on the outside we are strong. On the inside however...'

He trailed off and stopped pacing. His eyes rested upon Xanthe. Staring. Could he see through her disguise? The pause lasted for a time that made members of the audience look to each other with raised eyebrows. He tenderly reached up and with a curled finger, he lifted her chin, momentarily considering her.

Lingering.

I saw her knuckles tighten. Her eyes stared back into his, like a daughter who had just been scolded by a father. He leant in close and whispered something into her ear. For the first time since the fire, I thought I saw Xanthe tremble.

He knows.

'... But I digress,' he turned to face his audience again. 'Words are indeed cheap and I don't believe you all came here with the intention of taking a tour of our city from the sky.'

'As long as the drinks keep flowing your Excellence, we could stay here all evening,' members of the audience chortled at the comment.

'Indeed. Nonetheless,' he stated as he moved back to his position beside the portrait.

The Governor motioned toward a doorway and from it emerged a tall and familiar figure. The red helm considered the crowd and I felt the need to shrink behind the shoulders of those in front. There was a collective gasp and murmurs as The Reaper stepped deliberately to the side of the Governor and stood to attention.

'I spoke of weakness. Internal weakness. Something which I have no time for within my borders. So, when I discover conspirators or would-be assassins lurking within them, I take them and mould them. What you see before you is one of the great achievements of the Regime, a marvel of science. I have taken a weapon from my enemy and improved upon it. Without the need for food or sleep, unable to feel physical pain, stronger than several of our fittest men, what stands before you is a shining example of the will of my nation. This weapon can stand against an entire platoon of soldiers and best them. He is unwavering, loyal and mine.'

There were gentle rumblings of shock and surprise at The Governor's statement. Various voices around me made comments about 'rumours being true'.

'Your Excellency, if he was once of the enemy, how can you be certain of his loyalty? Why would you not simply utilise one of our own who has already shown their dedication to the nation?' a voice spoke out from someone behind me.

The Governor's eyes looked directly through the doubter. He turned his head slightly and gave a gentle nod.

'Behold what our science has achieved. A mere taste of the Regime's power.'

The Reaper removed one of the sharp looking swords that crossed his back, the same one I had seen up close before. Without the slightest of hesitations, he dragged the blade across his own neck. Blood squirted onto the floor. The audience gasped, someone retched and a woman fainted nearby – a handful of gentlemen rushing to her aid.

The Reaper's head tilted forward and he returned his sword to its sheath. There was a rasping and gargling sound as he gasped for air through his newly ventilated throat. With his other hand he removed a vial from a pouch on his waist and pressed a button upon it. A sharp metal prong ejected from the tip and he plunged the device into his own neck. The blood flow began to slow immediately, and within moments had stopped altogether. The Reaper raised his head and returned to his original stance from before the gory display. The wound was all but gone.

'Why you ask? Because I can,' the question seemed to rile him up. 'I can take the enemy's most loyal servants and turn their internal weakness into my strength. Turning what was once theirs against them. Blood against blood.'

He removed a golden dial on a chain from his pocket and opened its lid. Appearing satisfied, the Governor's demeanour settled, becoming almost relaxed.

'It is time. Ladies and Gentlemen, however poignant this display has been, it is not the reason I have gathered you here. If you wouldn't mind joining me upon the outer decks, there is a more impressive display I would like to show you.'

Joining his hands behind his back, the Governor strode through the open doors, leaving the crowd to follow obediently. No matter how badly I didn't want to join them, I could see that the Reaper had not followed him, and I certainly did not want to stay inside a room with *that* and some body guards for company. I stepped in behind the men who had propped the fainting lady onto a chair in the corner. Doing my best to blend in with the crowd.

Outside was a stark contrast from the room from which we had just been. Warmth, music and the smell of food was now replaced by a chilling breeze and the drone of the very large engines to the rear. The wide timber decking was wet with condensation, leaving many in the crowd to shuffle carefully to the railings to avoid slipping over.

'Gather around,' insisted the Governor, now raising his voice over the propellers. His airship gently descended toward the water.

After some more awkward shuffling, the mixture of dignitaries had moved to various points to look out over the bay and the surrounding city. The sun had almost set beyond view, casting the bay in an eerie glow.

'What you saw just now, had been an example of combined efforts of our scientists from across the Regime's lands. But one man can only do so much. Until recently, I had another. One that I was quite fond of. But failures on our behalf and a lack of funding meant that she was internally weak and our nation cannot afford weakness...'

His eyes began to search the crowd briefly, as though he had lost something or someone. After a moment he continued, remembering his train of thought.

'Most of all, our nation cannot afford weakness at sea. Remember if you may, that we have enemy fleets trying to gain control of our waters? Why would I allow such a thing? Why would I let them have control of what is mine? Because warfare is based upon deception. They think they can smell weakness. They think they can smell blood in the water. They will be lambs to the slaughter. May I present to you, the latest weapon of the Regime – my Juggernaut.' He gestured downward, and almost as if in response to his command, powerful lights shone down upon the biggest ship I had ever seen.

She was the size of three Man'O'Wars, and clad in what looked like armour, defying everything I knew about 'things that float'. Only a single giant mast poked skyward, flanked by two massive chimneys belching faint trails of steam. With no sails in sight, I guessed it moved like my father's steamboat, which meant the engines it used would have to be monstrous, buried somewhere deep within her hull. Huge cannons, larger than anything I had seen, poked from various points on her decks. Each one seeming to be able to aim without the help of a crew. Speaking of, there appeared to be no crew on her at all. No one was manning a station. No one ran the rigging. This was something different.

'Recently, we began to own the very skies with our airships. Something which our enemy cannot compete with – yet. But the seas, the seas need to be controlled from the water itself. If one man, like you just saw, can be forged into a weapon of the land and take down many men, then our great nation can forge a weapon of the ocean that can withstand and defeat entire fleets. A force of nature that can attack fortresses from beyond the horizon.'

He gestured for everyone to look again. More lights, shining from various airships in the bay, lit up several tall ships surrounding the Governor's Juggernaut. Ships, just like the 'Kraken Krusher'.

Almost immediately they fired broadsides upon the large metal-clad ship. Smoke spewed forth from their cannons as they belched iron balls across the bay. The cacophony echoed upward as copious amounts of smoke from the hundreds of cannons replaced our view.

Moments passed, and the audience strained over the railings to witness the expected carnage below.

It didn't take long for the strong breeze to clear away the mess. As it did though, the giant form of the vessel remained. There were no gaping holes, no toppled masts, no crew jumping for the safety of the drink.

The Governor reached into his lapel and removed a rectangular metal device, with a variety of buttons and its own lights. He looked down and pressed some of them. The massive cannons aboard the Juggernaut began to turn in a variety of directions. Each one lining up on a ship that had just fired upon her. The crews aboard the tall ships, pre-empting what was about to happen began to scramble. Sheet sails dropped and they each began to make as much distance as they could from the monster nearby. Some had managed to make it beyond cannon range, yet the Governor seemed unbothered by this fact.

'Your Excellency, there are men and women from our nation on those ships!' came a pleading protest.

'Some – yes. It was a wager. Those Captains and a few members of crew refused to accept our move into the future. They had their chance, and now they will witness what happens to everyone else who refuses to embrace our ideals, or evolution. As for the other members of crew? Made up of the remaining prisoners of war - for I have closed The Gulag and repurposed the inmates. You see, I'm not unreasonable, this is their chance at freedom. If they succeed, I will order them safe passage from the guns that guard our bay. I will no longer waste money keeping enemies of the state fed and housed within our city. I need every sovereign I can get for our future.'

What? No! That means that dad... No!

'But enough from me...' He turned to soak in the visual spectacle that was about to occur.

'Ladies and Gentleman, may I present to you - the Juggernaut,' his voice was cold as he pressed upon the device.

There was an almighty chorus of blasts as the giant cannons replied to their would-be attackers. A single shot from each metal tube was enough. Every ship exploded in a mix of splinters and flames. Even the ships that had seemingly almost escaped were burning wrecks slowly slipping below the waves.

My hands trembled. Eyes welled with tears. What kind of cruel fate would this be? To make it all this way to rescue my father, only to have just possibly witnessed his death in the carnage below.

I looked at the Governor, as the massive bonfires below illuminated him. His face held a satisfied smirk as he vicariously absorbed the display that he had just orchestrated. He didn't gawk like those around me. A chill ran through me, but whether it was from the prevailing winds up here or his complete disregard for the lives of his own men that he just claimed, I wasn't sure. Embers floated and swirled past him, the final glowing remains of those from below.

An older man with a square jaw spoke up from the crowd. 'Your Excellency, this is an incredible invention indeed, but how have you managed to build this without the approval of the panel of representatives? Surely this cost more than we can afford?'

The Governor's eyes never left the destruction from below, yet in his moment of seeming absence, he spoke, 'The magnificent invention you just saw demonstrate its power - was created within that large building over there. It took almost a year to manufacture and all staff working on it were sworn to secrecy. Now though, with the investments of the fair people gathered here tonight, we will expand our operations and two more should be completed by the end of the coming winter. Loose lips were our only threat. Nothing from outside these walls is a threat to us anymore. The panel will approve once they see her power. As for cost...'

He turned slowly and strode toward the gathered dignitaries.

'Now you have seen what I am capable of. Understand this, the Regime has lined your pockets for long enough. It is now your turn to give back for the betterment of our purpose. Each of you has ridden on the coattails of this nation, through industry, resources and trade. Now those profits which you have taken will be signed over to me this evening before you leave, so that the Regime can continue to build these fine machines of war and extend our reach unquestionably. There will be no more leeching from our lifeblood.'

There were disturbed murmurs through the crowd that quite quickly turned to anger. One of the men, the one that had called out previously, piped up, 'You expect us to simply sign away our life's work. What, so we can become paupers and beggars on the streets? I suppose next you will expect us all to sign up to join the ranks of your soldiers then too? For what? So we can meet the same fate as those poor souls down there? We earned that money fair and square. Regime or no regime,' the man gestured towards his entourage of bodyguards inside. They immediately began to file towards the doors.

The Governor's eyes narrowed. He pressed another button upon the device.

The glass doors to the entertaining room slammed shut.

'Let me make myself perfectly clear, *leech*,' the last word sounded of pure venom.

It began. Muffled screams came from inside the entertaining room. Red streaks of blood sprayed across the glass as the Reaper began to cut through the bodyguards on the other side. Fists banged in desperation, their hardened owners more stricken with fear of the nightmare they were now trapped with. A petrified scream rang out from the woman who had fainted earlier. It didn't take long at all. The Reaper had had his fun. I was reminded of the demonstration with the ship mere moments ago. Just like wrecks slipping away, the last bodyguard's eyes glazed over as he slid down the glass leaving a chunky smear upon the pane.

'Let me remind you, that you can sign over your fortunes and live or, you can die and your funds return to the Regime as default. Personally, I would rather not waste a sovereign on any of your funerals.'

'Are you mad?' came a cry from another member.

The Governor flicked another switch and the glass doors opened once more. The metallic smell of blood was overwhelming, and already the well drilled wait-staff had begun rolling the bodies and various body parts into the large thick carpet and scrubbing the windows with buckets of soapy water.

The Reaper, now covered in the shining red slick of his dissected opponents emerged onto the deck. Steam rose from the warm blood as it met with the cold night air.

The Governor strode past him and gestured toward a small table and chair that were hurriedly being placed upon the deck by more servants from inside. Within moments, a thick ledger book and a quill and pot of ink were placed ready for the gathering to sign upon.

'Now, who would like to be first?' The Governor asked.

CHAPTER THIRTY-TWO

The gathered crowd looked around at one another nervously. An older man with a bushy twirled moustache stepped
forward with a huff and picked up the quill. He was shortly
followed by an elderly woman with a fluffy animal fur draped
around her neck, as a queue began to form. I scanned around
for Arnesto and Xanthe, having lost them both since moving
outside. Looking up and down the lines, I became more and
more frustrated at the crappiness of the current situation. I
was trapped all over again, although, this time, the ship in
question was floating a considerable height above the bay
below.

The Reaper remained standing between the dignitaries and
the railings. His head turned slowly and mechanically, likely
inspecting the people gathered before him. I tried to subtly
jostle in behind a couple to avoid his attention but I felt it was
too late. I sensed his empty eyes on me. Studying me.

Surely, I was being paranoid. The costume I was currently
wearing was one of the best disguises I had ever seen.

I dared a sideways glance.

The hollow slits looked directly at me.

Like a deer staring back at a predator, I became stricken.
My heart thumped inside my chest.

His head tilted sideways.

Locking onto me, The Reaper strode forward and grabbed me by the arm. Hard.

'Hey! Let go of me!' I yelled.

He wrenched me from the line, lifting me from my feet.

'What are you doing? Leave the boy alone!' The Governor ordered calmly, still overseeing the steady stream of signatures before him.

The Reaper ignored his command.

'Did you not hear me? I said, leave the boy alone.'

Still his grip remained firm, causing my arm to ache in his vice-like grasp.

From over the Reaper's shoulder, I saw the Governor stand and begin toward us. A slight spark of anger flickered in his expression at having been ignored.

'I command it.'

But the Reaper didn't listen. His grip tightened. I winced in pain. My bones felt like they were grinding together.

'Ungh,' was all I could manage.

A metallic growl emanated from within the horned helm.

'I know you,' the metallic voice rumbled from within his helm.

'Really? That's nice. Now let me go,' I replied. His grip was unrelenting.

'I know you,' he repeated.

'I said unhand him. There is no need for violence until I say. Do you hear m...' The Governor's last words were cut short as a girl from the queue held the sharp point of the feathered quill against his throat.

'Let him go! Now!' Xanthe's voice found a strength I hadn't heard before.

The wind kicked hard across the deck and the propellers of the airship continued to hum away. With my free hand, I began to feel through my pockets for something useful. But what would a snooty rich kid have in his coat pockets that would possibly help. The pins and needles made the task all but impossible.

The Reaper's head turned to consider what was happening, but his grip never loosened.

'Oh my, this *is* interesting,' mused the Governor. 'So, you two know one another. I see now.'

My free hand squished against the gel filled pastry I had saved for Xanthe. Not the useful item I wanted. I continued my search.

'Order your lapdog to obey, or this quill will soon be tickling the pink mushy stuff in your skull,' Xanthe directed.

'Do you mean my brains?'

'Let's not get too far ahead of ourselves,' she replied.

Despite the discomfort, the Governor seemed unperturbed by the situation. His hands remained frozen in place. He began to chuckle.

Xanthe's eyes grew wild, 'Tell him!' she screeched wildly.

The Governor calmed down. Smiling, he looked at Xanthe through the corner of his eyes.

'No.'

He looked toward the Reaper. As if through silent communication, the Reaper understood his intentions and reached back for his sword.

Xanthe screamed and her body tightened. She prepared to plunge the quill into the Governor's neck. The Reaper turned his attention rearward as his master was threatened.

The Governor remained stoic. With a smirk, he uttered another phrase. It wasn't loud enough for me to hear, but suddenly, Xanthe stopped.

Her eyes glazed over.

Her head lowered, causing her hair to fall over her face.

She dropped the quill like it weighed a hundred pounds.

Still standing, Xanthe's mind seemed to have left her body. A hollow shell, motionless before the stunned crowd and The Governor.

He stepped aside and turned toward her, between his finger and thumb, he lifted her chin and examined her carefully, leaning in as if he were smelling her.

'Welcome home,' he purred.

Taking a moment, he studied her up and down with his eyes – leering.

I felt an unease grow in my stomach. But my concern for her would have to wait if I wanted to find a way out of this situation.

With the Reaper's attention rearward and the Governor's fixated on Xanthe, I seized the opportunity. After already having the experience of thoroughly inspecting his last utility belt and all its pouches, I now had in depth knowledge on where he kept his various 'handy' items. Flicking the target latch gently, I slipped my hand into the pouch he had accessed earlier. With the speed and delicacy of a surgeon, I pilfered two round metal objects that I guessed were the explosives that Xanthe had been so excited about on the cart. As subtly as I could, I slipped it back into my pants. Fighting the pain, I went in for a second 'dip'.

Big mistake.

A hand snapped forward and another strong grip was immediately applied to my wandering light fingers. Within a moment, both of my arms were pulled outward in a crucifix pose. Sharp pain raced through my shoulders.

Gods dammit.

'Reaper, you should be thanking the young man right now, not hurting him. He has delivered one of our family back to us as an act of providence,' The Governor's words were like oily secretions of a kraken on the surface of the ocean.

'You heard your boss. You can ease up on the old grip there,' I added hopefully.

'So, you are the one who has given my troops some trouble over the past few months, hmm? I must apologise for my manners. You seem to know my name, or at the very least my title... and how may I address you?'

'You can call me whatever you like, just consider letting old mate here ease up, yeah?'

The Governor paced deliberately toward us and placed an arm on the Reaper's shoulder.

I was lowered and my feet touched the deck, blood returned to my arms and the pain alleviated somewhat. But the Reaper remained holding me. Again, with the holding? Seriously, like I had anywhere to run to. It was just the same situation, different goon.

'I must say, I have heard some tall tales regarding you. So tall in fact, that I had quite a few of my men executed for spinning such rubbish. Yet here we are. I'm not sure what to expect really, never having given it much thought as I never entertained the idea we would have the pleasure of meeting one another.'

I wasn't sure if the pause that followed was intended for me to say something, but considering I now had two of the most influential figures this side of the globe in front of me, I kind of felt I had to.

'Yeah well, crazy happens hey.'

Wow. Just wow. Seriously, that is all you could put together at a time like this?

He paced slowly back toward Xanthe.

'I don't...' his teeth gritted, '*believe* in that word. So, tell me, why did you come here this evening? Is this some sort of half attempt at an assassination?'

'Pure accident, really. Just happened to be strolling through the city and, well yeah, the rest is...'

'History?'

'Exactly. Crazy.'

He twitched at the word again.

'And you expect me to believe that?! My patience wears thin, boy. The only thing that is keeping you alive right now is my fickle curiosity as to who in the hells you are. Entertain us, without the lies and I will refrain from having my friend here, tear you in half. So, for the last time, who are you?'

He stared intently into my eyes. There was something slightly unhinged in his expression.

'Uh, Governor, is it? Look, you're kinda wasting your time with all the theatrics. This isn't my first 'ship boarding' if ya catch my drift. I've seen it all before.'

'Have you just?'

'Yup.'

'Well, then do tell me more.'

'It's... a long story.'

'It's a long fall.'

'Yeah, I gue-' the last words were trapped inside as the Reaper grabbed me by the throat and drove me backward. One moment, I'm being held firmly off my feet, the next, I'm dangling by my neck, hundreds of feet in the air above a very long fall into the harbour below. I clawed at the forearm of the Reaper, trying to wiggle enough to bring some much-needed air into my lungs. Spots and stars began to form inside my eyes.

A metal door at the rear of the deck squeaked and slammed open loudly.

There was giggling and laughter from inside.

Giggling? Now?

The Reaper's grip loosened as his attention shifted. Air rushed into my lungs. Blood pumped. My senses flickered back to life.

Then came a familiar voice soaked in theatrical flair:

'By the gods, is this how you treat all your guests?'

CHAPTER THIRTY-THREE

The loud, confident voice of Arnesto made the Governor snap his head around.

Stumbling, Arnesto emerged out of the small riveted doorway with the lady from earlier, her hair ruffled and her lipstick smeared.

'- because, I must say it leaves a lot to be desired,' he continued.

'Esmerelda?!' gasped the Governor.

Immediately she paused mid-step, her giggling gone and her face turned from one of enjoyment to guilt. Her eyes were unable to meet those of the Governor.

Arnesto however, failed to miss a beat. 'Oh, where are my manners? Allow me to introduce myself, ladies and gentlemen, standing here before you is none other than –'

'Arnesto Dubois!' spat the Governor. In response to the name, the wait staff from earlier left their tasks of cleaning the entertaining room and began pouring onto the deck, now armed with small handheld crossbows. Each one aimed steadily at Arnesto, thin red streams of light beamed from each weapon and rested steadily on Arnesto's chest, like red stars in the night sky.

Arnesto paused mid-sentence, with a sudden look of mock relief. 'Thank you, finally, someone after all this time remembers who I am.' Having procured another glass of red wine, he took a sip and toasted toward the audience, as though completely unaware of the danger he now faced.

Excited murmurs rustled through the crowd of dignitaries. The Reaper reeled me inward onto the safety of the ship. Relieved, I considered shuffling back into the crowd once more, but before I could, his meaty paws locked onto my arms once more.

'Seriously? Aw come on,' I whined, with a slightly dry crackle in my voice from the earlier choke.

'So, you and this mongrel cur here are working together?' the Governor's veins in his forehead began to bulge. His face reddened, the cool demeanour from earlier, having slipped away at the appearance of my comrade.

Arnesto's attention was currently on the task of kissing Esmerelda's hand and whispering something in her ear, she nervously locked eyes with the Governor and let slip a giggle before stepping nervously into the crowd near the rail, away from his scrutinizing glare.

'Hm? Oh, yes! I would consider that artful young rogue there to be my protégé.'

He sauntered past the ledger that had been laid out for the signatures and casually spilt a solid portion of the red liquid across the pages. 'Oh, how clumsy of me. I'm always destroying things ever so carelessly,' he feigned sincerity, whilst picking up the book in his hand and flicking off the remnants of wine, smearing the signatures beyond recognition in the process.

'*My* things as it would appear.'

'Yes, *your* things would be correct. I do like them. Quite fond of taking some of them for my own pleasure in fact,' he turned back and winked at Esmerelda.

'Well, allow me to return the favour. I find I am no longer interested in this boy now that I know he means something to you. So, observe as I have my friend here dispose of him like the filth he is.'

The Reaper's grip tightened at the threat. I muffled another wince.

'I wouldn't do that if I were you,' Arnesto gestured toward me.

'You *aren't* me.'

'True, I am far better looking, but there is another reason. You see, on a large airborne craft like this one, there are so many places one could hide an explosive. And seeing as this craft floats on air - and I am taking a calculated guess here - it uses trapped gases. Trapped *flammable* gases.'

A forced smile made its way across the Governor's face. His eyes narrowed.

'There is no way you could have smuggled such a large item on board this craft.'

'Ah, it needn't be large. But it is certainly more than enough to create fireworks,' he winked at Esmerelda once more and the crowd. She blushed and looked away. 'And as for the matter of sneaking things aboard? Who am I again?' he gestured toward himself.

'Arnesto Dubois,' The Governor growled, like a reluctant dog begging for his dinner.

'That is right, my friend,' a smile so confident, a bard would blush - smeared across his face. 'Now let's make a deal.'

The Governor's eyes narrowed sceptically. A smirk appeared on his face.

'You mean to tell me, that you would sacrifice yourself and your protégé here just to take me out? You have gone soft, old man.'

'Tis true, I have lost a step. But what better way to give one final performance with a hell of an explosive finale? Or we could both rewrite the script if you would be so kind as to unhand my friend here, I tell you the vague whereabouts of the device and we will be on our way.'

The Governor studied Arnesto's expression carefully. He paused and seemed to be trying to read his thoughts.

'You're bluffing,' he announced finally.

'Maybe, but is that a risk you are willing to take?'

'You'll be killed as soon as you step off of this craft.'

'Perhaps.'

'I'll see to it that you are all skinned alive and fed to the sharks.'

'Mm hmm. So, do we have a deal? Or are we going to stand around flexing our muscles all evening?' he took another sip. It was interrupted by a sudden and explosive series of coughs. Arnesto dropped the glass and covered his mouth. Red wine spilt through his fingers and he clutched hard at his chest. The red beams of light, nervously twitched as the wait staff became jumpy at his sudden movement.

The Governor wasted no time, taking advantage of Arnesto's slip up. 'Reaper!' he cried.

Within a moment, I was dropped to the deck. The Reaper swept forward toward Arnesto with his blade raised, closing the distance in a mere moment.

With speed that belied his condition, Arnesto reacted by stepping forward to meet the Reaper. He moved within the overhead swing of the blade. The muscled figure of the attacker stalled suddenly.

Trembling.

The Reaper fell to his knees. Two small wooden darts protruded from the armpit and neck. I recognised them immediately– the same darts that had made Xanthe sleep when we set off the traps in Arnesto's cave. It seemed he had not come unprepared after all.

Infuriated, the Governor ordered his men to fire. Arnesto too reacted, bringing the large ledger up in front of his chest. Muffled twangs rang out and the thick book became peppered with a dozen or so quarrels.

Now this was a display to behold. A far cry from the clumsy Arnesto I had met back in the tavern, I thought to myself.

One of the Governor's men rushed toward Arnesto, I recognised him as the deliverer of the tasty pastries from earlier. There was a crunching sound as Arnesto slammed the thick book into the bridge of his now flattened nose. The others hesitated, just having seen one man stop both the Reaper and one of their own.

'Flynt!' yelled Arnesto.

Having been somewhat stuck for some time, my mind clicked into gear. I jumped up and pushed past the Governor making my way toward Xanthe.

I shook her hard. 'Xanthe! Snap out of it!' her glazed expression didn't change.

'What did you do to her?!' I yelled at the Governor.

He responded with a satisfied smirk.

'What did you do?!' I repeated, but his eyes left mine as he turned his attention to Arnesto and his current joust with the members of the wait staff who were game enough to try their luck in subduing him.

He snubbed me. He bloody snubbed me. My jaw clenched and my breathing sharpened. I reached for the Reaper's goods I had cached in my pocket earlier. Drawing out the two metallic balls, I quickly inspected them for the right coloured strip. One red and one grey. That'll do. I chose the one with a red strip and pocketed the other.

I held the round device up in front of me. My eyes met with the Governor. He considered me for a moment. I turned the dial without looking away.

His eyes widened.

'Know what this is? Now tell me, what did you do to her? Undo it now! Arnesto may have been bluffing, but I am not.' My veins pulsed hot through my body. If my father had just been killed before my eyes, this would be a fitting revenge.

The timer clicked away in my hand. I was now two paces from the Governor.

'Calm down, boy. You are most certainly out of your league.'

I continued to hold up the explosive between us. It ticked some more.

'Am I?'

The clockwork ticking maintained. Still, I didn't look to see how long it had left.

Sweat beaded upon his forehead. His mouth sneered.

'I've got nothing left to lose, Guv. Is it worth it for you?'

His teeth grit.

'Stop!' yelled the Governor.

The sounds of the fracas behind me ceased.

He continued, talking to me as though he were trying to calm a wild beast, 'I simply used my failsafe on her. It'll wear off shortly. The girl is fine.'

'Remove it.'

'I can't.'

'Do it now.'

'You don't understand. It is a complex science.'

I had heard enough. I had no reason to believe him, but then again, he didn't really have a reason to lie. Too much was at stake. Sooner or later Xanthe would return to normal. But my father. Sensibility crept back into my mind. If I ended us both now, there was a chance the Reaper would revive the

Governor with one of those bloody devices – and what of
Xanthe and Arnesto? How could I help them? They had come
this far for me. Right now, they needed me. Right now, I had
the power to help them. I turned around. Remembering what
Xanthe had said about airships and their propellers, I lined up
a large distant prop in my mental sights. With my best throw,
I launched the small round explosive at it.

'No!' Yelled the Governor.

But the explosive didn't hit the propeller. Well, at least not
the way I had intended. I kinda figured it would strike it and
there would be an explosion and the ship would slowly drift
downward so we could escape. Yeah, nah.

It didn't.

Instead, the small ball-of-boom, bounced off the propeller
and ricocheted upward.

Into the big sack of flammable gases. There was a smaller
bang, followed by a much louder one, as the small grenade
exploded and ignited like a primer firing off the main charge
in a cannon. The airship veered sideways and giant flames
spewed from the side of the airship. All on board the deck
turned and watched with mouths ajar as a lethal lightshow
took shape in front of their very eyes. It appeared that airships
don't necessarily 'blow up' when ignited. The Regime had
apparently engineered some fail safes for just an occasion.
The Governor yelled instructions which were hard to hear
over the roar of the flames. 'Cut away segments eight and ten.
Extinguish the flames on six. Quick or we will all perish!' The
Governor had his mechanical device in his hands once more
and was pressing at various buttons. Water began to spray
forth from metal mouldings both inside the ship and upon the
deck.

Those members of the crew that had been fighting with
Arnesto, now turned to man their stations. Chaos ensued as

the crowd outside all began scrambling up and down the exterior deck, screaming and unsure where to go. Grown men abandoned their partners, others considered jumping over the rails and taking their chances with the sharks in the bay.

Someone grabbed me firmly by the arm. I turned to see Arnesto, blood had run down the side of his face from a large cut on his forehead. 'Flynt, I'm afraid we need to go!'

'Go where? This is a floating prison!'

'Yes, but from what you have told me in the past, I hear you have escaped a floating prison once before. How hard can it be to repeat said feat?'

A large burning portion of the airbags above made a mechanical popping sound as the crew pulled it from its position and tumbled downward. Flames and ash spilled across the deck as it crashed and rolled outward, carrying with it the majority of the inferno that I had inadvertently caused. The release of such a massive section of the ship's floatation caused the deck to groan and tilt outward. Members of the crowd that had been near the rail considering whether to make the jump or not, had their decision made for them, the sudden jolt sending them overboard.

That's when I saw Xanthe. Still unable to move, she was thrown violently to the deck. She began to slide towards the rail. Bumping along the planks as she picked up speed. There was nothing to stop her.

My legs responded before my mind did, I skidded across the deck on my side and grabbed wildly at both her and something to anchor to. Unceremoniously I caught her by the hair. Kicking out, my boot connected with the railing and we slammed to a halt. My heart thudded like a series of cannon blasts within my chest. My eyes wildly looked around for some sanctuary, for some way to get off of this steaming heap. I saw Arnesto, further along the railing and concentrating on his grip. Just beyond him, the broad form of The Reaper lay splayed across the rails. I could almost swear I saw his arms slowly move. Cries rang out as members of the crew and passengers alike fell from the safety of the ship into the darkness. Their grips not holding as firmly as my own. The glow from the fires underneath showed the long drop into the drink below. I doubted whether many could survive the fall, let alone the swim to shore.

I heaved Xanthe upward, making the most of the conditioning training she had forced me to endure over the past few weeks. Pulling her limp form in tight, her head dangled in the swirling winds and embers.

'Xanthe! Snap out of it! Xanthe! Can you hear me?' I shook her hard. There was no response.

'Cut away segments seven and nine! Level this bastard out before she tumbles!' ordered the Governor over the screams of those not lucky enough to hold on.

Two massive bladders of air ejected outward and up from the opposite side of the craft causing the violent and sudden levelling of the airship. I spilled backward onto the deck, still holding Xanthe on top of me. I could feel a lurch in my stomach as the airship began falling steadily, now unable to maintain its former altitude.

'Put out the fire on the bloody deck!' ordered one of the crew.

More cries echoed from the crew, the curtains to the entertaining room were well alight. Smoke billowed forth from various fires now surrounding us.

I turned back to Xanthe and lifted her face toward mine. I studied her blank expression. The flicker of the flames reflected in her open eyes.

Flames.

That was it. It just might work.

I gripped Xanthe's face and angled it toward the fire. An orange glow covered her, the tendrils of light danced before us.

She blinked. Her pupils focused.

'Xanthe, I need you to snap out of it! Look around us, we are surrounded by flames. You know, the big scary hot things you are scared of?! Xanthe!'

She blinked again. Her mouth began to form a shape.

'R-r.'

'What? R-r? What are you trying to say? Are you with me?'

'R... Reap... Reaper...' she managed.

I turned my head in the direction she was facing. From within the flames near the railings, a silhouette began to shakily stand up. His broad back rose upward. He paused and cracked his neck before turning our way, scanning for his prey. The blaze raged and swirled around him. Those empty sockets locked onto us and he began to lumber toward us, one trembling step at a time.

'Oh damn. Why can't he just stay the hells down?!' This time the ship didn't move, but my stomach certainly did. Even in his weakened state, I would still back any money I had on the Reaper besting the likes of Steiger in a one on one fight. 'We need to get out of here. We need to get off this bloody airship, Xanth. Got any ideas?'

'Es- escape gondolas...' she pointed toward one of the outdoor struts. It had a button inside some glass.

'Escape gun dolas? What is that? You mean I need to press that button?'

She nodded.

I looked toward the Reaper before I moved. Not wanting to leave Xanthe, chances are I could get him to follow me instead and buy us some time. I saw Arnesto nearby still jousting with a few members of the crew.

'Arnesto! Stay with Xanthe. There is a way off of this thing!'

He momentarily turned and nodded in understanding before planting a solid uppercut on the final guard. By the time his opponent had hit the deck, Arnesto was over by Xanthe and helping her to her feet.

'My dear, it is nice to finally be able to return the favour...'

Leaving them to it, I sprang forth from my spot beside Xanthe and made my way through the panic toward the button. Dodging members of the crew and dignitaries alike I was almost upon the little glass box.

Almost.

The double-breasted uniform of the Governor side stepped into my path. His shoulder catching me in my sternum and knocking the wind from my lungs. I spilled backward onto the deck in a painful sprawl. My chest wheezed. His gloved hand wrenched me by the hair and pulled me upward. While the Governor was certainly no Reaper, he was still a formidable man and he was fuelled with what I guess was anger at the kid who had almost destroyed his airship by pure chance. He had no trouble whatsoever in rag-dolling me.

'You snot nosed brat...' he spat, winding up for a punch.

Again, it hit me in the same spot on my chest. The cracked rib cage that had only just healed from my brief run in with the Reaper, rattled under the strain.

I spat blood on his boots. Not intentionally mind you. Just because.

'Who even are you?'

I reached into my pocket one last time. I felt the smooth metal surface of the other grenade I had pocketed from the Reaper before.

A big bloodied smile formed across my face.

'That's just it, Guv. I'm nobody,' I spluttered.

I turned the grenade barely and slipped it inside the lapel of his buttoned jacket.

'Could ya hold this? I don't know if it's one that goes bang or not.'

His reaction was immediate and panicked. I was dropped to the floor once more as he wrestled at the gold buttons trying to free the orb. There was a loud pop, and a hissing sound. Thick smoke poured furiously from every opening of his attire and blanketing the deck. Adrenaline allowed me to briefly ignore the pain in my chest. I scrambled on my hands and knees in the direction I had last seen the button on the wall. My head struck a timber strut and through the smoke, I felt my way upward to the glass box. I punched it hard, the glass cracking easily.

The sound of mechanical cogs turning began. I heard a series of shots, not unlike those of cannons firing. Using the glow of the fire through the smoke, I stayed low and like a rat making its way through a busy galley of sailors, I found my way back toward Xanthe and Arnesto.

A member of the crowd cried out. 'Quick, everyone aboard those things. We can get off this cursed craft.'

The smoke thinned and I could make out the shapes of the people bustling about towards the railings. The source of the noise from before revealed itself. Three metal ropes, as thick as a man's leg had fired from the ship's anchors. Small craft, like metal boats, had detached from beneath the deck and using a pulley system were dangling from each cable precariously over the long drop into the waters below. People had wasted no time, and already the 'gondolas' as Xanthe had called them, were looking rather full of the desperate and scared. They screamed at one another and arguments had erupted as one of the craft had already filled to capacity and could no longer take any more bodies.

I searched desperately for any sign of Xanthe or Arnesto. My eyes darted across the features of each face within the floating cages.

No more than a few fathoms away, someone else was doing the same.

The Reaper stood looking into each craft. Unsatisfied with his hunt, he reached into his pouch. He removed another grenade and without the slightest hint of emotion he turned it sharply and tossed it into the gondola before him. There was a mixture of screams and confusion before a deafening blast erupted into flame, the flash causing me to shield my eyes. Metal groaned and squealed. I looked back to see burning bodies, still writhing, spill over the edges into the darkness. The gondola itself was a flaming basket that looked as though it had been kicked to the bazaar and back. With one final squeal of shearing steel, the mangled wreck broke from the metal rope and plummeted downward. The Reaper having seemingly recovered from the effects of the poison, paced to the front of the next gondola.

He reached into another pouch. Again, he removed a smooth metal bauble of destruction.

I looked into the horrified faces, as the people aboard that craft realised their fate. This time, one of the women reached forward and pulled a lever inside. The gondola lurched and began to drift at speed away from the airship. The crowd inside began to cheer and hug in celebration at having escaped the Reaper's intentions.

However, the Reaper was unbothered by the escape, continuing with his task. He twisted the clockwork parts and wound up for a throw. With an explosive movement, he launched the copper coloured ball with a force similar to what I had seen from a small ship's swivel gun. There was a distant metallic clunk, a brief scream of despair and finally another explosion.

My heart thumped hard and fast within my busted chest. Had he just killed off my friends?

The Reaper made his way to the final gondola. Two members within the craft wrestled at the lever. I saw at once, it was Arnesto and a larger gentleman. Arnesto was trying to stop him from pulling the lever, likely trying to buy me some more time.

The Reaper stopped before the craft.

Arnesto noticed me standing on the deck. He head-butted the larger man, letting him fall down clutching his nose and motioned wildly for me to join them.

The Reaper reached into his pouch.

They wouldn't make it. There was no way, after the ease at which the Reaper had dispatched the last two craft.

I had to do something.

I too reached into my pocket and was met with the squishy sugar dusted pastry from my exploration at the buffet from earlier. It was stupid. It was immature. It was all I had.

As the Reaper moved his hand over the clockwork explosive, I pegged the jam filled delight. It popped against his helm with a squelch and a puff of dusted sugar.

He stopped. His fingers inspected the smear, like he was checking for an incontinent pelican in the sky above. Turning he faced me.

Oh damn, it worked.

He began to move toward me at speed.

Now usually, I wouldn't consider myself a fast person, but this current moment in time, death itself was at my heels. I moved with a speed I hadn't before felt. However, the large man that Arnesto had recently given a 'Carvian Kiss' to, had regained enough composure and pulled the lever. The gondola dipped and began to slide from its dock beside the rail, moving down the metal ropes.

The gap grew.

I leapt at the railing and used the metal bar for one last ditch vault at the ever-distancing craft. The void passed below me.

My sternum connected with the edge of the metal flooring first. The air expelled painfully from my guts. My hands slapped hard onto the cold metal floor briefly and began to slip. I flailed, body slipping backward. Hands grabbed me, and for the umpteenth time this evening, I was pulled to my feet. The faces of Arnesto and Xanthe met mine.

'Thanks...' I managed, 'for a second there, I didn't think I was going to make it.'

Xanthe stared into my face briefly, for the first time since we met, I saw tears in her eyes. She wrapped her arms around me tightly.

'That was a fine escape, young man. One for the history books I believe,' Arnesto pat me enthusiastically on my back.

The sudden joviality reminded me of the fate of the last gondola.

'The Reaper...' I began. I turned to look back up at the flaming deck of the shrinking airship. Smoke and Flames danced around the shadowy form of the Reaper as he wound up for another delivery of explosives.

'Xanthe...' I began, but I needn't bother.

Xanthe pushed past me and faced the Reaper, her hair whipping in the strong winds. Something was different about her.

The distant form of the Reaper moved sharply. I could barely see the incoming projectile, but I saw Xanthe. With reflexes like a steel trap, there was a loud slapping sound as she caught the clockwork device and proceeded to throw it back in one smooth movement. There was a glint. The Reaper swatted at the bomb. It deflected downward. There was a fiery eruption just below the airship, the detonator finally igniting the chemical mixture inside.

Xanthe panted in the doorway of the gondola, holding onto the open doorway. Her eyes refusing to leave the Reaper, as though daring him to try again.

'Well,' chimed in Arnesto. 'We may have escaped the airship, but we are far from having escaped. There is still work to do I am afraid.'

'Arnesto, it's over. The Gulag, the prisoners, the-'disappointment crept heavily into my words causing me to trail off.

'Ah, I believe that is where you are wrong,' he said reaching inside his lapel and removing what looked like a very thin book with papers protruding from inside. 'I went for a little self-guided tour of the Govenor's airship while everyone was busy watching his display. I stumbled across this dossier inside his study with your father's name upon it. Would you believe he had it just carelessly lying around ... in a locked safe... behind a painting... in a guarded room? Much of the important information has been redacted, but one thing is certain – he was moved from The Gulag to an experimental facility within the Capital some months ago.'

'You mean?'

'Yes, young Flynt. Your father is still very much alive. And *we will* find him,' Arnesto smiled.

I couldn't help myself. My spirits lifted - I lunged forward and embraced the surprised pair of Arnesto and Xanthe. The feeling was reciprocated – Xanthe's affectionate hug being exceptionally bone cracking.

'Thank you, both of you,' I said.

Arnesto nodded. Xanthe smiled.

It was then that I became very aware of the other passengers sharing our gondola.

'Ahh...' I cleared my throat.

Arnesto seemed to weigh up our situation momentarily. He turned to the remaining passengers within the craft.

'Ladies and Gentlemen, I am sure that tonight's events have left you feeling quite worn down. Despite the fact that we have once been enemies with one another, may I take a moment to point out that we now have a common foe, and I humbly request that you turn a blind eye to our escape?' Arnesto was loud and confident as we approached the outlines of some buildings near the shore. The lights within showed silhouettes of onlookers gawking at the spectacle in the bay and the sky above it.

Eyes of the various remaining dignitaries and their partners looked at one another. No words were exchanged. An older lady wearing a fox fur around her shoulders, steadily turned her back to us, then her monocle wearing husband did the same. Slowly, one by one, they all turned their backs to us.

Needing no further encouragement and Arnesto taking the lead, we leapt from the gondola before it came to a halt.

With a splash, we entered the cold waters of the harbour and began our swim into darkness.

CHAPTER THIRTY-FOUR

'And that my friend, is the story of how your father and I sabotaged an entire legion of mechanical golems and foiled the Governor's plans of attacking the eastern settlements,' Arnesto smiled charmingly before swigging the last remaining contents inside his glass.

Xanthe and I sat cross legged before him in the 'gentlemen's lounge' (as he referred to it) back in his cavern hideout. Xanthe leant forward, wide eyed and mouth ajar, hanging off Arnesto's words. My attention though - wandered. I stared upon the damp sheets of my father's dossier as they hung to dry on a makeshift clothesline near the serpent oil fireplace. Thick black lines blotted out most of the information, but Arnesto assured me it would still prove valuable. I needed to be patient. If I was to try and read it now, the paper would smear and tear from our time in the waters of the bay. Relieved that my father hadn't been on ships decimated by The Juggernaut, I now wondered if the paperwork would reveal the location of the 'Experimental Facility' Arnesto had referred to upon the gondola.

I was aware that The Governor's *eyes* on the streets would be on alert for our presence. For now we would need to bide our time until things 'cooled off' as Xanthe had called it. My body did ache from the excitement of the night and I could use the rest.

But my mind was restless.

Finding my father was important to me but something else also niggled at my conscience – the Juggernaut. If that massive warship were to ever set sail to the Allied Nations, they wouldn't stand a chance. Every ship, every coastal township, like my old home – would be obliterated. My mind flashed images of the Governor's demonstration. The burning ships. The screams.

A slap across my shoulder, snapped me out of my musings. 'See kid, didn't I tell ya he had some great stories! And your old man, jeez he really stuck it to the bloody Guv now, didn't he?'

She was right. My mind was still coming to grips with the stories Arnesto had told me over the last few weeks since he had somewhat recovered from his injuries. I found them both informing and inspiring to say the least.

Arnesto interrupted politely, 'As I have said previously, your father found me and turned me from a decent thief, to one of the most famous enemies of the Regime. Thanks to him, I was '*The Thorn*' of the Regime.

Xanthe mouthed every word of his last sentence. She loved hearing each story, almost more than I did.

'Yeah, the way you two cut out the brake cable before blowing the train tracks was a stroke of genius, sir. Absolute,' Xanthe said staring into the alchemical hearth, its glow radiating across her face.

I noticed a look of concern on Arnesto's face at her comment. His eyes narrowed slightly, and he leant forward to study Xanthe carefully.

'Yes, the brake cable. What did I say we used to cut it again?'

'Oh, you used a shaped charge to blast through it,' she added helpfully.

His moustache twitched at the comment.

Arnesto's attention rested solely on Xanthe as she rocked back and forth hugging her knees before the hearth. I was the only one who noticed this change.

'Everything alright, Arnesto?' I asked.

'Oh, me? Ah, yes. Yes indeed. Say young Flynt, would you mind joining me in the Galley for a moment? There are one or two things I would like to ah... discuss with you, if you don't mind, Xanthe?'

'Hmm? Go ahead, sir.'

Arnesto swirled the remaining dregs inside his drinking glass before taking a final sip. He had been drinking quite a lot since recovering from his injury. He insisted it helped with the pain and sleeping. I could hardly blame him. Only recently had we stopped needing to change his dressings regularly as the wound had begun to scar over.

Standing up he winced in pain and clutched at his chest quickly before trying to hide his discomfort. Now wearing robes of fine silk and wool, he turned and steadily walked from the room, pausing momentarily to see if I was following. And perhaps, that I wasn't being followed by the impulsive Xanthe.

When we entered the Galley he turned once more, looking past my shoulder.

'Are you okay, Arnesto? You seem a bit distracted.'

'Flynt, tell me. How did you and Xanthe meet?'

The question caught me off guard. I hadn't seen Arnesto so stony faced before.

'I told you this before. She pulled me ashore while she was on the run from The Reaper and his troops.'

'Yes... yes I suppose she did.'

He stared at the floor, stroking his new goatee, care of weeks of sleeping recovery.

'Arnesto, what is this about?'

He pulled his attention to me. His eyes looking firmly into mine.

'Flynt, do you trust Xanthe?'

It didn't need a second thought. 'Of course. I trust her with my life.'

He stared intently at my expression and response. Slowly he began to nod.

'Has she told you anything about her past? Did she work for the Regime?'

'She has told me everything. I know she used to work as a soldier.'

Well almost, I thought.

'Flynt, I don't know why I hadn't picked up on this earlier. Perhaps it was the fatigue of recovery, but I know her.'

'What do you mean by that?'

'I mean, *I know her*. She wasn't just some grunt of a foot soldier for the Governor, Flynt. She was his key agent. His assassin *before* the Reaper. That girl in there was tasked with hunting down me and my gang years ago. She managed to assassinate every member, bar yours truly. Thanks to her, I fell into one of Mortlock's traps. It was a case of 'be captured and have a chance to escape' or cross blades with *her*,' he motioned toward the doorway. 'I only saw her once, half a decade ago. She hasn't aged at all, but it is definitely her.'

My head spun from the accusation. Sure enough, Xanthe didn't look like your average girl, she didn't act like anyone I had ever met. Xanthe Bones was clearly extraordinary, but she was perhaps my only friend, Arnesto aside.

'How do you know it was her?'

'She knew about the charges your father and I used on the train. I didn't mention that in the story. The only people who knew about the explosives on the brake cable were your father and I,' he spoke softly as though worried the walls would hear him.

'She was responsible for removing threats to the Regime, and she was very good at her job. Chances are, your father was on her list at some stage or another.'

I looked at him carefully, unable to respond. The smell of alcohol on his breath and the slight slur in his speech made me second guess his statement.

'If that were all true Arnesto, consider this. Xanthe saved me. Xanthe has helped me survive, avoid capture and has even trained me for these last few weeks. She is clearly helping me and without her, I'd likely be captured or dead.'

He looked at me intently. He considered my words.

'You don't think that if she wanted you dead still, if that's what she ever wanted, that you wouldn't already *be* dead? She changed your dressings, she saved you from drowning in your own blood. Don't come to me with this crap. The Regime changes people. I have seen hawks with clockwork parts implanted in their brains, forcing them to act against their own free will. What if that was something they could do to her? To me? To you?'

Arnesto looked downward. He nodded slightly.

'You have said yourself that the Governor has been investing heavily in new technology for his military. Heck, only months ago I was aboard a tall ship sailing the seas. Now he has airships! Air ships that fly in the bloody sky and shoot cannons. You just finished telling me a story about legions of mechanical gols... gaols... dammit.'

'Golems,' Xanthe insisted.

'Thank you, Golems... you just finished telling me a story about ... Xanthe?' her interruption had taken me by surprise. More than ever, in these last few weeks, I bared witness to just how quiet she could move about when she wanted to. A skill that she had been trying to teach me for our upcoming mission.

Arnesto and I both looked at the hurt expression on her face. She stepped forward into the room between us. Arnesto stared at her and I noticed his hand wave past the small filleting knife we had used when cooking earlier. I looked again and the knife was gone.

'Look, before you go jumping to conclusions, I guess this is as good a time as any.'

'For what?'

'To explain myself, Flynt. Jeez, I thought that much was obvious.'

'Xanthe, you don't have to explain anything.'

'Shut up, Flynt,' she had tears in her eyes. 'Just shut up and let me speak.'

She was trembling, just like the night we were surrounded by flames.

'You're right, Arnesto. About everything. I was *his* assassin. But I never did anything by choice. For years that old coot forced me to do things. Horrible things. Unforgivable things,' she looked at me, a tear trailed down her cheek.

'I never had a choice. He took me when I was a child. There was this fire in our district and it spread to our home. I woke up and I couldn't find my family. Everything was crashing in around me. It was so hot. It burned and burned. Everywhere I looked, there was smoke and flames. I screamed out for my mother and father but there was no one. A wall fell inward and trapped me, burning me. He pulled me out. The Governor. He said he saved me. He picked me up. I remember the pain, the burns. When I woke up, I was attached to a whole buncha tubes and contraptions. They held my eyes open and made me see things that I didn't want to see. I got strong. Real strong. And my burns healed quickly. They poked and prodded me, taking blood, making me sick, hurting me, all to see how I would react. After that, I was kept in a cell. He would visit me and watch me. Call me his little girl, his *left* hand. But he would say things, weird things and my mind would lose control of my body. I couldn't stop it. It was as if someone was flying me along like an airship. I was a prisoner in my own mind. I did horrible things. I couldn't stop, but I could always remember. Whenever I returned to my cell, they strapped me down and injected me again and again until I went to sleep. But I never slept. I always saw the things I did over and over. The faces of the people that I hurt. The Governor would always talk about me being his favourite. I was the one who was sent to kill those on his special list. The bloody list. He never shut up about it. For twenty years, I hunted his enemies. Each one of your team Arnesto, I remember them. I saw them die by my own hands and I didn't stop it. I couldn't stop it.'

'Twenty years? Xanthe, that's impossible,' I said.

'With that monster, anything is possible. With his influence and reach, he can do anything. Harm anyone. I haven't aged a day in twenty years. If I get cut, I barely bleed and I heal fast. The Reaper is the same, only better, stronger and faster.'

I struggled to absorb everything she was saying. It seemed so farfetched and yet, it all made sense. I looked briefly at Arnesto, his face remained fixed in an icy stare at Xanthe.

'That is why I'm so sorry. Your father was on my list. On *his* list. I'm sorry, Flynt.'

'You don't need to be sorry. You didn't capture him, Xanthe.'

She paused and looked at me desperately. She nodded unable to get her words out.

'I.... was there. When you and your father were out fishing. I was the one that led the raid on your village. I'm the reason... I'm the reason your mother and sister...' she trailed off.

I couldn't move. I stared at her in disbelief. Realisation was making my stomach twist.

'What? But how?'

'We received intel that your father was there. My mission was to eliminate him and anyone he had connections with. That included your family, your village and even you. But when we arrived, he was nowhere to be seen. So we continued with the secondary objective. We wiped out your village. I didn't realise the connection until you told me your village name aboard the airship. I'm sorry. I'm so so sorry.'

A thousand feelings came flooding in. Logic and emotion fought within me and I felt as though the walls of the cave were collapsing all around me. Dazed, I stumbled past Xanthe and made my way to the door.

'Flynt?' Xanthe asked softly behind me.

I paused.

'I need some air,' was all I could manage to say before running from the room.

CHAPTER THIRTY-FIVE

It's strange how the mind reacts when faced with a crushing reality. Some people get angry and want to fight those around them. Some get sad and hide themselves away. Me? Well, I turn numb and occupy myself with boring tasks, almost in an effort to appear unbothered, or to try and forget as quickly as I can.

After leaving the cave, I had run and scrambled over the rocks around the point until the path ended at a ledge over-hanging the ocean. Sitting down, I felt a slight comfort in the sunshine outside, as I perched upon a ledge looking out over the sea. The fresh air and the waves lapping against the rocks in the water, helped me to forget – well kind of. Images kept creeping into my mind. Disturbing flashes of Xanthe, leading groups of Regime Raiders ashore in my village.

Stop it.

Xanthe bee-lining for my family's home.

My stomach began to twist.

Stop.

Xanthe kicking in the door and dragging out my mother and crying little sister.

I tried hard to push the images from my mind. I looked out beyond the crashing waves to the deeper waters. In the distance, a massive splash erupted as a serpent breached from the depths.

'Ah, the sea beasts are migrating north again,' came the soft voice of Arnesto somewhere behind me.

I kept watching the distant performance in silence.

'Do you mind if I join you, Flynt?' Arnesto asked politely.

I didn't feel like responding, but I felt as though the questions were merely a formality. I picked away at the untarnished cogs of the bracer on my wrist.

Another Serpent erupted sideways from the water and landed with a massive splash. The dorsal fins of several others emerged and sailed along the surface before returning below the waterline again. The same signs the crew of the 'Kraken Krusher' had always looked for.

I distracted myself with the thought. If they had still existed, we would be following the migration patterns northward through these same waters, trying to pick stragglers that had grown too tired from their journey. We had to time it perfectly. The kraken herds trailed a day or so behind, following their prey north. If they ever caught us, we wouldn't stand a chance.

The Captain would have had extra sailors in the rigging and kept a constant lookout.

Good riddance to him, I thought.

I felt a deeper hatred for the Regime now than I ever had before.

'Flynt, I know how you must be feeling.'

The comment made me tense. Arnesto paused a moment considering me and offered me a sip from a freshly opened bottle of whiskey.

Without a response from me, he accepted his own offer, taking a swig and dangling his feet over the ledge beside me.

'But if I have learnt anything over the years, it is that people deserve a second chance. You were right, I do know what the

Regime is like, how it finds ways to manipulate and control. If what she says is true, that she was forced against her will, then there isn't much she could do to stop them. Your father and I – '

'Will you shut up?!'

His mouth clamped shut at my sudden outburst.

'What could you possibly know about how I feel, or what I am going through? I might be a kid, but I've suffered enough crap to know what the Regime is bloody capable of. Don't come out here and try to 'enlighten' me with your tales or experiences or how you had an adventure with my father that reminds you of this messed up situation. You lost your friends to her? Brilliant. They knew what they were doing and what risks there were when they started. You could say that they deserved it.'

His lip pursed at my comment. I could see the words hurting him. I wanted them to hurt some more.

'My mother had nothing to do with them. She was innocent. Elaina, she was only five years old. She was just a kid! I saw them when we returned. Dad holding them both. He was never the same after that. He left me. He left me locked up and never came for me. I was their bait on that ship. They used me like a worm on a hook to catch monsters like those,' I pointed at the distant breaching giants. 'And you're telling me you know how I feel?! Sod off. I'm sure I can hear another crate of whiskey calling your name.'

The crashing waves below echoed around us. I picked up pebbles and began flicking them, watching them bounce from boulder to boulder before plummeting into the swirling waters below.

Arnesto waited until I was done.

'You're right, Flynt. You have had to deal with a lot. More than most. You have every right to be angry. Forgive me. I never knew my family, I never had anyone to love. One thing has had the opportunity to best me, and that is time. Years have passed, where I had been too busy to find real love, to settle down. I had been too involved in my own ambitions. But these last few weeks have made me realise what I have missed out on. Life's true treasure; *a family*. I regret not having had someone to teach, to care for. I know it may not seem like much, but you have given me that opportunity.' He placed his hand gently upon my shoulder.

'I know I'm not your father, but what I do know is this; if I had a son like you, I would be a very proud man.'

I heard every word, but I didn't respond. I felt him slowly leave me be.

Within moments, I was alone again with my thoughts and the view.

My anger had somewhat subsided, and it began to be re-placed with pangs of guilt for my comments. I tried to bottle it up again, but my feelings had a different agenda. I removed a match from the packet I now kept inside the smelly confines of the bracer and placed it between my teeth, chewing at the wood in frustration. I felt the folds of my pants for the locket. Pulling it out, I turned the tarnished trinket over in my hands. The locket did nothing but remind me of a painful past. It burdened my mind every time I thought of it, showing me images of a family I will never be able to have again. My hand loosened its grip on the chain. I looked to the swirling waters below. If I just let it go, I could move on. Those memories could return to the sea. I raised my hand and prepared to toss the locket and my worries away. Lost to the tides.

A cry carried through the rocks from the direction of the cave.

I was snatched from my self-pity and my body reacted without even thinking. I strung the chain around my neck.

Scrambling across the gravel, I snaked through the cover of the boulders back around the point toward the cave entrance. Another cry, clearer than before.

It was Xanthe, and she was in trouble. Again.

CHAPTER THIRTY-SIX

I was learning every day. My latest lesson; 'Airships are bloody quiet'. They *putt* along like fat sharks and by the time you hear them, they are already on you, circling - hungry. In this instance, when you consider the loud sounds of waves crashing below, they can sneak up quickly and ruin your day.

Consider this day ruined.

I had leapt from my 'brooding' ledge and rounded the corner of the winding cliffs as fast as I could. Xanthe's training stopped me however, and I slowed myself enough to move through the concealment of the boulders below me. Snaking through the gaps, I found a cramped nook to conceal myself and observe the commotion ahead.

Sixty fathoms before me, three large airships had anchored themselves to the cliff face with their cables. Ropes dangled down from their bellies, Regime soldiers slid from the crafts and positioned themselves around a figure draped in heavy rope nets.

Xanthe.

My eye caught a familiar shape perched from the wing of the larger airship.

'No – way,' slipped from my lips as I almost lost my matchstick.

With his red horned helm and the blades criss-crossing his back, the Reaper leapt from the strut. Falling the considerable distance, he landed gracefully in a crouch, before standing up, his blades in his hands. The soldiers surrounding the nets stepped backward at the Reaper's gesture. The nets on the ground writhed and stood up as Xanthe found her feet. The Reaper moved forward, in an explosive twist of his torso, he struck the upright mass with the hilt of his sword. The 'crack' of metal on bone echoed through the rocky landscape. I winced at the sound. The figure of Xanthe, was thrown backward into a heap and lay motionless.

'Cheap shot and certainly no way to treat a lady,' muttered a voice behind me.

Startled I turned with my fists raised, only to meet the familiar face of Arnesto. His eyes looked past me to the spectacle ahead.

'Well, this is certainly not ideal,' he whispered mostly to himself. 'Lesson time, Flynt. I know what you are thinking right now. You want to run out there and save the girl. Don't. You've come too far. Push those emotions aside and focus. What can you see?'

I followed his orders and scanned the scene. Something in his voice was different. A sense of seriousness and command that I hadn't witnessed in Arnesto before.

'Five airships. Three anchored with one reeling in to dock and one patrolling the coastline.'

'Why?'

'It's looking for us.'

'What else?'

'Soldiers. Lots.'

'Flynt...' he said.

'I'm counting...' I rolled the matchstick into a new position for better chewing. 'Most likely three platoons. A mixture of elite infantry and aircrew, all being led by The Reaper. There are teams stacked near the cave entrance and small groups patrolling the cliffs slowly. There is one aircrew from each airship providing cover from above on swivel guns.'

'Well, it seems the Governor is taking notice of us. He must feel threatened,' he smiled. 'Elite infantry, you say? Those masked ones I take it?'

I nodded and continued to scan.

'Most of the soldiers, sorry, about five squads are preparing to enter the cave. Each one is armed with new weapons. They seem to be the same as the pneumatic crossbow Xanthe and I used when we found you... only black.'

'Hmmm, newly issued weapons too? We ARE a threat.'

He sounded almost pleased at our predicament. Arnesto began rummaging through his robes. I went to look back, but he motioned for me to keep looking ahead.

'What are you doing?'

'I ask the questions here. What's happening now?'

'Their teams are going in.'

'Well good luck to them, there are still some surprises in there for this occasion.' He began to count quietly to himself, nodding slightly to each number. 'I reckon the first group should be getting to the door about...' He continued the nods...

'Now.'

There was a rumble from within the cavern followed shortly by a plume of dust and smoke erupting violently from the entrance. Within moments a handful of soldiers stumbled out, now covered in dust and blood.

'What was that?'

'Just a little something I put in place. Pressure plates on the floor outside the main door. Set for the weight of more than four fully armed soldiers either side. The floor gives way an inch, which sets off the main charge and the barrels of whiskey and gun powder near the entrance ignite. That's your next lesson. If you're going to go out, Flynt, go out with all guns blazing.'

The last comment struck a chord with me. Was this it? Were we about to 'go out' as he had put it? I was so close to busting out my father and after all we had been through, only to be stopped before we could hatch a proper plan.

I watched as the Reaper ordered another five squads to go into the cave. Some men looked shaken and were hesitating to follow orders, their squad leader obviously relaying their concerns to the Reaper. With a quick swing of his blade, the squad leader was relieved of his worries and his head for that matter. No more discussion was necessary and the soldiers poured into the cave like prey running from a predator.

The numbers of soldiers outside were thinned substantially from earlier. Now only a few remained scattered around the cliffs, their attention drawn to the spectacle at the cave instead of their patrolling and security positions. This was the opening I needed to save her. Momentarily, I had forgotten about the confession, about Xanthe's past and what she had done. My instincts now told me that my friend, the one who had saved me time and again over the short period that I had known her, needed me now.

'Arnesto, I need to save Xanthe. I know you said to wait, but they are distracted. If I go now, I can slip in closer and...'

There was no response.

'Arnesto?'

I began to turn, but was met with cold metal pressing at the nape of my neck.

'Gotcha, you little bastard. Lay down and don't move.'

I now knew why Arnesto didn't reply. I searched frantically through my peripheral to see if he was there. *How could I be so stupid?* I thought to myself. *I was so close.*

'I said get down. Move that head of yours and I'll punch a bolt through it,' the owner of the voice pressed the weapon harder in the back of my skull to emphasize his point. The tip of a loaded bolt scratched at my skin.

'Raise your hands... slowly.'

My arms lifted reluctantly. I tried to remember the lessons Xanthe had covered for this very situation.

'Private, secure the little turd. Private? Priva-'

I could feel his attention waver through the weapon as he searched for his comrade.

Distraction.

My momentary shock was replaced with anger and frustration. Xanthe's training kicked in. I rolled quickly to the side. Enough to be out of his aim. I turned, grabbed the front of the weapon that had been pointed at me and kept it aimed away. At the same time, I struck with all the strength I could muster at the attacker's throat.

Instead, my punch hit Arnesto's arm. It was firmly wrapped around the soldier's neck. I watched Arnesto's calm exterior as the soldier's eyes rolled into his head. I was left holding the pneumatic black crossbow as the soldier's grip softened and let go. Arnesto held him firm a few seconds longer before laying him down between the rocks. Behind Arnesto, I could see the slumped form of another soldier. My attacker's comrade no doubt.

Arnesto noticed me staring and flicked his fingers in my face. 'Flynt, if you wouldn't mind, these old eyes aren't quite as sharp as they used to be. Would you continue to tell me what is going on ahead of us? What are they doing with Xanthe?'

I followed his directions and returned to observing the goings-on ahead of us. Arnesto made himself busy. I could hear him struggling behind me.

'Flynt, you were saying before?'

'Eh?'

'Before you were rudely interrupted by our friends here. I thought I heard you say something.'

I was reminded of my intentions.

'I said, I need to save Xanthe.'

The gravel shifted as Arnesto lay back beside me in position amongst the boulders.

'Ah, I was waiting to hear you say that young Flynt, you can see that you need to overcome the past in order to save your future. This is good. But first, let me correct you on your statement.'

'Correct me?'

'*I* will save her. You will wait for my signal,' he said as he leant forward giving my cheek a playful double pat.

'What? No, Arnesto. I –'

'You have done enough, young Flynt. Sit back and watch. I have a plan. If it goes bad, then at least you have a chance to get away and fulfil your goal. If it doesn't, we can escape and count our losses at a later time.'

'What is your plan?'

He grinned. He was no longer wearing the comfortable garments of a healing individual, instead he was now wearing the uniform of the soldier he had just throttled.

'Arnesto, are you crazy?'

'Always. Flynt, I need to do this alone. You are too short and... slim to be mistaken for one of them. You need to *trust* me. Besides, if you are half as good as our young lady friend was with one of those,' he gestured to the crossbow I was still holding from the soldier, '... then I'd feel much safer having you covering me from here.'

I briefly studied the crossbow. It was all black and brushed metal. Not flamboyant like the one we had swindled from Balgowan. It was also lighter in the hand and it had a small version of a Captain's looking glass mounted on top. I lifted it and peered through the tube. Immediately, everything appeared closer. I could see the eyes of the soldiers in the distance. The twitches of their limbs and the folds in their uniforms. Two lines criss-crossed in the middle of view, something which I imagined had to do with aiming the thing. No matter how brilliant this piece of equipment was, it didn't feel right letting Arnesto go it alone. I turned to protest his choice, to say sorry for my earlier comments, but I was gesturing to empty space. Arnesto was gone.

Quickly I began to look for him.

My eyes ran over the scene in front. I scanned back and forth for anything out of the ordinary. The sun was beating down upon the chalky cliffs and a breeze kicked out clouds of dust revealing the locations of several pockets of soldiers. With their uniforms and masks, the task of locating Arnesto became rather difficult. Something caught my eye. One soldier was moving along the trails lining the Cliffside, past the other patrols. From what I had been taught of Regime tactics, this was their 'cordon' – a sort of outer security area where they can catch anyone trying to escape. They weren't however, trying to stop their own coming in. Arnesto exploited this and moved confidently past the groups of soldiers tasked with providing this security role. It appeared that it was made even easier due to their distraction from the commotion down at the cave. To them, he was just another one of their soldiers, doing, you know, soldierly things.

Well, at least I *think* it was him.

I used the looking glass atop the crossbow for a closer look.

I watched as he moved closer and closer. Before long, he had casually manoeuvred himself mere fathoms from Xanthe's still unconscious and wrapped form. He removed shackles from inside a pouch on the soldier's vest and moved to the pile of heavy nets encasing Xanthe. I guessed they were the restraints meant for me from the missing private from earlier. Arnesto began to remove a few nets and withdrew one of Xanthe's limbs.

The Reaper turned and faced Arnesto, his blades still drawn from before.

Arnesto continued to work, with his back to the Reaper. He confidently clicked on the shackles and retrieved another limb.

The Reaper carefully paced closer behind him.

Inspecting his work.

My heart's pumping became stronger. I had been so invested in the scene that I had forgotten to swallow. Dried out, it was an effort to do so.

The Reaper rested a blade on Arnesto's shoulder. He stopped what he was doing. Turned. He stood up facing the threat who was a good foot taller. At this distance it was impossible to determine what they were saying, but I could sense suspicion from The Reaper. Arnesto was almost standing to attention before him. The emotionless visage of The Reaper said nothing, but he lowered his blade from Arnesto's neck. He turned. He left Arnesto standing beside Xanthe.

I almost couldn't believe it. It worked.

'How good was he?! Arnesto, you absolute legend!' I thought to myself.

Arnesto returned to his task of 'restraining the prisoner'. Within moments he stood up and held her over his shoulder like a sack of potatoes and began to walk toward the airship which had now docked and laid out its gangplank. It was then I noticed him wince, even despite the mask. He clutched briefly at his chest and coughed a noticeable spray of red. His slowly-healing wounds having gone beyond their tether, a slight splatter of blood trickled from the mouth of the mask.

The Reaper lifted his head.

'Arnesto Dubois!' came the loud metallic voice. It boomed over the noise of the waves.

'Lay the girl down and surrender yourself,' he continued.

Arnesto paused. He slowly lowered Xanthe's still unconscious form to the ground and placed her gently in front of him. He reached up and removed the soldier's mask from his face. Sweat having matted his silver hair down, he breathed in as though it were a relief to be free from it. In response, soldiers that were positioned around the cliffs turned their attention and weapons in his direction. There was an echo of clicks as their weapons were readied.

No, no, no, no. This wasn't good. Surely this wasn't part of his plan. I began to feel too far away, too useless to help. I searched desperately for a new position that I could provide fire support from. I noticed a route through the rocks ahead that could possibly get me rather close. I took one last look at the scene through the looking glass before moving. It was then that I realised Arnesto wasn't looking forward at the threat. His gaze rested on me. He seemed to consider me for a long moment, a solemn look upon his face. As though he were reading my thoughts, he stared directly at me, like I were only feet in front of him. Slowly and subtly he shook his head. He mouthed the word '*don't*' at me followed by a slight smile.

I was confused.

Arnesto turned his head slightly and looked out to the sea, breathing in deeply. He reached inside his armoured vest and slowly removed the bottle of whiskey from inside one of the pouches and with it, something small and stick like. Somehow, I wasn't surprised. Ever since the sword-through-the-torso incident, I struggled to remember a time I hadn't seen him with some sort of 'high proof' spirits in his possession. Arnesto placed the tiny object between his teeth and smiled. I recognised it as the matchstick I had been chewing on earlier. He must've swiped it when he pat me on my cheek before. *Cheeky sod.* I couldn't work out his intentions. Why would he bother to do that? What was he planning?

Arnesto turned to face the Reaper, nodding his head. He pointed the bottle toward the emotionless helm, as though inviting the agent of death to share a drink. Satisfied that the Reaper wasn't interested, Arnesto indulged in a long swig on the bottle. Bubbles of air replaced the emptying contents.

'Great,' I thought, 'he plans on drinking now. *Now* of all times. Arnesto would possibly make a great sailor if he ever wanted to change career paths. He certainly could drink like one.

The Reaper appeared to grow tired of the display and moved forward to put a stop to it. Arnesto held up a finger in a manner of a father asking his impatient child to wait. However ridiculous a request, The Reaper paused. Arnesto turned and faced me once more and our eyes met again through the looking glass. His expression was sincere. I had seen that look once before. The look my father had given me the day we were separated upon the 'Kraken Krusher'. The last time I ever saw him.

No.

Arnesto, don't.

He tilted his head forward in a gentlemanly nod. Like a performer signing off at the end of an exceptional street performance.

'NO!' I shook my head furiously. 'No, no, no, Arnesto don't.'

I knew what was coming, but I couldn't stop it.

The Reaper flashed his blade.

Arnesto spun. A spark. The match struck along the bottle. A gout of flame erupted from Arnesto's mouth as he spat the whiskey across the igniting wick. A flash of light. Engulfed, the Reaper swung wide of his target. Flames enveloped the Reaper's mask and torso. He began to slice wildly. Arnesto danced away, throwing the remaining bottle at the feet of the thrashing bonfire to his front. Again, there was a flash and the echo of breaking glass against the cliffs. The potent alcohol burned furiously as the Reaper clutched at his own face, dropping his blades.

Arnesto ducked down and grabbed Xanthe. He lunged toward the lowered ramp of the docked airship. Enemy crossbow bolts began to pepper the ground around him, as he moved away from their commander.

A blur leapt from the fire. A spinning cord honed in on Arnesto's legs. It struck. The weighted ends causing the cable to wrap around his limbs. He toppled and dropped Xanthe hard next to the ledge, kicking up dust.

I recognised the weapon immediately.

A bola.

The flaming form of The Reaper marched forward through the fire, as though the *King of Devils* himself had joined the ranks of the Regime. He towered over the dazed figure of Arnesto. The alcohol fueling the flames had begun to subside across his body. Only his helm had the slightest lick of spark as smoke billowed from his wide shoulders.

'Arnesto Dubois!' he roared. The crossbow bolts immediately ceased in response.

No, no, no. My hands trembled. I fumbled around for the trigger of the crossbow. I couldn't steady the aiming marks in time. The Reaper reached down and grabbed Arnesto by the throat and lifted him up, face to face, preventing me from a clear target.

Arnesto's feet dangled from the ground. He clawed in vain at the Reaper's smouldering armour.

The Reaper turned slightly, holding Arnesto over the long drop to the crashing swell below. An opening was beginning. But if I hit him, what of Arnesto? He had a better chance with the seas. I steadied my aim. Just a bit more movement. A bit more and I would be able to see his torso for a clean shot.

The Reaper reached behind his own head with one hand. His other effortlessly held the full weight of Arnesto. I adjusted the looking glass, as I had seen the Captain do previously if he had wanted to more closely observe a sea monster. Now I too, needed to better see a monster. I couldn't afford to miss and hit Arnesto. With a click, my view became their upper bodies.

The helm popped forward. Smoke billowed from inside. The Reaper shifted slightly right. The crossed aiming lines rested on his neck. The pair were almost side on to me.

My finger tightened on the trigger.

Arnesto's eyes widened.

The smoke shifted. Through the looking glass, I saw the face that had been hidden all along. The face of the Reaper of the Regime.

The face of my father.

***

What followed shortly after is an image that will haunt me.

I became paralysed. Disbelief numbed me.

I watched.

My father.

Crush.

Arnesto's neck.

Like a snapping twig.

I did nothing, as he tossed Arnesto's limp, lifeless body from the cliff into the swirling waters below.

I did nothing as he picked up Xanthe and ordered his men to return to the airships.

I didn't pull the trigger at the man who raised me, as he paced up the gang plank toward his ship and ordered the crew to fire upon the Cliffside.

I watched.

As my only home was obliterated by chorus after chorus of broadside cannons, turning the cave and surrounding landscape to dust and rubble.

I heard the drone of the airships as they peeled away to return to their hive within The Capital.

I remained.

As the day drifted slowly into night. Beating sun was replaced by chilling winds through the darkness.

Shivering and alone. I wept.

Chapter Thirty-Seven

I don't know the moment when I drifted off to sleep. Stricken, I hadn't moved from the spot where Arnesto and I had last spoken. As though, if I remained in place, there was a chance this was all a terrible dream and my friends would be here again. At some moment, through my grief, exhaustion consumed me and I had fallen into slumber. The moments from that day played over and over in my mind. Images of Arnesto speaking to me before slipping away. The soldiers. The Reaper on fire. My father. Each time, I was paralysed. Passive. Useless.

Arnesto's neck snapped.

A squall of icy rain pulled me suddenly from my dreams. I sat up, gasping from a mixture of cold and adrenaline.

Words kept circling through my head. Xanthe spoke to me.

'If the Regime ever capture me alive. Which they won't.'

'The Regime are good at a lot of things, kid. That's why they control so much of the lands. But what they excel in the most is *torture*. They have turned it into an art form.'

Arnesto's words.

'If you're going to go out, Flynt, go out with all guns blazing.'

Grief slowly began to be replaced. Anger birthed in the pit of my stomach. It slowly rooted itself into my gut and sprouted into me. I screamed at the rain clouds and heavy seas.

I was angry at myself for not taking my chance when I had it. I was angry at Xanthe for what she did to my family. I was angry at Arnesto for telling me to let him go and having faith in me. I was angry at my father for succumbing to The Governor.

That was it.

He was to blame.

The one person who had orchestrated my pain and suffering over the years.

The image of his face flickering in the flames of the burning ships began to permeate through my mind.

Moonlight peeked through the clouds and illuminated the newly shaped cliffs around me. Below, the waves had responded by crashing heavily against the rocks. I noticed the area where the entrance to our cave once was, crumbled and filled in with rubble, but at its base the waves made a hollow slapping sound. The same sound a ship makes when a hole has been punched in its side.

Curiosity began to lead my actions. I navigated through the slippery rocks down to the water line. Their surfaces became rougher, barnacles and oysters giving them a crust as I neared the water. The hollow slapping sound became louder and echoed, drawing me nearer.

Between the heavy sets, I made out a small inlet between two massive chunks of broken Cliffside. Wind howled through the opening giving it a haunting sound.

There was the slightest of chances, that maybe there was still a way into the cave. If I could just find my way in, then I could possibly salvage something, or find the entrance to Arnesto's caves. But the waves crashing amongst the rocks spelled disaster if I was wrong. Even if I timed it right, all that effort would be wasted if I became trapped in an underwater dead-end. The strong currents would push me in and prevent me from coming back out. Essentially, I would be fish food.

Like Arnesto.

Stop it. Get that out of your head.

No, use it. Make it your strength, I thought. Don't let him down. Not again. Never again. Xanthe needed me. My father, perhaps he could still be saved. If Xanthe managed to break free of the Governor's control once before, then it could be possible.

There was a sliver of a chance. I had to take it.

I breathed in deeply. Again and again. Filling my body with the air that I needed to get through the waves. I observed the surging swells, as I edged closer to the small cave entrance. Trying to figure out their timing. I needed to dive in moments before a wave struck, then I could use its force to give me a boost through the dark passage.

I removed the clothes Arnesto had gifted me, leaving only the pants, which I rolled up above my knees. I folded them neatly and placed them between some nearby rocks. My boots soon joined them. I couldn't afford to have anything slow me down, even the soldier's crossbow joined the cache. Just as I had arrived on land after all those years at sea, I now perched upon a large rock above the inlet, wearing only my pants, bracer and my trusty fish bone lock pick. I considered the locket hanging around my neck. I removed it and once again stowed the trinket away within the lining of my pants.

My inner voice drove my actions. What did I have to lose? Nothing. If I died here tonight, no one would know. No one would care. I am nobody.

Wrong.

I am 'the nobody' who will stop the Regime.

With one last inward breath, I tracked an outward surge of current being overrun by another large incoming wave.

I leapt into its path and below the surface.

—·—

CHAPTER THIRTY-EIGHT

The sharp cold of the waters almost sucked the air from my lungs. I stretched out my arms and stroked as the power of the incoming wave took over, propelling me toward the gap, which was still visible in the moonlight.

I breached through the entrance and was met with fierce swirls of bubbles from the smashing waves. I braced my arms in front of my face as the force behind me decided my direction, running my flesh against the rough channels of stone. Sharp slicing pain made me wince, an edge cutting my ribs. Barnacles grated my shoulders and forearms.

The surge slowed and just as powerfully as it had pushed me, it began to retreat toward the ocean, pulling me back with it. I scrambled and clawed in the darkness, feeling for a hold on a submerged ledge. Finger tips from my left arm clipped a slight indent and I held firm resisting the force of the current.

Another wave crashed into the wall outside and within an instant, the current pushed me forward once again.

The underwater battering was taking its toll. The air in my body was beginning to turn into a niggling reminder that I would soon need to breathe again. The further forward into the darkness I stroked, the more I had to fight the urge to panic in my mind.

Calm yourself, I thought. You need to do this. Life outside is forfeit. Calm yourself.

Now without the ambient light from the moon, I had to feel my way forward, running my hands against the rocky surface. Tendrils of vegetation licked at my fingers and face, making my path all the more disorientating.

The sensation in my body was becoming overwhelming. I had been holding my breath for a considerable amount of time, but by now, I had passed the point of no return. If I tried to turn back, to find my way or fight the currents to get my air, I would surely pass out and die. I just had to push forward.

Small bursts of light began to pulse before me. I recognised the colours as the cave dwelling luminescent shrimp. I was in the cave. I pushed upward, the glow allowing me to see that I was still inside a tight space of no more the three feet wide. My head struck rock. I was still under the water with nowhere to breach. Panic began to set in. My thoughts no longer held reason. Air - where was it?

My hands clawed desperately at the ceiling of stone above me, as though I could push it upward and find some space. My fingers breached a small gap in the rock. A pocket of air.

With no time to think, my mouth found the gap. I gasped. A small, almost insufficient bubble of air made its way into my lungs. Swimming upside down, I felt for more pockets of air. A few more fathoms and there was another, slightly bigger. And another. I moved now from gap to gap inhaling these gifts as I did. Calming my mind again, I navigated the corridor as it steadily shifted its course upward.

The underwater life around me paved my way, the light they created as I disturbed their underwater home would have almost seemed beautiful if I weren't trying to survive.

I struck something soft and heavy that was lodged between the cracks. Momentarily startled, I turned to face the underwater predator.

I grabbed outward to defend myself, only to grab leather.

A soldier's leather vest.

I held firm, my eyes adjusting in the dim light to see what it was.

The dead eyes of a man gazed through me. The skull with which they sat dangled at an unnatural angle. The face had a familiar goatee.

The last of my air spewed out in a cloud of bubbles - I realised I was holding the corpse of Arnesto. I pushed away and stroked hard from the body, kicking my legs to propel upward.

My head broke the surface. I gasped and spluttered violently trying to replace the bad air in my lungs with the good stuff. Glowing light from still burning fires lit up the small stone jetty and staircase inside the cave. Timber support beams and bits of whiskey-soaked-barrels providing a steady slow burning fuel. I flopped onto the stone jetty like an exhausted bear seal and lay there gulping in as much air as I could. Dust and rubble rained down every so often as the roof of the cave steadily struggled to hold up from the earlier explosions.

There was a *glubbing* sound as Arnesto's body surfaced beside me, now that it had been freed from below. Feeling pangs of guilt from my earlier reaction underwater, I leant over and grabbed onto the rear of the vest, using a final reserve of strength to pull him up beside me. The least I could do was pay my respects and stop my friend from becoming crab crap.

I knelt over my former mentor and closed his eyes one last time and said my goodbyes. I distilled the pain, for I needed it for what came next. A plan was beginning to form within my mind.

Struggling to my feet, I could hear the steady crackle of the flames and the creaking of the struggling cave. My eyes followed the scorched staircase to the heavy iron door, which now lay strewn open from the force of the blast from Arnesto's booby trap.

My fists clenched. Panting, I made to steady climb up the stairs, past charred bits of enemy soldiers to the tunnels that would lead me back to the Capital.

The show was about to begin.

Chapter Thirty-Nine

The streets of the Capital had been easier to negotiate in the darkness. Shadows stretched from alleyway to shopfront to rooftop. Coupled with what must have been a strict curfew enforced on the local civilians, it meant that only the odd patrol of guards needed to be avoided. Easy. Within minutes, I had swiftly made my way to the area I felt most comfortable in my enemy's backyard.

The cold, murky waters of the harbour.

Having left the now almost empty bazaar, the waters gently lapped at the stone jetty, welcoming me into their darkness. I pushed past the initial chill - tensing up, I forced myself to endure the less than tropical temperature. I focused on my breathing, deliberately slowing it down. I had a decent swim ahead of me, in waters that were most definitely thriving with underwater predators like those I had seen hanging in the markets the day before. After their recent indulgence from the victims of the Governor's demonstration, I was banking on the chance their bellies were now full of prisoner bits and their hunger would be sated. Now another predator was being welcomed home. Well kind of - more of a flea than a predator, I guess.

Using the moonlight to guide me, I quietly paddled away from the dull lights along the jetty. I scanned the waters to my front, analysing the shape of each boat, craft and ship within the harbour. It wasn't until I rounded the man-made headland that I made out the tell-tale silhouette I was looking for. Anchored in the heart of the bay, she dwarfed every ship nearby. Possibly every ship – ever.

The Governor's new plaything - The Juggernaut.

CHAPTER FORTY

From the surface, The Juggernaut was even more intimidating. From the sky, it had appeared much smaller, even though I had seen its size compared to other ships. The massive barrels of the cannons protruded from the deck like fallen masts. The Governor had been correct, this would be a man-made force of nature. Any naval resistance wouldn't have a hope. I tread the surface beside the enormous vessel, filled my lungs with air and dipped below the waterline. I had an idea that needed some time to manifest. I busied myself in the darkness, using only touch to manipulate my surroundings.

Anger had not been the only thing drawing me back to the city. True, the pain and suffering I had been forced to endure over the last few years of my life manifested themselves into fuel. Every lash, every beating, every cold and hungry moment spent within the 'Kraken Krusher', they all had hardened me. Lashings lose their impact once scar tissue thickens the flesh. At least I learnt to escape my cell and make life hell for those around me. What would be worse is having no control whatsoever - losing hope. It occurred to me what a cruel genius the Governor was. Having my father as a captive was one thing, but if what Xanthe had said was true, he was now a prisoner of the worst kind. Trapped inside a body unable to die, committing heinous deeds against those he once saw as

allies. What could be a worse torture than that? The Governor
had managed to manufacture his own version of the hells. A
prison that would be harder to help him escape from than the
now obsolete Gulag. Regardless, I had to try.

But, how?

Now without somewhere decent to stow my fishbone lock
pick, I had placed it firmly between my teeth before beginning
the climb up the ship's anchor chain. Cold and slippery, I
straddled the factory fresh chain, untarnished or barnacled
from life at sea. The offshore winds had picked up, and my wet
pants began to chill immediately against me. With chattering
teeth, I pushed upward.

A distant putting sound became louder above me. An airship, bearing the banner of The Govenor was rounding for another lazy lap above the harbour. Far smaller than the massive
regal airship he had been on the previous evening, it must
have been a temporary replacement as his preference was
repaired. However, it still had the appearance of a sleek shark
slipping through the sky, surveying the city he had helped
build.

I considered for a moment if he would be awake. If he
had known the suffering he had created beyond the confines
of his city. Did it keep him up at night, filling his mind with
nightmares or regret? Or did he simply not care? Chances are
he was fast asleep, with a belly full of those pastries having
spent another evening devising more ways to ruin the lives of
those not willing to bend to the Regime. Most likely, Xanthe
would be aboard that vessel. She had to be. With the Gulag
now out of commission and the Governor's clear interest in
keeping Xanthe from escaping once more, his airship would
be the most likely location to keep the things he was most
fond of.

I reached the edge of the starboard banister to the deck. Locking my leg around a thin metal strut, I peered over and quietly observed the deck for any sign of crew. Although it had appeared to have no one aboard during the Governor's demonstration, I still suspected that something this large and complex had to have some sort of specialised sailors. Ones that were trained in fixing issues the ship may have in its upcoming maiden voyage.

I paused to gather my bearings. The Juggernaut was different from almost every other ship I had been on, with the exception of a few noticeable similarities. One, was that it had the 'parts' of a ship, the decks, some masts, and cannons (albeit huge ones) but it was heavily plated in thick sheets of metal, reinforced by steel struts and rivets – not timber. The other was that it was shaped somewhat like a ship, with a bow and stern and just a supremely large hull. I guessed that inside, it still had ship's magazine, a galley, holds, stores and even massive bilge pumps keeping it afloat.

Brilliant, I thought. This will make the next steps of what I want to do just a tad easier, as I used my hands to wipe off the excess water. I didn't want to leave a trail of puddles that may alert a member of the crew that something was amiss.

Moving from shadow to shadow, I made my way to the main mast. The same area the Governor had pointed his hand held device toward during the demonstration. That mast must contain something that allowed him to control the ship from above. His flexing of military might had given away a weakness. Sabotage was in order.

Even with my eyes closed, I could've found the parts of the ship that I needed. Slipping to the rigging ropes, I began my climb upwards. Climbing had always been a strength of mine, especially when the Captain of the 'Kraken Krusher' had sent me out for dangerous errands where losing a sailor was rather likely.

Voices made me stop. Two to be exact. So, there *were* members of crew aboard. Possibly a skeleton crew, with the rest on shore leave before heading underway to months on the open sea.

A sharp smell cut through the salty air. A distinct odour that I recalled from my days spent aboard the 'Kraken Krusher'.

Carvian Tobacco.

Officers, I thought to myself.

They leaned against the railing looking out over the harbour, lighting their pipes and sucking back on the innards. Xanthe would have had no trouble dispatching these two, possibly using that trick she had been trying to show me back in Arnesto's cave. A pang of guilt distracted me. I had been so quick to judge her. I knew now, if the Governor had succeeded in controlling my father, someone who hated the Regime so much, then she was clearly at his mercy. Yeah, if she were here, she'd slide down that rope and dispatch those two within a second. Easy for someone like her, but I couldn't run that risk. I had work to do. Moving slower and more deliberately, I continue upward. Before long, the winds picked up and whistled about my head, as I neared the very top of the mast.

Coming to the end of the cargo rope, a small platform used for look outs provided some respite from the dizzying height. I know I said I was often used for the dangerous tasks up high, but it still caused a slight lurch in my stomach whenever I was up where the birds fly. Now was certainly no different, considering it was even taller than what I considered a reasonable distance upward. I gripped onto the metal grill and pulled my legs up onto the flat structure. Twinkling lights, like bright stars lined the shoreline from various households and buildings. Plumes of factory smoke still continued their billowing from the overworked factories, now likely being pushed even harder to meet the deadlines set in place by the Governor and his investors. I made a mental note on the location of several before turning my attention to the metal mast behind me. I hadn't been terribly sure what it was I could do or look for up until this point. I had figured that if the Governor was indeed aiming his device at this part of the ship to allow him some sort of distant control, then messing with it could possibly sabotage it enough to cause some grief to his current plans. Good thing I did, because a rectangular panel, complete with outward hinges and a rather simple looking lock promised to give me what I wasn't even sure I was looking for.

I removed the fishbone lockpick from between my chattering teeth and set to work. Within seconds the several tumblers had been shifted and the lock sprang outward an inch. I muttered angrily to myself about the shitty design and those responsible for it obviously not considering the inevitability of salt hindering any metal moving parts. This was going to be a noisy affair. I snuck a brief peek downward at the two officers. Having finished their pipes, they still lingered and chuckled to one another, seemingly reluctant to return to their roles upon the ship.

I cursed quietly through my curled lip and turned back to the panel. Gripping the curved metal plate firmly, I closed my eyes, breathed in sharply and wrenched it open.

There was a loud metallic squeak.

They had to have heard that. Oh gods, why couldn't I have just waited.

I peeked downward through the grill. One of the officers was looking directly at me. Even from this distance, I could see his eyes squinting hard, looking for the origin of my amateur move.

Speaking of, I didn't budge another inch. I perched there like an oversized sea bird and waited.

And waited some more.

Laughter erupted from the second of the pair and he jovially slapped his comrade in the shoulder. The watcher of the two, broke his investigation at the jibe and began to stroll back to the metal structure that I would have once consider the quarter deck, but considering the vast size and design changes, this section was something else with three levels to it. The sound of a metal door shutting, reminded my brain that I was once again allowed to breathe. Holding my pick, I turned to study the innards of the panel which I had just exposed. Organised chaos lay before me. A mish-mash of coloured metal strings jutted in and out of various points and numerous fine copper panels. I had some previous experience tinkering with bits and pieces the Captain of the Kraken Krusher had needed help with over the years, but I felt way out of my depth with the sight before me.

I considered my options briefly. Time was not on my side and I had to make something happen. So I did. I'd like to say I finely tuned the bits and bobs to my liking with my exquisite intellect, but that couldn't be further from the truth. Instead, I just began sawing, hacking, plucking and pulling at everything and anything that looked very, mildly and kind of important. Like a lion shark in a frenzy, I tore through the finery within seconds. There was a spark at my fingertips, sending a jolt through my body, followed by a bang and a sizzle. Blinded, I waited for my eyes to readjust to my surrounds. Smoke spewed forth from the panel and my hair stood on end.

I listened briefly for the tell-tale sounds of metal doors swinging open, or crew members yelling out, but to my relief, there were none.

Man, you just can't get good help anywhere, I thought. Admiring my handiwork, I considered how effective my attempt at sabotage had been. In the absence of Xanthe, I had begun to speak to myself. Equally for affirmation, condemnation and company. 'Not bad at all, I reckon. Let's see the Governor work his magic on this hunk now. Now for the next step,' I cracked my knuckles in anticipation, 'kicking these monkeys off the ship.

CHAPTER FORTY-ONE

I slipped easily through the darkness toward the section of the ship that would usually be considered the helm. The area where the ship's navigation and steering would take place. With a bit of luck, the Captain and his officers would be in their sleeping quarters for now, resting up before they left port.

The doorway, as I should have guessed, was riveted metal, with a wheel welded through the centre - quite similar to the one aboard the airship. That meant it was sealed tight, with no cracks for me to peep through to see if the coast was clear on the other side. Dammit. Time was starting to fade. The night was fast approaching dawn and I still had much to do before then. I would have to be a little more reckless in my approach through the ship.

I cracked the wheel a half turn and two metal struts released the door from its firm hold. It popped open with a slight creak, and I stepped inside.

Big mistake.

Several sets of eyes locked onto me from various well-dressed individuals throughout a large room, complete with panels and dials, like a massive version of the airship's 'cockpit' as Xanthe had called it. Two of the faces I saw were those of the officers who had enjoyed a smoke out on the deck but moments ago. Each member wore the signature garb of Regime Naval officers.

'Who are you?' demanded one of the men. He was a short bald man from the distant Isles. Wearing more embellishments than the others, a scar ran from his temple to the corner of his mouth. His dark complexion revealed a glint of outrage at my appearance.

The Captain. An experienced Captain.

My stomach lurched. This was a tight spot of bother to be in. I remembered Xanthe's words of encouragement.

'You're smart, kid. That brain of yours has done a good job keeping you out of trouble so far.'

I breathed in, and quickly composed myself.

'Seize him,' continued the Captain.

Three of the nearest officers drew their Flintlocks and began toward me, eager to follow their superior's directive.

'I wouldn't do that if you value the life of your crew,' I stated as confidently and menacingly as I could. Surprisingly my delivery was potent enough for the officers to pause briefly and look back to their Captain.

I took the opportunity to continue before he could reinforce his order.

'Consider this instance right now, Captain. Why would a half clothed, skinny boy be standing so confidently in your presence unless he had something dire that needed to be heard?'

The Captain raised his hand to silence his already quiet men. 'Do go on.'

I noted, that despite his appearance, the usual accent one would expect from the people of the Isles was replaced with the same accent as the Governor himself.

'I came here to warn you that this ship, The Juggernaut, is but mere moments away from sinking to the bottom of the harbour.'

The Captain and his fellow officers looked briefly at one another and erupted into hearty laughter.

'Which one of you men set this hilarious prank up?' The Captain demanded between laughs.

His men each looked at one another and slowly began to shake their heads, their forced smiles barely hiding a sense of concern.

'It is no prank Captain, I assure you. I am part of a small team of operatives tasked with sabotaging the Regime's assets. For example, I am sure you are aware of the incident recently aboard the Govenor's private airship?'

'How do you know about that?' he interjected.

'That is confidential. But I can tell you that my partner Arnesto was effective in achieving his mission.'

'Arnesto Dubois?'

'You know of him?'

'The thorn of the Regime.' His eyes stared at me, as though searching for the slightest whiff of a lie. I locked my eyes directly with his, as though we were the only two in the room.

'Then you know that my colleague's reputation precedes him. And you also know how serious I am when I tell you that he and I have just placed a small but powerful explosive within your ship's magazine. Very soon it will blow, and you and your crew will meet your makers, that is unless you demonstrate this ship's evacuation procedures and make the safety of shore immediately.'

The Captain eyed me suspiciously. I felt slightly guilty having used Arnesto in my ruse, but I had a feeling he would be enjoying the show if he were still able to bear witness to it.

'How do you know Arnesto?' he began.

'I helped him escape from the Warden Mortlock.'

Still he studied me carefully.

'So you know Mortlock?'

'Sure, husky voice, metal arm, newly acquired burns thanks to yours truly.'

The other officers began to murmur to one another.

'Shut it,' ordered the Captain. 'You were the one who gave him those burns?'

'The one and only.'

The Captain turned his head slightly. The nearest officer, a tall meaty man with a slick hair, stepped forward and leant in close. The Captain maintained his gaze on me and whispered something to his subordinate.

'If you are thinking of searching the ship, I will tell you this. You don't have enough time. Frankly, the device is due to detonate any moment now,' I pushed.

The Captain and his officer both looked back at me. His lips tightened and I watched as his jaw pursed. He was becoming frustrated.

'Well then young man, why would you endanger yourself by waltzing in here and telling such a tall tale? You must know how hard this is to believe and the stakes at which I find myself.'

'Because unlike your Governor, I am not a monster - yet. I would choose to stop the Regime with as little casualties on both sides as possible. There has been enough bloodshed, and I am no leech. If you need further evidence to help in your decision, try to communicate with your boss right now. I guarantee that you will not be able to, nor will your guns be able to be controlled by him from his... let me guess... new, less regal airship as it circles the harbour? Ask your two men right here, they almost saw me sabotaging the device in the top mast while they smoked their Carvian tobacco.'

'You know Carvian?'

'Our intelligence agents know many things.'

He looked at the two officers that I gestured to. With a slight strain in his voice, the one who had tried to spy me blurted out, 'It's true, sir. I heard something at the top of the aerial. I thought it was just a large sea bird.'

The Captain sneered at him, before turning back to me. He considered me a while longer. Beads of sweat breached his brow and trailed past his temple. With less confidence than before he nodded to one of the officers near the panel covered with dials, switches and buttons.

Indiscernible murmuring began as the sailor began in vain to speak with someone through a strange metal vase.

Despite his complexion, the colour seemed to have drained from the Captain's features.

'Captain. There is no radio communication with The Governor's airship,' came the awaited response.

A ray-dee-oh. So that is what they call it, I thought. I had seen a panel like that before on the airship, but it had been severely damaged from Xanthe's raid on the cockpit.

'Time is ticking, Captain. Think of your crew and what is at stake. You have already been beaten, but it isn't your fault. The design of the ship is to blame for not having better security on board. Right now, investors are pumping their coin into producing more of these ships to own the seas. After all, your demonstration the last evening was definitely impressive. I'm sure the Governor, whilst annoyed at your defeat, would forgive you for saving the crew and would allow you a chance at redemption, perhaps on a Juggernaut Mk II? You would gain a reputation as the Captain who chose his crew's lives over the ship. Think about it. Any crew to serve under you from now on would see you as benevolent and trustworthy. There wouldn't be the slightest hint of mutiny under you - ever.'

I couldn't help but seem cocky. Judging from the expression on his face and the panicked movements of the officers around him, the Captain had already folded.

He looked down at the floor momentarily, likely considering his options. Rolling his eyes in his head and jutting his lower jaw outward, he appeared to decide upon a conclusion.

'No.'

'No?'

'I will not give that order. I would rather die upon the ship I have been tasked with protecting than crumple to the tale of some half naked child. And I expect my men feel the same way.'

I felt a slight sense of panic flutter in my belly.

Oh.

It was my turn to sweat, although I tried hard to not show it, this wasn't exactly where I thought this conversation would go. I had failed to deceive the Captain of the ship.

The officers however had failed to respond. As if sensing this, the Captain's wild eyes flitted between them.

'Wouldn't you agree, men?' his words were firmly enunciated through clenched teeth.

At that moment, one of the officers, one that had been closest to the doorway, lunged forward in an attempt to escape.

There was a 'boom' and a puff of smoke as the Captain withdrew his naval issue Flintlock and shot the deserter in the back. He crumpled into a heap, feet from the door, a red flower of blood blossoming through his jacket. Another boom erupted as the officer with the meaty build fired a blast into the neck of the Captain in a split-second mutiny. Chunks of flesh sprayed forth and the Captain turned, eyes bulging at the traitor. The smell of burnt black powder filled the room as the officers showed their true colours. I scrambled across the floor and dove behind the chair of the Captain. Soon the smoke began to settle, and the wooden floor lay strewn with the slumped and bleeding bodies of the Captain, his supporters and his deniers. The ringing in my ears dulled enough that I could hear one voice. It was the Carvian tobacco smoking officer from the deck earlier. He leant forward over the radio holding down upon a button. A loud buzzing sound began to repeat throughout the ship. Red lights lit up and flashed as a sign of warning.

Through a gargled voice, he began his orders, 'All crew, evacuate the ship immediately. I repeat, all crew... evacuate the ship... immediately. Captain Crenshaw is deceased, this is Lieutenant Commander Smirnoff. Evacuate the ship... immediately.'

His head dipped forward and bumped the radio mouth piece, as his arms slipped from the button and fell limp by his side. A small trail of smoke escaped from a hole in his red jacket, however it smelled of burnt-off black powder rather than his Carvian blend.

My mouth hung open in disbelief. It wasn't what I had expected to happen at all, but the outcome was the same. The sounds of men and women yelling echoed down the hallways. I forced myself to focus. Now was no time to sit back gawking at the carnage I had semi-orchestrated... kind of... accidentally. It was nothing compared to what I had planned for the next step.

I now had uninterrupted access to what seemed like more than just the helm – it was like the brain of a sea monster. Seeing as the large panel seemed to be the means for controlling and communicating with most of the ship, I went to investigate. I unceremoniously wrenched Smirnoff from his temporary throne, his dead weight slapping against the newly-stained timber floor. I gave the panel a quick study. It was similar to the one aboard the airship Xanthe and I had commandeered, but bigger, and with more buttons, and more switches, and glass windows, and... oh jeez, this was a mess. I gathered myself and looked at the dark glass windows that were built into the panel. They had a striking resemblance to the device the Governor had used aboard his airship. Each one had a switch and two levers embedded directly in front of it. Taking a gamble, I flicked the switch on the window nearest me. It produced a muffled crackling sound before filling with artificial light. Within a few seconds an image appeared through the glass. In the middle, it had similar markings to the aiming points in the looking glasses of the Regime's newly issued pneumatic crossbows. But the image itself showed the waters of the bay. Unlike any images of water I had seen before, the waves moved and lapped in the frame.

A moving image.

Surely enough, small boats filled with crew from the ship appeared in frame as they followed the final orders from the smoking commander beside my feet. Reaching down toward the levers, I moved one suspiciously to starboard. Almost immediately there was a humming and cracking sound of mechanical gears within the ship. On deck, one of the massive guns began to slowly move in its starboard direction. Feeling a sense of understanding, I moved the lever upward. The gun did the same. The glass panel revealed the distant shoreline. I manipulated the other mini lever at the base of the window. Just as the switches on the weapon looking glass had given me a closer image, so too did the screen before me. The shoreline now revealing one of the massive factories, instead of distant sparkles of gas-lamps lighting the streets. This contraption allowed the officers to have control over the guns. Wow, what a way to take sailor error out of the mix, I thought.

I leapt along the panel, flicking the switches before the several windows. Each one crackled into a new perspective of the harbour.

The picture was as clear as looking through a window, with some exceptions. Each image was a different perspective of the bay. I moved from screen to screen - centring the aiming marks upon the various points the lookout's information board had so proudly and carelessly pointed out to me during my time upon the city lookout.

'The 'Stravovich Arms Company' is the factory where all of our latest weapons and armour are produced. Some two hundred units per day, creating the latest and most deadly weapons for our soldiers.'

Numbers on a dial signified the distance at eight hundred fathoms. I aimed the criss-cross on the factory.

'Standing at well over one hundred and sixty feet tall – one of the tallest buildings in our fair city is the factory for manufacturing our airships. Currently it produces six a month, which with new found resources and man power will eventually produce double that volume, making it the foremost producer of airships in all of the Regime's territories.'

Dialled and centred.

'Our major protector from any threats - the fortifications to the bay, combined with the impassable natural cliffs surrounding the city, provide complete protection – particularly from Allied Navy and the occasional sea behemoth.'

Three guns, dialled and centred on each of the stone structures.

Another building had remained burned firmly into my memory from that evening. The Governor's oily words still sent a shiver down my spine.

'The magnificent invention you just saw demonstrate its power, was created within that large building over there. It

Nothing outside, no. You should've been looking closer to home.

Three guns, dialled and centred.

I remembered his words about the Gulag. I dialled in the final gun on the base of the towering structure on its lonely island, figuring its own weight would work against it if the foundations were rocked. Its destruction would bring me a small sense of closure. No one would suffer his terrible mind-altering experiments again.

No more Xanthe's, no more Reapers.

My heart pounded, threatening to open my ribs and escape the room. It had been a stupid, stupid idea, fuelled by anger and hurt and years of cruelty, but now it was so close to actually working.

I breathed in deeply and held it. I focused on the pain of Arnesto's death, the fear Xanthe must be feeling and the betrayal of witnessing what my father had become. The putting sound of the Governor's latest airship became louder. Likely drawn to the Juggernaut at the sight of the evacuation of its crew.

Good. Time for him to watch *my* demonstration.

I moved to the first screen, whispering the words 'For Arnesto,' I flicked the red switch. There was an almighty boom that rocked the vessel and shook the glass window panels. A flash of orange light illuminated the room and cast dancing shadows across the walls, as the round exploded inside the factory walls.

Adrenaline spiked within my guts. I felt exhilarated by the power unleashed from the massive cannon. I smirked at the thought of the look on the Governor's face right now. I could imagine a contortion of anger and confusion as he watched his own creation lay waste to the things he loved.

Just like you took away those that I loved.

I danced along the panel and flicked all of the red switches, like an excitable child, a pocketful of money to spend at a toffee stall with rows of their favourite boiled sweets.

'For Xanthe!'

'For Elaina!'

'For my mother!'

'For my father!' Each name sounded of a drum beat of doom. The chorus of destruction that followed threatened to rattle the rivets from their resting places. Each screen flashed before revealing the targeted structures erupting into debris. Looking through the windows of the officer's room, the sight was even more spectacular. Huge fires spewed forth from the targets on the shores. An excited cry leapt from my throat, hoarse and angry as I punched at the air.

There was a beep from each small window. Words across the top flashed 'loading', followed shortly by the word 'armed'. Wow, this ship runs almost by itself, I thought.

Knowing that my time aboard was running out, I ran along the panel once more and fired off another volley of shots. If the targets hadn't been levelled before, then the repeat effect from the 'tom toms of doom' surely would change that.

Without stopping to admire effects of the second volley, I moved into the empty hallway. I guessed that time was even more fleeting and I had a floorplan to memorise before it did.

Chapter Forty-Two

It wasn't long before the Governor's airship closed in on the Juggernaut. Seeming somewhat reluctant to move closer until they were sure that they couldn't be targeted, the vessel finished its lingering hover above the harbour and finally approached.

By now, I had familiarised myself with the ship's various sections and I had returned to the controls to target a few more valuable assets of the Regime. Major sections of shoreline were either alight or smouldering. Massive plumes of dark smoke now rose well into the early morning sky, blotting out the orange and peach colours of the new day. Airships littered the water, the flammable gases inside burning furiously as they slipped beneath the waves.

As the Governor's ship lowered into view, he appeared far from composed. No longer did he exude confidence or a stately demeanour, instead stood a red-faced savage swearing loudly and striking his fingers firmly upon his mechanical remote device. He angled it in a variety of positions, pointing it at the mast that had been responsible for receiving his instructions. Still the ship didn't respond. Finally giving up, he threw the contraption upon the deck and began stomping on it repeatedly.

I couldn't help but smile.

With his rant over, he breathed heavily and turned to survey his precious ship. His view settled on the doorway I was in. I responded by waving casually. Our eyes met. His widened and the wildness rekindled within them once more. My waving hand turned around and protruded the middle finger in confirmation of his suspicion. He called out to somewhere within his airship.

Two figures emerged.

I recognised the first – My father; 'The Reaper', as he moved to the edge of the airship's rails.

The second one was different. It too moved to a rail, but the bulbous floatation sac of the airship cast shadows across it, obscuring the distinguishing details. The airship lowered some more till it was but fifteen fathoms above the deck. Slowly it turned sideways and the early morning rays painted its surface in a bright orange glow, lighting up The Governor's minions and revealing the second of the pair.

My stomach dropped as I witnessed the familiar white hair of Xanthe whipping in the updraft. She appeared like a smaller, leaner and more feminine version of the Reaper, decked out with the tell-tale darkened armour and sporting two new criss-crossed blades across her back, giving the appearance of small angelic wings in the sunlight. Her mouth and nose were covered in a type of muzzle, leaving her pale eyes to stare vacantly downward.

The Governor had gained control over her mind and body. She was his prisoner. His puppet. I had guessed there was a reason for his wanting so badly to retrieve her, and now it lay before me plain as the new day. The Governor now had his left and right 'hands' back. One Reaper was bad enough, but now...

Guilt tore through me. My smile disappeared as my teeth gritted. I had considered the consequences of Xanthe's capture previously. I had realised that the risk for her freedom was far greater than the risks I faced. Still, I had pushed her at the start, almost using her. But she proved to me that despite her past - a past she was trying to flee - she was willing to risk everything to help me. For what? For a friend? Now she stood above me, living her personal hell. Something she had feared more than death.

The Governor called out something and pointed at me. Xanthe's autopilot mode vanished and her eyes locked onto me. Her and my father leapt simultaneously from the airship, landing deftly upon the deck of the Juggernaut. I snapped from my depressive thoughts and quickly inspected the waters of the bay. Satisfied that I still had some time to spare, I disappeared through the doorway into the ship.

Now they were entering *my* territory.

CHAPTER FORTY-THREE

I heard the metal door clang open at the end of the narrow hallway as the pair of assassins trailed me in hot pursuit. I turned and waved, cheekily inviting them to hurry up, before ducking behind a corner and sprinting far more desperately than the cocky demeanour I was feigning. A pair of crossbow bolts whistled past my head and punctured a copper pipe nearby. It released a gout of steam behind me. Jeez, time to go.

'Ha ha ha, Reaper, you're getting slow. Some super soldier you are,' I taunted.

Truth be told, they were gaining on me faster than I had expected. This would be close, and if I slipped up, I would be gutted like a kraken on the deck.

I turned again into a noisy hallway that split port and starboard. Steam hissed and large turbine motors idled in a deafening cacophony. Earlier, I had decided this engine room of the ship would be important if the Governor had sent in multiple troops. Having previously removed the grill that covered the walkway, I slipped under the floor, between cramped pipes and pulled metal lattice over my head. Considering the fact the two of them had exceptional hearing, I felt compelled to try and stifle my beating heart and heavy breathing despite the loud background noise. No sooner had I shut the grill; my two pursuers slipped into the hallway and paused. Now here comes the interesting part. They had two separate directions I could have gone, leading to two different ends of the ship. Through the linear peepholes above me, I watched as the Reaper turned and looked at Xanthe.

Come on. Come on. Do it. Do it.

It was then that Xanthe did something I didn't expect. She began to sniff the air through the muzzle upon her face.

Uh oh.

I had witnessed firsthand, the keenness of Xanthe's senses. My only hope was that the sailors of this ship had demonstrated a similar hygiene to those aboard the 'Kraken Krusher'. Even if this was slightly the case, there was a decent chance my scent would be lost in the mix of fermenting body odour and machine lubricant from the Engines below.

Still, she sniffed.

The Reaper became impatient and growled at her, 'Inferior model'. Turning on his heel, he made the decision for her and stalked toward the port side of the vessel.

Yes.

Xanthe watched as he left before turning to leave in the opposite direction.

She paused. Waited.

What was she doing? Had she actually detected me?

Her feet buckled slightly and she braced her arm against the wall to stop from falling over. Her other hand clutched at her temple, almost clawing at her skull briefly as though she were in the midst of an internal struggle. A moment passed and a vacant look swept over her once more, leaving her arms to fall at her sides. Just as quickly as it had begun, she poised once more and returned to her hunt. Leaving me wide eyed and relieved mere feet behind her.

Brilliant, I thought. Divide and conquer. I now had them divided. 'Conquering' would be a different and much more difficult task.

— · —

CHAPTER FORTY-FOUR

Empty metal and timber hallways, as it seems, are brilliant for echoing one's voice. Simply calling out through a few lengthy corridors creates chaos for someone if they are trying to find you. I had already tested the acoustics during my limited reconnaissance before the Governor had arrived and was well aware of the disorientation it could cause. And that is what I did. Choosing to follow Xanthe, I now lured her back toward my current location – the ship's galley.

I had previously ignited the cooking fires and poured a mixture of oil, fats and spices into the many pots and pans now lining the stoves. I had ensured the heat remained low to avoid stifling the air with thick burning smoke and setting off the ship's irrigation system. Now the smell was rather pleasant and hunger inducing, within the narrow cooking space.

Upon entering the Galley again, I poured left over cooking oil across the entrance to the room, creating a slick surface for the next person through the door.

'Xanthe. C'mon, Xanth, I thought you were better than this. It can't be that hard to find little old me,' I laughed tauntingly.

It didn't take long. Even though I had expected her, I still jumped slightly as she appeared suddenly in the doorway.

But she didn't enter.

'C'mon Xanthe, I'm right here. What are you waiting fo-'

She flinched. A crossbow bolt whistled and thunked into me, knocking air from my lungs. I say 'thunked' for good reason. I held a cast iron frying pan in front of my torso just in time. The bolt punctured just barely into the metal.

'Woah! Woah! Come on. Really? You can't just take me down with your bare hands? Seriously, I'm just a kid, remember? Is there any part of you still in there? Any little bit of the Xanthe I knew?'

Her blank expression twitched. Momentarily she considered the galley before her, as though looking for anything unusual.

'Last chance, Xanthe. Snap out of it, or I will have to do something I will regret.'

With a slight shake of her head she moved forward over the threshold. The oil did its job.

Both of them.

Firstly, Xanthe lost her footing, almost comically, before falling onto the metal studded floor – hard. Second, it covered her in the grease I needed to win her back.

'I'm sorry to do this, Xanthe,' I shakily stated, hesitating to do what needed to happen next. The mistake cost me.

Realising her error and before I could enact my next step, she pushed off the metal threshold and slid across the floor on her stomach toward me, swiping at my feet. But it was too late. My hand was already on the pot of oil and fat. I tipped it across the open flames of the stove's top. With a flash, the galley and everything covered in oil ignited, including Xanthe, and my side.

Pain erupted through my body as the flames licked upward. I slapped wildly at it trying to douse the blaze. Xanthe screamed loud and shrill. As though pure fear attacked at her mind while the fire cooked at her body. I watched in shock as she writhed about completely alight, knocking over the remaining pots of oil and fat and causing a small inferno before me. I scrambled to the wall and pulled on the lever within a small red box labelled 'Fire'. Immediately jets of white powder sprayed forth from nozzles and pipes overhead, smothering the flames and causing me to lose sight of Xanthe.

I should've stayed. I should've checked to see if she were okay. I should've seen if fire was the one thing that could 'snap' her from her mind prison. But I couldn't. The commotion this caused, would've alerted The Reaper and he would be right around the corner. Already, I thought I could hear his boots pounding across the metal grills down the hall over the dying overhead extinguishers.

'I'm sorry, Xanth. I'm really sorry, but you left me no choice,' was all I could manage before slipping into the adjacent hall-way. The pain running through my scorched side was nothing compared to the guilt I was now feeling in my guts.

With watery eyes I looked back once more into the hazy Galley to see any sign of Xanthe's current state. A tall shadow moved through the smoke, two sword hilts protruding from its back. The Reaper was coming.

It was time to go.

CHAPTER FORTY-FIVE

On board the Kraken Krusher, I had known the handful of ways to sneak from my cell to the Galley and back again. Sometimes, on calm nights when the ship creaked less, I would slip through a gun port and shimmy along the outside of the hull to the other end of the ship. On rougher nights, when the waves tackled the front and sides of the vessel, I would be forced to scamper through the various shadows, ducking under sailor's hammocks and behind crates. Either way, I knew the routes almost as well as a physician knows medicine. The Juggernaut wasn't much different. Sure it was bigger and had more hallways, but it didn't take long for me to navigate my way into the darker depths of the ship's hold to the cells. I had taken time to break the lamps that lit up the hallways and rooms nearby, to help me hide.

The cells aboard the Juggernaut were only slightly different from the one I had called 'home' for the past few years. Each one was rather small, nothing different there, but there were five cells in total. The cages had solid metal walls between each of them, but bars still criss-crossed the ceiling some nine feet above. Less of a spacious luxury and more because the cell's shape was dictated by the ship's anatomy. A small narrow hallway led to each door before heading back toward the main furnace and boiling kilns responsible to fuelling the vessels giant turbines.

Although I was fast, I sensed the Reaper was gaining on me. Like the moments in deep water, when you can tell a large shark or sea monster has your scent and is preparing for that final ambush - my body told me so. The hairs on my neck stood on end and my eyes felt like they couldn't widen enough. The adrenaline surged through me and was almost enough to make me forget about the pain in my side, which now throbbed as though I were still on fire.

I turned a corner and listened briefly. Blood pumped through my ears so loudly it felt as though I were deaf. But I heard him. The long strides of his boots connecting on the floor as the Governor's weapon gave up stealth in place of speed.

'Come and get me, Reaper. Bet you never had someone give you this much of a run around,' I kept up the taunting. It had the duel effect of irritating him while making me feel just the slightest bit more in control of the situation.

I was almost at my destination.

'Boy, I will take great pleasure in dissecting you and feeding you to the sharks in the bay. Piece by piece,' his metallic roar echoed from around the last corner I had just turned.

Crap. Really close.

'Many have tried already. History lesson for you, do you recall a man by the name of Carter Cunningham? I reckon you can. I reckon you know him better than you think.'

His footsteps stopped. I waited for a second before continuing.

'You see, he was a good man. A family man. He cared for his wife Aylah, his little girl Elaina.'

'Shut up, boy!' he roared. His footsteps quickened to a charge, pounding hard across the metal underfoot.

I arrived at the doorway that led to the cells, just ten fathoms from the last corner to the long hallway where the Reaper would emerge from any second. Turning, I picked up a metal crowbar I had previously cached and began to strike the metal pipes that lined the walls. I needed them to break.

Bang. Bang.

Nothing.

Bang. The curved tip of the metal bar wedged firmly between the pipe and the wall. It stuck hard. I worked desperately trying to release it. Sweat on my palms causing the metal to slip between my fingers.

'Care to continue your history lesson? Or perhaps this is another ruse in order for me to drop my guard?' purred the voice from the corner.

Wide eyed, my head snapped around to see the full form of the Reaper blocking my only chance of escape.

'Uh, sure,' I said, a tremble finding its way into my voice. 'He also had a son. Or I should say 'has''

'No, you were correct the first time. 'Had''

He raised the crossbow slowly.

A tear escaped down my cheek.

'Dad. Don't.'

He paused.

'It's me, dad. It's me, Flynt. Don't you remember me? You're Carter Cunningham. You're my father.'

He stopped briefly and tilted his helm. The hollow slits of the mask considered me for a moment.

'Dad? Don't you remember me? I was left as a prisoner aboard that sea monster hunter. I escaped.'

He faltered. The crossbow dipped, the tip angled downward. A free, trembling hand moved up behind the mask, struggling as though it were trying to lift an anchor. A metal clink sounded, followed by the mask popping ajar. The hand removed the helm and it clunked carelessly onto the metal floor beside him.

'F-Fl-Flynt?'

'Dad, it's me.'

'You escaped,' a slight smile formed from his lips. It had been so long since I had actually seen his face up close. So long had I been aboard the Kraken Krusher, I had almost forgotten what he looked like. The day he revealed himself before Arnesto - whilst I recognised him, it just... wasn't dad. Like a puppet of flesh, he was driven by something else. Now, standing mere feet from me, his expression was worn away – as though in constant nauseating pain. The smile turned to a wince, as he tried to fight something, or someone within his head.

I felt the need to lunge forward and hold him, but my legs trembled. My body still sensed danger. My mind couldn't make it move.

'Flynt – I, I can't stop. I don't have control.'

'I know, dad. Try to fight it.'

'No, Flynt, you need to get out of here. He'll make me kill you. He'll make me watch. Flynt, go.'

'Dad, I'm not going anywhere. I know you can fight this. I can help you. I can help you escape.'

His head dropped. Veins bulged in his neck, dribble escaping through gritted teeth.

'I don't – deserve it. I'm trapped in this hell. Go.'

'Dad.'

Tears rolled from his eyes. A tremble began across his whole body.

'Son, I love y-'

The words caught in his throat as he stalled. Dad didn't move. His body seemed to shut down in position, each muscle fibre refusing to budge an inch.

'Dad, are you in there?'

A crackle, like the one on the ship's radio began from somewhere on the armour. Roaring laughter erupted from a small hole punctured box strapped to his shoulder.

'Oh, this is lovely, isn't it? Now it all makes sense. My boy, thank you for enlightening me on this little situation. I must say, you are an interesting find indeed.'

Recognising the oily words immediately as The Governor's, I snapped back, 'What have you done to him?'

'Well, I merely reset him, of course. Your father, as it were, is now mine to control. I did have my suspicions of late that he was becoming faulty like the previous model.'

My eyes narrowed at his description. 'Xanthe,' I corrected, gritting my teeth.

'Yes, yes. That thing. You must have realised by now her weakness to fire. One unfortunate moment during a mission allowed her to escape. I could have let her go, but it is far more resource conscience to regain her and start over. She was, after all, an investment of time and money. But your father - as I said, I had my suspicions, it was merely through the coincidence of seeing you that he had begun to overcome some of my control. So, I took the liberty of reprogramming him to combat those little indiscretions - like a safe word - and look at you, once again, you inspired him to fight back. My boy, you cannot undo what has been done here. You cannot stop the Regime.'

'I think I did a pretty good job tonight, wouldn't you say?'

'That? Minor setback really. With the Allied Forces Navy just outside these waters, I can blame a sabotage attempt from an elite team of experimental enemy soldiers committing an act of terrorism. We will therefore be given extra funding, more resources and have the 'red tape' as it were, removed so the Regime can move forward through the south and expand even further. You didn't think a few factories or airships would really stop us, did you?'

'Yup, kinda did.'

'Well, that is what happens when a young mind is allowed to wander.'

'By the way, how is that view from up there? I would imagine the skyline of your fair city is now looking a little more 'open' and 'well lit'. That is what happens when a young mind is allowed to wander. Matter of fact, you should tell me what you did to my father and undo it, or I may just take a wander back to the gun controls and open up that city a little more. I might even shoot down a particular Governor's airship. How does that sound?'

'Listen here, leech. I'm done talking. Enjoy some quality time with your father. I'm sure you both have a lot to catch up on and you can help him create some new memories,' he purred the last words, sending a cringe through my neck. 'Reaper, ubiystvo,' he ordered. I didn't know what it meant, but I could guess it wasn't pleasant.

Immediately my father's head lifted upward. His empty eyes were now filled with rage as they locked onto me. Any semblance of my father had once again been replaced by a monster. He raised the crossbow swiftly. I reached for the jimmy bar. There was a twang, pain jolted through my hand – a crossbow bolt slammed into the pipes behind me spraying forth steam and fire retardant. I stumbled backward, landing upon the metal floor, a moist white cloud enveloping me. The weapon continued to fire blindly into the mist, each bolt briefly whistling as it flew overhead where I had been standing a split second ago.

I turned to crawl across the floor, hoping to enter the safety of the holding room cells. Placing my hand onto the floor, my right arm buckled under the weight, my teeth grit to the point of breaking – the bolt had punched through the meat and bone of my palm. I slipped on my own blood as it spread across the metal floor. Half slipping-half scrambling through the fog, I made it over the threshold, marking the entrance to the cell block. Feeling for the wall, I let myself be guided by touch. I stood up to the side of the entrance. My back pressed up against the cold steel wall. So often it had been dark within the hold of the Kraken Krusher, I had learnt to get about blindly like an expert.

'Dad, resist it. I know you can,' I yelled.

The weapon fired his response. Three bolts peppered the metal wall behind my head. Dammit, it wasn't working and now he knew where I was. I ducked away from the wall to the cell nearby. I felt its cold metal bars. Smearing my blood onto the metalwork, I made sure to give the door a squeak upon entry – some crumbs for him to follow.

I paused. The hissing of the pipes began to slow till they had all but stopped. I listened to deft footsteps moving through the entrance, into the cell block. Reaching up, I leapt, clawing to the bars that criss crossed the ceiling above the doorway to the cage. Pain spiked through my hand and my right side slipped downward. I couldn't close my fingers around the bar. Like bait on a hook, I dangled by one arm as the footsteps approached the front of the enclosure. Adrenaline and strength coursed through me. Using my one good arm, I lifted my body upward and carefully and quietly looped my legs through the other ceiling bars. Holding both my weight and my breath, I mouthed a quiet 'thank you' to Xanthe - her weeks of ordering me to complete my chin ups had paid off.

If my calculations were right, the Regime crossbow would be harder to use inside the confines of a cell. If he entered, he would have to sling it and focus on hand-to-hand combat. Not that that was giving me much of an advantage at all. I mean, if he spotted me, he could always just riddle my body full of bolts from outside the cell. I shivered at the thought.

The calculations were right.

The mist had cleared enough for me to spy from above. He wavered at the entrance to the cell and inspected my fresh blood upon the bars. Looking downward, he stepped inside – with me. Machinery hissed somewhere in the bilge, causing him to snap his helm around in search of its origin. He stalked further, scanning through the mist as it billowed along the floor.

This was the opening I needed.

Remembering my training with Xanthe, my legs locked as my anchor, I slowly leaned backward, before hanging precariously upside down. The obvious threat was the crossbow that dangled upon its sling almost within reach. My left hand reached for it, but paused. I remembered the gruesome demonstration the Governor had commanded my father to do in front of the nobility. I thought of Xanthe and what I had just done to her. The loud machinery hissed again. I made my decision. With a slip of my fingers, they returned my enemy's possession to my ragged pants pocket.

I winced and risked a look at my hunter. He stepped further inside, opening up more space near the entrance. I squeezed my stomach muscles and lifted upward. Holding the bars with the good hand, I unhooked my legs and slipped to the floor – never taking my eyes from the monster.

This time, there was no noise to stifle my quiet movements. A slight *ping* sounded as my feet connected with the floor. I flinched. He spun, hands reaching. I leapt backward, through the cell door, slamming it behind me. The Reaper, once again wearing the red helm of the Reaper, crashed into the metal bars. His reach was further than I anticipated. A powerful hand grabbed me by the throat. My feet left the ground as

I was lifted. The blood flowing between my head and body blocked. My eyes bulged, dots starting to dance behind them. I gurgled and pawed at his arm. The grip was like iron.

An image of Arnesto flashed in my mind. The loud echo of his snapping neck.

His grip tightened.

The radio upon the Reaper's chest crackled 'Not yet Reaper. Don't make this too quick. I want to savour this moment, as should you,' The Governor commanded.

The grip lessened around my throat. Air and blood circulated just enough to stop me passing out. 'It isn't every day you get to revel in the strength of your own creation. Nature versus science. Science wins every time. The strength of the Regime demonstrated between a father and son. Bring him closer to the camera so I can see his expression.'

I was wrenched toward the bars. The Reaper held my face before a dark circular piece of glass embedded beside the radio box. An aperture moved slightly within it. This is how the Governor could see me?

'Any last words you would like to say to your father, boy? Any weakness you want to show before he ends your life just like he did with that pest Arnesto Dubois?'

I gurgled.

'What was that? Speak up boy, you're disgracing yourself in front of your own sire. Reaper, hold him closer, I want to hear the little bastard's neck snap.'

I was pulled completely to the bars. Cold iron grated against my skin.

'Slowly now. Take it all in.'

The grip began to tighten once more.

My good hand slipped through the bars into the Reaper's belt pouch. Feeling the cold metal sphere, I removed it. The bones in my neck shifted slightly and my fingers tingled. My windpipe crackled. The hand with the hole slipped wildly at the bauble. I had to twist it to activate it.

Or did I?

'Look at those eyes, Reaper. Do you think he has your eyes? Or more the eyes of your dead wife?'

Forcing a smile at the camera, I held up the explosive before it.

The Reaper's head jolted back.

'No! Stop the boy,' the Governor ordered desperately.

Before the other arm could stop me, I dropped the bomb inside the cell. So too was I dropped as the Reaper dove away from the rolling ball. I hit the deck in a crumpled heap, gasping and clutching at my throat. The Reaper picked up the ball and deftly threw it through the bars.

It landed at my feet. Reaching down, I plucked it up with shaking fingers.

I stared at him, my mouth ajar.

That thing before me was no longer my father.

Hoarsely, I croaked, 'It wasn't armed.'

'You clever little bastard.'

'What? What? It wasn't armed? What are you doing then? Shoot him,' the Governor's voice sounded slightly panicked.

I held up my finger in protest.

'I wouldn't if I were you. Consider that as a demonstration to what can happen if you don't follow my next request.'

'You aren't in a position to negotiate, boy. If you try to blow him up, I can just use the serum to revive him. You saw it yourself.'

'Do you mean this serum? Or the one you manufactured in your now levelled laboratory?' I held up the metal syringe I had pilfered when hanging from the cage.

'That's right. So, listen carefully or I will blow the both of us up and leave a sizeable hole in this ship that will send her to the bottom of the harbour, leaving your beloved Capital absolutely defenceless to the Allied Naval fleet you referred to in your... demonstration the other night.'

'You're bluffing, boy,' scoffed the Governor.

'Am I? Ask yourself Guv, what have I got to lose? You took everything from me. On the other hand, you have already lost so much, just not your two favourite weapons. Both of which are at stake.'

The ship rolled slightly while I waited for his response.

'What do you want?' crackled the Governor. I could hear his teeth grinding through the device.

'First, remove the crossbow and slide it through the bars. Keeping your fingers away from the trigger.'

There was a pause.

The Reaper remained motionless.

I held up the bomb before me, cocking my eyebrow.

The radio crackled, 'Do it.'

The hollow sockets of his helm stared at me. The Reaper moved forward and slid the crossbow across the floor. It stopped at my feet.

'Now what?' asked the Governor as I stooped and slung the crossbow.

I pulled out one of the dead officer's time pieces from my tattered pocket and flipped the lid, making sure he could see that it was indeed of Regime manufacture.

'You little –'

'Now,' I interrupted, 'If my calculations are correct, we will very soon be seeing the results of the battle you keep referring to.'

'And what battle is that?'

'Nature versus science,' I responded.

'Nature versu–'

I fired the crossbow. The bolt punctured through the camera and embedded in the Reaper's armour plate.

The Reaper looked at the stuck bolt before plucking it from his armour.

'I just couldn't stand that crumb any longer,' I said.

'What now, boy? You intend to shoot me in here?'

'No.'

'What then?'

'I've been asking myself the same question over and over since I realised who you were. To be honest, I didn't think it'd ever get to this. I just kind of had an idea and made the rest up as I went along, and now here we are.'

'Here we are.'

'I came to this city with the intention of finding you and helping you to escape the prison the Regime were keeping you in. But I realise your prison isn't iron bars and stone. You're trapped in your own body and forced to spectate. I know this, because I know Xanthe.'

'The girl.'

'Yeah, the girl. She escaped. And just before, I saw a glimpse that you could too. You just need the right push.'

Reaching into the folds of my pants, I removed the tarnished silver locket and held it before the bars.

'What are you doing? Stop. You think you can stop this?'

'That's why you had to be behind the bars. I couldn't risk this not working, like before.'

'You know what, boy? I will find a way out of here, then when I get a hold of you, I won't hesitate. I will tear those scrawny arms from that body –'

My fingers unlatched the locket before his lifeless sockets. He stopped.

'Elaina and Aylah, surely you remember them.'

'Stop.'

'You gave this to me the day they took you away. So I wouldn't forget. Don't you remember Elaina and how she used to follow you like a lost puppy? How you would read stories to her in front of the fire?'

The Reaper screamed. His helmet bashed against the iron bars like a madman trying to escape his bindings. The room quaked at the echo.

I pushed harder, 'Or mother - how you two would talk well into the evening after Elaina and I had fallen asleep. The day you met her in the fishing village selling your catch. How you were wed in spring and the rain threatened to stop the ceremony, yet you both didn't care. You said your vows in the downpour, as happy as the day you met. Do you remember?'

He fell to his knees. I moved closer to the bars and knelt before him, laying the locket on the floor for his eyes to see. Reaching through, my fingers gripped the helm by the clasp that held it. With a flick, my hand removed it. His body had become pliable and weakened. Staring at the images before him, his hair dangled over a face cast in shadow.

My trembling hand rested upon his shoulder.

'Dad.'

He lunged forth and grabbed me. I plucked the fishbone lockpick, and stopped it before his throat. His face lifted before mine.

'Son.'

— · —

Chapter Forty-Six

The galley reeked of burnt oil, hair and seared meat. We found Xanthe, still breathing, lying where I had left her. Seeing her now, I was racked with guilt. Her hair had been singed into a short bob, her pale flesh now blackened with dabbles of pink exposed muscle underneath. As I watched, the marks seemed to knit themselves back together. It was slow, like a sea snail trailing along a rock, but it was still happening before my eyes, which meant one thing - she was still alive.

'I'm sorry, Xanthe. I will make it okay.'

Removing the pilfered vial of serum, I pressed the lever and a long prong of metal ejected forth. As he had done the night aboard the Governor's airship, I plunged the metal needle into her neck. It hissed as an amber liquid released into her veins. It snaked forth into her body.

The blackened flesh withered. The pink mottling of exposed muscle disappeared, tissues knitted back together at an accelerated rate. All of her exposed flesh repaired within seconds. Her body convulsed and sat bolt upright, sending me reeling backward. She gulped air.

'It's okay. It's okay. Xanthe, look at me. It's me, Flynt,' though I were reassuring her, I still empathised with her panic. The last things she must have seen were the flames engulfing her body.

'I'm sorry. It was the only way.'

Xanthe's eyes looked at me. Fear turned to relief and she wrapped her arms around me.

'Kid, you did it, you-' her eyes darted from me to my father. 'Look out!'

I was wrenched behind her, a knife finding its way into her hand from somewhere on her outfit. Like a wolf defending her cub, Xanthe bared her teeth at my father.

'Xanthe, it's okay. He's with us. You know him as the Reaper, but I'd like to introduce you to my father. Carter Cunningham.'

Her demeanour changed, eyes darting back between the two of us.

'You mean...'

'Yup...'

'And he...'

'Mmm hmm.'

'And now...'

'Yuh huh.'

'Great,' she threw her hand forth, 'Xanthe. Pleased to meetcha... properly. You know, without all the mind-y wind-y stuff going on.'

'Likewise,' responded my father.

I took the moment in like a proud parent watching their child achieve their first milestone. I wanted the moment to last - to appreciate having my father in my life once again, but time was not our friend.

'I hate to interrupt the formalities. But I have a few other tricks up my sleeve that have yet to take effect, and well, that should be happening any moment.'

'That, and the fact that The Governor will have called for reinforcements by now. Chances are whole teams of troops will be dropping onto the deck presently,' said my father.

'How many Reap- Carter?' Xanthe asked.

'Well, considering how many buildings Flynt has laid waste to out there, and the locations of the various barracks – at least three platoons worth.'

'That isn't so –'

'With more on the way, from the second battalion.'

'Oh.'

'And there is one more thing you should know, Flynt. The Governor saw to it that he had a failsafe installed into my mind. You may have snapped me from the 'brainwashing' but all he need do is say a particular word and I will be back in his command.'

'Oh,' I gulped.

'So, what was that trick you had up you sleeve, kiddo? Say, you look just like the day I dragged you from the water. Cept there is something different bout ya... Where is the neat bracer?' Xanthe asked cheerily.

I smiled, rubbing my bare wrist, 'Well see, that's the thing.'

CHAPTER FORTY-SEVEN

'That's a lot of troops,' Xanthe marvelled through the port-hole.

'And airships,' I added.

'And airships,' Xanthe corrected.

The three of us stood shoulder to shoulder within the narrow hallway. We peaked through the small circular window in the riveted steel door that led to the open deck outside.

It was organised chaos. Several airships floated above various points of the deck, navigating around the masts and rigging as their propellers droned away. Teams of Regime troops were sliding from thick ropes onto the massive deck of the Juggernaut. Obviously well drilled, no sooner had they landed upon the planking, they moved for the nearest cover, their weapons trained on the various windows and ledges of the ship. The Governor had positioned himself on the foredeck and was barking orders to the officers nearby.

'What happens now?' I asked. Despite my efforts to help them from their mind control, I still felt rather naive when it came to military situations such as this. The two members beside me were a bevy of knowledge.

'Now they will prepare breaching teams. The Governor won't be taking any chances. He will want this to look like a hells-of-a battle,' stated my father.

It was surreal seeing him like this. Comfortable in the midst of a pending combat. He certainly wasn't the fisherman I had always thought him to be.

A series of clunks sounded above us.

'What was that?'

'Breaching teams fast roping onto the upper levels. Seems like they are preparing for a synchronized entry,' he said.

'That means, as many entrances, all at the same time, kid,' Xanthe simplified winking at me.

I nodded in understanding.

'If we could get to one of those airships, we could use it to escape,' I thought aloud.

'Bad news is, if we step foot on that deck right now, we will be dropped where we stand. We need a distraction. A big one.'

'Say kid, you used those big guns on the shoreline earlier. If we get to the bridge, could you use them again?'

'The bridge?' I asked.

'The room that controls the ship.'

'Oh... ahhhh, I kind of sabotaged the cannons so they couldn't be used if I was killed or captured.'

'Wow, kid, I'm impressed. How did you do that?'

My mind flicked back to the memory of me standing astride the control panel and urinating across all of the buttons, switches and screens as I whistled a sailor's tune. Sparks and smoke crackled from the switchboard and let me know it was a job well done.

'Ah, nature called,' I smiled sheepishly.

I looked back at Xanthe, she giggled slightly before turning her attention back to the porthole. Dad was watching me intently, his eyes studying me.

'Everything ok?'

He nodded with a slight smile.

'You've grown.'

'So have you.' I slapped his broad shoulder, trying to make the situation a tad more light-hearted. Whatever the Regime had pumped him full of had really beefed him up. Even though I understood I had broken the 'mind control', I still felt somewhat unsure about him. The image of Arnesto's neck snapping still fresh in my memory. I was not yet at ease.

'Hold on.' Xanthe said. Reaching into my pant pocket, she removed a water proof match and placed it firmly between my lips. She winked at me before turning to my father.

'It's kinda his thing,' she explained without a question to answer.

I exchanged a look with him. He smiled in understanding.

'We've got company. Breach team has moved up to the door,' Xanthe updated us.

Dad immediately turned the wheel, sealing off the doorway.

'Now they will have to use a breaching charge. That'll buy us a little time,' he stated firmly.

'What's that?'

'An explosive attached to the door. It'll cut through the metal and send the door inward. Then they will pour in and drop anyone or anything that moves. Seeing how riled up you have made the Governor, he won't be taking any chances. Consider yourself a wanted man, son,' he smiled at me.

It was the first time anyone had referred to me as a man. The notion wasn't lost on me. But something itched my thoughts. I imagined what the doorway would look like as it blew inward. The metal wrenching and twisting. Just like the doorway upon the airship that Xanthe had bent open.

'We could fight them in the hallways. Force them into choke points and take them out, so numbers won't really help,' Xanthe chimed in.

'No, the bodies will pile up and he will just keep sending them in. We are running out of time.'

I remember Xanthe using the soldier as a human shield the day we had met. She had managed to stop a whole volley of crossbow bolts with him. A shield would work perfectly.

'You could use the door,' I suggested.

'What, kid?'

'The door, just like the day you used the soldier as a shield against... well... him,' I pointed to my father sheepishly. 'Rip that door off and use it as a shield.'

'That's... a good idea,' Xanthe's eyes looked past me, a smile creeping across her face.

'It's better than nothing. But without a distraction, they will still outmanoeuvre us aboard the deck out there. But we will need to move soon. Xanthe, a little help?' Dad asked. His commanding voice snapped me from my thoughts.

'With pleasure.'

We had arranged a way of ensuring that the Governor couldn't use his failsafe against my father, once again turning him into the Reaper and dashing our chances of staying alive. It wasn't going to be pretty, but he had insisted that simply stuffing his ears wouldn't be enough. He closed his eyes and leaned his head forward. Xanthe held up her hands and in one swift movement clapped them hard against his ears. He flinched briefly, gritting teeth and squeezing his eyes. A trickle of blood exited each ear canal. Blinking, he adjusted his jaw a few times and nodded.

Xanthe flicked her fingers beside his ears. He shook his head and gave a thumbs up before slipping his helmet over his head and locking it in place. To me, he once again took on the persona of The Reaper. A slight unease came over me.

The handle of the door moved slightly, but the wheel lock held it in place. There was a subtle clunk against the door.

'Move back, they are attaching the breaching charge. When it blows, we don't want to be here,' Xanthe held her hands up and motioned us backward. She shot a few hand signals to my father who nodded his understanding in return.

A sound reverberated through the metal hull. A familiar dull lolling noise, deep and loud. The ship buckled as something huge slammed into its side, sending us stumbling against the walls. Men began yelling from outside the doorway.

'What was that?' blurted Xanthe before turning back to me.

I grinned in response.

Another bang against the ship sent us sprawling about. The hallway began to slant as something began to lift it from the water.

'That is our distraction,' I called excitedly. 'Xanthe, this is it. Go!'

Realisation swept over her, without hesitating she turned and slapped my father on the shoulder, giving him another hand signal. They both turned and ran for the doorway, sabres drawn from scabbards. I tried to keep up, with the pair, sprinting for the doorway.

With a bang, Xanthe and my father both shoulder barged the door with their combined strength. The metal screeched, shearing from the hinges and barrelling outward. I caught a glimpse of a soldier's body launching through the air – a victim of the sudden outward swinging barrier. Both enhanced warriors didn't miss a beat, utilising the surprise generated from the unexpected attack, they began to slash and bash in unison at soldiers from either side of the doorway. Xanthe leapt forward to retrieve the busted metal door and brought it before her as a shield.

I arrived shortly afterward to witness a spectacle that - should I live - would stay with me to the moment I die. Yelling and screaming erupted from all around, as soldiers were attacked on multiple fronts. Massive black tentacles from what had to be an alpha Kraken waved about the ship, slamming into the decking, and testing the ship's strong metal structure. Black, slimy and thicker than a ship's mast, one tentacle slapped at a team of soldiers before sweeping along the surface, dragging with it any poor souls stuck to its giant suckers. Other sets of the creature's appendages followed suite, reaching and snaking around whatever couldn't be pulled into its gaping maw below the surface. Soldiers fired their bolts into each faceless predator but to no avail. The bolts didn't have enough penetration to do much more than irritate the beast and give it more hope in finding prey. It simply grew more aggressive.

Airships had retrained their cannons and fired upon the Alpha, moving lower for a closer target. One overzealous crew crept too close for a full broadside. I could see the mistake before it happened. Alpha Kraken's don't work alone, with many females in their charge. Within seconds, another set of humungous tentacles erupted from the water and pulled the airship downward. The crew fired a salvo, which ignited the gases escaping the floatation bladder. There was a flash as the craft exploded rocking everyone on deck and sending flaming pieces of kraken tentacle and airship parts raining from the sky. The female began to feast upon the crew, unbothered by a few missing tentacles. Beyond the deck, there was even more carnage. The bracer had done its job and done it well, attracting an entire school of Kraken for a feeding frenzy. With the Capital's coastal defences decimated from the Juggernaut, the clockwork lure I planted during the night had activated on the ship's hull and lured in an entire migrating herd from the waters beyond. Now the harbour, in the wake of the work of the massive guns, was being devoured piece by piece - ship by ship. The Kraken demonstrating what carnage nature could inflict over science.

'Get with it, kid!' mouthed Xanthe over the din of the battle.

My musings had been but a moment, yet I had fallen behind my allies. Taking full advantage of the panic aboard, The Reaper and Xanthe cut a swathe through the enemy soldiers. I watched as Xanthe used the door like a battering ram into three enemy, still raising their crossbows to meet her. The force of the heavy hunk of steel echoed out a crunching sound of breaking bones before launching them backward several fathoms to break a few more. The Reaper had returned his swords to their sheaths. Dipping his hands within his pouches, he pulled out metal ball after metal ball. Flicking their clockwork timers with his thumbs, he leapt over a crate and launched them with the power of a ship's swivel gun. Explosions erupted across the deck sending Regime troops flying through the air. Well, mostly. Sometimes it was just... parts. Others began to drape the deck in thick smoke obscuring the aim of the soldiers on the high ground behind us.

'Kid, use that thing, will you?' Xanthe yelled again.

Her voice went from muffled to clear in a blink. My mind snapped to attention, the butt of the Reaper's crossbow found my shoulder. I scanned the deck in front for any threats, but the soldiers were too scattered. My head spun. It was sensory overload.

That's when I heard his voice - the Governor.

Standing on the bow of the ship, he had begun to pull back – withdrawing to his airship. Still commanding his troops to attack, while he left the fray. He yelled to his personal crew. Confident that I was behind cover of the guns and concealed from behind by the smoke, I brought the aiming glass before me. Wobbling, I tucked my elbows in and steadied. I watched as personnel cast down a rope to their commander. Desperately he latched a metal loop onto his own belt. The rope began to retract, and quickly he lifted from the deck of the ship. Using the ascent to his advantage, he picked out Xanthe and his former Reaper as targets upon the deck, obviously having realised his creations were no longer under his influence. I flicked the safety switch upon the side of the crossbow. The aiming lines levelled on his chest, wobbling ever so slightly - I squeezed the trigger. With a 'chink' of the firing mechanism, I fired a single bolt across the deck. It struck the belly of the airship. I had rushed the shot. His head spun to see what had struck inches from him, the shaft of the bolt almost pointing directly back to me. Peering down, his stern expression met mine. His hand pointed directly at me. *No, he wouldn't, not with his own troops in the firing line*, I thought. Who am I kidding, if 'The Reaper's' actions under his control were a reflection of his thinking, then of course he would.

He did.

Lining up a second shot of the crossbow, I could see his instruction. His lips mouthed the command – 'Portside guns... open fire!'

The airship crew echoed his command. Now side on, the cannons aiming upon the Juggernaut's deck replied. Smoke and flame spewed forth in quick succession from several cannons. The air whistled. Timber shattered and splintered all around me. Pain spiked in my neck and side - raked by shrapnel. My body lifted and the world spun as I rag dolled upward. I hit the deck hard, air forced from my lungs. Feeling as though my whole body were broken, I tried to stand and faltered. A pair of hands grabbed me from behind and held me steady. Ears ringing, I turned and was met with the gore covered mask of The Reaper, a skerrick of flesh still dangling from one of the upturned metal horns. It would seem he had been rather busy. I flinched involuntarily, caught off guard by the sight.

'It's okay, son. It's me. It's me,' he reached back and removed the helm, letting it fall. 'I'm here and you're okay. A little bit banged up is all.'

His voice calmed me. Breathing heavily, I found my feet.

'You good? You with me?' he asked, offering me his hand.

I grasped his in reply and nodded, spitting out a mouthful of blood. Reaching down, I regathered the crossbow and quickly checked it over. It still seemed in working order. Regime quality assured that is, I thought.

Slipping through the smoke and still sporting her latest heavy metal accessory, Xanthe sidled up beside us, smiling.

'This is fun and all, but how do we get out of here?' she asked far too jovially for the current situation.

My father pointed to his ears and shrugged.

Before I could answer, a response came from somewhere below the ship. The Alpha Kraken groaned. The same sound males would make when fighting over territory, it must have confused this new massive ship as a threat now, rather than food. Tentacles rained downward, slapping and grappling the mast, guns and bridge of the vessel.

'What's it doing?' Xanthe cried out confused, stumbling sideways.

'It's doing what male Kraken's do. It's going to wrestle the ship to the bottom of the harbour. We better hold onto something quick,' I ordered.

My father watched as Xanthe and I leapt toward the railings and held on. Quickly he followed our course of action. The stern of the ship bucked violently downward at the same time lifting the bow upward. Anything that wasn't bolted down upon the deck began to slide toward the rear of the ship. Bodies of troops, living or otherwise, tumbled past. One of the massive gun turrets buckled and popped before the giant cannon broke free and barrelled toward the salt water now looming downhill from us.

I looked upward. The bow of the Juggernaut now all but touched the Governor's airship. The rope used to rescue him still dangled precariously before the vessel's raised bowsprit.

'Xanthe! Dad!' I pointed to the front of the ship some twenty fathoms away from where we held on. 'That's our ticket out of here. Follow me!'

That's when I should have seen it. The one detail amongst the chaos. My old man nodded back at me. But I failed to see it.

Like running up a steep hill, I leant into the decking and scrambled with my hands and legs toward the bow. My muscles ached as fatigue set in. I had been so tense during the battle that my lungs were parched of air. Now I worked as hard as I could toward the airship. I slipped briefly, only to be caught just as quickly by the hands of my father as he kept watch over my climb. Just like he had when I had fallen from the roof as a kid or when Elaina had learned to walk. He pushed me upward and kept behind, letting me climb but acting as my safety.

'Look out, up ahead!' yelled Xanthe.

I did. Ahead of us, upon the deck of the airship, the Governor had noticed our approach. Several crew members had joined him, unable to bring the cannons to bear on such a sharp decline, they now aimed a variety of muskets and crossbows in our direction. The Governor yelled forth his command once more.

Without anywhere to go and completely exposed, no more than ten fathoms from the bowsprit, my eyes shut and I held myself close to the deck. As though being closer to it would save me. No clever tricks. No cover.

A weight pressed down on me, shielding me from above. The shots rang out. The armour and the body within it bucked as lead and bolts riddled it.

It was him. The Reaper... my father had saved me from death. Still he remained, encasing me.

At that moment, a shadow cast over us. Using a rope tied to the railing, Xanthe swung before us, bringing the door to bear as cover. The metal tinged and rang as the projectiles deflected or shattered against it. Peering through the porthole Xanthe drove forward and upward toward them.

Encouraging hands from my old man firmly steered me behind her. A warm wet sensation trickled down my back. I managed to catch up to Xanthe, her progress slowed by the consistent barrage to her front and the weight of the door. I held her shoulder and raised the crossbow over to rest upon the top of the shield. Looking through the porthole, I pulled the trigger. Bolts sprayed forth at the unprotected group. Three troopers dropped, before several reeled backward. The Governor turned and fired his crossbow at those who broke the line, before turning his attention back toward us with his four remaining men.

'Get down, kid!' yelled Xanthe, wrapping the rope around her leg with a swift spin of her ankle.

I dropped against the angled deck. Xanthe lifted the door and twisted sideways. Using both arms she spun and launched the metal door toward the group. I was reminded quickly of the time she had done so, using me. This time was far more destructive. The door punched forth, and cut down the remaining soldiers and toppling the Governor out of sight.

Seizing the opportunity, the three of us covered the distance in a flash. Xanthe led the way up the bowsprit and leapt for the dangling cord. Now at a considerable height, I tried to focus on the rope as I made my way forth. One slip, and it was a long fall into the waters below and the waiting tentacles of the Kraken herd.

I held onto the metal strut and cursed quietly at the Regime's newly chosen slippery building material as opposed to the good old 'grippy' timber. I reached for the rope, only to watch it slip away. The airship began to lift and pull away from the sinking Juggernaut. The last chance to escape to safety, disappearing from my reach in a moment. Xanthe's head appeared over the edge of the craft. Her face contorted in shock.

I was grabbed by the scruff of my neck. Looking back, I saw the face of my father consider me. He shook violently. Blood escaped his mouth and he wheezed quietly. His back was littered with several bolts, having finally worn down the integrity of his armour. The wetness upon my back had been his own blood. His body taking the Governor's barrage to save me.

'Dad… you're…' I couldn't get the words out. 'Quick, get one of those syringe thingies out. It'll fix you.'

I fumbled desperately through his pouches, but each one was empty.

'No, no, no. There has to be something,' I exclaimed.

He forced a smile through the pain. Unsteadily he leant forward, touching his forehead against mine. I saw the face of the man who raised me. The same man who had provided for and protected his family all those years ago. Pulling away, there was a softness in his weary expression.

'Dad, I'm sorry. I'm sorry.'

He turned me about toward the airship. I could see his intentions.

I forced back against his guidance. 'No dad, please. We can escape together. There has to be another way. I can't do this without you. I can't lose you again.'

Unable to speak, he slowly shook his head, before forcing me to face the craft again. With one last grunt, he launched me upward. I was propelled toward the airship like a shot. The world below me shrunk. The airship became large - fast.

I slapped into the decking on the airship in a sprawl. Unable to get a decent grip I began to slip backward. I slapped and clawed for something to grab onto. A powerful grip wrenched my punctured hand upward.

'Welcome aboard, kid. Gotta say, that was one helluva jump,' Xanthe said cheerily.

'I didn't...' my voice came out between heavy breaths.

'Wait, where's old mate Carter?'

Pulling away from Xanthe, I dove on hands and knees toward the edge. Moving forward, I looked downward. My father was no longer on the bow of the ship. I searched for any sign of him, but there was none to be seen.

'He's... gone.'

'What?'

I stifled tears in my eyes and grit my teeth. Once again, I had to bury pain inside my guts.

The Juggernaut's compartments had begun to fill as the ocean found its way inside. The Alpha Kraken began to wrangle the massive craft deeper and deeper into the sea. From above, the gigantic ragged beak ripped and tore at the ship.

There was no way one man could survive, not in that state and not in that water right now.

All around the bay the waters churned in turbulence as tentacles claimed the corpses of ships of the sky and sea. Fires burned furiously along the surrounding coastline, sending pillars of thick black smoke into the heavens. The remaining airships, resigned to the fact they couldn't stop the chaos, had limped back toward the further reaches of the city.

'Flynt, I'm sorry,' Xanthe's hand rested gently upon my shoulder.

'Don't be. It wasn't your fault.'

The airship banked starboard and began to accelerate. Bodies of unconscious troops littered the narrow deck like the morning after first harvest, outside a tavern.

'Who's behind the helm?' I asked.

Xanthe shrugged, 'I've only cleared the deck. I don't know how many more are inside, but this isn't a big airship, so there can't be many.'

She was right. This airship was even smaller than the one we had stolen months ago. Fitted out with three propellers, already it had accelerated much faster too. With the absence of a particular person of interest, I already knew of at least one member still inside.

I stooped and picked up one of the many crossbows that littered the deck and checked it was loaded. A few bolts remained.

'Then let's... let's hunt this monster.'

CHAPTER FORTY-EIGHT

'Now let's talk about this, shall we? There is no need to make any rash decisions in the heat of the moment. I have a proposition for you, young man.'

We found him behind the helm, blissfully unaware of the company he now shared. His eyes remained on the horizon, giving away his intentions of escape. Standing there, The Governor nursed a limp left arm and leaned wearily against the wheel. Both side hatches lay open, allowing a salty breeze to blow through the airship's internal bridge. After deliberation with Xanthe, I entered alone.

I took a moment to announce my presence by laying down the crossbow with a clunk a few feet behind him. It was for no other reason than to see the horror upon his face. Sneaking in to finish him would have been too quick. Too easy. He didn't deserve easy.

He must've sensed my intentions, so he did what The Governor did best.

He talked.

'Go on,' I said, patting the crossbow.

Encouraged by my change of tone, he continued, 'We could use people like you.'

'Like me?'

'Yes. Driven, passionate, strong. You are no leech. You see what you want and you take it. If only more of my men had your conviction. No man could've done what you did here tonight. No man. But you. A child - you defied it all. My city may lay in waste and ruin, but cities can be rebuilt. The Regime, she is strong. This is but a mere hiccup in the grand scheme. You could be part of that. Come with me and I will deliver you safely to my superiors. Once they hear of your exploits, you will be treated with respect and envy. Together, there would be no stopping us. You exude potential, it is clear. I can make you faster, stronger – unstoppable. I can make you powerful, boy.'

'That is an interesting proposal. Tell me, do you feel powerful?'

His face contorted at my question.

'I mean, you *had* all the power,' I continued. 'You *had* an advanced military. You *had* technology at your disposal. You. Had. Everything. But what do you have now, except words and empty promises?'

'You haven't listened, young man. Right now, I am headed for the major airway shipping lines of the Regime. Each ship carries with it resources and personnel, completely uninterrupted by the Allied nations, like healthy veins pumping blood without disease. Once I meet up with a small fleet, I can arrange reinforcements and resources, redirect them back to the Capital. In the meantime, we can work with the other leaders from the West, East and South. The pillars that hold our nation up. You caused quite a stir indeed, but as I mentioned, it is a mere set back. Regrowth will be swift. Consider your attack as an audition of sorts. One that has made me sit up and take notice.'

'You say the shipping lanes are in the air?'

'Yes.'

'And that they transport the 'life blood' of the Regime? Completely free of disruption?'

'Indeed.'

'Interesting.'

'Well, what do you say, young man? Do we have a deal? One survivor helping another?'

'You know, I believe we've gotten off on the wrong foot, Governor. What say we shake hands and put this all behind us?'

I moved away from the crossbow and offered my bleeding hand forward to shake. His eyes looked at the crossbow, then back to me. His meaty paw shot forward and grabbed at me. I slipped under the thrust and stepped sideways away from his next lunge. Like I suspected, the greedy Governor saw the opportunity and took it, bounding to the crossbow and claiming it.

His eyes flared wildly and he lined me up, the weapon aimed from the hip.

'You little leech, you think I would actually let you get away with something like this? I will ruin you.'

He pulled the trigger. There was a clunk as the weapon failed to fire. Careful and quick inspection would reveal one of my matches jammed in the firing mechanism, but the Governor was clearly more inclined to cucumber sandwiches than knowing the inner workings of a soldier's weapon. He pulled the trigger again and again.

I smiled. 'Having issues, are we?'

'You little leech. I'm not beneath killing a child.'

'Look, I'd love to stay and chat,' I said stretching my neck and shoulders, 'but I fear what happens next is not my sort of game. I've had my fun blowing up your city, sinking your fleets and stuff, but there is someone else who would like to have a word with you.'

'Someone else?' his eyes began to widen.

A spider-like shadow lowered down from the ceiling behind the Governor. A bolt of white hair dangling just inches behind his shoulders.

'Just remember, I offered my hand,' I warned.

I stepped outside the doorway and shut the door behind me. It was best to let them both have some privacy I thought.

I heard a muffled phrase being screamed louder and louder. It was obvious things just weren't going The Governor's way today. First with the Juggernaut, then with the crossbow and now his very own 'fail-safe' phrase wasn't working on Xanthe - having slapped her own ears before slipping in through the ceiling panels. Man, some people just can't catch a break.

The airship drifted past the confines of the bay, the ruins of the Governor's Coastal guns still smouldering below.

There was a gargled scream from within, before the half-dressed body of the Governor was launched at speed through the nearby window a few feet from me. A long rope followed, waving wildly as it unravelled. It pulled taught over the railing. Panicked screams rang out from below. The Governor was dangling upside down from his feet. Alive, bleeding – possibly missing an eye - but very much scared out of his wits.

It didn't last.

The knot – rudimentary at best - unravelled, and he screamed falling into the distant, kraken infested waters below.

Numb, I watched.

But he never resurfaced.

I waited a moment before stepping inside. Xanthe was standing proud before me, her hands bunched behind her back.

'I have a surprise for you, kid,' she grinned at me.

Considering the fact she wasn't quite yelling at me, I took it as a sign her ears had almost healed.

'It doesn't have something to do with the half-naked Governor you just threw through the window, does it?'

'Aw no fair, you peeked. I mean... maybe,' she quickly added, her eyes full of hope that I believed her.

'What is it?'

'I just wanted to say, 'thank you' and well, here ya go,' she thrust the semi folded coat, clothing and boots of the Governor in my direction. 'Looks like you could use some new clothes. These are good ones.'

'Thanks, Xanthe.' In all honesty it was the first gift I had been given in years.

She threw her arms around my neck, '-And thanks for coming back for me.'

I smiled. 'Well, my old man always told me the importance of keeping my word. And from what I remember, I still owe you a ride on my ship.'

Her confusion soon switched to realisation. Xanthe began to jump on the spot.

'You mean?'

'Yup. So where do you want to go?' I asked.

'Everywhere. No. Anywhere. No. I just want to have some fun and see amazing stuff.'

'That, I can do and I know just the place.'

I limped over to the helm. Adrenaline had subsided in my body and a calm swept over me. I had always wanted to command my own ship one day. I just never thought that it'd be a ship in the sky is all. Tenderly gripping the wheel with my injured hand, I turned the ship toward the eastern sun. Light crept through the windows and over the controls before me.

Xanthe pulled up beside me with the ship's first aid box. She began fishing out gauze and bandages for my burnt side and punctured hand.

'Flynt?' Xanthe asked cautiously wrapping my knuckles with a linen bandage.

'Yeah?'

'Why did you let me fight the Governor one on one? Didn't you want to - you know - finish him yourself?'

I mulled over the question.

'It was a fair fight,' I said thoughtfully. 'The only way to settle differences.'

— · —

ACKNOWLEDGEMENTS

Apparently, there is a specific way an author should 'create' and set out their acknowledgements section in a novel.

Apparently...

On the other hand, I have such a tremendous amount of people

who have steered me in the direction of writing that I would feel it a great injustice not to mention them or their influence upon me. So, like a wedding speech that drones on for far too long, buckle yourself in for the ride if you are interested – otherwise, skip this part and enjoy the tale I have created for you.

It all started when I was born...

Kidding, I won't go back that far. In all seriousness though:

To my wife – thank you for your ongoing love and support. Without your patience, company and organisational skills, I would not have had the confidence to continue this creation. You are my rock and your tolerance of my ramblings about writing is commendable. You gave me the confidence to write

and to back myself when doubt crept in. This story simply wouldn't exist without you.

My girls, Isla, Eden and Halle – my muses. I wrote this tale for you. For when I am gone, I still want to be able to entertain you with stories of fantasy and adventure that inspire you to stand up for what you believe in – no matter the odds. The roots of this story were created during the long nights nursing you girls – pacing the room for hours in the darkness, leaving marks from my footsteps in the rental home carpets, then the same on first home we owned. Sometimes I would whisper my ideas to you for your input. Silence was good. A fart was disapproval. Maybe one day, you can pass these tales onto your own children.

Mum and Dad, you supported my ideas throughout rearing me from a young pup. You taught me the value of persistence and nurtured my imagination. Without these, a story will never be told. From comics and 'Goosebumps' books as a kid, to the adventures of 'Handsome Grant and Liam', I learned that embellishment and adventure are great ways to entertain a young mind. I will never forget. Mum, I wish I could have finished this tale sooner, so that you could have enjoyed it.

Trent and Carrie – my *much older* siblings. You both spent so much time helping me to improve our family forte – writing. From the times playing Scrabble to sitting patiently beside me as a teen and helping me polish my stories and assessments to suggesting new novels to read, it shaped my imagination and writing. If you were wondering; 'FAUST Eric,' by Pratchett from Carrie and 'The Hobbit' by Tolkien, from Trent, were the first fiction books you gave me.

My Critique partners – Binnie and Lesley. Cheers for your patience and support throughout this process. You provided insight, confidence and guidance – all of which I certainly needed to tell this tale.

To my BETA readers; Broady, Tim, Bec, Wes, Sharleen and Hunter. Your excitement, honesty and feedback have been greatly appreciated. Cheers also to Jasper for your hype and encouragement. Your constant enthusiasm was contagious.

The goal is not to live forever, but to create something that will. – Andy Warhol

ABOUT THE AUTHOR

Liam Porter resides in Hervey Bay, Queensland with his wife Renee and three young daughters Isla, Eden and Halle. Together they make the most of living near K'gari (Fraser Island), often travelling there for an adventure. Liam has always been an avid fantasy reader – a love which led him to start a career as a High School English teacher back in 2009 and still enjoys to this day. He is also an Australian Army Reservist, serving as a Rifleman with the 9th Royal Queensland Regiment since 2010 – a job that has provided plenty of excitement and action over the years. He looks forward to the opportunity to keep telling the tale of Flynt Cunningham and Xanthe Bones – a story which planted its seed in his mind during the nights settling his girls as newborns.

Follow @writer_liamporter on Instagram.

www.ingramcontent.com/pod-product-compliance
Lightning Source LLC
Chambersburg PA
CBHW031742180726
48283CB00005B/1623